THE
Business Card
BOYFRIEND

KRISTA SANDOR

USA TODAY BESTSELLING AUTHOR

CANDY CASTLE BOOKS

CHAPTER

One

HAILEY

"HAILEY, you've got some nipple action going on, babe."

Nipple action?

"Wait, what?" Hailey Higgins exclaimed, dropping the cherry licorice twist she was about to eat onto the dressing room table. She clutched her cell and stared at the woman on the other end of the video chat.

Panic flooded her system. Her palms grew sweaty. The phone bobbled between her hands like a digital hot potato. After a few precarious wobbles, she regained control and zeroed in on her picture on the top corner of the cell's screen. Her face matched the color of her auburn hair. But her flushed cheeks were the least of her problems. She inspected her cleavage. And there it was—the rogue nipple peeking out like the boobie version of a Peeping Tom. She could not be flashing her nips. Not today. Not on her wedding day.

Wiggling from side to side, she flicked her gaze from the cell phone's screen and frowned at her reflection in a chipped mirror. With a jagged crack down the center, it resembled a prop straight out of a horror movie. In an act of fashion desperation, she wrestled with the bustline of her figure-hugging dress, attempting to negotiate a ceasefire with her C cups, reminding them that they were dealing with a budget-friendly polyester version of satin—a fabric that wouldn't take kindly to any boobie diva misbehavior. She shimmied and shook, channeling a seizing mermaid while sucking in her stomach like she took pleasure in tormenting her internal organs.

She winced. "This is so tight I had to go commando. And I shouldn't have eaten all that cherry licorice. It can't be helping with the fit. I wish I wasn't a licorice stress-eater," she lamented, executing another shimmy shake as the ivory fabric rose a forgiving inch.

She wiped her wrist across her damp forehead and breathed a sigh of relief. Nipple crisis averted.

Marginally satisfied with the coverage, she was about to return her attention to the video call when something flickered in her peripheral vision. She glanced around the event center's bare-bones bride's room and eyed a piece of torn wallpaper. The faded floral strip quivered beneath an oscillating fan's weak puffs of air. The blades creaked, guiding the stagnant air in another direction, and the strip went limp. Hailey took a step toward the drooping paper. Something was written on it. One sentence.

He's not meant for you.

Yikes! That wasn't a message any bride wanted to read on her wedding day. Then again, a place called Stu's Weddings and Funerals 4 Less wasn't exactly her dream venue either. But it was the best she could do on short notice and a meager budget.

Hailey took a bite of her cherry licorice twist and focused on the video call with the woman who'd been her best friend since grade school. "Izzy," she whispered, like she was trying to keep that torn wallpaper from hearing their conversation, "do I look like a hooker bride?"

Isabelle "Izzy" Adaire's brow creased. She chewed her lip, then tucked a golden lock of hair behind her ear.

Was the woman buying herself some time to come up with an answer?

Hailey checked her reflection again. Did Izzy's hesitation mean she *did* look like a hooker bride?

The mortification inferno roasting her cheeks intensified. "Iz, talk to me."

"No, Hails," Izzy assured her, "you don't look like a hooker bride. I'm simply surprised to see you in that body-hugging, boobalicious number. Last time we talked, you said you wanted a modest neckline. You emailed me a pic a few days ago. That boatneck dress with the cute three-quarter sleeves looked great on you."

Oh, how she wished Izzy could be with her. But with her bestie crusading for endangered species and protecting natural habitats across the globe, video chat was how they'd connected over the last few years. And they'd been logging in quite a few hours since Grant, her former boyfriend and now present fiancé, had proposed two weeks ago, which wasn't much time to find a dress.

Hailey tugged the clingy fabric. "That dress was my favorite, but—"

"Let me guess," Izzy interjected, her expression souring. "Grant didn't like it."

Hailey plastered on a plastic smile. "He did like it, but he liked this one better."

Okay, that was a lie. Grant hated the boatneck dress. He thought it was frumpy. But what was so wrong with taking her fiancé's advice and choosing something that made him happy? It was called kindness.

Izzy pursed her lips. "Uh-huh."

Hailey mirrored her best friend's expression and pointed the licorice twist at the phone. "I can hear the disapproval in your voice, *Isabelle Adaire*."

"I know that's not your real smile, *Hailey Higgins*," Izzy tossed back.

Hailey locked onto her friend's gaze, then looked away,

cracking first. "I like to think it was sweet that Grant took an interest in the dress selection."

Izzy's expression softened. "All right, I'll give him one begrudging point for that."

Her friend's lack of enthusiasm for Grant wasn't a secret. But Izzy had never been impressed with anyone she'd dated. Still, how was she supposed to find the man of her dreams if she didn't date? She'd been searching for true love since she could say the words.

Hailey flashed puppy-dog eyes at the screen. "I need you to be happy for me. I've always wanted a relationship like my mom and dad." The thought of her parents mooning over each other lifted the weight off her shoulders as if the drab dressing room momentarily became a brighter place.

"And you're sure Grant's the guy?" Izzy asked.

Hailey peered at her diamond ring. It didn't sparkle quite as much since he'd slid it onto her finger during a commercial break while they watched some TV show about vintage sports cars.

She'd kept that nugget from Izzy, too.

"Hails?"

"Yes, Grant is . . ." A tickle in her throat halted her reply. She coughed. "Why are you asking me this now?"

"I'm not trying to upset you. I love you. And you love *love*."

"What does that mean?"

"Your obsession with reading that love and relationship website you started going gaga over in college. What's it called? Stardust Romance? Or is it called, Yes, I Guess?"

"It's Shooting Stars Love Stories on the I Said Yes website," Hailey corrected, pretty much making Izzy's point that she was a little obsessed with it.

Izzy's brow furrowed.

"What is it?" Hailey asked, pretty sure she knew what her friend would say.

"You've got the biggest heart of anyone I know, Hails. You

deserve a love story worthy of that site. I want to make sure you see the full picture with Grant."

"What's so bad about believing in people?" Hailey shot back, her voice rising an anxious octave. "Sure, Grant can be a little distant, but nobody's perfect. I'm certainly not. And I'm tired of dating. I've kissed so many frogs. Why couldn't Grant be my Prince Charming? He's . . . great, and he's doing well at his new sales job. He enjoys the work and spends quite a bit of time with his coworker, Joe. They often work through the night. He's doing this for me, for us, and for our future."

Izzy raised an eyebrow. "He said that?"

Hailey popped the last bite of the cherry twist into her mouth and tugged at her bustline. "Not in those exact words. But he wants to marry me. Nobody's wanted me like that before." She paused, her throat growing thick with emotion. "What was I supposed to say when he proposed? I couldn't say no."

Her friend glanced off-screen.

"Isabelle?" Hailey said softly.

The woman's brows knit together as her concerned expression returned. "Didn't he propose because he wants to buy a dented Porsche 911 from the nineties off some dusty used car lot, and he thinks married people get better car insurance rates? Isn't that why he fast-tracked the wedding?"

Ugh! She'd forgotten she'd shared that with Izzy.

Hailey's plastic smile widened. "That might have been the reason we *started* discussing marriage. But it's not the only reason he cares for me. And the dent on the driver's side door isn't so terrible. Grant says it's an easy repair." A coppery taste invaded her mouth. She grabbed a water bottle from her bag and took a gigantic swig. "We'll grow into our love story."

Did she believe that, or was she saying it to appease Izzy?

Of course, she believed it. She had to believe it.

Hailey Higgins believed in love—even before discovering the website's love stories. Since she was a girl, she'd pined away for an all-encompassing, heart-thumping, pulse-pumping whirlwind of a romance. Just because she and Grant weren't on that level yet didn't mean they couldn't get there. She silenced the part of her that fantasized about being swept off her feet and focused on her friend.

"Come on, Iz. I don't have anyone else to cheer me on today."

She didn't.

She'd lost her parents a few weeks before she started college. Besides some wayward extended family she'd never met on her dad's side, her mom and dad were all she had. With Izzy overseas, she didn't have any guests waiting in the chapel to watch her get married.

Thanks to Grant's ever-changing career choices, they'd moved three times during their eleven-month courtship. That's how they'd landed in a dusty town in southwest Kansas five months ago. She couldn't expect friends from high school and college to drop their plans to attend a wedding with two weeks' notice. As for Grant's parents, they were currently on a cruise to Acapulco. That's what Grant told her, and she had to take him at his word. She'd never met or spoken to them. When she suggested inviting Joe, Grant rejected the idea.

She lifted her chin. She couldn't dwell on the negatives. She had to stay positive.

There were good parts to her current situation. Moving wasn't that bad—especially for someone with a degree in elementary education. She could always pick up substitute teaching jobs here and there. Would she love to settle down and have her own classroom? Yes, but kids were kids, and she loved what she did no matter where she did it. As long as she and Grant were together, she'd be fine—no, better than fine. She'd be terrific. And soon, she'd be happily married to a man with a Porsche—not that she cared much about cars. Her little sedan, rocking nearly one hundred thousand miles, suited her just fine. But Grant liked cars. And she supported him in his endeavors like a good partner should.

Yes, that was it. She was supportive. That was a quality worthy of the I Said Yes website.

But did Grant support her?

As the thought materialized, a prickle spider-crawled down her spine like she was being watched. She peered at the torn bit of wallpaper. It flickered as if it were desperate for her attention.

It was a silly piece of old paper. Nothing more. Still, her heart sank. She scanned the dreary room and inhaled the scent of mildew and floor wax. Even with a boatload of positivity, she had to admit this wasn't how she'd pictured her wedding day.

Stop!

She couldn't go down that road. An unpredictable life was an exciting life. Her parents had met in an adorably unconventional way. The stars had aligned to bring them together.

What did it matter if she was getting married at a place called Stu's Weddings and Funerals 4 Less?

Who would care if the initial talk of getting hitched was triggered by a fire engine red sports car built in 1997 that was on hold until noon today?

Thirty years from now, she wouldn't be worrying about the aesthetics. She'd be too much in love. Yes, that was it. Love would persevere.

"Today is the day my life will change forever. I'm chasing the dream of having a relationship like what my parents shared."

Izzy offered her a grin, but its warmth didn't quite reach her eyes. "I know, honey. I hope you get exactly what you want today. And I'm sorry I can't be there."

Another wave of emotion hit, and Hailey blinked back tears. "You don't have to apologize. You're protecting animals. I can't think of a better reason to miss a wedding."

Izzy leaned in. "Did you bring the jar?"

The mere mention of the treasured item had Hailey smelling pickles and eased her apprehension. She pointed her cell at the one-gallon glass vessel and studied the slips and scraps etched with scribbled text stored inside. The sunlight filtered through a grimy window and illuminated the unique snippets of paper. Nothing was uniform about the textured fragments besides the flecks of pink and purple dotting the cream to ecru to wheat-colored bits of fibrous paper. As a girl, she'd remove the lid and dip her fingers into the sea of fibrous-textured goodness.

Hailey traced a heart on the glass. "It's like having my parents with me. I've been thinking about them a lot with the wedding planning."

Izzy rested her chin on her fist, her grin now reaching her eyes. "Your dad sure was crazy about your mom. How many notes are in that pickle jar?"

Hailey started in on drawing her second invisible heart, warmth radiating through her chest. "Two hundred and twenty-two."

"And they're all on that special paper?"

"Yes, there's something unique about it I've always loved," Hailey replied, the muscles at the base of her neck relaxing. "It's got character. And my dad wouldn't use anything else for the jar notes. I guess that's why he kept the paper in a special box in his desk drawer."

"Where'd he get it? I don't think I've ever asked?"

"An eccentric uncle on my dad's side would mail it to him. I found a lone sheet while clearing out the house after they passed away. I've kept it with me for the last six years. Today, I gave it to Grant."

"To Grant?" Izzy exclaimed.

"I asked him to write me a note and tell me what our first kiss meant to him."

Izzy fiddled with a lock of her blond hair. "What did Grant write?"

Hailey shrugged. "I don't know. I told him to give it to me at the altar before we got married." She glanced at the clock hanging cockeyed on the wall. A shot of adrenaline hit her system. "And speaking of getting married. I have to go. I only have a few minutes before our wedding time slot."

"Time slot?" Izzy repeated with a crease to her brow.

"That's how it works at Stu's Weddings and Funerals 4 Less." It took everything Hailey had to say that with a straight face and keep her bottom lip from trembling.

Buck up, girl!

This was no time for wavering. Her love story started today. It had to.

A wedding was a wedding—even if it was being held at a dilapidated event center in a half-vacant strip mall.

"I love you, Hails," Izzy said, her voice cracking. "I'll be in the field and out of cell phone range for the next week or so. But I'll be thinking of you. I'll call you the minute I can."

Hailey brushed a tear from her cheek as the weight of this day sank in. "Love you, too. Be safe."

The screen went black, and a heaviness hung in the musty air. With the oscillating fan in the corner clicking and rattling like it was gargling rocks, Hailey attempted to center herself in the least Zen room on the planet.

Forget about the fan. Forget about the peeling wallpaper message.

Teetering on the sky-high heels Grant picked out, she went to the table on the other side of the room, dropped her cell into her oversized canvas tote, and examined the contents. She needed to be prepared for what came next.

Once she and Grant purchased the Porsche, he'd promised to take her to a bed-and-breakfast a few towns over. She'd thrown her clothes into his large overnight bag but snuck a couple of packs of licorice and the lingerie she'd purchased for her wedding night into her tote. She fished around her purse, reaching past a stack of letters that had come in the mail yesterday. She'd worry about bills later. She pushed her makeup bag aside and spied the lacy panties that were sure to do a number on Grant tonight—her wedding night.

The prickling sensation returned.

Was that a normal reaction?

"It's nerves. Wedding day nerves," she whispered.

She went to the mirror for another boob check and caught the jar out of the corner of her eye. Forgetting her bustline, she picked up the precious keepsake, closed her eyes, and unscrewed the lid. Like she'd done a million times before, she lowered her hand into the crush of paper and let fate decide which message she'd read. Reveling in the texture, she chose a remnant, opened her eyes, and skimmed the message. The breath caught in her throat. What was scribbled on the slip of paper had to be a sign.

"Julianne," she read, concentrating on the faded ink, "the first time I kissed you, I knew—"

Bang, bang, bang!

Hailey shrieked and lost her grip on the jar. Panic tore through her as the container dropped an inch. She heaved forward and clutched the slippery glass to her bosom.

This jar cannot break.

Clenching with every ounce of strength, she didn't breathe. She didn't twitch. The only movement came from the gasping fan on electrical life support. She waited for a beat, then another, before loosening her grip. "Thank God," she gushed, her heart pounding as she cradled the jar.

She barely had a second to get her bearings when the door opened with a creaking whine. A tanned, crinkly-faced woman with pale blue eyes and a cigarette dangling from her hot pink lips surveyed the room. "I'm Flo. I'm the bridal consultant at Stu's Weddings and Funerals 4 Less," the woman barked.

Hailey remained in her contorted position.

Act normal.

She released a feathery laugh. "Hi, Flo. I'm—"

"I know who you are, Miss Higgins," the woman said and flicked ash onto the worn hardwood floor.

Hailey nodded. "You probably saw me when my fiancé and I met with Stu to book the wedding ceremony. My fiancé had to step out and take a call. Perhaps you only saw me," she replied, again taking note of the woman's unique eye color.

Had they met before?

"I don't worry about the scheduling. That's Stu's job. My job is to keep us running on schedule. And listen, toots, I don't mess around. My sister is in town, and we've got plans to take my granddaughter to the park. I'm not staying a second later than I have to. Do we understand each other?"

Yikes!

"We do, ma'am," she stammered, not wanting to inconvenience this fiery-tempered senior citizen.

Flo took a drag off her smoke. "Leave your creepy pickle jar and bag in the bride's room and push your titties back inside your dress—unless you want to get married with them on display. We don't mind the kink around here. But it'll cost you another twenty bucks."

Hailey gulped a breath of stale air as she caught her reflection in the mirror.

Heaven help her! What a sight!

The jar remained securely lodged between her dislodged cleavage. Blushing like a hooker bride, she set the jar on the dressing room table, then crossed her arms to shield her breasts. "I most definitely do not want to get married topless."

Flo exhaled a stream of smoke and shrugged. "Then stuff your girls back inside your dress. We don't have all day. You like kids?"

Hailey blinked. Going from boobs to talking about children was quite a leap. But it was an easy question to answer. "Yes, very much. I love kids."

Flo's expression hardened. "Then you won't want me to keep my sister and grandbaby waiting."

"No, ma'am," Hailey replied, wiggle-worming her breasts into place, which was significantly harder now that she'd broken out into a nervous sweat. Flapping her arms like a chicken to get some air circulating, she mouse-stepped toward the apoplectic fan and silently cursed the formfitting gown. The wallpaper flickered, and she zeroed in on the faded flowers with the succinct message scrawled in black ink.

He's not meant for you.

A line like that would never make it onto the I Said Yes webpage.

Stop!

Her vision grew glassy as an out-of-tune piano hammered out the first few notes of the "Here Comes the Bride" melody.

"Is that for me?" she asked, ignoring the foreboding message.

"Are you supposed to marry a sandy blond called Nimrod?"

"It's *Rimnod*." Hailey teetered toward the door in the sky-high heels. "And yes, that's my fiancé, Grant Rimnod."

The old lady smirked.

Hailey disregarded the woman's reaction. It wasn't Grant's fault he had a last name that lent itself to mispronunciation.

"If you're sure you want to marry the nimrod, then the music's for you."

Hailey stood there for a beat and glanced at the wallpaper strip.

"You taking decorating notes, honey? Studying the wallpaper?" Flo tossed out, circled by a cloud of smoke.

"No, I'm . . ."

"Wasting time," Flo supplied with a sly twist to her lips. Without another word, the woman headed down the hallway.

In a flurry of clickety-clacks, Hailey followed the tiny woman. "So, should I walk down the aisle now?"

Flo dropped her spent smoke onto the scuffed floor and ground it out with the sole of her flip-flop. "Walk, skip, do a few cartwheels. I don't care how you get to the altar. If you want to do it nude, it's—"

"It's twenty dollars extra. I got it," Hailey supplied, exhaling a shaky breath as her nerves kicked in.

Flo pursed her lips and gave her a once-over. "I have a feeling you're smarter than you look, but you don't look very comfortable."

Hailey drank in her heaving cleavage and cringed before tugging at the bustline. "This dress isn't really me."

Flo cocked her head to the side. "Then who are you?"

Hailey parted her lips, but nothing came out, not a peep.

The wedding consultant shrugged and opened the door to the chapel, and the choppy piano music flooded into the hallway.

Hailey tried to steady herself as everything went topsy-turvy. The music was too loud. A flickering fluorescent light had her eyes twitching. The scent of stale cigarettes and sweat hung in the air.

Flo thrust a bouquet of fake red roses into her hands. "Your fella's waiting at the altar with Stu. Go marry your nimrod."

Hailey clutched the plastic stems. "Right, yes, this is my wedding day."

"Unless you keep lollygagging. Then you'll have to wait until next Thursday to get hitched." Flo eyed her wristwatch and removed a pack of cigarettes from her pocket. "You've got eleven minutes before your time's up."

Hailey swallowed past the lump in her throat. "Eleven minutes."

Flo pressed a fresh cigarette between her lips and checked her watch. "Ten."

Back to clickity-clacking, Hailey ignored the empty pews, and sexy-dress shuffled her way toward Grant. She'd expected him to greet her, but the man was glued to his phone. A series of beeps and pings cut through the jarring piano notes as he stood beside a droopy-faced officiant whose eyes were closed beneath his bushy gray brows.

She nodded to a skinny old man playing the piano in a T-shirt printed with a tuxedo.

At least somebody noticed her trip down the aisle.

She switched to a side-step, moving in time with the chimes emanating from Grant's cell, bobbing down the worn carpet in sync with the rhythm of the "Here Comes the Bride" tune.

Ping, ping, ping, ping!

Ping, ping, ping, ping!

Who was he texting?

Yet to acknowledge her, he kept his eyes on the device and

raked his free hand through his hair. It was probably a work-related issue. He was always working. He was truly a dedicated employee.

"Stu, wake up! It's go-time," Flo hollered.

The droopy-faced man sputtered to life and wiped a bit of drool from his lip. Grant looked up like he'd been caught with his hand in the cookie jar. She waved to him. But he didn't wave back. Wide-eyed, the guy turned the shade of the faded wallpaper in the bride's room.

Be positive!

She slapped a grin on her face as he peered past her.

What was he looking for? She was right there.

She glanced over her shoulder. The space was empty. All that remained was a thin trail of Flo's lingering cigarette smoke.

She focused on her fiancé. Was he okay? Could he be coming down with the flu? No, it had to be nerves. It was a monumental day. A massive milestone in their relationship.

"Oh, hey," Grant sputtered, his gaze bobbing between her and his phone.

She maneuvered her polyester-bound body up the step to the orange shag altar and caught her breath. Mummy walking was no easy feat. But she'd made it. She gestured to his cell, then stretched her grin to the brink of splitting her lips.

"I'll put it away," he stammered, shoving the device into his pocket.

"Are we ready to begin?" Stu asked, rubbing his bloodshot eyes.

"Not quite yet," she replied. She gazed at Grant. "Don't you have something for me?"

This was the moment her swoon-worthy love story would begin.

Her fiancé's brows knit together. "The rings are in my pocket."

"No, I'm talking about the special paper. I asked you to write about how you felt after our first kiss."

The guy grimaced. "Yeah, about that . . ."

"Yes?" she whispered, eagerness coating the word.

"I had to use that piece of paper for my gum."

The heady anticipation zinging through her body fizzled. "Your gum?"

"We've got a no gum policy," Stu explained, joining the conversation.

Grant gave her a half-shrug. "Nothing I could do."

"Where's the paper now?" she eked out.

"There." Grant pointed to a cracked stained-glass window.

Hailey gasped as a man dumped the contents of a trash can into the back of a grimy garbage truck. Her mouth opened and closed like a flounder before she could speak. "My dad's paper is in there," she whispered as the trash collector hopped into the truck's cab and headed down the street. She studied her fiancé's vacant expression. It had to be an honest mistake. There had to be a way forward. "Did you write to me on another sheet of paper?"

Grant recycled his grimace and inhaled a tight, hissing breath. "I was pretty drunk the night I met you. I couldn't narrow down our first kiss."

A bead of perspiration trailed between her breasts. "You didn't seem that drunk. You were at the bar with some friends. You'd said you'd only had a few beers."

"And mixed drinks. And shots. And this stuff my pal made in his mom's bathtub," Grant countered, counting the alcoholic beverages on his fingers. "I guess I forgot to mention that."

Hailey shifted her stance. Her dress was getting tighter by the second. "But you remember the night we met in Phoenix, don't you?"

"Uh, yeah," the man offered, but a tinge of doubt seeped into his tone.

She pressed her hand to her chest, ignoring his shaky reply. "Good."

"Well, I recall pieces. I remember seeing you at the bar."

"Okay," Hailey replied, her spirits rising.

He chuckled. "My buddies dared me to talk to the lonely

redhead eating candy out of her giant bag and nursing a sad little umbrella drink."

And she was back to nervous sweating. "Lonely girl? Sad umbrella drink?"

"You stuck out like a sore thumb, Hailey. Everyone else was drinking and laughing. You were—"

"I was grading spelling tests and snacking on cherry licorice," she supplied, recalling her last steady teaching position and her precocious, inquisitive second-grade class back in Arizona.

He nodded. "I asked if I could buy you a drink. But then I couldn't find my wallet. I left it at the table with my friends. So, you covered our tab."

Had she built up this moment in her head? Grant had been a bit wobbly. His speech could have been described as slightly slurred. Still, he'd charmed her with his laser-focused attention.

Emotion thickened in her throat.

He hadn't been trying to impress her. It had been a show for his buddies.

But what did that matter?

Even if his motive for meeting her had been less than ideal, they'd forged a relationship.

She twisted the rose's plastic stem. "You never told me you talked to me because of a dare."

He cocked his head to the side. "That's not quite true."

Her spirits lifted. "It's not?"

"They dared me to see if I could score with you. And I did. We went back to my place that night. After that, you stuck around. I moved to Utah, and you came with me. And then I got fired from that job, and you moved with me to Oklahoma. And then I got fired again, thanks to another pesky surveillance camera."

"I thought you quit because you were offered a better job?" she stammered.

"Oh, yeah, right, that was the reason." Grant tugged at his collar. "And then I got this new gig, working in Kansas, and you came along."

Hailey's bottom lip trembled. "You didn't want me to come with you?"

Grant shifted his weight from foot to foot and checked his watch. "I didn't *not* want you with me."

Tears pricked her eyes, but she blinked them away. There had to be a way to salvage this. She'd have to work harder to help him see they were meant to be together.

"Listen, Hailey," Grant continued, "I know you wanted a letter, but I can't remember our first kiss. That night is a blurry mess in my head. But I did write something."

"And what's that?" she asked with bated breath.

He pulled a torn sheet of notebook paper from his jacket's breast pocket. "The improvements I want to make on the Porsche. First up, fix the dent. Second, get a fresh paint job. Doesn't that sound amazing?"

Hailey clenched the fake flowers. The plastic nubs holding the artificial leaves in place cut into her palms. "That sounds . . ."

What was she supposed to say?

Before she could utter a word, a side door near the altar opened.

Flo peeked out. "Seven minutes."

"Um . . ." Hailey stammered as a wave of nausea washed over her.

Her situation couldn't be as hopeless as it seemed. Grant wasn't a big communicator. It wasn't his way. And he never told her that he didn't want her around. By default, that must have meant he enjoyed her company. But he'd never said those three little words to her—words she'd thought he'd say today.

She studied his face. "Do you love me, Grant?"

He shrugged. "I don't *not* love you."

Another line she'd never read in the Shooting Stars Love Stories.

The breath caught in her throat as Stu cleared his.

"All right, let's get this going. We can't piss off Flo. She's got plans with family. Here we go, folks. We're gathered here today to witness—"

The chapel door swung open, emitting a shrill, ominous screech. A platinum blonde charged inside. Her rapid-fire footsteps pounded against the worn carpet runner. "Let me finish that sentence for you, preacher man," she called, chomping on a mouthful of gum. "We're gathered here today to witness my positive pregnancy test. And the baby is yours, Grant Rimnod." She stopped a few paces from the altar, waving a plastic pee stick in the air like the Statue of Fertility.

The baby is yours, Grant Rimnod?

If Hailey wasn't standing, she would have sworn her heart had stopped beating. She faced her fiancé and posed the dreaded question no bride ever wanted to ask at the altar. "Grant Rimnod," she eked out, "who is this knocked-up wedding crasher?"

CHAPTER

Two

HAILEY

"UM . . ." Grant mumbled, avoiding eye contact.

"Um?" Hailey repeated. How could uttering *um* be his only reply?

She closed her eyes, praying she'd hallucinated. But when she blinked them open, the scene remained unchanged. A blonde with her hair in a high ponytail decked in neon yellow knee socks, a pair of barely-there shorts, and an electric blue sweatshirt stood there like she'd planned to hit a roller derby after she finished busting up weddings.

Grant turned the color of pea soup. "Jo, what are you doing here?"

"Joe?" Hailey repeated as her stomach dropped. "That's Joe? That's who you've been with night after night? I figured Joe was a guy."

"It's short for Josephine," the woman chimed, her platinum ponytail swinging from side to side as she donned a ditzy grin. "And lady, I didn't know Grant had a fiancée until I saw a note on his calendar that said *marry Hailey to get the Porsche.*"

"Marry Hailey to get the Porsche?" Hailey repeated.

No, this could not be happening.

Grant returned to fidgeting with his collar. "Well . . . yeah. Two birds. One stone."

Hailey drank in the scene as her heart broke and a truth cracked wide open.

The wallpaper was right.

"You've never introduced me to your parents. We've never hung out with your friends. Does anyone in your life know about me—about us?" she asked, needing to confirm her worst fears.

Grant wiped the perspiration from his forehead. "Um . . ."

There was that *um* response again.

"You don't love me. You're marrying me to get a better car insurance rate." She cringed. Had more pathetic words ever been spoken?

Grant shifted his weight from foot to foot like a toddler about to wet his pants. "And because your credit is great if I need someone to cosign the loan, and I care about . . ." He paused like his brain was a webpage having trouble loading. "You," he finally blurted. "I care about you."

One part of that word salad of a response was true—and it wasn't the caring part.

A sickening feeling took hold.

How had she not seen through the guy?

"Just say it, Grant. Tell me the truth," Hailey pressed, willing her voice not to shake.

He returned to tugging at his collar. "The car lot guy is holding the Porsche for another hour. You know I've always wanted that model. And it's in my price range. The car dude said he had another buyer if I pulled out. You know what they say. Desperate times call for desperate measures."

Hailey pictured the slips of paper in the jar and couldn't imagine one saying, *I married you to get a decent insurance rate on a sports car priced to sell because desperate times call for desperate measures.*

She pointed to Jo. "Why don't you marry the woman who's having your baby?"

Grant's shoulders slumped. "I didn't know she was pregnant. And I can't marry her. She's got a boyfriend."

"Had a boyfriend. I dumped him," the woman chirped in a singsong voice.

Grant perked up. "You broke up with him?"

Hailey dropped the plastic roses and stumbled backward as Jo and Grant made googly eyes at each other.

This had to be a joke.

Her stomach hardened into a knot.

No, this wasn't a joke. This was her life, and she was the joke. She'd put everything she had into making this man love her and look where it had gotten her.

Screwed over at the altar.

The wallpaper was right.

"I can't marry you, Grant," she whispered, humiliation piercing her heart.

"I can," Jo called, waving the pregnancy pee stick like a Fourth of July sparkler.

Did this gal come off as the sharpest tool in the shed? No way. But Hailey had no room to judge when it came to emotional intelligence—or even regular old intelligence.

"Hailey," Grant rasped, taking her hand.

"Yes?" she replied, hating that her stupid love-chasing heart still held out hope he'd choose her.

"Could I have the ring back since you can't marry me?"

What's worse than getting blindsided at the altar? Getting blindsided, then getting replaced in under thirty seconds.

Trembling, she yanked her hand from his grip. She glared at the ring, her gaze growing glassy. She had to get it off. She couldn't stand the sight of it. But thanks to the flush of mortification, her fingers resembled bloated hotdogs. "Come on, come on," she begged through gritted teeth as she pulled on the bit of gold, pleading with the recalcitrant jewelry. Her body heaved. Her muscles quivered. She leaned over and growled, "You're not meant for me!" With a vicious twist and one final tug, the ring scraped past her inflamed knuckle. Breathing hard, she reared back and was met with a chorus of gasps.

What were they looking at?

"That'll be twenty bucks, sugar tits," Flo called from the side door.

Twenty bucks? Sugar tits?

Jo pointed at her with the pregnancy test. "Nice rack."

"You do have great tits. It's the main reason I agreed to the dare," Grant added.

No, no, no!

Hailey looked down, and *yes, yes, yes,* her breasts had come out to say hello.

Really, universe? On top of everything she'd endured, now she'd get fined for public indecency.

Talk about adding an R-rated insult to injury.

And she wasn't about to stick around to see what else fate had in store for her.

Yanking on the dress's bustline, she corralled the girls, then tossed the ring at Grant. "Have a nice life. Enjoy your Porsche." Turning on her heel, she side-stepped off the orange shag altar. A furious clickety-clack ensued as she sashayed out of the dank space and back to the bride's room.

Alone, the tears spilled down her cheeks. The wallpaper fluttered, taunting her as she grabbed her treasured jar and placed it in her tote. She fished out her wallet and eyed the bills. Three tens. She left two on the dressing table as cringe-inducing piano notes echoed from the chapel. She didn't know the official name of the tune. But she'd heard it in nearly every movie that included a wedding. It was the popular song played for couples as they walked down the aisle after they'd said their I dos.

Jo and Grant hadn't wasted a second. Then again, they probably only had thirty seconds before the time was up.

Her belly did a flip-flop as another revelation hit. She'd footed the bill for their wedding.

Oh, forget them!

She brushed the back of her hand across her tear-laden eyes, smearing her mascara. She observed the black streaks on the back of her wrist. Done being played for a fool and currently rocking raccoon eyes, she had to figure out an escape route. She surveyed the room and glared at the door. She wasn't about to hightail it toward the main entrance. She couldn't bear to see Grant and his pregnant wife—Porsche bound.

There had to be another way out.

Grabbing her tote, she shuffle-hopped to the window. She used every ounce of strength to open it. Dust fluttered in the sunlight as she scrutinized her formfitting dress. She could not blow this rundown event center wrapped in polyester like a bridal bratwurst. Luckily, she didn't need to look her best. She gripped the hem and tore the fabric like one of those oiled-up fake wrestlers ripping off their T-shirt. The material snapped and popped. The sound of her dreams unraveling. She stopped ripping a few inches above her knee and shimmied out the window with her tote. Blessedly, the dressing room looked out onto the parking lot. She spied her car, and relief flooded her system. It barely took a minute before she was safely inside and cruising the streets aimlessly.

But where was she supposed to go?

She didn't know anyone well enough in this town to crash at their place.

Turning down a side street, she pulled up to the curb and shifted into park. Her gaze landed on her naked ring finger, and she grimaced. What was wrong with her? How on earth had she talked herself into marrying Grant Rimnod? How had she been so blind? She collapsed forward and rested her head on the steering wheel. Like salt hitting a wound, the greatest hits of her dating life carouseled through her mind. Wait! Scratch calling them her greatest hits. Gut-wrenching dating catastrophes was a better descriptor.

Her past relationships could be described in two words.

Epic failures.

She'd endured cheating, gaslighting, and having her heart broken time and time again. Despite doing everything she could to make these guys love her, she'd failed. The hole in her heart—the hole that had formed after her parents' deaths—expanded, eating away at her. If things got any worse, her heart might disintegrate, leaving a gaping, soul-sucking void.

She lifted her head and concentrated on the jar peeking out of her tote. A heaviness set in. She'd been deluding herself. She'd never find a love like her parents shared. They had a spark—a rare connection blessed by the stars. What did she have? A jerk who wanted to use her to buy an old sports car.

Pathetic.

Her phone chimed an alert. She slipped it from her tote.

A new Shooting Stars Love Story has posted.
READ IT NOW!

"*Gah!*" she shrieked, frustration gripping the syllable. She tapped the link, scrolled to the bottom of the page, and found what she was looking for.

Unsubscribe.

She tossed her phone back into her tote and pushed the top of the glass container deeper into the bag. It was too hard to look at it. It was too difficult to know she'd failed. She opened her glove box and removed her secret stash of cherry licorice twists. She ripped off a piece and popped it in her mouth. Chewing and stewing, she understood what she had to do. "I'm done chasing love," she said, talking to the piece of candy like a deranged person. "I'm finished letting jerks break my heart."

She waited for the candy to reply and, of course, got nothing.

Lonely and heartbroken, she sank into her seat and stared at a stop sign at the end of the block.

"Stop," she whispered.

That was it!

That was the answer to her predicament. She'd stop dating.

She'd forgo courtship. She'd end her pursuit of matrimony. Today made one fact crystal clear. A love story would not be a part of her future.

Love freaking sucked.

But what would she do now? Where would she go? It wasn't like she was rolling in cash. She didn't have a steady job. Not to mention, she'd footed the cost of the wedding, and it had drained her savings. She fished her phone from her tote and opened her banking app.

She sucked in an audible breath, hardly able to breathe, as her account balance blazed across the screen.

$122.22

How did a person start over with a few packs of cherry licorice twists, a ten-dollar bill, and a bank account low enough to induce hyperventilating?

Tap, tap, tap.

Hailey jumped at the sharp sound and dropped her candy in the crevice between the seat and the center console. She peered out the passenger side window. A woman holding a dog bowl filled with loose change smiled.

Hailey pressed the button to roll down the window. "Yes?" she asked, taking in the round-faced woman in a T-shirt covered in little stars interspersed with the silhouettes of dogs and cats. *Rescue Pet Alliance* was embroidered across the front.

"We're out asking the town to donate to an animal rescue organization. Would you be willing to help us save animals?" she asked warmly, jiggling the change in the bowl.

"Sure, of course. Let me get my wallet," Hailey stammered, emerging from her heartbroken fog. Back to fishing through her purse, her fingertips brushed past one of the letters. A tingly déjà vu sensation took hold. *Weird.* She brushed off the odd reaction and removed her wallet from the cavernous bag. Her heart sank as she spied her last ten.

At least this money wouldn't go toward Grant and Jo's big day.

She zeroed in on the crisp bill, then placed it in the dog bowl.

"Thank you, honey," the pet rescue volunteer gushed. "Would you like to adopt a kitten today? You look like you could use a kitten—or two—in your life."

"No, ma'am, I can't because . . ." Hailey glanced around her compact car, which now appeared to be her residence. She was not going back to the apartment she'd shared with Grant.

"Don't you worry," the volunteer offered gently. "I can tell you've got a good heart. You'll figure it out."

"What will I figure out?" Hailey asked, desperate for clarity—even if it came from a stranger.

"Why, whatever's got you here, drying your tears on the side of the road," the woman replied, then continued down the street.

Hailey watched the volunteer disappear around the corner, then deflated into her seat. "I might have a good heart, but it's a stupid heart." Exhaling a heavy breath, she rested her hand on the gear shift, prepared to pop it into drive. But she didn't move. That odd déjà vu feeling took hold again. A breeze blew in, and the air crackled with . . . hope.

How strange for that to occur at her most hopeless moment.

She examined her bag. It was as if something inside it was calling to her. She plucked the textured envelope from the stack. But this letter didn't look like a bill or junk mail. It had been forwarded a few times and had taken over two months since it was postmarked to make it to her in Kansas.

She ran her fingertips over the return address. "Why would I be getting a letter from the mayor of Starrycard Creek, Colorado? And where the heck is that?" Again, she drew her fingertips across the textured surface, speckled with tiny flecks of green and brown. Earthy and light, the paper had character—no, not exactly character. It had a presence. She turned the envelope over in her hands. A slim, solid object dropped from corner to corner. With a delicate touch, she peeled the flap. It opened as if it had been waiting for her. She peered inside, then emptied the contents onto her lap. A folded piece of paper with the same texture and coloring as the envelope and a battered silver key, like something from a long-lost treasure chest, landed on her polyester-bound lap next to a small rectangular card.

She held the key in her hand, assessing its weight. A pounded copper circle was attached to the top with a dry twist of brown twine.

"Higgins Hideaway," she said, reading the words etched into the tarnished metal.

She returned the key to her lap and picked up the letter. Unfolding the flaps, she inhaled a fresh woodsy scent.

> **Re: Estate of Albert Austin Octavius Higgins, Deceased**
>
> **Dear Ms. Hailey Higgins,**
>
> **I am writing to inform you of a legal matter pertaining to the estate of your late great-uncle, Albert Higgins. I regret to inform you that he has passed away, and you are the sole living relative entitled to inherit his cottage located at 222 Starryview Lane, Starrycard Creek, Colorado, known informally as Higgins Hideaway, and miscellaneous assets associated with the property.**
>
> **I understand this news may come as a shock, and I offer my condolences for your loss. Please do not hesitate to contact me if you require any additional information. I've added the business card for a local handyman as a courtesy. The cabin is situated in a remote location and may require maintenance.**

The rest was just pleasantries.

She rested the paper in her lap. "I own a cabin?" she uttered, then picked up the business card. She traced a line across four words. "Finnegan Starrycard, Local Handyman." She concentrated on the letters. They weren't printed. They were embossed onto the paper like this handyman and the card were one and the same. What a peculiar thought. While it was like the envelope and stationery in appearance, the texture—the curious unruliness of the fibrous paper—left her oddly spellbound. She tapped the card against her bottom lip, then licked it.

What was she doing?

Why had she tasted a business card? Did she like it?

She inhaled the card's woodsy scent. It reminded her of freshly chopped lumber, and a lightness took over. "Albert Austin Octavius Higgins," she mused, resting the business card against her chin before going stock-still. Like the morning sun burning off a lingering fog, her muddled mind cleared, and a memory surfaced—something from when she was five or six years old. She'd heard of this Albert before. Her father had mentioned an Uncle Albert after a package wrapped in brown paper and twine arrived on their porch. He must have been the one to send the paper to her dad. She'd twisted the coarse brown string around her index finger as she'd inquired about the sender's identity. The memory was fuzzy. She couldn't recall her dad's complete response, but one word stood out.

Recluse.

She'd looked up the term in the behemoth of a dictionary that had lived on the bottom shelf of the bookcase in her father's study. Tabling the memory, she touched the key nestled in the ivory folds of her dress and stroked the bit of twine.

Her great-uncle Albert might have been a solitary hermit, but today, he'd become something else. Her salvation—at least until she could get back on her feet and figure out where she wanted to start over.

That was it. That was the plan.

She required a complete life reboot—a life void of romance. A life where she wasn't tempted by the false promise of stupid, blessed-by-the-stars true love. And to do that, there appeared to be no better destination than the isolated former residence of a recluse.

There was no turning back.

She reached for her phone. With precise, measured movements, she opened the navigation app and entered an address.

A map and a number appeared on the screen.

A little over six hundred miles was all that separated her from the ideal location to shun love and shut out the world.

But she wasn't ready to go quite yet.

She studied the business card, then wiped the tears from her cheeks. Straightening in her seat, she caught her reflection in the rearview mirror. She focused on the puffy-eyed woman. "You're nobody's fool. Not anymore. Love isn't in the cards for you. You're done with relationships." She'd spoken the conviction-laden words but didn't dare look at the jar in her tote. What would her parents think of their daughter committing herself to a loveless existence? She banished the thought.

She peered at the business card, drawing strength from the tiny rectangle. With renewed purpose, she tucked it into her cleavage, near her heart, and set her phone in the center console. Enchanted by the lingering woodsy scent, she raised her gaze to the open road and shifted into drive. "Starrycard Creek, Colorado. Here I come."

CHAPTER

Three

FINN

"UNCLE FINN, you need to get some."

"Get some?" Finnegan Starrycard exclaimed, nearly falling on his ass. He eyed his freckle-faced six-year-old niece. The child sat cross-legged on the floor with a stuffed frog to her left and a Teddy bear to her right. A dainty tea set littered the space in front of her. He had to have misheard her. "What did you say, McKenzie?"

"I said you need to get some. It'll help you be less like this." She scrunched up her face as if she were taking a massive dump.

"Why do you look like that, Kenz?" He stepped back and glanced out the door, praying none of his siblings had heard the kid's jaw-dropping advice.

McKenzie huffed, and her golden-brown pigtails brushed past her shoulders. "It's what you look like because you need to get some."

Christ! He had heard her correctly.

He shifted his stance and cleared his throat. Granted, it had been a while since he'd gotten any, but there was no way on God's green Earth his precocious and plucky niece would know that. Let alone know what the slang term *get some* meant.

"What exactly do you think I need to get more of?" he asked, praying for a PG-rated answer.

She held up an ivory cup. "Tea. You need to get some tea. Tea makes everybody feel better. That's what Mommy says if I eat too much ice cream, and I heard Mommy telling Daddy that Grandma says you're eating *copious* amounts of cherry chocolate chip ice cream. I asked Mommy what *copious* meant, and she said it meant a lot, a lot, a lot. But I only like tea party tea. Real tea tastes like grass water." She cocked her head to the side. "What did you think I was talking about?"

He ran his hands over his cheeks, feeling the scruff beneath his palms. "We're not going there until you're thirty years old. No, forty. And I eat copious amounts of other things." Was that the truth? Not exactly. But he wasn't about to go there either. Instead, he inspected the display of cups and saucers. "Do we have to play tea party? We could rustle up some paper and make a paper tower. I could help you build it super tall and strong. We don't even have to do towers. We could make . . . a paper staircase. We could even make stuff shoot out the top. Doesn't that sound fun?"

He was grasping at straws.

"Uncle Finn, I want to play tea party. And you promised I could pick the game we'd play. Watch me so you know how to do it. You have to make your pinky stick out when you hold the teacup. That's the fancy way to drink a cup of tea." McKenzie lifted her chin and extended her pinky finger like a pint-sized aristocrat. The child sipped the imaginary liquid from the dainty ivory cup and then picked up a scrap of textured paper. She dabbed at the corners of her mouth, using it like a napkin.

Finn pursed his lips and emitted a low growl. He'd agreed to play tea party because he needed a break from the festivities going on downstairs. Get-togethers used to be his thing. Social settings were once his stomping ground. But not anymore. Not after what happened exactly a year ago today.

Warily, he eyed the delicate tea set laid out on the hardwood floor of his sister's childhood bedroom. "I'm not very fancy,

McKenzie." He gestured with his chin toward a pile of toys in the corner of the room. "Didn't you say the front door was squeaking the last time you played with your mom's old dollhouse? How about you enjoy your fake tea with your stuffed animal buddies, and I see what I can do about the hinges?" He removed a screwdriver from his tool belt. Was it weird to wear a tool belt everywhere he went? He honestly didn't give a fuck. Years ago, the old hermit who used to live in the cabin on the property adjacent to his used to walk around the woods buck naked. A tool belt was useful, practical even.

"Who cares about hinges?" McKenzie quipped.

"Hinges are a critical component to door usage. Without them, the door couldn't function properly," he lectured.

McKenzie rolled her eyes, unimpressed.

His not-giving-a-fuck attitude must have rubbed off on the kid.

"Sit down across from me, Uncle Finn. Don't mess with the components. I like the squeak," the child replied with a determined set to her jaw—a Starrycard family trait. She shifted on the floor. "It's too bad we don't have the *floofy* rug I told you to buy here at Starrycard House. Do you like it in your cabin? Do you sleep on it? I bet it's super soft like sleeping on a furry cloud."

He grumbled at the mention of the *floofy* floor covering. *Floofy* was Kenzie's word. And as silly as it sounded, it was an accurate descriptor.

The rug in question was an item Kenz had seen in a shop window when he'd taken her out for ice cream. White and fluffy, the faux sheepskin rug looked like it belonged in a sorority house, not a rustic cabin. Still, he had a soft spot for his niece, so of course, he bought the outlandish and *floofy* floor covering.

"When can I come see the cabin?" the child pressed.

He gave her a half-shrug. "When the cabin's ready."

"When will that be?"

He lowered himself to the floor and emitted another low growl. "Are we playing tea party or what?" he asked, channeling a surly schoolboy.

McKenzie looked him over and frowned.

"What?" he shot back.

"You used to be super fancy, Uncle Finn. You used to wear fancy businessman shirts. Now your clothes are wrinkly with bits of paint and wood stuck to them. You used to have shiny black shoes. Now you stomp around in muddy old boots, and you're never at the paper shop. I heard Uncle Owen say to Uncle Kieran, 'It's been a year. What if he never comes back? What'll we do?'"

Finn rubbed his temples. It was a fair question. Too bad he didn't have any answers. "Any other observations about my life, Kenz?" he grumped.

"I don't see you very much anymore."

The kid's comment hit like a punch to the gut.

He swallowed past the lump in his throat. "That's because I'm helping people around town with their projects, and I'm still fixing up the old Starrycard Cabin. It's a lot of work," he lied. He'd completed the renovations months ago. He stared past her. "Anything else?"

"You used to smile. Maybe you need to write your heart's wish on a piece of Starrycard paper."

He pinched the bridge of his nose. He didn't have the energy to get into Starrycard paper folklore.

He frowned, making her point, but he couldn't help it. It had become his default setting. "I smile, sometimes."

McKenzie took a pinky sip of fake tea. "No, you don't."

"Yeah, I do. See." He flashed the kid his pearly whites.

She set the delicate cup on its saucer and waved him in. "That doesn't count."

"What do you mean? This is a real smile," he countered, dialing up the grin-wattage.

She cringed. "That's not a real one."

"Says who?" he balked.

"Me. McKenzie Fiona Starrycard-Dunleavy."

His niece was too smart for her own good. It had been one of his favorite things about the girl until she focused her powers of perception on him. This is why he'd walled himself off. This is why, whenever he did come into town, he busied himself with fixing whatever problem du jour he encountered.

"Do they make you write that mouthful of a name on the top of your homework?"

"No, Uncle Finn. I'm in first grade. I only have to write my first name. McKenzie. *M-C-K-E-N-Z-I-E.* You have to write your whole name in second grade."

"I can tell you one thing, kid. You won't be smiling next year when you have to write thirty-one letters across every page of schoolwork."

The child's brows knit together. She stared at her fingers, mumbling as she counted. She got to seventeen and blew out a frustrated breath. "My name has thirty-one letters in it? Your brain added up all the letters that fast? Are you sure that's right?"

"I'm sure." It was how his mind worked. It wasn't always easy, but once he figured out a solution, he could visualize the parts of anything and see how they went together. He could order them. Arrange them. That's what made him a successful mechanical engineer and inventor. Scratch that. That's what *had once* made him a successful mechanical engineer and inventor. He examined his calloused hands, then eyed the dollhouse. "One of the shutters looks like it's about to fall off. I could fix it."

McKenzie poured fake tea into a second teacup. "You sure love fixing things. Is there anything you can't fix, Uncle Finn?"

The vice clamped around the pieces of his shattered heart tightened. "There's one thing I haven't figured out how to fix."

"And what's that?" the kid asked, offering the cup.

He returned the screwdriver to his belt and accepted the tea. "It's not important."

It wasn't—not anymore. He was done with matters of the heart.

Fuck love.

Two words. Eight letters. One hundred percent his new mantra.

"Well, what do we have here?" his sister, Eliza Starrycard-Dunleavy, asked, leaning against the doorframe with a sly twinkle in her eyes.

He startled at the sound of her voice. But he shouldn't have been surprised. Even when she was a toddler, his little sister had been uncannily stealthy. She was also cut from his mother's cloth when it came to her powers of wit and perception.

He took a sip of fake tea. "How long have you been there, Liza?" he asked, trying to play it cool.

"Long enough to hear about you *getting some*."

God help him. He could feel his cheeks heat.

Eliza cleared her throat and coughed.

Worry creased Kenzie's brow. "Are you okay, Mommy? You've been coughing a bunch. Want some pretend tea?"

"Aren't you sweet, little star. But it's nothing. A tickle in my throat. What's going on up here?"

"We're playing tea party. I'm showing Uncle Finn how to hold a teacup the fancy way."

His sister zeroed in on him. "How's he doing?"

"He's not fancy anymore, Mom. He's something else."

"What's that, honey?"

"He's a handyman."

"That's news to me," he said, despite looking every part the handyman.

"That's what Grandma says," McKenzie explained.

He attempted to flick a few wood shavings from his sleeve. "Grandma's wrong."

The child narrowed her gaze. Her green eyes sparked with curiosity. "Then what are you?"

Another question he couldn't answer.

"Kenz, sweetheart," his sister said, strolling into the room, "Starrycard Creek's mayor requests your presence. She requires your assistance with the cake."

"It's cake time, Uncle Finn!" McKenzie exclaimed, springing to her feet. "Grandma Maeve said I could cut the cake and pick the first piece. But we can't eat yet."

"Why not?" Eliza asked, collecting the teacups.

"I have a surprise. It's my paper project. I told Grandpa Hank I wanted to make him and Grandma a special anniversary present. He said I could use anything in the recycling bin at the shop."

"Get to it. But you better check the cake first. Your Uncle Owen's been circling it like a chocolate-gobbling vulture. He might try to sneak a little icing," Eliza added with a conspiratorial air as she lowered her voice.

Finn studied his sister. She had something up her sleeve, and he'd bet his last dollar it didn't have anything to do with his brother sneaking cake.

"No icing thieves on my watch," the little girl called and took off like a shot.

"Hiding out up here?" Eliza asked, looking him over as McKenzie had done.

He picked up the bear and the frog and emitted a low growl as he rose from the ground.

His sister bit back a grin as she collected the rest of the tea party items. "All that time holed up in the old cabin has improved your communication skills immensely."

"At least I'm here," he grumbled. "Caroline is who-knows-where, finding herself, whatever the hell that means, and I assume Christian is cavorting with supermodels between doubleheaders, as professional baseball players do."

"Kieran's here, but he might as well be somewhere else," she added as they left the bedroom and headed downstairs. "He's been on the phone since he got here. City Council business. So, it's you, me, and Owen holding down the Starrycard sibling fort."

"What about our grandparents?"

"They're three scotches in and might have pre-partied before sauntering inside Starrycard House. But they did bring cherry turnovers and orange marmalade, so we'll forgive them any boozy remarks."

His grandparents, Goldie and Rex Starrycard, had retired from the family's artisan papermaking business. They'd opened a restaurant and were embracing their eighties like college seniors hitting spring break.

Finn glanced down the hall. "Where's your husband, Liza? I thought I heard him come in."

Eliza twisted her light brown locks into a bun and sighed. "A dog at the rescue sanctuary decided to go into labor. So inconsiderate of the animal, I know. Jack left the party to make a house call."

Finn nodded, then paused at the bottom of the staircase, taking a second to study one of the many framed family photos on the wall. A few of the images were faded, sepia-colored prints from over a hundred years ago. But the photo that caught his eye this evening was only about fifteen years old. The picture in question was a shot of him and his five siblings at their family's artisan paper company. Tall with dark hair, sage-green eyes, and sharp jaws, the Starrycard boys took after their father. The girls were petite like their mother, sharing her sparkling emerald eyes and caramel-brown locks. In the picture, taken at the papermaking company, the brood smiled at the camera, their hands dripping with damp pulp, dotted with pink and purple flecks, from one of the papermaking vats. A warmth he rarely felt these days emanated from his chest. It was so simple back then. All he had to concern himself with was school, tinkering in the garage, and working at the family business, The Starrycard Creek Paper Company. They'd spend hours helping their dad and grandfather make the Starrycard textured paper in the same way their ancestor William Starrycard had done it back in the late eighteen hundreds when he and his wife founded the mountain enclave with a roaring creek cutting through the heart of the town.

Finn flicked his gaze from the photo and peered at his sister. "Kenz says Owen is grumbling."

Eliza straightened the picture. "All the Starrycard bachelors seem to be grumbling these days."

He frowned. "Starrycard Bachelors?"

"Yes, that's my new name for you guys. And I'm giving you a heads-up."

"About what?"

"You know how much Mom wants a house filled with grandkids."

He sighed. "She's been bringing it up since we were kids."

"I have a feeling she wants you to get out more and meet somebody."

"What? No, that shit's not for me. Never again."

"Looks like I'm carrying the load. You boys owe me big for giving our Mother Mayor a granddaughter."

"What about Caroline?" he mused. "Have you given up hope on her?"

Eliza waved him off. "She's the baby. She can barely take care of herself. And speaking of self-care, my big brother Finnegan desperately needs some."

"Technically, every Starrycard brother is your big brother. You're number five in the lineup," he answered, attempting to redirect the conversation.

"Which makes me the oldest and wisest Starrycard sister."

"At twenty-eight?" he shot back.

"Hey, I'm a school principal married to the town's beloved veterinarian. You've become a thirty-year-old recluse." Eliza's teasing expression dissolved into concern. "Listen, Mom's worried about you, Finn. We all are. But when it comes to Mom, I fear she's about to take extreme measures. You know how she feels about love. Well, how the whole town feels about love."

Oh, he knew.

Love is always in the cards in Starrycard Creek.

Thanks to the Starrycard that founded this town, the locals had been spouting that line for over one hundred years.

Finn sighed.

Eliza rested her hand on his forearm. "You know what happened wasn't your fault. You should stop punishing yourself.

It's been a year, Finn. It's not good for you to still be spending so much time alone."

A muscle ticked on his jaw.

Who else's fault could it be?

"I'm not alone. I get out. I fixed the Town Hall's front steps this week. I patched the leak in your husband's vet office two days ago. There's barely a business on Main Street that I haven't patched up or improved in some manner. And I'm still working on the cabin."

Eliza crossed her arms. "Really? You're still working on the cabin?"

"On the property," he stammered. "There's a hell of a lot of brush to clear out. But it's April—mud season. There could be a foot of snow, or it could be warm enough to break out shorts and T-shirts. It's slow-going work because of the unpredictable weather."

Eliza raised an eyebrow, and rightly so. He didn't have to explain mud season to a seasoned Starrycard Creek Coloradan. They'd lived their entire lives in the lush valley surrounded by mountains a little over two hundred miles southwest of Denver.

She parted her lips, most likely to call bullshit on his explanation. Luckily, her phone pinged.

"This might be the answer to my prayers." She pulled her cell from her pocket, checked the screen, and frowned. "Dammit! Another no. I swear, Finn, running a school is not for the faint of heart."

"You know what else isn't for the faint of heart?" Owen Starrycard remarked, sauntering down the hall toward them.

"Let me guess. Running an artisanal handmade paper company?" Finn snapped.

Shit! He needed to dial it down.

Owen ignored him and met Eliza's gaze. "Did you talk to him?"

"You sent Eliza to talk to me about work?" Finn snarled, then inwardly cringed. His brother was carrying the load at the paper shop. He was the last person who should be giving the man shit.

"No, to let you know Mom's on a love-is-in-the-cards rampage."

Finn glanced away. "Why don't you find a nice girl, fall in love, and make some little stars?"

Owen emitted a low growl.

"See, you're all like this," Eliza lamented, shaking her head. "And there's something else, Finn. Owen didn't ask me to say this, but anyone can see, he could use your help. You guys were always the best together."

Yeah, before his life went to shit. He was no good to his brother at the shop.

The muscles at the base of his neck tightened as he shoved his hands into his pockets.

"I've left you a ton of messages, and God knows how many texts," Owen said.

Finn peered at his work boots. "I'm not much for phones these days. And I'm not ready to come back quite yet. I've got too much on my plate with . . ." He gestured to his tool belt.

"I'm not asking a lot, Finn," Owen pressed, running a hand through his dark hair. "I'm burning the candle at both ends with Dad phasing out his role and Kieran tied up with the town council."

Finn rubbed at the knots in his neck. Yes, he shared the responsibility of running the business with Owen, but he couldn't set foot in the shop. Not yet. Still, he could hear the frustration in his brother's voice.

He held his brother's gaze. "I'll make some time to come into the shop. I will."

Was that the truth? Probably not. And yeah, that made him a shit brother. But he couldn't help it, and he couldn't divulge why he couldn't stomach entering the place he'd once loved.

"There you all are," his mother crooned. "My little stars."

"Make way for Mother Mayor Maeve," Eliza murmured, using

the teasing term they'd started calling their mom when she was elected to the position after Goldie stepped down.

"McKenzie kicked us out of the kitchen to decorate," his father explained as he came to their mother's side.

His dad wrapped his arm around his mother's waist.

Finn watched the pair. A pang of envy struck. When he pictured his parents, it was always like this. Touching, like two halves of a whole drawn together. He'd loved that about them and had once craved finding his equal—his Mrs. Starrycard. Now, ice trickled through his veins at the very notion.

Fuck love.

"What was that, Finn?" his mother asked, her emerald eyes trained on him.

He shook his head. "Nothing."

"Well, I'm so glad you came down from the mountain to celebrate with us, Finnegan. I know it's not the most ideal day," his mother added, sharing a look with his father and then with Eliza and Owen.

Freaking perfect! It wasn't just a gathering to celebrate his parents' anniversary. It was a Finn Starrycard pity party.

If he had to spend much more time in this house, his head might explode.

He crossed his arms. "I'm fine, Mom."

"Is he fine, Hank?" his mother asked, turning to her husband.

"Hard to tell, honey," his dad replied, then brightened. "Want me to put on some nineties music? Your mom and I can cheer you up with our dance moves."

God help him! The last thing he needed to see was his sixty-something parents bust out a terrifying move they called the running man.

"No!" Finn exclaimed as Eliza and Owen joined in.

"Our Finnegan looks like he showers in wood chips and hasn't touched a bar of soap in weeks, but he left that musty old cabin. That has to be a good sign," his sister offered, sharing a look with the others.

And hello, full-on Starrycard ambush.

Now, the entire party of four looked him over warily like an oozing elementary school science project.

"Listen, I'm fine," he reiterated.

His mom pursed her lips. "You need to meet someone."

Here it comes.

"I don't want to meet someone, Mom. I'm happy being alone. This is who I am."

"Finnegan," his mother continued, "our family's legacy is built on love conquering all. Love is always in—"

"The cards. I know," he supplied with a heavy sigh.

"Your mother is right, Finn," his father agreed. "William Starrycard wouldn't have been able to accomplish what he did without his wife Fiona by his side. Our family has understood the power of love since eighteen eighty. That's one of the reasons people continue to purchase our paper and visit the Starrycard Creek Wishing Wall."

Finn should have expected this. Leave it to his parents to throw in the line about love always prevailing, thanks to the legend of Starrycard paper.

"Who could we set Finn up with?" his mom asked, plowing ahead like a freight train. It was her way.

"I don't want to be set up. Starrycard Creek is a small town. We know everyone." He had to change the subject. He rested his hands on his tool belt.

His tool belt. His projects. That was how he'd change the subject.

"Dad, can I borrow your axe?" he blurted. "The one up at the cabin is rusted, and the wooden handle has splintered."

His father watched him closely, narrowing his sage-green gaze. "Sure, it's in the shed. Need to take down some trees?"

Finn nodded and breathed a sigh of relief, grateful the conversation had veered from his love life. "A few aspens have bowed toward the road that need to be removed, and I want to thin out a spot near Old Man Higgins' drive. The entire property is a mess since nobody's been there for ages."

"That might be changing," his mother remarked with a sly twist to her lips.

He wasn't expecting that.

He studied the woman. "What do you mean?"

"I tracked down Albert Higgins' only living relative."

"When?"

"A couple of months ago. I included your card with the inheritance letter and the key."

"My card?" Finn asked, confusion coating the words.

"Your mom asked me to make a box of them," his father replied.

"I started giving them out," she gushed, removing a slim rectangle from her pocket. "There's a pile on my desk at the town hall and some in the library."

Finn stared at the textured paper, inhaling the woodsy scent.

Finnegan Starrycard, Local Handyman

"Really, Mom? I've got a master's degree and a lucrative patent under my belt."

"And yet, you walk around wearing a tool belt. You're a handyman with questionable hygiene, darling. We might as well embrace it."

Finn grumbled his displeasure. If there was ever a time for the floor to cave in and swallow a person whole, this was it. He stared at the ground. Unfortunately, there was no chance in hell of a structural catastrophe. The moment William Starrycard hammered the first nail into place, Starrycard House was built to last.

"I'm ready. Come and see the surprise," McKenzie called.

And thank Christ for that.

He allowed his parents and siblings to walk ahead of him. He leaned against the wall and rubbed his eyes.

Would it ever get easier?

The thought barely materialized when the clap of footsteps ceased, and a round of gasps peppered the air.

"McKenzie, your surprise is . . ." Eliza began, her words laced with concern.

What could the kid have done that was so bad with a few worthless scraps of Starrycard paper?

He entered the room. Instantly, he smelled the hint of roses. Nausea washed over him. His mouth went dry. He peered at a banner made of paper triangles held together with brown twine. The letters in *Happy Anniversary* were printed atop much smaller letters embossed onto the paper.

Paper that he'd made.

He narrowed his gaze and read a line.

The pleasure of your company is requested at the . . .

Dammit!

Of course, he knew what he was looking at. He carried a piece of that horrible day with him everywhere he went as a hidden reminder of his failure. He'd kept it on purpose as if allowing the wound to fester would keep him from making the same mistake. But he sure as hell didn't expect this reminder to be on display for all to see tonight.

"I didn't realize those were in the recycling bin, son," his father said softly.

"Neither did I," Owen added. "One of the part-timers must have put them in there."

"Are you okay, Uncle Finn? Your face is super red." McKenzie asked, her bottom lip trembling.

He had to hold it together. This wasn't her fault. She probably couldn't even read the letterpress cursive words on the oatmeal-colored paper dotted with dried red roses.

"I'm great, Kenz," he lied. "I'm blown away. I can tell you worked hard on your project." He checked his watch and feigned surprise. "Wow, look at the time. I should go. There are some trees near the road I need to chop down. One could fall and block the street. It's a safety hazard. I need to fix myself. I mean . . . fix the tree situation. It can't wait another second. I'll get the axe and be on my way. Happy anniversary, Mom and Dad," he stammered, making damned sure to keep his focus on the floor.

Without waiting for anyone to reply, he pressed a quick kiss to the top of McKenzie's head, shrugged into his coat, and bolted from the house.

Finally alone, he focused on his breath and the thud of his boots hitting the ground as the night air bathed him in a chilly reprieve.

If only the crisp breeze could numb his pain.

The one thing that would help him now was a project—work, anything that needed to be fixed. He hit the shed, got the axe, and tossed it onto his truck's bench seat. But adrenaline still coursed through his veins. He just needed to get back to the cabin. He climbed into his truck and his hammering heart began to settle as he hit the gas.

With the lights of the town behind him, he wound his way up Starrycard Mountain Drive and took a left onto Starryview Lane as a drizzling rain blurred the windshield. He turned on the wipers and took comfort in the misty darkness enveloping the truck. Exhaling a slow breath, he loosened his white-knuckle grip on the steering wheel.

Just breathe.

He exhaled another slow breath as the headlights illuminated the leaning cluster of aspen trees. The winter winds and heavy snow this season had bowed the slender trunks. He took his foot off the gas and glanced at the axe. Was the dark of night the best time to chop down a tree? Hell no. But it would keep his mind occupied.

Axe in hand, he ignored the whisper of rain and exited the truck's cab. His boots crunched against the damp gravel road. His frazzled nerves settled with each step until a slight yowling caught his attention. But he wasn't concerned. It could be anything. It was early spring, and the forest was slowly awakening from its winter slumber.

He positioned his hands, reared back, ready to swing when the sound returned. Instead of landing the first blow, he stilled, listening as a frantic scraping overlapped with the animal's low whine.

"That's a kitten! Don't you dare hurt it!" a woman yelled, her voice piercing the air and freaking him out.

Who the hell was that?

He shielded his eyes and squinted as a white form stepped into the beams of light.

Wearing a torn ivory dress speckled with mud, her hair fluttered in the breeze. Raindrops trailed down her bare shoulders. A large canvas tote bag, big enough to hold a spare tire, hung from her shoulder, and she had something furry clutched in her arms.

Holy shit! Was he hallucinating?

Was she a ghost? A hauntingly beautiful yet relatively irate supernatural being? There was a decent amount of folklore when it came to Starrycard Creek. But he'd never heard about the spirit of a woman with a thing for kittens roaming the hills at night with a gigantic purse.

She scowled at him. "You can't hurt it. I won't let you."

He wiped the rain from his brow. "What are you talking about?"

"The kitten you're about to murder."

Meow, meow.

He lowered the axe and pushed aside the dripping aspen leaves. There it was—a wet-to-the-bone ball of fluff curled beneath the tree. He scooped the kitten into his hand.

Meow.

He held it to his chest, and the tiny beast purred.

"I think it likes me," he murmured.

"What are you doing here?" the woman demanded, snapping him out of kitty cuddle time.

Dammit, that's right. She was pissed. But so was he. This was his mountain escape. She had no business being here.

"What are you doing here?" he lobbed back.

She lifted her chin defiantly. "That's none of your business."

He took a step toward her and deepened his scowl. "You're making it my business by interrupting my evening, lady."

"Your evening of murdering defenseless animals?" she exclaimed.

He didn't answer. He took a beat to study her. He'd never seen anything like her. Tourists and nature lovers would make their way up the mountain, but they usually didn't pop up until the summertime. And he'd never come across a wayward bride wandering Starrycard Creek's dark and twisty mountain roads.

Christ on a cracker. She was wearing a wedding dress.

"You're a bride," he mumbled, every muscle in his body tensing.

Why would a random bride be standing in the middle of his street? There was no wedding venue on this side of the mountain. The Starrycard Creek Bed and Breakfast was closed for mud season. If there were a wedding going on in town, his mother would have mentioned it. She knew everyone. She probably would have been invited.

He drank in the newcomer's slim waist and hourglass curves. A ragged rip in the material fluttered with each gust of wind, revealing toned legs. She was petite and frighteningly stunning. The dress left little to the imagination. The tips of his fingers tingled. His pulse quickened. And then there was his cock. He shifted his stance. Sweet Christ, he could not pop a boner.

Focus on the situation.

She was probably deranged—an escaped mental patient who robbed a bridal store. And she had to be cold. The temperature was only a few degrees above freezing.

Seriously, what was she doing out here?

He might as well find out.

"Are you dressed like that because you're looking for a husband?" he barked.

Shivering, she set her bag on the ground and straightened her posture. Shoulders back and chest forward, she looked like she was preparing to go into battle. "The last thing I want in this world is a husband. I'd rather you swing that giant axe and cut me up into a thousand tiny pieces than be subjected to a nimrod of a husband."

Nimrod of a husband?

Well, even if she was crazy, he agreed with her sentiments regarding matters of the heart.

She wobbled back a few feet, teetering on a pair of high heels —the absolute worst choice of footwear for the rugged terrain.

She pointed to the axe, then chewed her lip, losing the battle-cry person. "Okay, that might have been a bit of an overstatement. I would prefer not to be axe murdered in the middle of nowhere, where I am currently without a working car, and my cell phone's out of juice." She gasped. "Oh my gosh! I just informed a mountain man axe murderer that I'm the perfect victim."

He shared a look with the cat. The animal looked as confused as he did.

"Lady," he said, softening his tone, "this is Starrycard Creek, Colorado, and I'm not an axe murderer."

"You've got an axe," she rattled off, her voice rising an anxious octave.

She had him there.

He took a step toward her. "But I'm not a murderer."

Her jaw dropped. "That's exactly what an axe murderer would say."

He stood there, speechless. How the hell was he supposed to reply?

She held the soaked kitten to her chest. "Just don't hurt the kittens, okay? You're not going to use the axe on them, are you?"

He reared back. "No, hell, no! What are you going to do with your kitten?"

"I'm saving its life. I found it on the side of the road."

"That's what I'm doing," he exclaimed. "People dump animals along this road from time to time. Or a pregnant stray could have wandered into the woods to have her babies." Unable to stop himself, he took a few more steps toward her. He glanced past her shoulder and made out a sedan on the side of the road. "Do you need me? I mean, do I need you?" *Jesus Christ, man! Get a grip.* He shook his head. "Do you need my help?"

"Don't come any closer, Mr. Axe Murderer," she warned. She moved away from him, then yelped as she tumbled backward.

With the kitten and axe still in his hands, he rushed toward her. He dropped the axe, then leaned in to help her, and oh no! He froze when he got an eyeful of her exposed breasts.

He averted his gaze. "Your top. Your upstairs lady parts are showing," he stammered. Panic shot through him as he spun around and shut his eyes. "Should I help you get up or should I keep looking away? I'm not sure what to do in this situation." *Fuck!* This was getting crazier by the second.

"I hate this dress. And don't you dare look at me," she shrieked.

This was insanity.

"Stupid dress. Ridiculous shoes." She sighed. "Are you okay?"

He exhaled an audible breath. "Honestly, I don't know how I'm doing."

"Not you, Mr. Axe Murderer," she chided. "I'm talking to the kitten."

Tiny, angry bride huffs mixed with crunches and scrapes as the kitten in her arms broke out into a chorus of mews.

"Are you decent?" he called.

"As decent as one can get in this getup," she growled.

He turned. With mud caked to the side of her dress and a twig in her hair, she looked like she'd gotten into a wrestling match with a mountain goat. And then he noticed she was missing an integral bride accessory.

This bride wasn't wearing a wedding ring.

"You're a whole-lot-of trouble in heels, aren't you?" he murmured.

She groaned. And rightly so. He'd uttered one hell of an insult.

"Get back!" she cried, glancing around wildly. "Don't come

any closer, or I'll call for my . . . my big, hulking . . . boyfriend. A boyfriend who hates red sports cars and will protect me and my heart at all costs."

He didn't have to be a genius to know she was lying. A smart man would get in his vehicle, call a tow truck, and be done with this ridiculous encounter. But he wasn't feeling very smart. In fact, he hadn't felt this alive in ages. "You're a bride with a boyfriend?" he tossed back.

She pulled the twig out of her hair and stared at him, wide-eyed.

He picked up the axe and rested it against a tree trunk but didn't take his eyes off her. "Let's try another question," he mused.

She lifted her chin. "What is it?"

"You said you hate love and don't want a husband."

"That's right."

"But you've got a boyfriend wandering through the forest?"

She chewed her lip, and damn if the move didn't have him half-cocked.

She looked over her shoulder. "He's . . ."

Finn took in the darkened lane as a surge of electricity zinged through his body. "Where is this boyfriend?"

"He's nearby."

"Is that right?"

She took a step toward him. "You don't believe me? Do you want to know his name?"

He shrugged, pretending not to care. But on the inside, every cell in his body vibrated with heady anticipation. He knew nothing about this deranged, love-hating, ripped-to-hell wedding-dress-wearing bride except that he didn't want this strange meeting to end. He schooled his features and took a step toward her. "Sure, what's this sports-car-hating protector of your heart's name?"

She moved closer. "I should warn you—I make up his entire

universe—the sun, the stars, the moon. He's hopelessly devoted to me."

"I'm sure he is. What's his name?" He took another step.

She resumed her soldier stance. "If you touch a hair on my head, he'll make you regret it."

She was stalling, and it dialed up his need to know what outlandish thing she'd say next.

"His name?" he prodded, closing in on her.

Her chest heaved with each breath. "You're sure you want to know his name?"

"I've asked you three times, lady. Clearly, I do."

She stroked the kitten's fuzzy head, then brushed the rain from her brow. "Fine. I'll tell you."

Less than an arm's length separated them. The air crackled. The hum of the woods at night muted as if Mother Nature herself were listening to their back-and-forth banter. His breaths grew ragged as the breeze picked up. It blew wisps of hair across her cheek, and it took everything in him not to reach out and tuck the errant locks behind her ear.

"Well, let's hear it," he rasped.

She shifted the kitten into the crook of her arm, reached into her cleavage, and removed something small enough to remain hidden in the palm of her hand. She stared at whatever it was. "My boyfriend's name—the man who'll make you sorry if you axe murder me is . . ."

"Go on," he coaxed, irresistibly captivated with the mud-caked, ring-less bride.

She pressed the item to her heart and squared her jaw. "His name is . . ."

"Yes?" he whispered, taking another step toward her and on the verge of exploding from his clawing need to know.

Barely a breath apart, the headlights kissed her shoulders. Raindrops glistened on her skin like beads of twinkling magic. She was a beguiling fairy tale come to life, who smelled of cherries.

And God help him, this fascinating creature came with a scent.

She lifted her chin another fraction of an inch and stood her ground. "My boyfriend's name—the man who shouts his love for me from the rooftop. The man who—"

"What's his name?" he growled, standing close enough to feel the heat of her body.

With defiance etched on her face, she narrowed her gaze. "His name is Finnegan Starrycard."

CHAPTER

Four

FINN

FINN'S JAW DROPPED. Were his ears working? Was his brain? What the hell did that deranged bride just say? Was he dreaming? Had she said that Finnegan Starrycard was her boyfriend?

He wanted to ask that precise question but couldn't.

His name flowing from her lips had left him speechless and damn-near spellbound. All he could do was stand there and drink her in. Raindrops trailed down her cheeks. He observed the gentle curve of her jawline. He studied her full lips and determined chin. And those eyes. He couldn't make out the color, but the intensity of her gaze left him mesmerized.

"Did you hear me?" she asked, her voice barely a whisper.

He snapped out of it. He could not allow himself to moon over this woman. He cleared his throat and stepped back, placing some much-needed distance between them. "Finnegan Starrycard is your boyfriend?" he asked, finding his voice.

She glanced away. "That's what I said."

Lying wasn't her forte.

He didn't take his eyes off her. "Does Finnegan Starrycard know this?"

"Of course, he knows this. I make up his entire—"

"I get it. And all the rooftop yelling, too," he supplied.

She wiped the rain from her cheek. "That's right."

He ignored his conflicting emotions surging and crashing, leaving a whirlwind of uncertainty in their wake. It was time to get some answers. He was done playing games in the rain.

"Who are you, lady?" he demanded in his best surly mountain man tone.

Unfazed by his gruff demeanor, she took a step toward him. "Who are you—besides the resident axe murderer?"

"I'm Finnegan Fucking Starrycard," he announced to the entire mountain.

Now, the bride's jaw hit the ground. "You're the local handyman?" She presented her palm and revealed the item in her hand.

He moved so the beams of light could illuminate the object. Holy shit! It was a card—a card he recognized. His mother had just shown him an exact replica at the house.

"Hello? Are you the handyman?" she pressed.

He stared at the drops of rain dancing on the rectangle's surface. "Yeah, sort of." He lifted his gaze and met her eye. "Who are you?"

"I'm Hailey Higgins. I'm looking for—"

"Higgins Hideaway. You inherited the cabin," he finished, connecting the dots.

She cocked her head to the side. "How do you know that?"

"My mother is—"

"Wait!" she exclaimed. "It's Maeve O'Leary-Starrycard, right?"

How the hell were they already finishing each other's sentences?

"How do you know that?"

"She's the mayor. She sent me the letter about my great-uncle's cabin."

Holy hell! This piece of work was his new neighbor. He'd barely processed the thought when a gust of icy wind rustled through the sea of evergreens. His deranged bride—no, she had a name. Hailey shivered. He set the kitten on the ground and shrugged out of his coat.

"What are you doing, Mr. Starrycard?"

"Mr. Starrycard is my dad or my grandpa. Call me Finn."

"What are you doing, Finn?" she asked, edging away from him.

"You're wet and freezing. I'm giving you my coat. Don't say no. Don't tell me you don't want to wear an axe murderer's jacket. Just take it, Hailey." It was curiously invigorating to say her name.

And perhaps it helped.

She didn't fight him as he draped the coat over her slight shoulders. He adjusted the collar, and his fingertips brushed against her rain-kissed skin. The breath caught in his throat. Butterflies fluttered in his belly.

Butterflies?

Reel it in, man.

This must be what happened when a guy locked himself away for a year. Every sensation amplified. Every emotion intensified.

He assessed her from head to toe. The coat was at least five sizes too big. It nearly reached her knees. But it would keep her warm. And for some damned reason, he wanted to keep this stranger safe, like it was his duty to protect her.

What was happening to him?

He picked up the kitten and took a step back. "There you go," he stammered, channeling the awkwardness of a gawky teenager.

She stared up at him. "I'm sorry I lied and said you were my boyfriend. If it's not already obvious, I don't have a boyfriend." She looked away. "I don't have anyone."

Her words hung heavy in the air. He could feel the weight of her loneliness.

"I panicked," she continued, "and then remembered your name from the business card."

He wanted to gather her into his arms and kiss her until they each forgot their pain. But there was no way in hell he could do that.

He zeroed in on the kitten in his arms, doing everything he

could to calm the hell down. "Don't worry about it," he mumbled, reverting to caveman communication.

"Before my phone went dead, the navigation app said I'd made it to my destination. 222 Starryview Lane. But I can't find the cabin," she said, and when she wasn't screaming at him, her voice was gentle like a tender melody.

"I can help you with that," he answered, fighting the urge to touch her.

She shifted the kitten in her arms, tucking it inside the folds of his coat. "Do you live up here?"

It should be an easy question to answer. But it wasn't.

"Yes, for now. I'm fixing up my family's cabin. It's on the property next to Old Man Higgins' place."

"Hailey's Place," she corrected with a whisper of a grin.

"What?" he asked, so damned enthralled with this woman.

"It's my home until I figure out what comes next. So, Hailey's Place for now."

Hailey's Place.

It had a nice ring to it.

Jesus, stop!

He kicked a small mound of wet gravel. "You don't want to live in Starrycard Creek?"

Her shoulders slumped forward. "I'm not sure what I want. I've never been so lost—literally and figuratively."

The knot in his belly tightened. What was going on with him? What did it matter if she stayed or left?

He cleared his throat. "I'll take you to your cabin."

"In your truck?"

"No, in the rocket ship I built. Can't you see it? It's in the middle of the road." Dammit, there was his gruff, recluse side rearing its ugly head.

He expected her to hurl a scowl his way or call him an axe murderer.

She didn't.

She giggled, and the sweet trill almost had him smiling—almost.

She picked up her giant tote bag from the side of the road. "I needed that. Thanks," she replied, a weariness creeping into her tone.

Not sure what to do or say, thanks to his gone-to-shit social skills, he nodded and produced an utterance that could be best described as a caveman-casual grunt as he gestured for them to head to his truck. Going through the motions, he secured the axe in the back, then opened the passenger door for her. "Here," he said, taking her hand to help her inside. And there it was again—freaking butterflies and that current of electricity he didn't know how to stifle.

It was nothing—misfiring neurons.

He closed her door and walked around the back of the vehicle, staring at the silhouette of the woman riding shotgun. Warmth filled his chest. Did he like having her around? No, of course, he didn't. This interaction was simply a neighborly act of kindness. He couldn't leave her wandering in the rain. Still, her presence threw a wrench into his plans. He'd come to Starrycard Cabin to steer clear of people, and he couldn't do that with this cherry-scented, mud-splattered, ripped-wedding-dress-wearing outsider living a damned hop, skip, and a jump from his cabin.

Jesus, what a mouthful.

He got in and handed her the kitten. "You'll have to use my driveway to get to your property. Old Man Higgins' driveway is overgrown with brush. There's a path that connects our land."

"It's Hailey's driveway, for the moment," she corrected.

"Sorry, old habits, you know," he mumbled.

Getting his head back in the game, he fired up the engine, and they rumbled down the bumpy road.

"That's my family's place," he said, pointing to the cabin nestled among a blanket of evergreens. The outdoor lighting he'd installed held the cozy home in a warm glow.

"It looks like something out of a mountain living magazine," she said softly.

"We're in the mountains, so, yeah, it's mountain living."

She chuckled again, that same sweet trill of a sound, like a contagious melody spreading infectious joy.

He glanced at her. "I wasn't trying to be funny."

She gifted him with a dazzling smile. "I know you weren't, Finn."

He looked away, unsure of what to make of her statement or his racing pulse. Determined to maintain his hardened facade, he glared ahead, then turned left onto a narrow path. The foliage scratched the sides of his truck as he navigated the darkened trail. The bush let up, and a lone cottage flanked by towering ever-greens loomed in the darkness.

"That's your place," he said and parked in front of the struc-ture. He frowned. He was on this side of the property recently and didn't like what he saw. Tonight's visit hadn't improved his assessment of the cabin. The roof had lost several shingles. The screen door hung cockeyed. It clanged against the side of the cottage with each gust of wind.

He kept his attention on the rundown structure. "Did you call ahead to get the power and water turned on?"

She fiddled with the cuff of his coat. "There wasn't a whole lot of planning ahead. I learned I'd inherited this cabin seven hours ago. I left Kansas and headed here. I'll figure out the utilities tomorrow."

Seven hours ago! And what the hell had happened in Kansas to make her bolt? He eyed her torn dress—her torn wedding dress. That had to be the reason. And she clearly didn't have anywhere else to go. But coming here wouldn't be like staying at the Four Seasons. Higgins Hideaway was no posh vacation spot. It had been vacant and left to the elements for a couple of years. Even when Old Man Higgins was still around, it appeared aban-doned and unkempt.

Hailey leaned toward him. The light from the dash lit her face in a golden hue. "Thanks for—"

"Not axe murdering you?" he finished.

When did he become a funny guy?

A slip of a grin tugged at the corners of her lips. "Yeah, and for the ride." She surveyed the animals sleeping in her lap. "What should we do about the kittens?"

"Leave them with me. I know a guy who can help."

She peered at him through her lashes. "Not an axe murderer, I hope?"

And God help him, there was that smile—that adorable twist of her full lips.

He glanced away. "It's a small town. We can only handle one potential axe murderer at a time. I can promise you that my best friend isn't the axe-murdering type, and he'll know what to do with the cats." He remained stock-still, feeling her eyes on him.

"You're a sweet guy, Finnegan Starrycard."

He sat there like a lump. Sweet? He'd been nothing but a grump for the better part of the last year—and a pretty big asshole to her tonight.

She reached into her bag. "I'd like to thank you. Would you like a cherry licorice twist?"

He wasn't expecting that, but it did explain the smell.

"Yeah, okay," he mumbled.

She handed him the candy, then shrugged out of his jacket.

He took a bite of the licorice and hummed his delight. "I forgot how much I like this stuff."

"Isn't it funny how something as simple as a little candy can turn your day around? Someone I loved very much used to say that every time she took a bite of a cherry licorice twist."

He nodded, intrigued at how this curiously beguiling woman could inject optimism into what must have been one hell of a tumultuous day.

She made a pillow with his coat and set it between them on the bench seat. Gently, she nestled the animals in the faded twill folds. Seemingly satisfied with the kittens' placement, she stroked the tiny beasts one last time, then held her tote to her chest. "I'll see you around, Finnegan Starrycard. Local handyman."

That was it? She would disappear into an abandoned cabin, and whatever the hell was happening between them would be over? A hollowness engulfed the cab of the truck. Or was it a hollowness in his chest?

She slipped out of the car and shut the door. He didn't say a word. He didn't even grunt or growl. The clap of metal meeting metal sent a charge through his body. The cherry fragrance enveloped the car. He peered ahead, watching her weave through the tangle of overgrown, spindly chokecherry bushes and a blanket of tumbleweed. She wobbled on those ridiculous shoes, and his heart leaped into his throat.

He cut the engine, threw open the driver's side door, and found his voice. "Hailey, hold up a second."

The gentle rain had stopped, and the scent of pine and earth permeated the night air. As the clouds parted, a shimmering streak of stars sliced through the sky. Hailey stopped and looked over her shoulder. A sliver of moonlight held the woman in an ethereal glow.

"How about I check out the cabin with you? I've got a tool belt with a flashlight. I adore tools. I'm a real tool fanatic."

Holy freaking Christ! He not only had tools. He was a tool.

"I'd appreciate that," she answered and gestured toward the ramshackle cottage. "It looks a little rough around the edges. Nothing wrong with that. I'm sure it's better on the inside." As she'd spoken the words, a blustery wind blew a forceful puff of mountain air. The precariously positioned screen door banged once, then twice, then . . .

Whoosh!

With a clawing whine, the damn thing flew off the lone hinge holding it in place. The metal door hit the side of the cabin and ricocheted toward them. He had to act. Sprinting, he scooped her into his arms and jumped back. The warped metal whizzed past them and crashed into a hulking blue spruce.

"Wow, thanks," Hailey said, breathless, clutching her bag to her chest as she nuzzled into him.

His heart beat like a goddamned drum. He inhaled and smelled cherry but also . . . pickles. He peered into her bag and spied a metal lid. "Do you travel with pickles and cherry licorice?"

"Not pickles. Just cherry licorice and an old pickle jar."

She was a deranged bride who roamed around with candy and an ancient pickle jar. Did she think that made her sound less nuts? He narrowed his gaze. What was in the jar? It didn't appear to be pickles. Then again, maybe he didn't want to know. What would a person carry in a giant jar? Forget being labeled an axe murderer. Shlepping around glass jars with questionable content was strange and bizarre behavior—something straight out of a serial killer documentary. That being said, since the moment Hailey Higgins crashed into his life, his world had become the embodiment of strange and bizarre. That had to change. As mesmerizing as she was, he needed to return to his dull, solitary life.

It was time to get this show on the road. He'd get her settled inside and return to his solitude.

Making sure the projectile screen door wasn't going anywhere, he carried her up the two steps that led to the porch. The warped wood gave off a spongy squeak. He growled his displeasure and eyed the paint peeling off the front door. "I'm not sure this structure is safe," he mumbled.

She leaned into him. "It doesn't matter. I'll make it work. It's all I've got."

His chest muscles tightened, or perhaps it was his heart clenching.

If she fell, nobody was waiting in the wings to catch this woman.

Jesus, when had he become a damned sap?

He grumbled and tightened his hold on her. A flicker of movement caught his eye. He glanced up and spied a canvas awning. That would need to be secured.

"Finn?" she said softly.

"Yeah?" he answered, still glaring at the drooping material.

"Could you put me down so I can open the door?"

Jesus, he'd forgotten he had a tiny woman in his arms. It was like she'd become a cherry-scented, pickle-perfumed appendage. He accessed his limited vocabulary and grunted a caveman version of yes. Feeling around with his foot for a less creaky spot, he lowered her to the porch.

She dug in her bag and produced an old key. "Here we go," she said, but she didn't insert it into the lock. Instead, she leaned against the door and drank him in. "Do you want to give it to me?"

He stared into her eyes. "Hell yes," he whispered.

She cocked her head to the side. "What did you say?"

Was he short-circuiting?

"Hell yes, I'll give you whatever you want," he stammered, attempting to recover his dignity and failing spectacularly. Thank God it was dark, and she couldn't see the flare of red heating his cheeks.

"I'd like the flashlight on your tool belt. Do you mind if I touch it?"

"I can't think of anything I'd like more." He shook his head, praying the movement would jumpstart his addled mind. "I mean, yes, touch it. Touch it as much as you like. I mean, no," he stammered, cursing his discombobulated brain. "I can hold it— the flashlight. We're talking about a flashlight."

"Yes, we are," she replied.

He could hear the thread of amusement in her voice. At least somebody was benefiting from his oatmeal brain.

He pulled the object in question—that he'd never look at the same way again—from its spot on his belt and clicked it on. "Flashlight," he said, like how McKenzie used to identify objects in picture books when she was a toddler.

Hailey grinned up at him. "Yes, that's your big flashlight."

Damned phallic flashlight!

His heart was back to thumping away in his throat. "Why don't you unlock the door, and we can see what we're dealing with here."

She inserted the old key into the lock and jiggled the knob. "It's a little rusty, but I think I've—"

Click.

The bolt retracted, and the locking mechanism released.

Eeeer!

The warped wood creaked open like it was auditioning for the role of *Spooky Door* in a scary movie.

Hailey exhaled a shaky breath and stepped toward him.

He had to put her at ease. "Don't worry. That noise is nothing. The hinges need a little lubrication. It's an easy fix."

"Okay, that doesn't sound like a major problem," she replied, relief coating her words.

He shined the light into the snug space. Old Man Higgins had been around long before he was born, but he'd never seen the inside of the hermit's cabin. He swept the light across the main room, illuminating a stack of old papers next to a tattered recliner.

"Did you ever meet your great-uncle?" he asked as they cautiously entered the cabin.

"No, I don't know much about him. My dad had mentioned he kept to himself."

"I'd agree with that. I'd only seen him a handful of times, and I've lived in Starrycard Creek my whole life—well, most of my life." A lump formed in his throat, but he didn't have time to let the past swallow him up.

Hailey scooted by and picked up one of the pieces of paper. "It's a mix of newspapers and loose sheets." She ran her hand over the top of the stack. "Huh," she said with a curious bend to the syllable.

But he couldn't worry about a pile of paper. He needed to make sure the place wouldn't collapse with the next gust of wind.

He squinted. Dust danced in the beam of light as a pungent scent pierced the cold, stale air. He surveyed the scene with an engineer's eye. She'd need a new floor and possibly a new roof. A built-in bookshelf was in rough shape, but that didn't affect the structural integrity.

He swept the light across the room again and took a step. *Creak!* Besides a few puddles dotting the floor, some peeling wallpaper, and a couple of cockeyed cabinet doors, nothing glaringly dangerous stood out to him.

The place was sparse. A recliner. A table with one chair. The kitchen and the bedroom had to be in the back half. The guy didn't appear to have a TV. Finn ran his finger across a wobbly end table and picked up an inch of dust.

He flicked the beam of light and pointed it toward Hailey. "We should take it slow. I don't want you falling through the floor."

Hailey stomped her heels on the hardwood. "It feels solid enough to me. And look, there's a stone fireplace and a bookshelf. How cozy! Can I take that?" she asked, gesturing to the flashlight.

"Sure. But seriously, be careful. Most of the improvements that need to be made seem to be cosmetic, but you never know."

She crossed the room in a cacophony of clacks and creaks. "This isn't bad at all. It's musty and a bit dingy, but there's a little kitchen with a fridge in the back. And look! A hutch. I don't see anything up top but there could be dishes in the bottom half behind those doors." She shined the light on a tarnished oval knob. "It's like a choose-your-own-adventure book. My students love those."

"Students?" he repeated.

"I'm a teacher." She glanced over her shoulder and waved him over. "Let's see what's inside." She swung open the door and gasped.

He crouched. Four pairs of eyes belonging to four very large raccoons peered at them.

He rose slowly. "Don't make any sudden moves."

"Maybe they're friendly?" she offered.

Grrrr! Hiss! Grrr!

Friendly raccoons? That would be a big hell no. The raccoon quartet snarled and snapped, growling and clawing. The largest one swiped its paw at her. Hailey shrieked, wobbled backward, and dropped the flashlight. It clattered against the ground, clicking off, leaving them in a sea of blackness.

"Hailey?" he called through the uproar of piercing squeals and growls. The swish and scuffle of the unwanted cabin occupants echoed off the walls.

A sharp thud cut through the animal's racket, followed by Hailey shrieking again. The frenzied scratch of claws meeting hardwood peppered the air. It was a madhouse! He took a few cautious steps forward, and his foot hit the flashlight—thank Christ. He grabbed it and turned on the lamp in time to catch the four interlopers hightailing it toward the back of the cabin, where he was ninety-nine percent sure he'd find a raccoon-sized hole.

"Ow, I hate these shoes," she bit out.

He pointed the light and found her prostrate on the floor, clutching her ankle.

He sprinted the few steps to get to her. "Are you hurt?"

"I slipped on something sticky. I may have twisted my ankle."

He shined the light on her foot and grimaced. Oh, she'd stepped in something sticky, all right.

She leaned forward, assessing the damage. "What is that? Poop? Is that raccoon poop?" she yelped, her words tumbling from her lips as anxiety gripped her.

He eyed the substance in question. "It's not poop."

"Thank God," she gushed. "What is it?"

"It's called scat."

"What?"

"Scat."

She focused on him intently. "Isn't that another word for poop?"

He shrugged. "Yeah."

She wiggled and squirmed, kicking like a gazelle fending off a lion. "Ew, ew, ew! Ow, ow, ow!" The scat scattered, pebbling off in a disgusting spray of fecal particles.

"Stop moving," he exclaimed. "You're making it worse."

He swooped in and scooped her into his arms for the second time in less than five minutes.

She clutched her giant tote to her chest. "I have to wash this off. Check the tap. See if this place has water."

Juggling a petite, scat-covered woman and a flashlight, he rushed her to the sink. Hold this," he said, handing her the light.

She focused the beam on the water-stained faucet.

He turned the discolored knob in a counterclockwise motion. The wheezing grind of metal rubbing against metal wailed as he wrestled with the cantankerous dial. An ominous sputtering accompanied a menacing vibration. A grating groan, something akin to a slumbering sea beast being rudely awakened, reverberated through the space.

He stared at the rusty faucet. "That is not a good sound for pipes to make."

"Should anything sound like that, Finn?"

He shook his head. "No."

The sound tapered to a low hiss. But that wasn't a reassuring turn of events either. He had a good idea of what was coming. And very little time to react.

"Look out!" he cried.

With an angry gurgle, water exploded from the faucet like a vengeful geyser.

"I'm turning this off. And we're getting the hell out of here," he called, wrestling with the knob as the spray soaked their bodies. He gave it two forceful turns. With a furious burble and what sounded a hell of a lot like a monster burp, the water stopped its catastrophic aqua eruption. He breathed a sigh of relief, but he wasn't about to wait around to find out what else this little cottage of horrors had to offer.

Running like their lives depended on it—because there was a decent chance something in this place could kill them—he bolted out the door. "We're going to my place," he rasped, adrenaline coursing through his veins. He threw open the passenger side door and guided her onto the bench seat. The kittens mewed excitedly, sensing the restless energy.

Hailey inhaled a sharp breath and winced.

He cupped her face in his hand. "Is it your ankle?"

She bit down on her bottom lip. "Yeah, but I'm okay. Let's go!"

He ran to the driver's side and bounced into his seat. Not wasting a second, he fired up the engine and threw the gearshift into reverse. The tires squealed, grinding into the layer of wet pine needles blanketing the ground.

Hailey gasped. "Finn, look at the roof."

Blinking the water out of his eyes, he stared at the cabin. Four raccoon forms sat atop the house like furry conquerors.

"The nerve of them," she huffed.

And he was right there with her. He rolled down his window. "You asshole raccoons! This is Hailey's Place."

"You are officially evicted!" she hollered.

As if the fuzzy creatures understood—and weren't at all pleased with the arrival of the meddling humans—the group descended from the roof like a raccoon Navy Seal Unit. The pack headed straight for the truck.

"Go!" she yelled.

She didn't have to tell him twice.

Pedal to the metal, he hit the gas. A cascade of mud sprayed from his back tires. Slamming the vehicle into drive, he floored it down the bumpy path connecting his property to hers. It barely took thirty seconds before they pulled up to his place.

"Stay there. I don't want you putting any weight on that ankle," he ordered halfway out the door. He sprinted to her side and hoisted her into his arms. "Are you in pain?"

She curled into him. "I think I'm in shock."

"That makes two of us."

He unlocked the door, flicked on a light, and placed her on the couch.

She stared out the door. "Don't forget the kittens!"

"Shit, the kittens!" Like a damned chicken with its head cut off, he sprinted out of the cabin.

His motion detection lights turned on with all the commotion. He skidded to a stop, scanned the property, and searched for four pairs of beady eyes. Blessedly, there wasn't a raccoon in sight. Catching his breath, he gathered the makeshift cat bed, ushered the pair out of the truck, then stilled. He gave his property another once-over. Trees. Rocks. More trees. No killer raccoons. He shut the car doors, leaned against his truck, and took a few slow breaths.

"What a night," he said to the kittens.

They stared at him and meowed.

Perfect! He'd made the move from growly loner mountain man to crazy guy talking to his kittens.

No, these weren't his kittens.

The last thing he needed were pets. Rolling his head from side to side to work out the kinks at the base of his neck, he entered the cabin, grabbed an old plastic milk crate, and set the pair inside. "That'll keep you safe and contained."

He stood and ran his hands down his damp cheeks. "Jesus, what a night, huh?" He waited for Hailey to reply. But she didn't make a peep. He peered over his shoulder at the couch. "What the hell?" he mumbled and scanned the room. The location where he'd left his bride was now bride-less.

CHAPTER
Five

FINN

WHERE THE HELL was Hailey Higgins?

How could she have disappeared in less than thirty seconds?

Finn walked through the living room into the dining room. The cabin was a large square with the living room, dining room, and kitchen stacked on one side and the bedrooms, bath, and utilities on the other. He grimaced. Littered with empty bowls, half-filled glasses, and his goddamned laundry piled on the dining room table, from top to bottom, his Starrycard bachelor pad was a fucking disaster. Was the laundry clean or dirty? He didn't have a clue. What he did know was that it looked like a tornado had drilled a path through the snug space. And what he still didn't see was his bride—no, not his bride. The bride. She had to be here. She wouldn't get far on that ankle. Having a stranger roaming around his cabin doing God knows what should have been alarming. But it wasn't. He could smell the hint of cherry. She was still here. The momentary reprieve gave him a second to take care of his damp clothing.

He eyed the laundry. Even if it was dirty, it was dry. And that beat soaked to the bone any day. He removed his tool belt and slung it next to the pile. An odd lightness took over as he glanced around. Still no bride. He stripped off his wet shirt, hung it over the back of one of the chairs, and slipped on a black T-shirt from the pile. He sniffed his pits, then shrugged. It was clean enough. Somewhat dry, he headed into the kitchen. No bride there either. Instead, a heap of takeout boxes piled precariously on a small island in the center of the space greeted him with the scent of stale French fries.

There were only three other places she could be. The bathroom, his bedroom, or the spare bedroom. She could have hightailed it out the back door onto the porch. But she hadn't. How did he know? The scent—her cherry sweetness—intensified. It soothed him, filling the air with a comforting aroma that put his mind at ease, reassuring him that she was still within reach.

"Hailey?" he called, reveling in how natural it felt to speak her name.

"In here. I wanted to clean up a bit and plug in my phone. I hope you don't mind," she called from behind the bathroom door.

He leaned against the wall across from it, eyeing the light and the shadows moving on the other side. "What about your ankle? You shouldn't be walking on it."

"It's tender. I think I tweaked it. No real damage done. And Finn?"

"Yeah?" His pulse kicked up.

"This might not be the most appropriate request, but I was hoping I could use your shower."

"My shower?" he eked out, sounding like he'd just entered puberty.

"To de-scatify myself. Between the mud, rain, and raccoon poop, I don't think I've ever been this filthy."

Filthy?

His filthy caveman brain flashed the image of her accidentally flashing him. Christ, she was alluring. What would those breasts feel like pressed against his bare chest? He shook his head, attempting to knock that dirty thought clean out of his mind. He could not entertain those kinds of thoughts. He squeezed his eyes shut like a two-year-old. "No, stop it."

"No?" she repeated.

He blinked open his eyes.

Jesus, he was a scattered clusterfuck of a mess.

He cleared his throat. "I was talking to someone else."

"There's someone else here?" Uneasiness coated her question.

He ran his hands down his face. "No, I was talking to the . . . the kittens." *Dammit!* He truly was a cat dude now. "Go ahead and take a shower. It's not a problem," he answered, praying he'd put the toilet seat down, which he probably didn't. His sister's assessment of him being a bachelor was dead on—not that he'd ever cop to it. And then it hit. Hailey was the first person to enter the cabin since he'd moved in a year ago.

The shower started, and he flicked his gaze back to the door. He pictured her slipping the dress down her torso, skimming the skintight material past her hips.

"Finn?"

He gasped, damn near jumping out of his skin. "Yeah, yes, I'm still here, but not in a creepy way." He grimaced. Saying he wasn't creepy was the defining characteristic of being a total creeper.

"The tile work in here is gorgeous. Did you do it?" she asked.

He breathed a sigh of relief. He could talk about this subject without the threat of sporting a hard-on. "Yes, I did it myself."

"Is this a steam shower?"

"Sure is," he answered, feeling pretty damned good about himself.

"And are the floors heated? They feel like heaven."

He stood a little taller. "They are. I put in a hydronic system. Water circulates through a polyethylene tubing. I like tubes. I'm good with tubes." He grimaced. "As in building materials."

Dammit! What the hell was wrong with his mouth?

"You really are a handyman," she remarked.

He stuffed his handy hands in his pockets. "That's what it says on the card that my mom had made for me." Jesus, he did it again. He hung his head. Now, he sounded like a tube-obsessed cat guy with mommy issues. He waited for a beat, then another. She had to be in the shower. There was a good chance she hadn't heard his asinine response and . . . she was probably naked.

Probably naked?

Of course, she was naked. She was taking a shower. Unable to stop himself, he pictured Hailey Higgins in his shower. At this very second, water would be drenching her hair, trailing to her shoulders and lower to her perfect breasts.

He stared at the closed door.

What was she doing now? Soaping up her legs? Running her hands through her hair? Puffs of steam escaped beneath the door as his breathing grew audible. The woman was likely hot, wet, and shrouded in a steamy cloud as she lathered up her slim, lithe frame.

So much for not being creepy.

He glanced at the pronounced bulge in his pants.

He could not let her see him like this.

He had to do something—anything other than fantasizing about a stranger in his bathroom while lurking in the hallway like a grade A creeper.

Waddling like his pants had gotten a wee bit tighter—because they had—he made his way to the kitchen, seeking something to occupy his mind and hands. And hallelujah, the answer was right in front of him. He'd scour the filthy thoughts right out of his head by engaging in a little de-hornification cleaning.

Moving like a lean, mean cleaning machine, he swiped the takeout boxes into the trash, loaded the dishwasher, and threw his laundry into a basket. The kittens mewed, and he went to work finding something for them to eat. He opened the refrigerator and sniffed a carton of milk. It was a few days past the expiration, but it smelled pretty much okay. Carefully, he poured the remaining liquid into a saucer and placed it inside the crate with the kittens. He peered at the ginger balls of fluff as they feasted on what he hoped wasn't sour milk. Getting into the groove of not imagining Hailey naked, he concentrated on a stack of wood by the fireplace.

He found his next task.

The mountain air still held a chill, and he could certainly go for the soothing crackle and pop of a roaring fire. Arranging the logs and lighting the kindling, he zeroed in on the doorway—the threshold that marked the entrance to his secluded abode. A curious revelation dawned. He'd carried a bride over it. Not his bride, of course, but a bride, no less.

"Wood, wood, wood. Focus on wood," he mumbled.

"Hey there, handyman," came a woman's purring voice that drew the attention of his man wood.

"I wasn't thinking about man wood. Just wood-wood," he blurted. *Shit!* It was Hailey, and he sounded like he'd been hit upside the head with a piece of wood-wood. He sprang from his crouched position and banged his head on the mantle.

Hailey gasped. "Finn, I didn't mean to frighten you. Are you okay?"

He rubbed his head and stumbled onto the floofy ivory sheepskin rug situated between the couch and the hearth. He groaned. That mishap would leave a mark. "I'm . . ." he began, then took her in. The throbbing noggin pain disappeared, or maybe his brain couldn't experience pain and process the scene before him.

She stood in the center of the room barefoot and toyed with the hem of a faded T-shirt—his T-shirt—that hit her mid-thigh. It was his old Starrycard Creek Paper Company shirt he'd had since he was sixteen. It had been given to him the summer he was officially hired to work at his family's business. The logo and lettering had faded over the last decade and a half, but he could still make out the curve of the creek and the stars from the image Fiona Starrycard had created all those years ago.

He continued his examination of his unexpected houseguest. Her hair was damp. Her auburn hair. She was a redhead with doe-like amber eyes. A smattering of freckles dusted her cheeks. Between the darkness and then the utter melee of escaping the cabin from hell, he hadn't had a chance to properly look at her. Christ, she looked like an angel. Was she sent to save him?

She released the hem and ran her hands down her torso. "This shirt was on the hook on the back of the door. I wasn't sure what to wear. I couldn't bear to put that dress back on." She touched the collar. "This shirt is so soft and comfy. It's the opposite of the ridiculous bridal monstrosity I've been stuck in all day. But don't worry. Even though I wasn't wearing any underwear, I had a clean pair in my bag. Not that I walk around with extra under-wear or gallivant around going commando." She chewed her lip. "That was probably too much information."

She was nervous.

That made two of them.

"I don't mind that you're wearing my shirt. And wearing clean underwear is . . ."

"Good hygiene," she chimed.

"Uh-huh . . . and that shirt is just a shirt I sleep in. But I haven't slept in it in a while. I haven't been sleeping very well this past year—mostly because I pass out on the couch in my clothes. Sometimes, I even forget to take off my tool belt."

She cocked her head to the side.

God help that mouth of his! Score another point for the tool of the year, Finnegan William Starrycard.

He raised his hands defensively. "I don't mean that I pass out like I've got a drinking problem. I do drink, from time to time, but normal amounts because I'm a normal non-creepy guy." He clamped his mouth shut. It wasn't doing him any favors. At this point in the evening, she probably thought a quartet of angry raccoons had to be more appealing company than a blathering, possibly alcohol-obsessed handyman with insomnia.

She mustered a weak grin. "I could use a drink."

"Christ, me too," he muttered on a relieved exhale and headed into the kitchen. He held up a bottle. "Tequila?"

"Perfect," she answered, following a step behind when her stomach growled. She gasped and pressed her hand to her belly. "Oh my gosh! That's embarrassing. All I've had to eat today is a few cherry licorice twists."

"I can help with that, too," he answered. He opened the fridge, and shit, it looked like a takeout container graveyard. He tried the freezer and eyed eight pints. "I haven't been to the market in a while. How about some cherry chocolate chip ice cream?"

She beamed. "It's my favorite."

"Really?"

"Yeah." She peered past him and grinned. "And it appears to be yours, too."

He felt a blush heat his cheeks. "Pretty obvious, huh?"

"What's so bad about liking ice cream?" she asked without even a hint of judgment.

He relaxed. "Absolutely nothing," he answered, again, finding himself spellbound with this woman.

She leaned against the island. "Can I help? You can make our drinks, and I can scoop the ice cream?"

"That works." He gestured with his chin toward the cabinet. "Bowls are in there, and the silverware is below in the drawer."

Side by side, they worked silently. He glanced at her and caught her looking at him.

She blushed, and sweet Jesus, the color pink never looked so alluring. But he couldn't tell her that. He needed to engage her in normal, non-creepy conversation.

"Do you have a suitcase in your car? I could get it for you," he said, filling the space with small talk.

She stared at the teeming bowls of ice cream. "I don't have a suitcase, just my tote." She looked up, and her eyes shined with emotion. "Can we have our snack by the fire?"

"Sure, should I bring—"

"The bottle? Yes, absolutely," she exclaimed, and the adorable blush returned. "And for the record, I'm like you. I drink a normal, non-creepy amount of alcohol, from time to time, when the situation calls for it." She toyed with a lock of auburn hair. "Do I sound insane?"

"No, not at all. Well, you do, but it's comforting. I like it." He cleared his throat. This was not him. He wasn't a tongue-tied fool, but her cherry-sweet vulnerability had turned him into a walking sitcom, spouting awkward lines and fumbling like a clumsy clown.

She closed her eyes and sighed. "This day has me feeling like I don't know up from down."

He understood that sentiment better than anyone.

"I don't know if tequila will help, but it can't hurt. Let's sit," he said, holding the two tumblers in one hand and the bottle in the other.

As if she'd done it a thousand times, she padded ahead of him, passed over the sheepskin rug, and set the bowls of ice cream on the coffee table. She settled in on the couch. There was something so natural about existing alongside her, like old friends sharing a comfortable silence.

Stop! Just drink the damned tequila.

He handed her a glass and joined her, making sure to put as much space as possible between them.

She held up the tumbler. "To not being an axe murderer." She pursed her lips, but there was a twinkle in her eyes. "You're not one, right?"

"If I am, I'm not a very efficient one," he said, clinking his glass with hers.

She took a sip, then eyed the liquid, shrugged, and knocked back the rest.

He followed her lead and tossed back the alcohol. The sharp burn soothed his nerves.

Hailey closed her eyes and melted into the sofa. "What a day."

"What a day," he echoed, taking another opportunity to observe her. Her beauty was captivating, and seeing her in his T-shirt stirred a yearning deep within him.

"Are the kittens all right?" she asked with her eyes still closed.

"I gave them some milk and set them up in a crate. They're a pair of ginger cats, like you."

She opened her eyes.

He shoveled ice cream into his mouth. "That came out wrong," he mumbled through the bite. "Their fur is similar to yours . . .

your hair. You don't have fur because you're not a cat or an animal. You're a person." He took another gargantuan bite, nearly finishing the bowl and praying the cold treat would numb his tongue to render him mute.

She took a bite of ice cream, grabbed her bowl and glass, and headed to where he'd left the kittens near the hearth. She sat on the sheepskin rug and peered at the animals. "You're right. A trio of redheads seem to have taken over your cabin." Her sunny disposition darkened. "And I seem to have quite a bit in common with these cats."

He watched her closely. "What do you mean?"

"They're unwanted and on their own in this world." She concentrated on the kittens. Her shoulders rose and fell as she took a heavy breath. "You haven't asked me why I was wearing a wedding dress."

He couldn't pull his gaze from her. He rested his bowl on the coffee table. "I figured that was your business."

She nodded and stroked the furry crate-dwellers. "Could I have a little more tequila?"

"You got it," he said, grabbing the bottle and joining her on the rug. He poured them each a generous amount.

She took a sip. "Can I tell you something?"

"Sure."

"When I woke up this morning, I thought by this time today, I'd be on my honeymoon as the new Mrs. Rimnod."

"*Mrs. Nimrod?*" he repeated, feeling the muscles in his face do something funny.

"No, *Rimnod*. My ex-fiancé's name is Grant Rimnod."

"What happened with the nim—"

"Rimnod," she corrected, shaking her head as the hint of a grin bloomed, but it disappeared. "Grant's coworker, who I thought was a guy named Joe, turned out to be a woman. Jo, short for Josephine. She crashed the ceremony with a positive pregnancy test. I'm betting you can guess whose baby she was carrying."

He raised an eyebrow. "Jesus, Hailey."

"It gets worse."

He scoffed. "What could be worse than that?"

"Grant asked for the ring back. I threw it at him, which led to my boobs falling out of that stupid dress, and then he used it to propose to Jo and marry her thirty seconds later." Hailey knocked back the rest of her tequila. "I haven't said that out loud yet. It sounded bad in my head. But it sounds really terrible saying it aloud."

"This Grant is a colossal idiot," he grumbled.

"That might be true, but I'm also to blame."

"Why the hell would you say that?" he barked, unable to dial down the sharpness in his tone.

She poured more tequila into her glass and took another sip. "He wanted to get married to qualify for a loan and get better car insurance rates on a sports car, and I still agreed to it. I gave him my heart and let him throw it away like a piece of trash. There were so many red flags. He'd never introduced me to his friends or family. We basically hung out at home. How could I not put it together? I guess I was love blind."

Finn's throat thickened with emotion. "I know what that's like . . ." His chest tightened, constricting his breath as waves of humiliation washed over him. But he couldn't start down that pathetic road.

She drank him in with those big, brown eyes. "Have you ever had your heart broken?"

He flicked his attention to the fire. "Let's just say love isn't in the cards for me."

Beaming, she bounced onto her knees. "That makes two of us. Love sucks. I'm done with it."

"I can drink to that," he replied, pouring them each another shot.

She raised the tumbler to her lips, then glanced at his couch. No, she wasn't focused on his couch. She studied her giant canvas tote bag on the floor next to it. She must have brought it out when she'd left the bathroom.

He spied the top of the jar, peeking out. "You don't have that nimrod's finger—or some other appendage—in that pickle jar, do you?"

"Why?" she asked with a flirty twist to her lips. "Would that change your opinion of me if I did?"

How could it change his opinion? He hardly knew her, right? He drank in her rosy cheeks and the slow slide of her smile. The tequila appeared to be kicking in. She didn't look like a stranger or a deranged bride. She looked like salvation.

Enough! He wasn't some starry-eyed teenager. No woman could be his salvation.

"What you put in your pickle jar is your business," he grumbled, plucking the tumbler from her grip. He finished the contents and then placed the empty glass on the coffee table.

"Hey, that's mine," she pouted, and Christ, even her scowl was adorable.

He schooled his features. "You've got a bowl of the best cherry chocolate chip ice cream in all of Starrycard Creek melting. Eat."

She watched him a beat, then picked up her spoon. She dipped it into the bowl and raised it to her mouth. "See, I'm eating," she said, parting her lips—her full, plump lips—as she took a slow-motion bite, savoring the ice cream like she'd been cast in an ice cream infomercial. "Are you happy?" she pressed.

He could hide it, but he couldn't deny it. For the first time in what felt like forever, he was.

She took another bite, eyed an old map of Starrycard Creek framed on the wall, and then pointed the spoon at him. "Your name is Finnegan Starrycard."

"Uh-huh." He had a pretty good idea of what she was thinking.

"And this town is called Starrycard Creek."

"That's right."

"Does your family own it? Is that why your mom's the mayor?"

"My mom got elected because she's a force of nature. Most

Starrycard women are. But we don't own the town. An ancestor of mine founded Starrycard Creek in the eighteen hundreds. His name was William—"

"Starrycard," she finished with that cute-as-hell tipsy grin.

"You can't be a teacher," he said, goading her.

"Why not?" she shot back with that adorable pout.

"You've got to be a supersleuth with skills like that."

She took the tumbler from his hand and finished his tequila. "You are funny, Finnegan Starrycard. Now, tell me about William Starrycard." She leaned forward. Tequila glistened on her lips— her very kissable lips.

Do not obsess over her enticing mouth!

He ran his hand through his mess of dark hair. "What do you want to know?"

"Who was he? How did he end up here?"

He surveyed her bowl. "Take another bite, and I'll tell you."

She watched him through her lashes—and Jesus, his pulse kicked up.

She set his empty tumbler on the table, then complied, taking another bite that made him wish he could morph into a scoop of cherry chocolate chip. She locked onto his gaze and raised an eyebrow.

Was she challenging him to go on?

There was certainly some sass to this woman.

He gestured to the map. "William Starrycard was born in the eighteen fifties. He was the second son of a wealthy papermaker in Liverpool, England. He knew the business would go to his older brother, leaving him with limited prospects. So, he set off for America and started his own papermaking business here."

She leaned against the coffee table and supported her chin on her hand. "Why did he choose Colorado?"

He pointed at her half-eaten bowl. "Take a bite. A big one."

She watched him closely.

He liked having her eyes on him more than he should.

"Will you be doing this all night, Finnegan Starrycard?" she asked, now the one grumbling, which was fucking adorable.

"Yeah, I will. You need something in your belly besides licorice and tequila."

That mischievous twinkle returned to her eyes. "Brace yourself." She lifted the bowl and inhaled the rest of the cherry chocolate chip. And sweet Jesus! Sign this chick up for an ice cream eating contest.

"Are you happy?" she asked again, licking her delectable lips.

"I'm slightly terrified." It was a lie, but he wasn't about to disclose the truth.

"Come on, Finn. Why did William Starrycard choose this place to start his business? I want to know."

Finn leaned against the coffee table and studied the map. "The creek was part of the reason. Thanks to the mountains and the geological wonders in the area, it's replete with minerals and ores."

She cocked her head to the side, her gaze trained on him. "Is that good for paper?"

"It is for handmade paper. It can add to the color and texture. But some people think there's more to it."

"Like what?" she pressed, hanging on his every word.

"They believe whatever's in the creek is powerful, persuasive, magical even."

"Magical water that creates magical paper? What did it do that was so special? There had to be something that got people talking," she asked, wide-eyed.

"That's the other reason William chose to settle here. But it's something you and I aren't fond of—and neither was William Starrycard, at least in the beginning."

"Love?" Hailey whispered.

He nodded. "Do you still want to hear the story?"

She set her bowl on the coffee table and scooted beside him. She sat for a few seconds toying with the hem of the T-shirt. "Yes, but not because there's an element of love. We both agree love isn't for us. Call it historical curiosity. I own property in this town. I should understand its history."

There was a decent helping of bullshit to her answer, but who the hell was he to judge when it came to love.

"Here's the part that's become something of a legend," he continued. "William Starrycard was adamant that he wanted to focus on building his company and remain a bachelor."

She frowned. "How do you know that?"

"We have his journal."

"What did it say?"

Finn knew the line by heart. "I shall shun love and seek to embrace bachelorhood, focusing solely on my business endeavors," he rattled off in a terrible British accent.

"But he didn't shun love, did he?" she asked, a sweet grin spreading across her lips.

"No, he didn't. In fact, he fell head over heels for a girl. William Starrycard had just gotten to this remote corner of the Wild West when he caught a glimpse of a nineteen-year-old redheaded Irish beauty and talented artist named Fiona Donnelly."

"Fiona Donnelly," Hailey repeated. "Her name sounds magical."

"Fiona was the only daughter of Brian Donnelly, a local rancher," he continued. "They lived about twenty miles from here in the valley. The story goes, the second William saw Fiona, his life changed. He knew she was the woman he'd spend the rest of his life with."

"Love at first sight?" Hailey asked with a thread of wistfulness.

"Something like that. It's said that minutes after setting eyes on Fiona, William applied for a land grant for the property adjacent to the Donnelly's place."

"And then they married?"

Finn shook his head. "No."

"What happened?" she asked, moving closer to him.

He paused. Over the past year, the mention of this story—the story that defined his family—triggered clawing, red-hot anger. Oddly, retelling the tale tonight didn't leave him wanting to punch a hole in the wall. He concentrated on the stunning redhead in front of him. Hailey Higgins was something out of a dream—a siren sent to distract him from his pain. It was as if her presence created a parallel world where his past couldn't touch him, giving the term Higgins Hideaway new meaning.

"Can you keep going?" she asked, edging even closer.

Her bare knee brushed against his leg, and the contact steadied him.

"William and Fiona wanted to marry. It's said she fell for him just as he'd fallen for her."

Confusion marred Hailey's expression. "Then why couldn't they be together?"

"Mr. Donnelly. You see, Fiona's father loved his daughter dearly and wanted her to be happy, but he was a strict man. He wasn't about to trust his beloved child's welfare to anyone—even to the man she professed to love. Before William rolled into the valley, the story goes that Mr. Donnelly had turned down more than twenty suitors who'd come asking for his daughter's hand in marriage. But William was persistent and had a skill set the others didn't."

Hailey perked up. "Papermaking."

"William had been doing it his whole life," he continued. "And he was damned good at it. Using the water from the creek, he incorporated wood from the Donnelly land, cattails, and the wildflowers Fiona wore in her hair into the pulp that eventually became a few sheets of paper. The whole process was—and still is —quite labor intensive."

Hailey brushed a lock of auburn hair from her brow. "What did he do with the paper? Did he gift it to Fiona's father?"

"Not exactly. He folded it into a card and wrote a letter to Mr. Donnelly, promising to love and provide for Fiona. Nobody expected the old man to give in. Men made bets on it. But it's never smart to bet against a Starrycard."

"Brian Donnelly agreed to the marriage," Hailey inferred, her grin widening.

"He did, and his cherished daughter married the young paper-maker the very next day. After people learned that Brian Donnelly gave William and Fiona his blessing because of a letter written on a handmade card, the legends and folklore around Starrycard paper exploded. People believed it was lucky."

"And magical, right?" she added.

"Yes. Folks were—and still are—superstitious. The rumors about the paper spread across the West. Everybody wanted a piece of the good fortune. Businesses wanted their contracts written on it. Parents wanted birth certificates printed on it. Universities and colleges use it for diplomas. My younger brother is a professional baseball player, and he—and his teammates—insist on printing their cards on our paper. To this day, numerous organizations, local municipalities, businesses, and families insist on using our paper to capture important occasions. And the folk-lore spread past the state's borders. People travel here from all over to write their aspirations and dreams on a piece of Starrycard paper. We've got a rock wall that Fiona and William built that runs along the creek. People slip fragments of the paper in the cracks and crevices, hoping their dreams will come true."

"Do their dreams come true?" she asked, soaking up the story like a sponge.

How the hell was he supposed to answer that?

He shrugged. "I guess it depends on the dream. When I was a kid, I was in the shop, and someone asked the same question. My grandma Goldie told them something William and Fiona used to say."

"What's that?" Hailey pressed.

"Your dream can only come true if whatever you ask for was meant for you. Whatever the hell that means," he mumbled. "And then there's what the locals say about love."

"What do they say?" she asked, her voice a wisp of a sound.

"Love is always in the cards in Starrycard Creek. It sounds cheesy, but . . ." He shook his head.

"But it's not in the cards for us," she said softly, filling in the blank.

A sliver of what felt a lot like regret wedged into the pieces of his broken heart. "Yeah, not for us," he repeated.

She nodded as if her mind were elsewhere and glanced at her tote. "Can I ask you a question about the paper?"

"Please, sure, absolutely," he replied, relieved yet also oddly disappointed to shift from the topic of love.

"Does the paper come wrapped in twine?"

"Yes," he answered, taken aback at the specificity of her question. "We sell and package the paper the same way it was done in the eighteen hundreds. Why?"

She retrieved her bulky tote. Without removing the jar, she unscrewed the top and removed a single scrap of paper—Starrycard paper. He could identify the telltale texture anywhere. He couldn't stop his gaze from lingering, and Jesus, the container appeared to be teeming with torn slips and ragged fragments.

He frowned. "You said you didn't know anything about Starrycard Creek. That jar says you do."

"I didn't—I don't," she stammered. "I just put it together. My great-uncle sent Starrycard paper to my dad. That's what's inside the jar. I knew the man had sent paper to my father. But I didn't know where it had come from."

He gestured to the piece in her hand. "What's written on the slip?"

Lovingly, she stroked the paper with her thumb. "It's one of two hundred and twenty-two love notes my father wrote to my mother."

He eyed the stash. "That's what's in the jar?"

"Yes, and I think my great-uncle has some of this paper left-over in his cabin. I touched a sheet before the raccoon fiasco. It felt familiar. I couldn't place it until now."

"It's your cabin now. Hailey's Place, right?" he asked, knowing better than to wish she'd want to stay, but he couldn't help himself.

She was back to chewing her lip. Without disclosing what it said, she placed the slip into the jar and secured the lid. "It's my place—at least until I decide what to do with it."

"What do you mean?"

She stared at the fire. "I don't know if I'll keep it."

"You might sell?"

She shrugged. "I don't know. Maybe."

Her statement hit like a kick to his gut.

He watched the shadows flicker on her face. "If you want to sell the cabin, you'll need it in good condition. I can get it into shape for you."

Where the hell did that come from? What did he care what she did with the cabin? Still, his drive to help her overrode his need for solitude. Or perhaps it was his need to exist in this alternate universe—with her.

She shook her head. "I can't pay you, Finn. After buying gas to get here, I've got less than fifty bucks to my name."

"You don't have to pay me."

Her shoulders slumped forward. "I'm sure you've got bills to pay. I couldn't monopolize your time."

All he'd wanted for the last year was something to monopolize his time.

"I don't need money."

"Does it grow on trees out here?" she teased.

"I have a patent that would allow me to live comfortably if I never worked another day of my life."

She reared back. "That's amazing. What's it for?"

He waved her off. "Boring stuff that has to do with the paper-making and the drying process."

"It doesn't sound boring. I'm genuinely impressed, but no matter your financial situation, I couldn't let you work for free."

He picked up the bottle and poured tequila into his glass. "You'd be doing me a favor."

She watched him closely. "How is allowing you to fix my cabin for free doing a favor for you?"

He tossed back the alcohol—not sure how much to disclose. "I do better when I have a project—something comprehensive to keep my mind and hands busy. It helps me sleep." That wasn't a lie. Since he'd finished renovating his cabin a few months ago, he'd been randomly picking up projects around town. It was exhausting searching for the weaknesses in structures to find something to do to get through the day.

She poured a splash of tequila into her glass and held the tumbler against her chest. "If I did agree to it, you'd have to let me help you. I'm not a total home repair novice. I share a deep connection with wallpaper."

"You commune with wallpaper?" He slid the bottle of alcohol away from her. "What's in your glass is all you're going to get tonight. I'm cutting you off."

"You are not cutting me off, mister," she countered, feisty and bright-eyed. She poured another splash into her glass and took a sip. She sighed a faraway wisp of a sound and stared at the tumbler, her expression dimming. It was as if a memory had washed away her sassy side. "When I was in the bride's room before the whole blind-sided-bride debacle," she said, seemingly locked in that moment, "there was a piece of torn wallpaper with a message written on it."

He watched her closely. "What did it say?"

She held his gaze. "He's not meant for you."

Finn reared back. "Holy shit!"

"It might as well have been a magic ball predicting my future," she continued. "But my connection to wall coverings is solid. I can put up wallpaper and paint. And use a drill. When I was a girl, I'd help my parents complete projects around the house. They were a real team." She paused, and her gaze grew glassy. "They adored each other. They did everything together. They were high school teachers who taught at the same school. They made taking out the trash look like a date night."

Her usage of past tense wasn't lost on him. "Adored?" he said, needing to know more about her life.

She finished her tequila. "They died in a car crash when I was nineteen."

"I'm sorry, Hailey. I can't imagine. They were all you had?"

She traced the rim of the glass with the tip of her index finger. "Yeah."

The woman had no family and barely had a dollar to her name. And Christ, there was something else she was lacking. Something he could remedy.

"You can't live in Higgins Hideaway—not until I make sure it's structurally sound," he snapped, his voice laced with unintended harshness but desperate to convey the seriousness of the situation.

Her shoulders drooped again as she clutched the tumbler to her chest. "I could always sleep in my car."

There was no way in hell he'd allow that.

Frustration surged through him like a wildfire. "You're not spending a single night in your car."

"I'm not?" she asked, curiosity welling in her eyes.

He steadied himself and set his tumbler on the coffee table. What he was about to say would change everything.

"Hailey Higgins," he rasped, his voice a velvety demand tinged with an unmistakable hunger.

"Yes?" she breathed, placing her glass next to his.

He leaned in, inhaled her cherry-tequila sweetness, and fell deeper under her spell. "You're not going anywhere. You're staying in Starrycard Cabin with me."

CHAPTER
Six
FINN

HOLY HELL! Did he just tell Hailey Higgins that she had to live with him? He might as well have tied himself to her leg and begged her not to leave. He couldn't help but cringe internally at the demanding proclamation. He sounded like a melodramatic soap opera villain.

Smooth move, handyman.

Hailey's mouth opened and closed like a beautiful ginger goldfish. "You want me to stay with you? I couldn't. I don't even know you."

He was wading into dangerous waters, but he couldn't stop himself. He was intoxicated—and not because of the tequila. It was Hailey and the promise of existing in this perfect bubble with an alluring, love-hating stranger.

He had to convince her that staying with him at the cabin was the only logical choice.

He dusted off his charming side. "What do you mean you don't know me? You said it yourself. I'm your boyfriend," he purred.

She didn't look away. Instead, she took his damned breath away with her sensual, slightly sloppy grin. It bloomed on her lips like the pink of the Shooting Star wildflowers that peeked through Starrycard Creek's late spring snow.

"Finn, you're not my real boyfriend. You're my . . ." She pursed her lips. "My business card boyfriend."

"Business card boyfriend?" he echoed.

"Yes, and only because I had to come up with a reason for you not to chop me up into a million tiny pieces. I simply blurted out the last name I'd read, which happened to be the name on your business card. You know this."

He offered a half shrug. "Fine, you can bunk with your business card boyfriend."

She shook her head. Skepticism rolled off her in waves, but he wasn't about to let her say no. It wasn't how his mind worked. When a solution materialized in his head, relentlessness took over, driving him to persist until he achieved perfection.

"You're in the mountains, Hailey," he continued. "You've got two choices. Freeze your ass off sleeping in a sedan every night or wake up to heated bathroom floors each morning. And I can fix your car. You can come and go as you please. Let me help you. It'll help me," he confessed, his voice brimming with the emotion he couldn't contain.

She twisted the hem of the Starrycard Paper Company T-shirt. "Finn, I—"

"Would be doing me a favor," he finished—no, pleaded.

Was he laying it on too thick? It didn't matter. There was no going back now.

She released the hem and sighed. "Okay."

He had to hold himself back from pumping his fist in the air like a meathead at a techno rave. "Okay? As in, yes?"

"Yes," she answered, returning to twisting, then releasing the hem. "But I should warn you. Every decision I've made lately has ended up a total train wreck." She held him in place with her deep amber eyes. "Have you ever felt like no matter how much you wanted to do the right thing, you know you'll probably screw it up? I've misjudged so many people."

She wasn't the only one.

"I'm not just anyone," he pressed. "I'm your handyman—and your business card boyfriend. There can't be any train wrecks for us because what happens between us is . . . transactional. You give me a project to keep my hands busy. I help you fix your cabin and give you a place to stay. Nothing more. Nothing less."

Was that true? It didn't matter. It had to be that way.

She stopped her assault on the T-shirt's hem and nodded. It was a barely perceptible movement, but he caught it. She wanted this. No, she needed this like he did. He could feel it in his bones.

"Transactional, nothing more and nothing less," she said softly, then went to her bag and removed something from her wallet.

What would she need in there?

She held out a card. "Here," she said, slipping it into his hand.

He scanned the small white rectangle. It was a business card. Her business card.

Hailey Higgins, Bachelor of Arts, Education
Certified Elementary School Teacher

Her cell and email were printed below her title.

He brushed his fingertips across the cheap cardstock. He sure as hell could make her a better card than this.

"Finnegan Starrycard," she said.

He forgot the card and met her gaze.

"You've got yourself a business card *girlfriend*." She swallowed hard, then looked down and studied her hand—her left hand.

"What is it? Talk to me," he said gently.

"I've never had a boyfriend who didn't break my heart."

He pocketed her card as he watched her wilt in front of him. He had to do something, say something. "I can't hurt you, Hailey. I'm not your real boyfriend." It was the truth. Why did it feel like a lie?

She nodded but didn't look up.

What was she staring at?

He noticed the faint discoloration on her ring finger.

The muscles at the base of his neck tightened. "Your last boyfriend, fiancé, whatever, did a real number on you."

She touched the strip of ivory skin. "I'd be lying if I said he didn't. And to think, I faked so many orgasms for that no-good, cheating jerk." She gasped, and her cheeks burned crimson. "I can't believe I said that. It's got to be the tequila talking."

"Is it the tequila, or is it the truth?" he prodded, unable to help himself.

She pressed her hand to her lips, then burst out laughing. "It's completely true. Grant was terrible in bed. He never caught on that I was pretending." She raised an eyebrow. "Or . . ."

"Or what?" he breathed. The mention of orgasms sent his pulse racing.

Wide-eyed, she sat back on her heels. "Maybe I'm a pro at faking it. Come to think of it, I must be amazing at it. It wasn't only Grant. I've dated a decent number of guys who were lacking when it came to . . ." She blushed that beguiling shade of pink that got his heart pumping. "Well, you know." She locked onto his gaze. "Do you want a demonstration?"

Now, he was the one with bugged-out eyes. "You're asking if I want to watch you fake an orgasm?"

"Yes," she replied with a little clap. "You could be an unbiased judge. Everything we do is transactional, right?"

He poured more tequila into his glass, downed the liquid, and returned the tumbler to the table. "Well . . . yeah, okay. Let's get transactional."

Christ on a cracker! He was back to talking like his brain was disconnected from his mouth.

"But you can't laugh at me, Finn," she warned, playfully jabbing her finger into his chest.

"I promise I won't," he replied, his voice suddenly strained as blood rushed away from his brain and headed south. "Go ahead, show me what you've got," he urged, fully aware that they were pushing unspoken limits, even if this demonstration was supposed to be a platonic transaction.

She closed her eyes. "Are you watching me?"

That fake rocket he told her he'd built could be headed straight for them, and he still wouldn't have been able to look away.

He swallowed hard, the muscles in his neck constricting. "I'm watching you."

She inhaled and exhaled a slow, steady breath, her breasts rising and falling beneath his shirt. She pushed up onto her knees. "Oh, that's so good. Mmm, just like that. Right there. Uh-huh. Oh, yes, I'm so close. So close." With her lips parted, she rolled her head to the side and swayed her hips like she was riding an invisible cock.

And holy hell! He'd been with other women—plenty of other women—but watching this woman fake an orgasm had him rock hard.

She hummed. "Keep going," she whispered and ran her hands through her hair. "Don't stop. I'm so close. You're so good. So big. So hard."

He couldn't take it. He was on the brink of detonating. He drew his fingertips down her jawline. "Hailey, you need to stop."

She dropped her hands to her sides and opened her eyes. "Why?"

"Because you need a handyman to intervene."

Confusion marred her expression. "I do?"

"Badly," he growled.

Concern creased her brow. "Am I doing something wrong?"

"Yeah, you are."

Her bottom lip trembled as she sank to the floor. "You said you wouldn't laugh at me."

"I'm not laughing. You're doing it wrong because you don't deserve to have to fake it."

The crease on her brow deepened. "I don't understand?"

He shook his head. "I changed my mind. We need to end this transaction."

"We do?" she asked, breathless.

He took a page from her nervous energy playbook and twisted

the hem of the Starrycard Creek Paper Company T-shirt around his index finger. His hand brushed against her leg. Every muscle in his body tensed. He inhaled a sharp breath, but he didn't pull back. He released the fabric and rested his hand squarely on her thigh. He drew slow circles against her ivory skin with his thumb. Raw desire tore through him. Touching her was like tapping into a current pulsing with passion.

He glanced at his hand. "Is this okay?"

She looked down and nodded. With that slight movement, the pain he'd carried this last year melted away. The weight of his anguish lightened. With the fire crackling and cherries, chocolate, and tequila permeating the air, the electricity pulsing between them transported him to another world—a place where he became a different version of himself.

He slid his hands up her thighs and gripped her hips. Under her spell, he drew her in. With Hailey in his arms, a switch had flipped. His vision went red, but not with anger. It was the fire, flickering and highlighting her damp auburn waves. Caught in a dream, he locked onto her amber eyes. "I asked you to stop because I don't want to listen to you pretend. I want to hear what you sound like when you're not faking it."

She pressed her palms to his chest. "How will I do that?"

Like Alice falling down the rabbit hole, he descended deeper and deeper into this fantasy world. And fucking hell, his body was on the brink of combusting. Lust coursed through him as he leaned in to press his lips to the shell of her ear. "You don't have to do anything. You're going to let your business card boyfriend take care of you."

Was this completely inappropriate and utterly insane?

Absolutely.

But he wanted her. He would have traversed a valley of crushed glass barefoot to have her.

Hailey Higgins was the opposite of the dark clouds that had followed him like a lingering shadow. Her nearness brightened his dreary world. Gravity lost its grip. The air crackled with a palpable energy, and the vice clamped around his heart loosened. Not to mention, from everything she'd told him about her day and her douchebag ex, it sounded a hell of a lot like she could use an escape from reality, too.

"It's simply a transaction," he added, recycling the term.

And there was the solution to his problems.

He and Hailey hated love but required companionship. He pulled back and studied her expression, but he couldn't read her. Was she contemplating hitting him over the head with the tequila bottle or throttling him with her pickle jar? Was he about to spend the night in a cell at the Starrycard Creek Police Department? A jagged sliver of hesitation threatened to puncture his fantasy land. He parted his lips, prepared to blame the alcohol for his behavior, when mischief glinted in her eyes.

"I could agree to engage in a transaction that keeps your hands busy," she supplied with a flirtatious lilt.

And boom! They were back in Finn and Hailey's Wonderland, aka Starrycard Cabin.

"Not just my hands," he said, his voice growing gravelly. "This transaction also requires the use of my mouth."

In for a penny, in for a pound.

Her gaze darkened. "Your mouth?"

"I have to kiss you first. It's called building a foundation. It's Orgasm Prep 101."

Orgasm Prep 101? Yep, he'd officially lost his mind. But insanity turned out to be one hell of an exciting ride.

She slid her hands past his pecs and wrapped her arms around his neck. "Are your tools up for the task, handyman?"

Winner, winner! The woman was down for his crazy 101 talk. And she spackled on a touch of tool belt naughtiness to boot. God help him. He was there for it.

With one swift movement, he slid her onto his lap.

She wrapped her legs around his waist, and the T-shirt crept up, revealing more of her creamy skin.

He shifted her lithe frame and rolled his hips, pressing his cock between her thighs. "I've got the exact tool for the job."

She inhaled a tight breath and moved with him. "It appears you do."

"Here's something you need to know about me. Your business card boyfriend is always prepared and up for the task."

She pressed her plump, tequila-kissed lips together. "Then I guess you better kiss your business-card girlfriend."

But he wasn't ready—not yet.

He slid his hand to the small of her back and cupped her face with his other hand. And then . . . he froze, a prisoner to those soulful brown eyes.

"Is something wrong?" she asked, her voice barely a whisper.

"I just want to look at you. Do you mind?"

She didn't answer. Instead, she smiled. She was the sun banishing storm clouds—a light that exploded into a rainbow, filling the sky with colors so vibrant he could taste them. He drank in her eyes—those deep amber wells that anchored him to this moment.

"In the fall," he said, utterly captivated, "we collect fallen leaves to add to the pulp. It creates these beautiful brown flecks in the finished paper. There's a cozy comfortableness about it, but also strength. The power of going dormant and then emerging stronger. That's what I see when I look into your eyes."

Why was he telling her this?

He didn't have an answer.

He brushed his thumb across her bottom lip. "Are you even real?"

It was a stupid question but a valid one. How could one woman work her deranged bride magic and turn his life blissfully upside down in less than an hour?

"If I don't drown in your eyes, those lips of yours might be the death of me," he added, giving in to this new, raw, vulnerable side. But why should he hold back? She was real, but they—*as a they*—weren't real. They were surrogates giving in to desire.

That's all it could be. He'd make damn sure of it. But for now, he knew what he wanted, and her name was Hailey Higgins.

She threaded her fingers in the hair at the nape of his neck. "There's one way to find out if I'm real—that first step in Orgasm Prep 101."

The lady wasn't wrong, and he wasn't about to wait another second.

He captured her mouth, hungrily tasting her tequila-cherry-chocolate kiss. Their tongues met in a dance fueled by deep yearning but also something lighter, something so decadently delicious it left him lightheaded. She tasted like hope and heady temptation. And just like that, she was everywhere. Freckles dusted her cheeks. Her warm chestnut gaze tempted him to lose himself. She came to him like droplets of spring rain trailing down his cheeks, soaking him, drowning him in her beauty.

This kiss would change him. He knew this with absolute certainty.

Drunk on the promise of temporary salvation, he deepened the kiss. She moaned against his lips, and the sound triggered his primal side to take control. Allowing lust to lead the way, he lowered her to the floor. No, not the floor, to the floofy sheepskin rug he'd never liked until that very moment. He hovered above her, balancing on his knees and forearms, careful not to crush her with his hulking, muscled frame. And what a view. Her auburn hair fell in waves, framing her face as she rested on the plush surface. She was a ginger angel, a handyman's ultimate fantasy girl, and his to pleasure.

He lazily dragged his fingertips down her torso. Lifting the T-shirt, he slipped his hand between her thighs. His fingertips were rewarded with a tiny scrap of smooth silk.

She tensed beneath him. "Those aren't what I usually wear. I'm pretty boring in the underwear department. I bought these for tonight. They were supposed to be for my honeymoon." She tensed. "I probably shouldn't have said that."

He had to put her at ease.

"I don't give a flying fuck about underwear. I'm too focused on my task."

"Which is?" she purred, relaxing beneath him.

"Giving you the honeymoon night that jackass Grant Nimrod never could."

She stroked his cheek. "It's Rimnod."

"I don't give a damn what his name is. I'm the one who's with you tonight."

It was time to make this woman forget she'd been engaged.

He massaged between her thighs, then pressed his palm against her most sensitive place, applying pressure with his middle finger to her slick entrance.

She arched her back like a greedy cat, moving her hips to his rhythm. "How are you doing that? How can it feel so good so quickly?"

A confidence he hadn't felt in ages took over.

"I know how things work. I'm a mechanical engineer who lives to make engines purr. I'm handy like that."

He worked her in slow, tormenting circles, listening to her breath hitch as he dialed up his speed. Tuned into her every move, he noted each buck of her hips and the lack of bullshit flowing from her lips. She didn't recite a stream of *oh yeahs* and *right theres*. Her response was intensely quiet. Profoundly internal. Her energy centered in her core—a core wet beneath his touch. A triumph that had him on the edge of losing it and taking her right there on the rug.

But it wasn't time yet.

His breaths grew heated as he observed her nipples tighten into hard pearls. They pressed against the cotton T-shirt beckoning him, begging to be licked and sucked and bitten. Her arousal fed his desire as the skin on her snowy white neck flushed scarlet. He studied this decadently delicious work of art that he yearned to devour.

"Can I taste you down there?" he asked against her lips.

"Yes," she breathed.

Electricity sparked through him like a live wire.

He kissed her through the shirt, teasing her nipples as he worked his way down. But he never let up between her thighs. Machines, like people, preferred a steady flow. Abrupt stops and starts welcomed frustration and thwarted completion. And there was no way he'd leave this woman wanting for even a second.

Lowering his lips to the delicate skin below her navel, he trailed a path of warm kisses and assessed the questionable state of her undergarments. The sight left him with no doubts. Those wedding night panties had to go.

A playful grin tugged at his lips as he toyed with the flimsy lace waistband, twisting it around his index finger. "Are you invested in these?" he asked, a hint of mischief lacing the question.

Her eyes sparkled with amusement as she shook her head. "I never want to see them again."

He leaned in closer. "I can help you with that. Do you trust me?"

It was an odd question, considering she'd compared him to a psychopathic axe murderer not much more than an hour ago. Yet, he sensed a glimmer of trust lingering in a corner of her heart.

As her hands threaded through his hair, a radiant smile graced her lips, speaking where words fell short.

There was his answer.

With a boldness fueled by their shared connection, he tightened his grip on the waistband and ripped the offending undergarment clean off her body. He tossed the panties aside, gripped her hips, and feasted on the beauty before him. Letting his tongue take over, he binged on a hot, wet, cherry-flavored erotic banquet.

He hadn't felt a spark or a glimmer of desire for more than twelve long, lonely months.

That ended tonight.

Hailey had set off a contagion of lust. His machinist's mind cataloged every way he could deliver carnal bliss to this woman.

"Finn," she eked out on a tight exhale.

As she writhed beneath his touch, his name on her lips sent his arousal into overdrive.

"Yeah?" he breathed against her smooth skin.

"It's so good. I didn't know it could be so—" She tensed, and he knew what was coming.

She bucked her hips, demanding more as she crashed into her release. And he was there to give her everything.

Fearless and glorious—and not faking it for some jerk who didn't deserve her—Hailey let go.

Now, did he deserve her?

He banished the intrusive thought.

His emotions were riding high, and the ample blood loss from his brain clouded his judgment.

He couldn't forget for a second what he'd promised himself. But before he could let his past pierce the perfection of this moment, Hailey exhaled an audible breath. She stilled, then pushed up onto her elbows. Blinking wildly, she glanced around like she'd been hit with a bout of amnesia.

She stared at the ceiling. "I'm seeing stars. Am I still on earth?"

The muscles on his face contorted again, basking in her sated sense of complete awe. "You are."

A slow smile pulled at the corners of her mouth. "And you're still Finnegan Starrycard, Local Handyman, and my current business card boyfriend?"

He drank in her sunrise-pink cheeks and mussed hair. Christ, she'd have him wrapped around her finger if he'd allow it.

He held her woozy gaze. "That I am."

She gripped the collar of his shirt. "Good! Get up here."

"Whoa!" he exclaimed. She was frighteningly strong for such a petite thing.

She yanked his ass up from between her thighs, guiding him to hover above her. He'd barely steadied himself when deft hands unfastened his jeans. "I want that again. But I want it with you."

He'd created a pleasure-hungry sex monster—and he was absolutely good with that.

She pushed down his pants and took him into her hands. "Ready for another transaction."

His equipment was more than ready. But if she kept up her handywoman work, he'd be out of commission in no time flat.

He held her wrist, and she stilled.

He studied her expression as a reality hit. "I don't have any condoms."

"I'm on the pill. I've been tested. But Grant hasn't touched me in months. If you're worried about . . ." She looked away, and her radiant glow dimmed.

Dammit!

"I haven't been with anyone in over a year." He flinched. He hadn't meant to share that pathetic nugget of information.

She peered past his shoulder. "I hope I don't disappoint you."

He stroked her cheek. "Hailey, look at me."

She complied, and those pools of amber grew glassy.

It had to be the nimrod. He wasn't about to let that asshat get into her head.

"If your ex couldn't ring your bell, then he has no business telling you that you're lacking when it comes to intimacy. This isn't about him. It's about you. Tonight is about me making your body writhe with pleasure. I'm going to leave you so spent, the last thing on your mind will be your ex. In fact, I'm going to bang him clean out of your head. You'll think you vacated your body and abandoned Earth for a heavenly plane. And as far as you getting me hot. You succeeded at that the second I saw you in my T-shirt. Do you want to know what you are?"

"What am I?" she whispered, tears no longer welling in her eyes. Instead, lust glimmered in her gaze.

He stroked her cheek. "You're cherry-scented fire, and tonight, you're all mine."

He waited a beat, then another, and there it was. She'd gifted him with her sexy twist of a grin. It sent a titillating jolt of arousal through his body. Yet, as much as he craved this sensual smile, it was time to kiss it off her face. He pressed his lips to hers and kissed her hard. The connection resonated with raw need, and an exhilarating notion reinforced what he already knew. There was a damned good chance he'd never be the same. It was as if the brush of her lips against his transcended the senses. But he couldn't stop. He deepened the kiss, addicted to her touch.

And he required more of her—all of her.

He shrugged his pants to his ankles, lined up his cock at her entrance, and thrust his hips. Her wet heat welcomed him into a velvety, smooth embrace.

Gasping, she dug her nails into his back. He felt it through his work shirt. His focus sharpened, and a determined glint flickered in his eyes as he set out to accomplish his one mission: to deliver a climax that would leave this goddess of a woman breathless and moaning in unadulterated pleasure.

He rocked his hips, making love to her in long, fluid strokes. He maintained the pace and kissed a line to her earlobe. He licked the delicate skin. "You're so damned sexy, and you feel so fucking good. It'll take everything I've got not to come in seconds," he growled, piling on a little dirty talk.

He pulled back and studied her expression. Lust and awe swirled in her eyes.

Precisely the reaction he wanted.

"You like taking every hard inch of me, don't you?" he rasped, filling her to the hilt.

She arched her back, pressing those glorious breasts against his chest. "Yes."

"What about this?" he bit out as he slipped his hand beneath her and palmed her ass. The movement changed the angle of penetration, tightening their connection. Delicious heat built between them, and the sensual friction ignited a firestorm. Caressing her sweet bud, he provided the perfect pressure and was rewarded with her lusty moans. He wanted to go slow and draw out the pleasure like the meticulous handyman he was, tightening each screw, savoring the process of bringing ultimate satisfaction with every precise turn. But Hailey's enthusiastic reaction had him on the brink of oblivion.

"That's . . ." she whispered, but she couldn't elaborate. She showed him her appreciation with her body, meeting him thrust for thrust and blow for blow as they set an erotic, heart-pounding pace.

The sweet slap of skin meeting skin pierced the air as he pistoned his hips, pounding away like a human jackhammer. A frenzied vibration tore through the room. All that existed was Hailey's cherry chocolate tequila taste on his tongue and the rhythm of their bodies, pumping and grinding. He moved like a machine built to exact pleasure—an instrument formed solely to fornicate and fuck.

He knew one thing for sure. Her ex was a terrible judge of sexual prowess. This woman was nothing short of glorious. A sexual temptress. And this siren was closing in on carnal rapture.

She tightened around him, heightening his pleasure as she rocketed toward another release.

And that's when it hit him.

The first time sleeping with anyone can be awkward, but this was the opposite. They moved like they were made for each other. Their connection was automatic, like breathing. Their bodies hummed, creating a frequency solely for them.

He tightened his hold on her ass, again altering her position. The slight shift was all it took to earn another low, breathy moan. Within seconds, she clung to him. Clenching her core and bucking her hips, she plunged into a sea of ecstasy. He watched her lose control. Entranced, he obsessed over her parted lips and flushed skin. He memorized the line of her jaw and the arch of her auburn brows.

"Finn," she breathed, "I want you with me."

The words shattered what was left of his dwindling resolve.

It was what he wanted, too.

With a primal cry, he joined her in the rollicking waves of carnal bliss. Delirious ecstasy washed over him. Momentous, this moment transcended time and space. His orgasm hit like an avalanche colliding with a tornado. A roar of sweat, heat, and breathy moans ripped through the cabin. Needing to intensify their connection, his mouth found hers. Panting and gasping, their lips, tongues, and teeth met in a tangle of kisses. Rising and falling, ascending and descending, he kept her close, maintaining that perfect pressure as he expelled every drop of energy to lengthen her release.

Around and around, like a carousel spinning out of control, he was on the brink of passing out from exertion when Hailey loosened her hold.

"Handyman," she said between audible breaths.

"Yeah?"

"I'm ninety-nine-point-nine percent sure we left the planet. What do you think?"

He wasn't sure of anything besides the fact that this woman was magic. Starbursts clouded his vision as he reveled in her warmth. The fire crackled, and he rested his forehead against hers, drunk with satisfaction as they remained suspended in this hidden world.

Reluctantly, he pulled out and shifted his body so she wouldn't have to bear the brunt of all two hundred and twenty pounds of him. He rested on his side, and she turned to face him. He touched the collar of her T-shirt—well, his T-shirt. Possessively, he drank her in, staking his claim without uttering a word.

"I don't know where we went," he said, his voice gravelly and loose. "But we're back in the cabin now."

"That was . . ."

But she didn't need to speak. Her sweet, sated smile spoke volumes. It left him light and airy as it penetrated his defenses.

She wiped a bead of perspiration from her brow, then threaded her fingers into his hair. "I might need another shower, and you look like you could use one, too."

This woman was brilliant.

"Good idea," he replied, stroking her cheek. "Since I'm giving you the wedding night you deserve, I suggest our next transaction occur in the steam shower."

She sat up, hugged her knees to her chest, and tapped her chin theatrically.

What did she have up her sleeve?

"The shower, you say?" she replied as she stood and headed for the kitchen. She glanced over her shoulder, then peeled off his Starrycard Creek Paper Company T-shirt. She dropped it onto the ground, walking through his place buck naked like a redheaded Lady Godiva, minus the horse.

Was he complaining?

Hell no!

He'd happily take in the view.

Still, he wanted to do more than watch.

He scrambled to his feet. Well, he'd hoped to scramble. Thanks to that mind-altering make-out session on the sheepskin rug, he moved like he had Jell-O for legs. It was a goddamned miracle he was able to pull up his pants. Newborn colts had more balance. He stumbled behind his naked houseguest, grateful his limbs could still support him. He regained his bearings and leaned against the wall. "Hailey Higgins, you are a petite package of complete ginger trouble."

She looked over her shoulder, flashed a sly grin brimming with nothing but complete ginger trouble, then opened the freezer.

"What do you need in there?" he asked.

"It's not for me. It's for us. To keep up our stamina."

She closed the door, then opened a drawer. In one hand, she held a pint of cherry chocolate chip. In the other, a spoon. She tore off the lid with her teeth, dunked the utensil into the creamy goodness, and took a monster bite. If a TV show featured this woman pounding ice cream, he'd be glued to the screen twenty-four seven.

"Come here," she mumbled through the creamy treat that now, thanks to indulging in another bite, coated her lips.

He shook his head and chuckled but did as he was instructed.

She scraped another spoonful from the container. "Open wide, business card boyfriend." She grinned up at him and held out the spoon, dripping with ice cream. "Eat," she ordered, just as he'd done earlier.

He was never one for cheesy acts of affection, like couples feeding each other. But that seemed to change the second this redheaded siren directed him to part his lips.

She slipped the cherry-chocolate delight into his mouth, and he hummed his satisfaction. Christ, even ice cream tasted better with her. Still riding the high of existing in this secret bubble, he tipped her chin and kissed the excess treat from her lips.

He licked a tiny chocolate flake from the corner of her mouth. "This might be my new favorite way to eat ice cream."

She took a step back and trailed the spoon between her breasts. "Is that so?"

And God help him, he was rock hard again.

She eyed the spoon like she and the eating implement shared a dirty little secret. "I think we can find a few ways our business card boyfriend will enjoy ice cream even more."

Yes, yes, and hell, yes!

In a burst of lust and laughter, he scooped his naked ice cream goddess into his arms.

"What are you doing?" she yelped, giggling as she attempted to keep the carton from tipping over.

He schooled his features. "We take ice cream trials very seriously here in Starrycard Creek, ma'am. There can be no delays in the testing process, which, due to the sticky nature of ice cream, would be best done in—"

"The shower," she finished, reading his mind as a cherry-chocolatey spoonful of ice cream fell from the container and landed between her breasts.

His cock twitched as he hungrily stared at the dollop.

She scooped the melting mass onto her index finger and held it to his lips. "This might get messy."

Why did he get the feeling she wasn't only talking about the ice cream? Or was he the one projecting?

He licked the treat off her finger. "Then we get messy. It's simply a transaction. Nobody but us will know. It's you and me, hidden away with a shit ton of ice cream."

Worry or possibly apprehension flashed in her eyes.

Was it something he said?

She blinked and the worry was replaced with desire. "Are you up for *transacting* with me all night long?"

He'd never wanted anything more.

"I promised you a proper wedding night."

"Yes, you did."

"You'll want to take another bite."

She pursed her lips. "Why is that?"

"Because I'll be transacting the hell out of you on every flat surface in this place. And that starts . . ." He paused, embracing his strange, new, playful side.

She grinned up at him as anticipation built. It lingered in the air with the chocolate cherry scent.

"Now!" he exclaimed, his voice brimming with excitement and passion. He dashed towards the bathroom, his heart racing, his mind unburdened, and completely focused on the woman in his arms.

What would tomorrow bring? Hell, if he knew. But tonight was theirs, and he wasn't about to waste a single second of it.

CHAPTER
Seven

HAILEY

"THIS IS how a girl should wake up," Hailey purred beneath a down comforter as Finn peppered her neck with nips and licks. Cocooned in the warmth of his king-sized bed, she kept her eyes closed as she rolled her head to the side, allowing him full access. She stretched and ran her hands down her torso to her hips—hips that had to have Finn's fingerprints emblazoned on her skin.

She sighed. Despite falling asleep in his strong, secure embrace, her head was still spinning.

In the span of mere hours, she'd lost a nimrod fiancé, gained a business card boyfriend, and met a side of herself she'd never seen.

A sultry, sexy, commanding side.

She would have never described herself using those words. What had gotten into her? Well, besides a couple of pints of ice cream, a touch too much tequila, and of course, Finnegan Starrycard's glorious cock.

Glorious cock?

Holy moly, who was this new cock-obsessed Hailey Higgins?

Maybe it was the mountain air. Maybe it was the crazy roller coaster of a life she was living. Maybe the bazillion orgasms from last night had scrambled her brain. Still, it was hard not to be a little cock-obsessed after last night's ecstasy-palooza.

Finnegan Starrycard was a sex machine—like, for real. From the bathroom to the kitchen table to the sheepskin rug—for rug sex round two—and then back to the bathroom before collapsing onto his bed only to have the man go to town on her like she was a pint of cherry chocolate chip ice cream, the handyman had made good on his promise to make her wedding night one to remember. The delicious ache between her legs was a testament to his stamina.

She hummed again. She'd never been so deliciously ravaged.

Twenty-four hours ago, she'd woken up in Kansas, assuming she'd be married to Grant by now. If someone had told her back then that she'd be lounging in an axe murderer's bed after letting the man work her body six ways from Sunday, she would have died of laughter.

Okay, Finn wasn't an axe murderer.

Well, could she answer that definitively?

She'd only known the man for a matter of hours.

And now she was living with him—as his business card girlfriend.

The wallpaper had been right. Grant Rimnod wasn't meant for her. But neither was Finnegan Starrycard.

She had to remember that.

Love sucks, and the last thing she wanted was to nurse another broken heart.

Luckily, Finn hated love as much as she did.

She detested love—couldn't stand it. There was no way she'd be losing her heart to another man. That's what she decided, and she was sticking to it. Yep, sticking to it like the sticky ice cream Finn had licked off her belly and breasts with that masterful tongue.

Seriously, the man should be classified as a sexual national treasure.

But that wasn't what had her clenching her core at the thought of the guy. A sleepy smile stretched across her face as she recalled when he'd dropped the grumpy mask and grinned. As goofy as it sounds, her heart had skipped a beat. She couldn't help it. The second he'd shed his growly demeanor, he'd transformed. His moss-green eyes sparkled. His dimples peeked out from behind his scruff. There was no denying it. In the looks department, he was mountain man perfection adorned with a tool belt and wrapped in faded cotton and broken-in denim.

Her treacherous mind lapsed to when he caressed every inch of her body with large, calloused hands. His hard chest pressed against her breasts. And that glorious cock. *Glorious*. There was that word again. She shivered and contracted her core muscles, longing to feel him thrust his hips and fill her to the hilt.

But that's all it could be. Sex. Phenomenal, toe-curling, multiple-orgasm-inducing sex.

Their arrangement was temporary. She was not in danger of losing her heart. Nope, no way. There were no pickle jars in her future, and that was totally fine—one hundred percent A-OK. What happened between them were transactions. Nothing more and nothing less. That's what he'd labeled them, and that's what they'd stay. They were roommates with benefits, and it appeared her roommate was cashing in on the situation at this very second.

Finn licked her earlobe, but the sandpapery slide across her skin gave her pause. Perhaps he was dehydrated.

"Good morning, business card boyfriend," she said through a yawn.

"Good morning," came Finn's voice—from the other side of the room.

The other side of the room? Who the heck was nibbling on her ear?

In a bluster of sheet-pulling and comforter-cavorting, she whipped her head toward the rogue licker and eyed her bedmate. "It's a kitten," she exclaimed, eye to eye with the tiny fluff ball. The animal mewed an agitated sound, clearly upset she'd interrupted his lick session.

"I didn't want to disturb your moment with the boy cat."

She sat up and scooped the wee beast into her arms. "You always look so grouchy, but you're a secret cuddler behind that kitty scowl," she cooed, then focused on Finn. Her handsome handyman stood there sporting worn jeans and a dark denim button-up over a gray T-shirt with a kitten in the crook of his arm. And yes, he was rocking his tool belt. The stacked Mr. Fix-It with a kitty combo left her breathless. It should be criminal to cart around a baby animal while looking like a do-it-yourself dreamboat.

"Are you okay? You're drooling," Finn remarked, biting back a grin.

Her cheeks burned as she dragged the back of her hand across her mouth. "I'm not drooling over you or anyone. That's morning saliva."

That mind-bogglingly moronic term earned her a Finnegan Starrycard panty-melting grin.

"Morning saliva, huh?" he remarked, only looking hotter when he added a devilish smirk to the mix.

Was the man trying to kill her?

"How long have you been up?" she asked, changing the subject as she touched the corners of her mouth to ensure she wasn't actively spritzing saliva like a broken fire hydrant.

"A couple of hours. I checked out your cabin and patched the hole the raccoons were using to gain entry. Then I went into town."

She frowned. "Why didn't you wake me? I could have come with you."

"Wearing your mud-caked dress and scat-encrusted heels?"

Good point.

She eyed her current clothing ensemble. Before they'd collapsed in bed, Finn had retrieved the Starrycard Creek Paper Company T-shirt for her to wear while he completed another business card boyfriend transaction between her thighs. And boom! Her blush returned. But it wasn't triggered by thoughts of carnal bliss. This blush was sparked by embarrassment over how she'd handled her flighty departure from Kansas. She hadn't been prepared for what happened after she executed the skip-town-with-nothing-but-the-clothes-on-her-back plan.

She slumped against the padded headboard. "I don't have any normal clothes, sensible shoes, or much cash to buy a new wardrobe. And you annihilated my lacy underwear."

He sauntered to the bed, cupped her cheek in his hand, and kissed her. The sensation was electric, a slow and deliberate dance of soft, parted lips that sent shivers down her spine.

Was this the beginning of morning sex?

It was certainly one way to deal with her problems.

She inhaled his crisp woodsy scent and tasted the sweet bite of coffee, chocolate, and cherries on his tongue as his scruff tickled the corners of her mouth.

"Did you have ice cream for breakfast?" she asked.

His lips moved against hers. And there it was again. She pulled back and drank in a Finnegan Starrycard grin. Heaven help her! He was a beautiful man.

He schooled his features. "No," he answered with a thread of amusement woven into the syllable. The mischievous glint in his eyes triggered a rush of tingles between her legs.

"Liar," she purred. "I can taste it."

He gave her a playful half-shrug. "It's all we have to eat."

We.

Her pulse kicked up.

Ignore it. Ignore every impulse to fall for this man. He only meant *we* as in roommates. She was off the love train. She needed to tattoo the words *LOVE SUCKS* on the back of her eyelids.

He ran his knuckles down her jawline. "What's going on in that head of yours?"

She shook that head of hers. "Nothing. It's just my morning brain fog burning off."

"Come with me," he said and offered her his hand.

She gestured with her chin toward the bed. "We're not staying here?"

His eyes smoldered with desire. "You can bet that perfect ass of yours that we'll be back here."

There was her heart, skipping a beat again.

Good morning, Swoon City.

No, not Swoon City. Sex Goddess Junction. Yes, she was only about the sex. All the sex. Nothing more.

"Hailey?"

"Yeah?" she yipped, snapping out of her sex-obsessed head.

"I need to show you something before I bend you over the dresser and *transact* your brains out."

What a statement!

She picked up her fluffy bedmate, then dragged her perfect ass —and soon-to-be transacted-out brains—from the bed and followed Finn into the kitchen.

"Will any of these work for you?" he asked, his gruff persona taking on a shyer demeanor.

He stepped aside and revealed stacks of women's clothing piled on the kitchen table.

She handed him the kitten and perused the items. She spied a few pairs of jeans, T-shirts, a couple of skirts, yoga pants, sports bras, and a denim dress. That wasn't all. A red fleece jacket, a few pairs of sneakers, and some boots rounded out the offering of clothing.

A jolt of panic shot through her.

Her mouth went dry. Her muscles tensed.

Why did he have a complete woman's wardrobe?

Holy smokes, he was an axe murderer!

She stumbled backward. "Are these from your last victim?"

"What?" he exclaimed as the kittens mewed and squirmed in his arms.

"Did these clothes belong to your last victim? Do you invite stranded women into your home, lavish them with orgasms, steal their clothing, then cut them up into tiny pieces?" Adrenaline coursed through her veins. Fight-or-flight kicked in, and fight it was. She reached for his tool belt and grabbed the first thing she could get her hands on. She stared at the item. A tape measure? Ugh! Why couldn't she have snapped up a screwdriver or a hammer?

Making the best of her weapon, she pulled out a foot or so and swung the flaccid ribbon of thin metal at the man. "Stay back!"

He stared at the ceiling and groaned. "I'm not an axe murderer. I went to town to get these from my parents' house. They're some of my sister Caroline's clothes."

Hailey shook the tape measure at him. "Your sister's clothing?"

"Yes," he huffed.

"And where is this sister?"

"Fuck if any of us know, honestly. Somewhere in Europe. Maybe Asia. She's finding her purpose."

"Isn't that convenient," Hailey bit out, slicing the air with the tape measure.

"Hold on a second!" he exclaimed. "You're upsetting the kittens."

The poor balls of fluff mewed wildly. They did appear distressed.

"Have they eaten?" she pressed.

"I gave them a little cream and a can of tuna I found in the back of my cabinet. And go easy with my tape measure, boss. I need that if I'm going to fix your cabin. Again, for the millionth time, I am not an axe murderer. You've got to trust me."

He'd said the same thing last night before he ripped her panties off her body.

Axe murderer or not—and possibly beyond her better judgment—she trusted him.

She clicked the button and reeled in the flexible metal strip.

"Jesus," he muttered, reverting to grumpy mountain man mode. He returned the kittens to the crate and opened a kitchen drawer. "Look at this. I can prove these clothes belong to Caroline. This is a picture of me and my siblings from a couple of years ago." He handed her a photo. "That's me on the far left. Next is

Kieran. He's the oldest. Then there's Owen, Christian, and Eliza. The woman on the end is Caroline. She's my little sister. She's twenty-five and about your size. I knew you had nothing to wear, so I grabbed some stuff from her room at my mom and dad's place."

Hailey chewed her lip. "That was . . . thoughtful."

"And not something an axe murderer would do—not that I'd know what goes on in an axe murderer's mind." He growled. "I'll shut up now. Just look at the damned picture."

She studied the photo of the smiling Starrycard siblings. Talk about good genes. The four brothers shared the same dark hair and chiseled features, while the two sisters had brown, honey-kissed locks and pink cheeks.

Hailey concentrated on Caroline. "Your sister is twenty-five?"

"Yeah."

"So am I."

He looked her over. "Really?"

"How old did you think I was?"

He shrugged. "You seem older than Caroline."

"How old are you?" she lobbed back.

"Thirty."

"And you're sure you're not an axe murderer?" she pressed.

He sighed—channeling the most put-out handyman on the planet. "Hailey Higgins, you are on the verge of making my damned head explode."

She couldn't help but get starry-eyed when he said her name. His gruff voice manhandled the syllables, triggering her to clench her core.

He took the tape measure from her and placed it on the kitchen table. She gasped, but before she could protest, he picked her up and plopped her on the hard surface. She gasped again as her legs parted like she was one of those motion-sensor doors. She couldn't help it. Axe murderer or not—every part of her body craved this man.

With her legs spread wide in front of him, Finn situated

himself between her thighs. He tucked a lock of her hair behind her ear. "I'm not a thirty-year-old axe murderer." He removed his tool belt and set it on a chair, then leaned in and kissed the corner of her mouth. "I'm your thirty-year-old handyman slash business card boyfriend."

"Uh-huh," she replied on a dreamy exhale. The man could have confessed to a string of homicides, and she'd still have been powerless to resist him. *Gah!* She had to up her game when it came to shutting down her libido.

He kissed the other corner. "I want you to touch something, Hailey."

And hello, Tingle City.

"I bet you do," she breathed as heat rushed to her core.

He chuckled. "Not that. Wait, strike that. Let's make one thing abundantly clear. I'm always up for you touching my cock. What I want you to touch—to prove I'm not an axe murderer and that these clothes belong to Caroline—is to your left." He pulled back and crossed his arms.

She glanced at the item—a folded red fleece jacket. She rested her hand on it. "Okay, I'm touching it. Do I get to touch your cock now?"

"You'll be the death of me, woman," he said through a chuckle. "Look at the picture. Look at what Caroline is wearing."

She'd forgotten she still had the photo in her hand. She concentrated on the petite woman. "She's wearing a red fleece jacket."

"Bingo," he said with a triumphant fist pump, then swooped in for another kiss. "I'm Finnegan Starrycard. Local handyman. Not an axe murderer." He drank her in. "It appears you'll live another day, Hailey Higgins."

God help her! Her name dripping from his lips left her dripping.

"That's something to celebrate." She wrapped her arms around his neck and kissed the man like she wanted him for breakfast because Hailey Higgins, the newly crowned sex fiend, was all about sex for breakfast.

He hummed his satisfaction, lifted her from the table, and pressed her back to the wall. She closed her eyes, giving in to the heat that drew them together. She rocked her hips, feeling his hard length through his jeans. He palmed her bare ass with his calloused handyman hands as delicious friction built between them. She moaned, so ready for what had to be her millionth orgasm in twelve hours, when a buzzing sensation added to the heady mix.

Finn stilled.

"What is it?" she asked, breathless.

He blinked like aliens had returned him to his body. "It's my cell. Probably my friend," he murmured, lowering her so her feet could touch the floor.

He turned away and pulled his phone from his back pocket.

"Yeah, Jack. Uh-huh. Now?" Finn sighed. "Okay. Give me fifteen." He glanced at her and pocketed his phone. "I need to head into town with the cats."

She peered into the crate at the cuddling balls of ginger fluff. "I'll come with you."

He shifted his stance. "Don't you want to take a shower or something?"

What was going on with her business card boyfriend? His transact-your-brains-out vibe had done a one-eighty.

"I can throw my hair into a ponytail. It's not a big deal. I want to be there to make sure the kittens are okay, and I'd like to see the town."

The color drained from Finn's face. "You want to go into town?"

She studied the man. What was so wrong with her wanting to get a feel for the place?

"Yes, I do. I live here—at least for now."

A muscle ticked on his jaw. He'd gone from wanting to take her against the wall to acting like a grumpy brick wall.

"I'll get the kittens and meet you in the truck." With his gaze locked on the ground, he picked up the crate and headed out the door.

She ignored the prickly sensation working its way down her spine. Exhaling a heavy breath, she ran her hands through her tangled locks and surveyed the scene. She didn't have a minute to spare. She better not keep the grump of the mountain waiting.

Moving at light speed, she stripped off the T-shirt and threw on a pair of jeans, a sports bra, and a white blouse. She caught her reflection in one of the windows.

Not bad. Not bad at all.

The items fit perfectly. She'd have to rock commando until she could find a shop selling underwear, but that was leaps and bounds better than shlepping into town in a mud-splattered, boobalicious wedding gown. She sent Finn's sister a silent thank you as she slipped on a pair of white canvas sneakers and grabbed the fleece jacket.

What else did she need?

Her bag. She removed the pickle jar from her tote, set it on the coffee table, then bolted out the door. The chilly morning air clung to her cheeks as she spied a scowling Finn in the driver's seat.

She climbed into the truck, channeling sunshine. "Starrycard Creek, here we come," she sang, pulling a hair tie from her bag and corralling her auburn locks into a ponytail.

And . . . nothing from her business card boyfriend.

He zeroed in on a point in the distance.

They rumbled down the drive and onto the road in silence. Rocks and gravel crunched beneath the wheels, providing a tactile backdrop to the awkwardness. She stroked the kittens and cautiously checked her handyman. With a clenched jaw, he remained in grumpy robot mode. Where had the man who insisted on making her wedding night one to remember gone? Where was the attentive lover who'd kissed her like she made up his entire universe?

Stop!

She could not slip back into her old lovesick ways.

Take it for what it was—the best sex of her life.

Surely, that could fill the void in her chest. She'd have to learn to live this way. As the directive materialized, she touched her mouth, recalling their first kiss. Their lips had collided with an electric intensity, revealing the depth of Finn's desire to claim her body and soul.

Enough!

Find a distraction.

She rested her hands in her lap and focused on her surroundings—her absolutely breathtaking surroundings.

Patches of snow dotted the vast sea of evergreens and budding aspens. Whispers of pink and purple adorned the muddy terrain on the side of the road as they snaked through the mountain paradise. A clearing emerged, and she caught a glimpse of a ski lift on a nearby outcropping of steep peaks.

This place was a mountainous nirvana.

They came around another bend, and her heart leaped into her throat. "It's gorgeous," she breathed as she got a bird's eye view of Starrycard Creek, Colorado.

A roaring creek cut through the town, nestled in a valley and framed by mountains. Two and three-story brick buildings lined a grid of roads with a series of bridges arcing over the rushing waters in what appeared to be the heart of the business district. Cozy mountain cabins and larger rustic homes fanned out from the center. A park with an amphitheater and a school were tucked along the creek. Further south, she spotted the town hall. "It's charming, like something out of a storybook," she said softly as they traded the rutted mountain road for a paved one.

She glanced at her companion. The man was white-knuckling it as he glared at the road.

"Finn?" she said, not sure she'd break through.

"What?" he rasped.

At least he responded.

"You seem tense?" she replied, hating the slight shake in her voice.

He must have noticed. He released a pained breath, then reached over the kittens and held her hand. "I'm not a fan of going into town these days."

She squeezed his hand. "You're doing a good thing. We're going down to make sure the kittens are okay. We'll be back on the mountain soon."

"Yeah, you're right," he replied, tightening his hold.

"Is your friend a veterinarian?" she asked, trying to distract him from his worries.

"He is. How'd you know that?"

"My legendary powers of perception. Remember, I'm a super-sleuth. Who would be able to examine kittens?" she teased, attempting to lighten whatever burden weighed him down. "A lumberjack? No. A construction worker? No. A vet? *Ding, ding!*"

"Jack—that's my friend's name—can check out the kittens, and he knows the folks who run an animal rescue outside town. I'm sure they can help us."

"Oh," she answered, peering at the sweet, sleeping puffs of orange fluff.

Would they be saying goodbye to the cats today? Probably. It made sense. What would they do with a pair of kittens? They weren't even a *they*.

Heartsick, she focused on a line of red brick buildings. "It looks like a movie set for a Wild West town."

"That's actually true," he said, not sounding so growly. "Starrycard Creek is one of Colorado's largest historic districts. We've got nearly fifty preserved buildings linked to the Wild West."

She took in a sunny flower shop, an outdoor adventure retailer with a line of kayaks adorning the sidewalk, a few funky art galleries, a clothing shop, a deli, and a cozy bookstore with a rustic exterior and climbing vines covering much of the storefront before an awning with Starrycard Legal Services written in bold lettering caught her eye. "Do you have a lawyer in the family?"

"Two. My mom and Kieran. Kieran runs the law office. He's also on the town council."

She nodded, grateful to converse with the man. And then she saw something she recognized—the logo from Finn's T-shirt.

"The Starrycard Creek Paper Company." She studied the two-story blond brick building perched beside the lapping creek. It almost didn't look real. The mountains and the rushing water framed the building like nature had carved out this exact place for the structure. She could sense the love and dedication that went into building the business. Warmth rippled from her chest. "William Starrycard built the paper company for Fiona, didn't he," she uttered, her words taking on a dream-like quality.

"Yeah, she inspired everything. That's how the story goes and why the locals started saying love is in the cards. A play on words that stuck," Finn answered, his tone neutral, which was better than growly.

Hailey craned her neck, taking in more of the town. "And I see the rock wishing wall."

The low, weathered stone barrier meandered alongside the rushing creek, its stones hugging a path not far from the water's edge. Slips of paper in a myriad of shades were crammed into cracks and crevices.

The view changed as Finn turned down a quiet side street and parked the truck. He cut the engine, removed his seat belt, and turned toward her.

She followed his lead. "Are we here?"

Again, he'd gone mute. He stared at her with a yearning in his eyes that sent her pulse racing.

"Finn, did you hear me? Are we—"

He didn't let her finish. He set the crate on the floor near her feet, twisted his fingers in her ponytail, and kissed her. And hold on to your hat! This was no peck. This was the kiss of a man unable to hold back. He devoured her mouth. Kissing her hard, like star-crossed lovers saying goodbye. He pulled her closer as if he wanted to merge into one being and lose himself in her. She trembled as she allowed him to deepen the kiss, tasting the insatiable hunger on his tongue.

He pulled back and rested his forehead against hers. "Hailey?" he whispered in a desperate, gut-wrenching rasp of a sound.

"Yes?" she answered, chest heaving as she steadied herself.

"We can't let anybody know about us . . . about this. Whatever this is."

Whoosh. Ice crystallized in her veins. She shivered like a gust of frigid sleet had ripped through her chest, widening the cavernous void in its wake.

"Hailey?" he said, pain woven through each syllable. "Did you hear me?"

Love sucks. Love sucks. Love sucks.

She repeated the mantra, praying the words would quell her hammering heart.

"Nobody has to know about whatever this is," she rattled off.

A flicker of desire danced within the depths of his gaze. She'd swear he was ready to pull her onto his lap and take her in the truck. Or perhaps she'd misjudged his intentions. He blinked, and it was gone, as if he'd flipped a switch and become the zombie version of himself.

"I'm helping you fix up your cabin, and you're staying with me—in my spare room—until it's safe for you to move into your place." His words dropped like lead weights. "When we're alone, I can be your business card boyfriend. But here, in town—"

"I understand, Finn," she blurted.

Message received. She couldn't take anymore.

He searched her face. "We're on the same page when it comes to . . ."

To hooking up? To roommates with secret benefits? To love?

She mustered a grin. "Absolutely. Love sucks. It isn't in the cards for people like us."

"Love isn't in the cards for people like us," he repeated, stroking her cheek with his thumb.

The air crackled on the brink of igniting. The world narrowed down to the intimate space between them, where every breath, every brush of skin caressing skin, became an intoxicating temptation.

She had to make it stop.

She cleared her throat and edged away from the man. Needing to busy herself with something besides falling under his spell, she scanned the street. "Where's the vet's office? I assume we're close by."

Finn snapped out of their love-sucks haze. "Two doors down. The green awning."

She grabbed her canvas tote, but she wasn't ready to get out of the truck. She needed a second to distance herself from the man. She flashed her sunniest fake smile. "I'll meet you inside. I didn't have time to fix my face before we left. I'd like to put on a little makeup before going in."

He observed her, and a boyish grin bloomed on his lips. "What's there to fix?"

Cue the stupid belly butterflies.

Her core clenched as her poor heart dialed up its raucous beat.

She reached into her bag. "Lip balm. Mascara," she announced, like she was auditioning for a cosmetics commercial.

He straightened and ran his hands down the dark stubble on his cheeks. "Sure, yeah, okay. I'll see you inside."

And hello, Awkwardsville. Population two.

Finn exited the truck with the crate and headed down the sidewalk. Once he disappeared beneath the green sign, she deflated into the seat and peered at the makeup. "I've been looking for love for so long, it's become a habit to seek it out in every situation with every guy I connect with. But I'm done with that version of myself. I'm breaking a pattern. It's like the beginning of the school year when teachers set fresh expectations for the class. It takes time to acclimate to a new routine. And, in my case, what better way to create new patterns than to do it with a guy who doesn't want me for anything more than a fling where he showers me with ice cream and orgasms. And that's fine because that's all I want from him. I'm entering an exciting new loveless chapter chockfull of extreme sexual gratification because love sucks, and diving into a pool of sexual bliss does not suck." She stared at the plastic tubes, but the makeup didn't reply. And why would it? She dropped the items into her tote and groaned. Terrific! In the span of twenty-four hours, she'd become an orgasm-obsessed lunatic who conversed with cosmetics.

She slung her tote over her shoulder and exited the truck. She inhaled the fresh air, praying it would usher in some clarity. The sun kissed her cheeks as she strolled down the sidewalk. It was warmer in the valley. The soothing sound of the rushing creek mingled with birds bidding good morning to the day. She studied her surroundings. What wasn't there to like about this place? A knot twisted in her belly. Finn was here. A truth that left her comforted and conflicted. She huffed a tight breath. She desperately needed to get out of her head.

Luckily, she had plenty to keep her mind busy. It wasn't that she had a lack of important matters to consider. She needed to have the cabin fixed, but she also needed a way to make some cash while she was here. She wasn't about to depend on Finn. He'd already gone beyond what she felt comfortable permitting him to do.

But first things first.

Focus on the kittens.

She skimmed the lettering on the door to the vet's office. Jack Dunleavy, DMV.

Her heart sank in her chest. Would she ever see the kittens again? She blinked back tears. What was wrong with her? Perhaps it was the elevation or the whirlwind of the last twenty-four hours catching up with her.

"Get it together," she whispered, then entered the office. The space was neat, bright, and deserted. An empty chair greeted her at the front desk. It was Sunday. It would make sense that the vet's staff was off.

Not sure what to do, she glanced down a hallway, then took a seat as a man's voice floated from a room with a half-open door.

"I need you to start from the beginning, Finn."

Hailey froze.

That had to be Finn's friend—the vet, Jack Dunleavy.

"You're not making any sense," the man continued. "You're telling me you picked up two abandoned kittens and a woman on the side of the road outside your place, and all three spent the night with you at Starrycard Cabin?"

She cringed. She'd graduated from hooker bride to town harlot in a matter of hours.

The door to the office opened. A woman in a blue ball cap slipped inside with a brown paper bag. She took a seat and glanced at her phone. She must be a delivery person. Hailey tried not to stare, but the lady looked familiar.

"I don't have a lot of time to talk. Hailey will be coming in any second," Finn hissed.

"Hailey, that's a nice name. Is Hailey a miss or a missus?"

"Jack," Finn growled.

"I know that face," Jack crooned. "Liza said she overheard McKenzie tell you to get some. I'm proud of you for going for it, man."

Hailey felt her cheeks heat as the young woman in a cap tossed a glance her way.

"We've known each other our entire lives," the vet continued. "Something happened to you. Something good. You're not giving off recluse serial killer vibes today. You look more like you. Well, the *you* before—"

"For Christ's sake, Jack, I'm here about the kittens," Finn grumped.

"What was Hailey doing up near the cabin?" Jack pressed, defying his friend's wishes.

"Her last name is Higgins. She inherited Old Man Higgins' cabin and needs a place to stay until it's fixed."

"Does it need a lot of work?"

"Structurally, it's fine, but the floors and the roof are a mess. The plumbing is ancient. The electrical needs some TLC."

"It sounds like this lady in distress requires the skills of a handyman—a handyman who, again, as his niece so adroitly put it, needs to get some."

Hailey slumped in her seat, wishing a sinkhole would open beneath her. And who the heck was this niece telling her uncle to *get some*? She unzipped her jacket. Had the heater kicked on? She was on the verge of melting into a pool of mortification.

"Excuse me, miss?"

Hailey jumped, nearly tipping over in the chair. "Yes?" she eked out, meeting the delivery woman's gaze.

"Lovely morning."

Hailey plastered on a wide grin. "Um . . . yes, it is."

"Funny how you can hear everything in a doctor's office," the woman continued—a woman who appeared to be suppressing a grin.

"Uh-huh," Hailey squeaked.

"Jack, you're way out of bounds," Finn bellowed. "Not to mention, you don't get to have an opinion on what I do and don't do. And may I remind you, you're damn lucky I let you marry my sister."

Sister?

"I'm guessing you're Hailey Higgins?" the woman in the cap said, rising to her feet.

Hailey froze, wide-eyed, as the pieces came together.

She was sitting across from Eliza Starrycard. She recognized the woman from the photo. What a way to meet one of Finn's family members.

She swallowed past the lump in her throat. "Yes, I'm Hailey."

"Well, Hailey," Eliza said, her eyes glinting with mischief, "you'll want to brace yourself for what's about to happen. I promise you, it won't be pretty."

CHAPTER
Eight

HAILEY

ELIZA HARDENED her features and lifted her chin. "Finnegan William *Jackass Extraordinaire* Starrycard, get your butt to the waiting room, and bring my husband—who you sure as hell didn't allow me to marry—with you."

Wowza!

Finn's sister was not messing around.

Eliza set the paper bag on the chair and swiped her cell phone from her pocket. "Listen, Hailey," she continued without looking up as she hammered out a message. "I love my big brother dearly, but I've got to put the kibosh on this letting-me-marry-my-husband business. Men don't get to dictate women's choices. You feel me?"

Feisty and headstrong, Eliza Starrycard-Dunleavy was a force of nature. The muscles in Hailey's chest tightened as if an invisible hand had gently squeezed her heart, reminding her of her late mom's fierce spirit.

Hailey's rocking pulse dialed down a few notches. "I agree completely."

"Good," Eliza replied and pocketed her phone as footsteps echoed from the hallway.

A tall man with cropped blond hair headed toward them in

green scrubs with *Dr. Jack* embroidered on the breast pocket. "Hey, babe, go easy on your brother," he said to Eliza, then eyed the bag. "Are those turnovers from Goldie's?"

"They are. I figured you'd be hungry after a long night at the rescue center, and I'll decide how I deal with my brother. Everything go okay with the mama dog?"

"Six healthy puppies. One tired veterinarian," the man replied and kissed his wife's cheek.

"Jesus, can you two tone it down?" Finn grumbled, bringing up the rear.

Hailey stepped back. All she could do was watch this family drama unfold. But she wasn't bothered by it. In fact, seeing another side of Finn—his cantankerous, brotherly side—left her utterly captivated.

"If you think this is naughty, Finnegan," Eliza added with a smirk, "you'll never believe what we had to do to end up with our daughter. And for the record . . ."

"Here we go," Finn mumbled.

"You didn't *let* me marry Jack," she continued. "It doesn't matter if he's your best friend. He vowed to love and honor me before our friends and families. So, I win," she proclaimed in riveting little sister fashion.

Finn rubbed his eyes and huffed. "Liza."

Hailey couldn't help but grin.

"Do you think I even had a choice, Finn? Who can say no to Eliza Starrycard?" Jack added, but the love in his eyes as he drank in his wife betrayed his teasing words. "You've got to excuse the Starrycards," the vet continued, meeting Hailey's gaze. "They're a rambunctious bunch. And where are my manners? You must be Hailey Higgins. I'm Jack Dunleavy. It appears you've met my wife, Eliza Starrycard-Dunleavy," he said, stepping closer to the woman.

"It's nice to meet you both. Thanks for examining the kittens. Are they all right?" she asked, then caught movement out of the corner of her eye. It was Finn. Her business card boyfriend mirrored Jack's behavior and took a step toward her. Did he realize he'd done it? Or was he simply shifting his stance to work out some of that grumpy energy?

"Their vitals look good," Jack replied. "I don't have any immediate concerns. We can get going on vaccinations, and I'll get them on deworming meds. It's a good thing you brought them in. They wouldn't have lasted long alone up on the mountain. Give me about fifteen minutes, and the kittens will be good to go."

Eliza's phone pinged. She glanced at the screen, and a sly grin graced her lips. "Honey, can you bring the kittens to Goldie's? McKenzie wants to see her uncle Finn."

"Sounds good. I'll be down in a bit. It was nice to meet you, Hailey." Jack looked from the exam room to the waiting room. "I'm not sure how long you were out here or if you heard—"

"She heard everything, honey. We both did," Eliza said, cutting off her husband. "These walls are paper thin. Don't you remember? We learned that lesson the hard way."

Jack pressed a kiss to Eliza's lips. "We sure did. The waiting room got an earful that afternoon."

"How many times do I have to say it? I do not want to hear about you and my little sister," Finn lamented.

Eliza patted Finn's arm. "If you haven't figured it out yet, Hailey, Finnegan Starrycard is tons of fun. And when I say tons of fun, I mean he's a walking, talking carnival of grump-tastic grumpiness." She gave the grump a once-over. "But not so much today."

"He's been nothing but kind to me," Hailey replied meekly.

It wasn't a lie. Finnegan Starrycard had given her a place to stay, food to eat, clothes to wear—and the orgasm buffet of a lifetime. But she wasn't about to cop to that. Jack had already inferred as much. But he was only guessing. A guess he'd made because Finn appeared different. What did the vet say? Finn wasn't giving off recluse serial killer vibes, and he'd attributed that change to her. A warmth spread through her chest until she recalled their conversation in the truck mere minutes ago. The heat waned. Finn didn't want anyone to know about them. And there wasn't a *them*. She was done with *thems*.

Love sucks. Love sucks.

Wash. Rinse. And repeat that mantra until it stuck.

But just as the faintly glowing ember in her chest threatened to fade into darkness, its weak glow burst into a vibrant flame. And who sparked this inferno? Mr. Growly Handyman himself, Finnegan Starrycard. He was looking at her. She could sense his intensity like a spotlight cutting through a pitch-black auditorium.

"Finn, the gentleman. Well, look at that," Jack said, catching Eliza's eye.

Hailey glanced at her handyman. "Yes, very much so. I was stranded on the side of the road, and Finn was there in my moment of need. He also saved me from a pack of angry raccoons when he went with me to check out my cabin."

"That sounds like one hell of a way to meet," Jack mused with an easy grin.

Finn rubbed his neck. "It was nothing."

"It wasn't nothing to me," she said softly.

A barely-there whisper of a grin tugged at the corners of Finn's mouth eliciting a rush of heady euphoria that left her lightheaded.

How did this keep happening? One second, she was the captain of the *SS Love Sucks*, and the next, she'd been catapulted into a sea of warm fuzzies courtesy of her business card boyfriend.

"Well, then, it's nice to hear Finnegan's been on his best behavior," Jack said, his words snapping her back to reality. "Now, I'll need to say goodbye. I'll catch up with you after I get the kittens sorted." He shared another look with his wife before snagging the brown paper bag and heading to the exam room.

Eliza studied her brother, who'd returned to donning a scowl. She gestured outside. "Shall we?"

Finn got the door for them. Eliza passed through and continued down the sidewalk. Hailey glanced over her shoulder as she followed Eliza. In that brief snippet of time, Finn flashed another ghost of a grin her way. *What was he playing at?* The question had barely formed when he reached for her hand. He brushed his fingertips along her knuckles for a fraction of a second. The brief contact sent a delicious charge through her body and triggered a memory. She pictured her father reaching for her mother's hand like a connection that transcended words.

But that wasn't happening between her and Finn. Finn didn't want her. And she was not in the market to have her heart broken.

End of story.

"You two coming?" Eliza called.

Finn stuffed his hands into his pockets. "Right behind you."

Hailey wiggled her fingers, then fiddled with her purse strap. She had to compartmentalize her emotions. In the cabin, she could give in to his advances. In public, they were . . . nothing.

But what was this touchy-feely business he was throwing her way? Why would he take the risk of his sister catching him in the act of stroking her hand? He could shrug it off and say it was an accident. Still, it didn't make sense. He was the one demanding absolute secrecy.

Oh, forget about it.

She had to break her pattern of reading into everything. She returned her attention to Eliza as they strolled down the sidewalk toward the creek.

"Hailey Higgins," Eliza began, then sneezed.

"Are you okay?" Hailey asked.

"I've been stretched thin at work, and now I'm fighting off a cold. Luckily, I refuse to get sick, but I don't want to think about that. Let's talk about you."

"About me?" Hailey stammered.

Eliza pulled a tissue from her pocket and patted her nose. "How much do you know about Starrycard Creek, Colorado?"

Hailey breathed a sigh of relief. She could do small talk. "I know a little bit about the town. Finn shared some of the history with me last night when we were in his cabin."

Eliza narrowed her gaze. "In *his* cabin? You've been inside Starrycard Cabin? Did you stay there with my brother?"

That's right! Eliza hadn't heard Jack and Finn rattle off that nugget.

Just play it cool.

"Yes, but only because . . ."

"Because Higgins Hideaway isn't habitable yet," Finn supplied. "I offered Hailey my spare room until her place is ready since it's mud season and the inn and the B and B are closed."

"You hired Finn to work on the cabin?" Eliza pressed.

"I needed a handyman, and I had his card," Hailey replied, grateful she could be quick on her feet.

"That's right," Eliza replied, sporting that sly smirk as her phone rattled off a series of pings and dings. "My mom put it in with the letter. Isn't that something?"

"What's going on, Liza?" Finn grumbled. "Why's your phone blowing up?"

"Just Starrycard Central, like always," the woman answered, eyeing the screen, then pocketed the device. "And here we are," she said, not missing a beat. "This is my grandmother's restaurant, Goldie's on the Creek."

Hailey took in the buzzing scene. Goldie's on the Creek did not disappoint when it came to small-town charm. A cheery marigold awning stretched over the outdoor tables, dotting a wide concrete walkway parallel to the gurgling creek. The scent of freshly brewed coffee and the clink of busboys stacking plates as they cleared tables peppered the air. A few lazy dogs sat beneath tables while their pet parents noshed on dishes teeming with scrambled eggs, fruit, and pastries. Children climbed on the sea of rocks and boulders that lined the creek bed. This must be the image that popped up online when the words *idyllic mountain town* were entered in the search box.

"Mommy! Uncle Finn!" came a child's trill of a voice. A little girl with golden-brown hair like Eliza's bounced from the table closest to the water. She zoomed toward them, dodging chairs, patrons, and waiters like a pint-sized roadrunner.

"Get ready for trouble," Finn murmured, but there was nothing but affection in his voice.

The little girl skidded to a stop in front of them and scanned the trio. "Who are you, red coat lady?"

"Manners, Kenzie," Eliza chided gently.

"Sorry, Mommy," the little girl replied, then nodded to herself. "I'm McKenzie Fiona Starrycard-Dunleavy, and I'm in first grade. Please, tell me who you are, red coat lady. Thank you."

Hailey beamed at the child. Moments like these were why she loved working with children. She offered her hand to the girl. "I'm Hailey Higgins. It's nice to meet you, McKenzie Fiona Starrycard-Dunleavy."

The girl shook her hand, then gave her an appraising once-over. "Is your name Higgins, like Old Man Higgins, who used to live on the mountain and walked around without clothes on?"

"McKenzie," Eliza said in a teacher-like voice Hailey could appreciate.

"What, Mom? They have the same last name, and Uncle Finn told me that Old Man Higgins would walk around without his clothes a whole bunch of years ago."

"We can always count on Kenzie to be direct and share her every thought," Eliza said warmly and wiped a crumb from the little girl's lip.

"I wonder where she gets it?" Finn murmured.

Hailey suppressed a grin. "You're quite perceptive, McKenzie. Albert Austin Octavius Higgins was my great-uncle."

"Wow!" the child exclaimed, wide-eyed. "I didn't know he had a bunch of names like me. I bet when his mom called him all four names, he knew he was in big trouble."

Hailey chuckled. "It's quite a name. But I don't know anything about his mother. I don't know much about him. I learned he left a cabin to me yesterday."

Confusion marred the child's features. "You never met him?"

"No, but my dad mentioned him to me when I was about your age. He used to send my father Starrycard paper."

The sparkle in the child's eyes intensified. "I know a lot about Starrycard paper. Everybody in Colorado uses it. But it's making my uncle Owen say things like, 'How am I supposed to keep up with this workload on my own? It's total bullsh—'"

"Kenzie," Eliza exclaimed, ending the child's imitation of her uncle.

"And it's the most special paper ever," the child continued, changing gears. "If you have a big wish, you write it on a piece of Starrycard paper and put it in the wishing wall." The girl released a pained breath, and the excitement drained from her expression. "I've been wishing for a stegosaurus for half my life, but I haven't gotten one yet."

"You know what I've told you about wishes, little one. It's the same thing William and Fiona Starrycard used to tell everyone who came searching for Starrycard paper, hoping to make their dreams come true," came a woman's voice, bubbling with energy like the creek.

Hailey took in the attractive senior citizen. Her sky-blue eyes glinted, matching her blue apron as she assessed the scene. With her silver hair fashioned in a long braid that trailed over her shoulder, she carried a keen air, appearing part gypsy and part chef. She removed a dishtowel from where it rested on her shoulder and wiped a dusting of white powder from her hands.

"But I really want my very own dinosaur, Goldie," McKenzie grumped, taking a page from Finn's playbook.

"You might want it, but a wish only comes true if what you desire is truly meant for you," the old woman replied.

McKenzie exhaled a frustrated breath. "I know, I know. You've told me a million times."

Goldie patted the child's cheek, then captured Hailey with her appraising gaze. "And who do we have here?" she asked like she already knew the answer.

"This is Hailey Higgins, Goldie. Her great-uncle was Old Man Higgins," McKenzie replied.

"Hailey Higgins," Goldie purred with a curious glint in her eyes.

Hailey pasted a grin on her face.

What could this woman already know about her?

"Ms. Higgins, it's nice to put a face with the name," another woman added, joining the group. The attractive newcomer looked like the sixty-something version of Eliza. "I'm Maeve O'Leary-Starrycard."

"The mayor. You sent me the letter about Higgins Hideaway," Hailey stammered.

"It took quite a bit to track you down." She tossed a glance at Finn. "And it appears you've used the business card I placed in the envelope to connect with our local handyman. Hello, Finnegan, darling," the woman added.

"Good morning, Mother," Finn answered with a wary touch to his tone and pressed a kiss to the woman's cheek. He looked between his mom and grandmother, then eyed his sister. "I think I figured out what the text storm was about."

Maeve smoothed a lock of hair near her forehead and turned up the wattage on her grin. "We're excited to welcome a new resident to Starrycard Creek. Tell us, how's Higgins Hideaway?"

"I'm afraid it's a little rough around the edges," Hailey replied.

"Good thing we've got a local handyman hanging around," Finn's mother answered. "Have you hired Finn?"

"He's kindly agreed to help me," Hailey answered, not lying but not telling the entire truth.

Maeve frowned. "I hope you're not staying there. That can't be safe."

Here it comes.

"No, I'm . . ."

"She's staying with me at Starrycard Cabin," Finn finished. "But I have a feeling you already knew that."

"Is she?" Goldie remarked, sharing a look with Maeve.

What was going on with these women?

McKenzie's mouth fell open, and she tugged on Hailey's coat sleeve. "Hailey Higgins, have you been inside the cabin?"

Had Finn not had any visitors—not even his family?

"Hailey's only staying at Starrycard Cabin because Higgins Hideaway isn't safe to live in yet, and there's nowhere for her to stay in town right now," Finn said to the gobsmacked girl.

"Did you see the floofy white rug I picked out for Uncle Finn?" McKenzie continued.

Hailey felt her cheeks heat. "I think I remember seeing it in front of the fireplace."

That's it. Play stupid.

Awestruck, the child gave her sleeve another tug. "I have a big question for you."

"Sure, ask me anything," Hailey replied, then glanced at Finn, who turned the shade of dirty dishwater.

What did he know that she didn't?

McKenzie rubbed her hands together like a pigtailed mad scientist. "What did you do on the rug, Hailey Higgins? Tell me everything."

CHAPTER
Nine

HAILEY

HAILEY BLUSHED beneath the weight of everyone's gaze, her mind spinning as she searched for answers. What exactly did she do on the sheepskin rug? How was she supposed to answer that question? Revealing that Finn had transported her to a state of delirious ecstasy, sprawled across the floor covering like a sex-crazed maniac, didn't appear to be a suitable response.

A beauty-queen-wattage smile stretched across her lips. "What, McKenzie? I don't think I heard you correctly."

The child tapped her foot, growing impatient. "What did you and Uncle Finn do on the big, floofy rug I picked out for the cabin?"

Hailey nodded, mulling over the question like the child had asked her to explain nuclear fusion.

Think, think, think!

She had to come up with something.

"We did typical rug stuff," Finn rattled off, swooping into the conversation.

"Yes," Hailey affirmed, finding her voice, "typical rug stuff."

"Like . . . ?" McKenzie prodded.

Hailey's nervous grin was millimeters from cracking her lips. She loved the kid's curious mind, but this was getting ridiculous.

She caught Finn's eye. They needed to tread carefully but convincingly.

"We walked on it," she said like she'd invented rug walking.

The man nodded, following her lead. "And we sat on it."

That's it! Stick to boring stuff. Kids at this age will grow bored of adults' tiresome replies.

"Did you lay on it?" the girl probed.

Maybe not every kid.

"What?" Hailey yelped and prayed her eyes hadn't popped out of their sockets.

"That's what I'd do," the child mused. "I'd roll around in the floofy softness—roll and roll and roll. I might even sleep on it. And that's not all. You could play on it. Or read on it. Or wrestle on it. It's a big rug. I bet you'd both fit."

Oh, they fit on it.

"Well," Hailey replied, sharing a look with the man who resembled a six-foot-four length of cherry licorice twist, "those are creative rug suggestions."

"Top-notch, Kenz," Finn mumbled and patted the kid on her shoulder.

"Do you like your bedroom in the cabin, Hailey? Is the bed comfy? What does it look like?"

Her bedroom?

McKenzie had stumbled onto an even more precarious line of questioning than rug activities.

Hailey swallowed hard. She hadn't even opened the door to the guest room.

"It's very . . . square," she offered, going for vague.

Finn shook his head. It was a minute movement, but she caught it.

"I mean, it's rectangular," she blurted, amending her statement.

McKenzie pursed her lips. The wheels in the child's head were turning.

"Hey, Kenz, I bet you can't jump from rock to rock like those big kids," Finn challenged and pointed toward the creek.

McKenzie squared her jaw and eyed her uncle. "I'm the best rock jumper in Starrycard Creek. Watch me, Uncle Finn," the child exclaimed and headed for the water.

Hailey tossed Finn a grateful look, conveying he'd done a good job, and that was a close one.

He eyeball-replied, love that kid, but holy hell, my head's about to explode.

Hailey chuckled, then froze. She shifted her stance as three generations of Starrycard women studied her and her eyeball partner in crime like they were the menu's special of the day.

"I best be getting back to the kitchen," Goldie said with a wry twist to her lips. "These turnovers don't make themselves, and I've got a mimosa with my name on it back there."

"Baking and drinking? Who would have guessed," Eliza teased.

"I'm eighty-three years old. I dedicated a good chunk of my life to this town. Now, I can do whatever I like. I can cook, drink, and sing 'The Star-Spangled Banner' in my birthday suit if I want to. As long as I keep the turnovers coming, nobody gives a hoot if I'm three sheets to the wind," Goldie proclaimed, then patted Eliza's cheek.

This family was a riot.

"It's nice to meet you, Hailey. I'm sure we'll be seeing more of you," Goldie added.

"Nice to meet you as well."

"Have you had breakfast yet, dear?" Maeve asked, sporting the same cat-who-ate-the-canary smirk as Goldie.

"No, ma'am, I haven't," Hailey replied, smack-dab in the center of a Starrycard tornado.

"Forget the ma'am business. Call me Maeve," the woman cooed. "Now, we've got a fresh pot of coffee and a platter of my mother-in-law's cherry turnovers at the table. They are delectable with a little orange marmalade. It sounds like a strange flavor combination, but it just works. Are you a fan of oranges and cherries?" the woman asked as she led them to a rustic rectangular table.

"She likes cherries," Finn chimed, then winced.

Everyone's attention flicked to the man as they took their seats.

He shrugged. "Hailey likes cherry licorice and cherry chocolate chip ice cream."

Hailey nodded. "I do."

"How do you know that?" Eliza quipped, settling into the chair next to her mother.

"I always carry cherry licorice with me. It was my mom's favorite—and mine, too. I offered some to Finn."

Finn nodded. "And all I have to eat at my place is ice cream, so that's what we ate."

Off her body.

Finn had eaten, licked, and sucked ice cream off just about every part of her. She couldn't help the sizzling tingle that settled between her thighs and suppressed a dirty little grin.

"Hailey, you look a little flushed," Eliza commented.

Oh no! No, no, no!

"Must be all that ice cream," Eliza continued.

And sex.

Hailey crossed her legs. She had to get her mind out of the gutter.

"I can imagine all that sugar can't be good for either of you," Maeve remarked. "They're worried about your level of ice cream consumption at the ice cream shop, Finnegan. I hoped your father and I instilled the importance of eating a balanced diet."

"Hailey and I aren't kids, Mom. What we eat is what we eat. And what's so wrong with a little ice cream?" he grumped.

We.

Hailey ignored her sappy side, but she couldn't leave Finn looking like an ice cream fiend. "A little cherry chocolate chip was exactly what I needed after a long drive."

Maeve sat back and nodded. "I see." She narrowed her gaze. "Your jacket looks familiar, Hailey. I believe my youngest daughter has one like it," the woman continued, like a seasoned prosecutor leading a witness to confess.

"It's Caroline's, Mom," Finn answered in his signature grump style. "I grabbed it this morning from the house along with a few other things. Hailey didn't have a coat, and she needs one, especially up on the mountain."

Maeve frowned as worry creased her brow. "You came to Starrycard Creek without a coat?"

Hailey was back in the hot seat. "Or shirts or pants or pajamas. You name it, I left most everything in Kansas because . . ." She scanned the faces gathered around the table. Maeve and Eliza's expressions spoke volumes, a mixture of genuine concern and empathy etched across their features. But the handyman sitting catty-corner from her put her at ease. He shifted in his chair, and his work boot brushed against the tip of her sneaker, a subtle connection that stirred something within her.

She relaxed and exhaled the breath she hadn't realized she'd been holding. She let in the town's peaceful energy and drank in the melody of the soothing creek accompanied by the joyous laughter of children playing nearby. A profound sense of calm took over, and another childhood memory surfaced. She recalled the many nights she lay tucked into bed, her parents' conversation resonating from the kitchen below. She'd loved listening to the cadence of their voices in the fleeting seconds before she succumbed to sleep, a gentle reminder that she wasn't alone in the world.

And at this very moment, surrounded by Starrycards and the comforting rush of the creek, she didn't feel alone either.

She gathered a bit of courage. "I arrived in Starrycard Creek completely unprepared because the day I got here—yesterday— was supposed to have been my wedding day."

"Supposed to have been?" Maeve echoed, raising an eyebrow.

"A woman holding a positive pregnancy test interrupted the ceremony and said my fiancé was the father."

"Yikes," Eliza remarked, wide-eyed.

"We broke up on the spot, but I didn't expect him to ask for the engagement ring, so he could use it to propose to her."

"What an absolute creep," Eliza lamented.

Maeve glanced at Finn, then returned her attention to Hailey. "My dear, how awful. I'm so sorry. Here, have something to drink," she said and poured a cup of coffee. She slid the steaming mug across the table.

Hailey took a sip of the warm beverage. "I'm okay. He wasn't the man for me—clearly." She traced the rim of the mug with the tip of her index finger. "After that happened, I didn't know what to do. I was sitting in my car, trying to figure out my next move, when I noticed some mail I'd left in my purse. I was drawn to your letter. I opened it and saw the key and the business card," she said, gifting Finn with a smile. "I couldn't believe I'd inherited a cabin. It felt like fate was steering me in this direction. I drove straight here."

Eliza leaned forward. "In your wedding dress?"

Hailey took another sip of coffee, hardly able to believe how much had happened in twenty-four hours. "Yes, in my wedding dress. I got several second and third glances when I stopped for gas."

"And then you met my son," Maeve supplied, connecting the dots.

"On the side of the road up by Higgins Hideaway. My car broke down. I thought he was an axe murderer."

"A what?" Eliza exclaimed through her bite of cherry turnover, amusement dancing in her eyes.

"An axe murderer," Finn repeated, dropping the grumpy demeanor. His sage-green eyes twinkled. "I had Dad's axe with me. I was about to chop down a cluster of aspens blocking part of the road. Just before I swung the axe, I heard someone yelling. I looked up and saw Hailey in my truck's headlights." He flashed that whisper of a grin that left her breathless. "This beautiful, deranged bride with a kitten in her arms."

Beautiful.

Had he said it, or had her mind inserted the word? It didn't matter. She couldn't concern herself with semantics. All she could concentrate on was her starry-eyed handyman. Time stood still as their eyes locked, the world shrinking to the space between them. He wanted to kiss her. She knew it as well as she knew her name.

Eliza cleared her throat. "And speaking of kittens . . ."

Hailey snapped out of her Finnegan Starrycard stupor. She followed Eliza's gaze and looked over her shoulder. Jack headed toward them with the crate in his arms.

"Two kittens, good to go," the man said and set the crate on the table between her and Finn.

Finn scratched the girl cat between her ears as she purred her delight. "Should we drive them up to the animal rescue now?"

"Nope," Jack replied, then greeted Maeve before taking the seat catty-corner to his wife.

Finn studied the animals. "Are they coming to get them?"

Jack poured himself a cup of coffee. "No."

The frown line between Finn's eyes deepened. "Why not?"

The vet took a sip of the steaming beverage. "Because you're keeping them."

"What are Hailey and I supposed to do with a pair of kittens?" Finn asked, his voice brimming with disbelief.

Unbothered by the grumpy handyman act, Jack relaxed into his seat, added a dollop of orange marmalade to a turnover, and dug into the pastry. "Foster them at the cabin," he said through the bite. "The rescue says they can't take any more animals. I put the supplies you'll need, along with some food, in the bed of your truck. It won't be more than a month. Maybe six or eight weeks."

"You're kidding," Finn scoffed.

"I'm afraid he's not," Maeve added. "I was talking with one of the volunteers the other day. They're well over capacity. They've been seeking more funding avenues to expand."

Hailey observed the balls of ginger fluff. How curious that she'd be fostering a pair of kittens. The pet rescue volunteer she'd met while musing over her life's terrible choices had mentioned that she looked like she could benefit from the company of a kitten. Now she had two—at least for a little while.

"I don't think they'll be too much trouble." She reached into the crate and scooped up the boy kitten. He mewed his displeasure until she held him to her chest. He nuzzled into her and buzzed like a content little engine.

"Is that a kitty?" McKenzie called, skipping over to the table. A man with an athletic build, olive skin, wavy black hair, and a canoe paddle tucked under his arm followed a few steps behind. The child peered into the crate then patted the head of the kitten in Hailey's arms. "Look, Nico, my dad brought me kitties."

"No, little star," Eliza said, shaking her head. "We have two dogs, two Guinea pigs, four fish, and a cat. We are not taking these cuties home. Your uncle Finn and Hailey are," she added, then leaned over and waved to the man. "Hey, Nico? Are you gearing up for kayak and canoe lessons?"

"I am. No better place to hit the water than the creek in Starrycard Creek," the man replied with a flowing Italian accent. Decked in a formfitting long-sleeved T-shirt highlighting his bulging biceps, an equally snug fleece vest, and shorts quite shorter than what most men usually wore, this guy looked ready to conquer the creek or pose for an outdoor adventurer magazine.

"Nico let me help him take the kayaks off his truck," the little girl gushed. "Will you be coming to my school again to teach us about water safety?"

"*Assolutamente*! Absolutely," the man answered, his focus trailing from McKenzie to Hailey.

"Are you new in town, *bella*? You must be. I'd remember meeting you," the man crooned and flashed one killer Casanova smile.

"That's Hailey Higgins, Nico," McKenzie announced. "She got here yesterday. She's living with my uncle Finn."

"Are you two together?" Nico asked, his gaze bouncing to a stone-faced Finn.

"No, no, no," Hailey answered. "It's nothing like that. I'm staying in his guest room until my cabin is safe to live in."

"Hailey's great-uncle, with four names like me, left her Higgins Hideaway," McKenzie explained.

"You inherited Higgins Hideaway? Are you making your home here?" the man pressed with a glimmer in his dark eyes.

"I'm not sure."

"I've lived in Starrycard Creek for a little over five years. It's a beautiful town with beautiful women," Nico gushed and gestured to Maeve and Eliza.

"Nico," Maeve cooed, waving off the man.

"What about me, Nico?" McKenzie asked, falling under the Italian heartthrob's spell, like her mother and grandmother.

"Beautiful children, too, of course, *bambina*," he continued and tapped the tip of the little girl's nose.

"Did you hear that, Daddy? I'm a *bambina*."

"Oh, I heard it, sweetie," Jack replied, suppressing a grin as he added another spoonful of marmalade to his turnover.

"It is true," Nico announced boldly. "Beautiful people, beautiful land, beautiful water, and beautiful mountains. So much to do year-round. I run the water sports program in the spring and summer and work as a ski instructor in the winter."

"What do you do in the fall, Nico?" McKenzie asked, beaming.

The man stilled. Slowly, he closed his eyes and harnessed a Zen vibe. "I meditate on my virility."

"I can tell," Eliza murmured to her mother.

He opened his eyes. "My routine gives me excellent . . . stamina," the man added, setting his sights on Hailey.

"How lovely for you," she stammered.

Finn emitted a low grumble.

"Listen, *bella*," the man continued, leaning in to pet the kitten in her arms. "I'd love to take you out and show you around. Take you on the water."

Tension crackled in the air. Hailey didn't dare look at her business card boyfriend, but curiosity got the better of her. She took a quick peek. And yikes! With clenched fists and a furrowed brow, irritation gushed from her handyman in palpable, roiling waves. And that wasn't all. Finn shifted in his chair, moving to allow his knee to rest against hers.

Hailey exhaled a shaky breath and mustered a grin for the dashing Italian. "That's very sweet of you to offer . . ."

"Nico. *Nico Romano,*" the man said, doing a little tongue trill with his last name that had Eliza and Maeve giggling and fanning themselves.

"You should let Nico take you out, Hailey. You're a single woman. Get out there," Eliza remarked, blotting her nose with a tissue before tossing a furtive glance at Finn.

"Everyone adores Nico," Maeve added.

Hailey shifted in her seat. "Um . . . yeah, okay, Nico. Thank you. That sounds fun."

"Okay!" Nico exclaimed. "Can I get your number? My phone is in my truck. You can write it on my business card. Our *bella* Mayor Maeve helped me pick out the paper." He reached into his pocket and produced a ballpoint pen and an off-white rectangle with flecks of blue.

He handed the items to her, and she studied the lovely card. Look at that. She was in possession of another man's business card. What kind of weird artisan paper-infused life was she living?

She jotted down the digits and returned the card and pen to Nico as a low, menacing grumble permeated the air, like Zeus, the god of thunder, had decided to drop into Goldie's on the Creek for a turnover.

"What's that, Finn? Did you say something?" Nico asked.

"It wasn't me," Finn lied. "It must have been the boy cat. I don't think he likes you, man."

"No, no, Finnegan Starrycard," Nico answered, waving off the growly mountain man. "All pussycats like me."

Wowza!

Hailey bit her lip to stop from laughing. That was quite an answer.

She stole a look at Finn. Was her handyman jealous?

"Boy cat?" McKenzie said, eyeing the kitten. "The cats don't have names?"

"They have names. Boy Cat and Girl Cat," Finn answered, gesturing from kitten to kitten.

"Those aren't real names, Uncle Finn," McKenzie chided. She scratched her chin. "You should call the boy cat Mr. Whiskerfrown because he's got a frowny face, and you can name the girl kitty Sweet Miss Marmalade because she's got a sweet face and has orangey fur that's the same color as Goldie's special orange marmalade, like the color of your hair, Hailey."

"Those are wonderful names, McKenzie, and so creative," Hailey replied and waved in the child. "You'll like this. I once had a student who named her grouchy cat Lord Crankypaws."

"Wait! Stop the presses," Eliza exclaimed, nearly knocking over her mug of coffee. "You're a teacher?"

"Yes," Hailey answered cautiously. Nobody usually got that excited to learn what she did. "I'm an elementary school teacher. I've mostly been subbing for the last year or so."

Eliza leaned forward, mesmerized. "What do you know about second grade?"

That was a specific question, but an easy one for Hailey to answer.

"It's a pivotal year. Children are transitioning from primary grades to intermediate. It's the year when students are required to progress from learning to read to reading to learn, but because of individual development and outside factors that affect children's learning, skills can vary. Second graders are embracing more independence and can take on more responsibilities in the classroom and at home. It's truly a magical time."

Eliza watched her for a beat, then whooped and clapped her

hands. She swiped another turnover from the plate and pointed the pastry at Hailey. "You're hired."

Hired?

Hailey stared at the ecstatic woman. "I'm sorry. Hired for what?"

"You're hired to substitute teach second grade for the rest of the school year at Starrycard Creek Elementary School. I'm the principal. Our second-grade teacher, Mrs. Kimball, left two months ago. Her daughter's twins came early, and she moved to Grand Junction to be closer to them. It's hard to find qualified educators. We'll get you an emergency substitute license. I know people, so don't worry about that. If it goes well, we'll talk about making it permanent," Eliza rattled off, hammering away on her cell phone.

"Wow," Hailey said on a stunned exhale.

"She can't work at the school," Finn mumbled.

Eliza glared at her brother. "Why not?"

"She's got work to do on her cabin—on Higgins Hideaway."

"You'll be doing all the work, Finnegan. Once you set your sights on something, you don't let anyone or anything stop you."

"What's that supposed to mean?" he barked.

"Remember the tree fort?" Eliza said and nudged her husband. "Jack, back when we were kids, who was supposed to build the tree fort?"

"All of us neighborhood hellions," the man answered.

A sly smirk bloomed on Eliza's lips. "And who ended up sneaking out of the house and doing everything in the dead of night so nobody could get in the way of his plan?"

Jack used a turnover to point at Finn—must be a Dunleavy thing.

"Hailey can help you on the weekends and after school," Eliza said, losing her teasing tone. "Having Hailey here in Starrycard Creek is like the universe answering my prayers. You heard her answer. She knows what she's talking about. I've been in a terrible bind trying to fill the vacancy, Finn. Hailey is a godsend. And it's not your call."

Finn shifted and broke their connection beneath the table. "You're right. It's Hailey's decision."

"What do you say, Hailey?" Eliza continued. "Will you let my brother work his magic on your cabin while you do me a huge favor? I've been teaching the class and continuing my role as principal. I'm running myself ragged doing two jobs. You're obviously well-qualified. We've got a thousand-dollar bonus for agreeing to work as a long-term sub, and our sub pay rate aligns with the rest of the area. You'd start tomorrow."

It was almost too much to take in.

Hailey glanced at her sullen business card boyfriend. But this wasn't about him. He wasn't her real boyfriend. They weren't building a life together. The only building that was happening was whatever needed to be constructed to get her cabin ready for her to live in—or sell. If her failed past relationships taught her anything, it was that she had to take care of herself. She couldn't depend on anyone. And that meant getting a job to make some money.

She met Eliza's gaze. "I accept. I'd love to get back into the classroom. Thank you."

"And I could take you out to celebrate," the local Don Juan crooned. "A night with Nico is always one to remember."

"That would be—" Hailey began when the kittens broke out into a frenzied chorus of mews and meows.

Finn rose to his feet, causing Nico to take a few steps back. "We should get the kittens to the cabin, and I need to walk you through the repair list for your place."

That was quite abrupt.

"Okay," Hailey replied, working to regain her bearings.

"Take the rest of the turnovers with you. Hailey hasn't even had one," Maeve said, wrapping the pastries in a cloth napkin and tucking a small jar of orange marmalade inside with the treats.

Eliza took the wrapped pastries from her mother and handed them to Hailey. "Can you be at Starrycard Creek Elementary around seven thirty tomorrow morning? School doesn't start until nine. That'll give us time to get you situated in your classroom."

Hailey cringed. Her vehicle was still on the side of the road. "My car is—"

"She'll be there," Finn said, answering for her and moving like the restaurant was on fire. "I'll have her there at seven thirty on the dot."

"Hailey, *bella*, I'll be in touch," Nico called, holding up the card. He pressed it to his heart, then slipped it into his pocket.

"Give it a rest," Finn grumbled.

Nico ran his hand through his perfectly coiffed hair. "What was that, Finn?"

"Nice vest, Nico. Great fit," Finn deadpanned.

The water sports instructor puffed up. "*Grazie!* My *mama* sent it to me from Italy."

"No kidding," Finn grumbled.

Hailey stood and placed Mr. Whiskerfrown into the crate with Sweet Miss Marmalade. "It was a pleasure meeting all of you. And thank you for the opportunity, Eliza. I'm beyond excited and grateful."

"Hailey, we need to go," Finn growled like a rabid beast.

"Goodbye, everyone," she added, placing the turnovers and marmalade into her tote.

Finn pressed his hand to the small of her back and guided her from the dining area onto the empty street where he'd parked the truck.

"Leaving like that was rude, Finn," she said, eyeing the man.

He huffed and grumbled like a cantankerous old bear as he picked up the pace.

She struggled not to break into a jog. "What are you? A handyman and a speed-walking champion?"

He opened the truck's passenger side door and rested the kittens' crate on the bench seat. She set her tote next to it, then started to get in when two strong hands gripped her waist and turned her around.

She gasped. "What are you doing?"

He didn't answer. Stone-faced, he took her hand and led her to a nearby alleyway.

"What about the kittens and my bag?" she exclaimed as he tightened his grip.

Finn came to a halt. He returned his hands to her hips and walked her back a few steps. She gasped as her heels hit a brick wall.

He glanced toward the truck. "The door's open. I can see the crate from here. The kittens are safe. Your bag is fine."

She looked from side to side. "Why are we standing in a deserted alleyway?"

He pressed his hands to the wall and caged her in. He lowered his head, his lips mere inches from hers. "Why did you give Nico your number?"

She held his piercing sage-green gaze. "Because he asked for it. He was being kind, offering to show me around town."

"Do you want him to show you around?" Finn rasped against her earlobe.

Her eyelids fluttered shut as his closeness enveloped her, intoxicating her senses with his woodsy scent. "I don't know what I want."

It wasn't a lie. It might even be the most truthful she'd been with herself in ages.

"I know what you want," he replied, unbuttoning her jeans.

She tensed, her core muscles clenching as heat sparked between her thighs. "You think that's what I want?" she whispered, trembling.

He pulled down the zipper and slipped his hand inside her pants. "It's what your body wants."

"How do you know that?" She tilted her head back and hummed her satisfaction.

"That sultry little sound is your tell. That's how I know," he answered, his words dripping with a self-assured arrogance that left her reeling.

She attempted to steady herself. "Regarding the underwear situation—or lack of underwear situation."

"Uh-huh," he purred.

She fought to keep her voice from cracking as he worked her with his hand. "I don't usually leave the house like this," she got out through heated exhales.

He smiled against the shell of her ear. "I know. I ripped your only pair of underwear off your body last night."

"Uh-huh," she got out, stealing his reply as she lost herself to the grumbly cadence of Finn's voice.

"Do you think Nico Romero can get you wet like I do?" he rasped, shifting from teasing her ear to taunting her lips with light, airy kisses as he worked her tight bundle of nerves with his rough hand.

"No," she breathed. She rocked her hips, and her pulse kicked up as her body responded to Finn's advances. Growing weak in the knees, she wrapped her arms around his neck, anchoring herself to him.

"We're the same, Hailey. We want the same thing. And I'm the only man who can make you feel like this."

Was he right? It didn't matter. She didn't have a second to answer.

He kissed her. No, it wasn't just a kiss. He devoured her mouth. And she greedily welcomed every brush of his lips. It was so easy to let go with him—so effortless to shut out the world when he touched her. In his hands, she became a delicate paper boat, floating on tranquil waters, drifting away from every worry and every concern. In this sacred space, she didn't second-guess herself. She surrendered to the pleasure her handyman provided.

He dialed up his pace, working her into a titillating froth. "Don't fight it, Hailey. I want you to come on my hand. I demand it."

Orgasms on demand? What was a gal supposed to say to that?

"Finn, Finn, Finn," she whispered, unable to convince her mouth to say anything but his name.

He kissed away her breathy utterances and nipped at her bottom lip. This man was knocking on the door to her pleasure palace, and she gladly handed over the keys. She moaned, and he muffled her lusty cries as the world faded into one tiny point of light.

"Hailey, you're so damned beautiful when you're teetering on the edge," he said between kisses.

Beautiful.

There was that word again.

It triggered her undoing.

Like a bow stretched to its limit, every muscle in her body tightened. He held her close as she crashed into her release. The microscopic flicker of light exploded into a kaleidoscope of colors, a breathtaking cascade of shimmering particles. And she was one of those tiny pieces, floating in space, weightless. All at once, she connected to the hum of the earth, the whisper of the breeze, and the beat of her heart. No, not her heart. Finn's heart. It thrummed from the tips of his fingers, cradling her most sensitive place.

Gasping for breath, she rested her head against his chest, allowing him to support her sated body. "That was—"

"The warmup, Sweet Miss Marmalade," he answered, his voice a velvety caress.

"Sweet Miss Marmalade? That's not me. It's the kitten," she said against his chest as the warm fuzzies threatened to take over her orgasm-addled brain. Nobody had ever gifted her with a silly nickname.

"We'll call the kitten Sweetie. You're *my* Sweet Miss Marmalade."

She threaded her fingers in the hair at the nape of his neck. "All right. Can Sweet Miss Marmalade ask you to expand on this warmup business?"

A wicked grin graced his lips. "This is round one of what I have planned for you. I'm taking you back to Starrycard Cabin," he continued, still touching her, but he altered the pace, drawing lazy circles against her oh, so sensitive bud.

"Keep talking," she sighed.

"You'll lose the shoes, then I'll peel off these jeans."

"And then what?"

"We'll say goodbye to the shirt and bra. I'll carry your naked body into that rectangular room, toss you onto the bed, and pound you into the mattress."

What a plan!

"That's quite a round two," she replied.

He narrowed his gaze, a man on a mission. "I'm going to make you come so hard you'll need at least two turnovers, several spoonfuls of orange marmalade, and a pint of cherry chocolate chip to recover."

Sex that included binging on pastries and ice cream? How could any red-blooded, sugar-loving woman say no to that?

"Will there be any *typical* rug activities?" she asked, embracing her brand-new, bad girl getting-off-in-an-alleyway style.

He kissed the corner of her mouth. "There's nothing typical about what your business card boyfriend is going to do to you on that rug."

Gently, he removed his hand from her pants and fastened her jeans. "Look at me." He raised the hand he'd pleasured her with to his lips, sucked the tip of his fingers, and hummed his satisfaction. "Hailey Higgins, I want your taste on my tongue. Then I want my cock buried so deep inside you, you'll ache for days."

Never had someone desired her with such voracity.

Still, she should say no—tell him she needed to prepare for her first day on the job at Starrycard Creek Elementary School. Was that the truth? Not really. She'd been substitute-teaching long enough that she'd become a pro at adapting to new classrooms. The real threat was what was happening to her heart. Her mind whispered warnings. *"This is only a transaction to him."* But when Finn's stony demeanor gave way to a boyish grin, her body defied her better judgment.

"What do you say, Sweet Miss Marmalade? Are you in?" he asked, his voice a raspy, growly caress.

And heaven help her, Sweet Miss Marmalade sounded damned sexy when he was referring to her.

Ignoring the voice in her head, she pushed onto her tiptoes and pressed her lips to his. "Yes," she said between slow, sensual kisses, "Your Sweet Miss Marmalade is all in."

CHAPTER

Ten

FINN

"THIS IS the Starrycard Creek Paper Company, established in 1880. We're happy to welcome you to our family's business. This tour will take you through the entire process. Now, most paper you see in the world is made from wood pulp. It's ripe with chemicals and processed by hulking machines. For all intents and purposes, it's a cookie-cutter, hands-off, homogenous process. I'm not saying that's bad. Mass-produced paper serves a critical function in society, but it's not what we do at the Starrycard Creek Paper Company. At Starrycard Paper, we follow handmade papermaking techniques that have been used for over two thousand years. Techniques brought to Colorado by my ancestor, William Starrycard, and perfected alongside his wife, Fiona Donnelly-Starrycard. There's nothing cookie-cutter about our handmade artisan paper," Finn's father, Hank, explained, speaking to a group of high school art students.

Finn narrowed his gaze and adjusted the valve on one of the Starrycard hydraulic paper presses, listening to the familiar speech his dad and grandfather had been making for as long as he could remember. His dad continued, rattling off the history of the town. His pleasing voice flowed effortlessly, captivating his audience. His words echoed softly off the concrete floor and hung in the air, held in place by the exposed blond brick walls. They rose above the hum of the conveyor belt and the churn and splash of the beaters, combining creek water and raw fibers in vats to create pulp for papermaking. His words mingled with the satisfying slice and swish piercing the air as workers cut stacks of Starrycard paper to their desired size. This myriad of layered sounds wove itself in with the aroma of the botanicals they used to accent and adorn their one-of-a-kind paper.

This symphony of scents and sounds had served as his child-hood's sensory soundtrack. It had always brought him comfort until last year. He could still recall the first time he'd entered the shop after his life had gone to shit. The scent of roses hit him like a punch to the gut. After that, he'd done his best to spend as little time here as possible. This translated into shirking his responsibil-ities at the shop and filling his days with handyman projects.

But today was different.

The second he walked through the door, he didn't smell the roses. He'd peered at the rows and rows of white-washed wooden botanical bins lining the wall where they kept the herbs, flower petals, leaves, stems, roots, and seeds used to craft their unique paper. He inhaled, and despite the frothy, earthy aroma of the pulp churning in vats and the hundreds of botanicals, one scent overpowered the others, delighting his nostrils and leaving him lighter than he'd felt in ages.

And what was that beguiling scent?

Cherries.

The scent of the petite redhead who'd spent the last six nights in his bed. His secret siren, Hailey Higgins.

Though it had been less than a week, he and Hailey had settled into a routine. They were early risers. They'd wake a little before their alarm was set to go off. But he was always up first. It was as if his sleeping mind needed an uninterrupted view of the mesmerizing redhead.

For those blissful few minutes, he'd brush the hair from her forehead and watch her sleep. Christ, she was beautiful. Ivory skin, pink cheeks, long auburn lashes, and a smattering of freckles like stars dotting the sky above Starrycard Mountain. Waking up used to be a nightmare—another gloomy day, more hours to fill until he'd pass out from exertion. Now, waking up was an extension of his dreams. Inside the cabin walls, she was his. When it wasn't enough to simply observe her, he'd stroke her cheek as anticipation built inside him. She'd sigh, and with her eyes still closed, she'd gift him a drowsy whisper of a grin.

"Good morning, business card boyfriend."

That greeting had him beaming like the morning sun.

Her first few words took on a breathy edge, a sultry purr that got his engine revving. Not to mention, the matter of her sleeping attire always had him waking up half-cocked.

Thanks to Hailey's new teaching gig, she had the cash to purchase pajamas, but he'd insisted she wear his Starrycard Creek Paper Company T-shirt to bed. Nothing got him harder than to see her in the bathroom each night, toothbrush in hand, while wearing the garment.

Each morning, between her sexy voice and that T-shirt, he couldn't help but want to start the day buried deep inside her.

After she'd greeted him with the business card boyfriend line, that slow slide of a sleepy grin would quirk into something decidedly dirtier. Under her spell, he'd kiss the corners of her mouth, inch up the worn cotton shirt, and caress her most sensitive place. Her sweet sighs fueled his need to possess her. When she was teetering on the edge, he'd draw her into his arms. Their heated breaths would mingle in the sliver of space between them as she opened for him, inviting him to thrust his hips. Becoming one with her happened like a key turning a lock. It was as if she'd been crafted for him. They'd make love slowly, basking in the first rays of light filtering in through the curtains, cherishing every whisper of early morning pleasure. She had become his sanctuary. His safe place. All that existed was her cherry scent and the rhythm of their bodies coming together.

"How's it *coming* with the hydraulic press, Finnegan?"

"What?" Finn exclaimed, praying he hadn't mumbled what was going through his head.

"Did you fall asleep back there, kiddo? You forget how paper presses work?" his grandfather asked with a wry bend to the questions.

Finn snapped out of his cherry-laced Hailey haze. He glanced toward the direction of his grandfather's voice. He spied the man past the large barn door that opened to a patio leading to the gurgling creek. It was the perfect place to unwind and take a moment to appreciate the flowing water that made their whole operation possible. And it was where his grandfather had decided to park his ass. Sitting in an Adirondack chair a few feet from the creek bed, the elder Starrycard soaked up the late afternoon spring sun. With a ball cap pulled low over his salt and pepper buzzcut, a whiskey in one hand and a cigar in the other, he was the embodiment of a happily retired papermaker. A sly smirk graced his lips. His grandfather had always had a dry sense of humor. He was a demanding man, but he never expected more of others than he did of himself. It made him an excellent role model and teacher. Finn couldn't help but recall his college thesis advisor, who shared the same characteristics.

Finn eyed the calibrated press and dusted off his hands. "I designed the valve for it and hold the patent for the design. It would be a damn shame if I couldn't fix it," he answered and leaned against the doorframe, taking in the creek and the burnt caramel scent of his grandfather's tobacco.

"You want one?" he asked, jiggling the cubes in the glass.

Finn checked his watch. "It's barely three o'clock, Grandpa."

"Is that a problem?"

"I have to drive."

The man eyed the creek. "Over to the elementary school to pick up Miss Higgins?"

"Yeah."

"Her car's still out of commission?" his grandfather continued.

Now Finn was the one concentrating on the waters. "I haven't gotten to fixing it yet. All she needs is a new battery."

Was that true? Sort of. He'd been busy working on Higgins Hideaway, but he liked, no, he needed to drop her off and pick her up from work. It provided the structure his pragmatic mind had craved over the last year. But it was more than that. It was knowing she was safe, knowing he'd see her come out the school-house doors in eight hours.

Rex Starrycard took a sip of his drink. "How's she liking it over at Starrycard Creek Elementary?"

Finn had to be careful. He had to go out of his way to insist his relationship with Hailey was purely platonic and leave no room for misunderstandings. He understood how inviting her to live with him looked. And knowing his sister, mother, and Goldie— the trio had to have been blowing up their group chat with predictions. And Goldie wouldn't keep their conversations from his grandpa. Still, his family was well aware that he was done with love. And he was. One hundred percent over the traitorous emotion. And so was Hailey. That's what made their situation so enticing. All the perks of a relationship with no fear of getting hurt.

When it was over, it would be over. Like it never happened. Like she was never his.

His stomach dropped. His throat thickened with emotion. He ignored the visceral reactions and focused on the creek.

"Well?" Rex pressed.

Stick to the facts.

He kept his features neutral. "The kids love her. She talks about them like they're her own, and she's only been there a handful of days. Parents adore her, too. They can't stop sending in baked goods. We've got two dozen cookies and three pies at the cabin that we haven't even touched yet." He pretended to rub his nose and cracked a grin. He couldn't help it. His body knew what was coming.

A warmth spread through his chest as he peered at his watch.

After only four days, he'd become intimately familiar with the minutes between 3:26 p.m. and 3:42 p.m. He'd park on the side of the road across from Starrycard Creek Elementary and wait for the school doors to swing open. Teachers and children would spill from the building like a burst dam, flooding the playground and grassy sports field with a sea of laughter and furious footsteps. They dismissed by grade level, starting with the youngest children at 3:30 p.m. Right on the dot at 3:33 p.m., the next batch of backpack-laden children exited the building.

And then, he'd see her.

The light would catch the shades of auburn in Hailey's hair as she emerged. Her second graders would trail behind her like a line of ducklings as she led them to the grassy area a few paces from the creek bed and gathered them beneath a great oak. A few hugged her goodbye, then ran to catch their bus while others waited to be picked up. She was masterful, conversing with parents while zipping half-open backpacks and keeping a close watch, making sure no one in her charge wandered off. And as much as he enjoyed watching her multitask like a pro, he could barely contain himself, waiting for the look that had started on her first day. Once she'd said her final goodbye to the last student, she'd hold her clipboard to her chest and lower her head like she could feel his eyes drinking her in. After a few seconds of smiling to herself, she'd look his way, meet his eye, and stretch that Sweet Miss Marmalade grin into something that left him breathless. It wasn't just any smile. This was a smile for him—a smile so brilliant and beguiling it left him mesmerized and ready to get her into his truck, find a deserted street, and kiss her like it had been a thousand years since his lips had last touched hers.

"Miss Higgins sounds like a quick learner," his grandfather remarked.

Finn cleared his throat. "She is."

"I talked to Eliza last night," the man added, eyeing the melting cubes in his tumbler.

Finn made sure his mask was in place. "Oh yeah?"

"She sounded terrible. That cold she's been ignoring might have gotten the better of her." Rex paused. "It appears Eliza and your Miss Higgins have become fast friends. Your sister said that Hailey might be one of the most gifted teachers she's worked with. Liza also says Miss Higgins has got a good heart—a tender heart—and that she showers her students with that gentle affection."

Finn shifted his stance. "I can tell she's dedicated to her work," he answered, keeping his tone neutral and staying the hell away from the heart comment. He knew when Rex Starrycard was spinning a web and he wasn't about to get caught in it. "I see her working at the kitchen table each night. She's committed to her work."

It wasn't a lie. What he didn't elaborate on was what dirty deeds occurred on that kitchen table after she was done with her grading and planning.

Rex took a puff off the cigar. "How's the Higgins cabin coming?"

Good! A question he could answer easily.

"Quite well. I patched the roof, upgraded the plumbing, and swapped out the hardwoods in the main living space." He reined in his excitement. He couldn't wait to show Hailey the new flooring. That would be their first stop after he picked her up.

"Sounds like you're making progress," Rex replied with a nod.

"I am. Surprisingly, the cabin is structurally sound."

Rex shrugged. "I'm not surprised."

"Why not?"

"Once upon a time, Al Higgins was an engineer," his grandfather said, dropping one hell of an info bomb. "He'd know how to build something that would last."

"I didn't know that," Finn answered, moving closer to the man.

The elder Starrycard nodded. "He went to your alma mater, I believe."

"He went to Golden Tech?" Finn exclaimed as the info drops kept coming.

"He invented something—a formula. I don't know much more than that. He was a private man. But there were whispers about him being on the top of his game and raking in the cash. Then—out of nowhere—I'd heard that he'd given away his fortune, built the cabin, and you know the rest—recluse and all. Higgins was on her father's side, I'm assuming," the man continued.

"Yes."

"I understand her parents passed away."

"When she was nineteen."

"Does she have kin on her mother's side?" Rex asked and took a sip of his whiskey.

"No, Grandpa, it's just her."

The man sat back. "Eliza mentioned she drove here in a wedding dress after her fiancé's lady-on-the-side broke up the ceremony with a show-stopping declaration."

"It's her ex-fiancé," Finn bit out with an edge to his voice. *Dammit!* He had to dial it back, but the mention of that jackass had his blood boiling. Or perhaps it was the mention of a wedding. He hardened his expression. He loved his grandpa, but the man had to know he was treading into dangerous waters. "And yeah, that's what happened. But she's here now," he finished, dialing back his fury.

"She sounds like a resilient woman," the man mused, taking another puff.

Finn nodded, knowing his grandfather wasn't done.

"Quite a character trait, resilience. You've got to be willing to take a risk and believe that what's before you is better than what's behind you. You know," Rex continued, "kind of like making lemonade out of lemons or cherry lemonade. Whatever suits your taste. Cherry lemonade was always your favorite as a boy. This Miss Higgins, is she comfortable in your spare bedroom? The square-shaped one?"

The Starrycard women strike again.

"It's a rectangle, Gramps."

A twitch of a grin curved the corners of the old man's mouth. "My mistake."

Finn adjusted his tool belt, then crossed his arms. "It's a temporary situation. I'm helping a person in need. Nothing more. Nothing less. I have a feeling Eliza and company are making more of it than it is."

His grandfather watched him for a beat, then another. "If you say so."

"I do say so. And you know why."

His grandpa's expression softened. And shit, pity was the last thing Finn wanted.

"Finn!" Owen called.

Thank Christ for the distraction.

Owen stood next to the press with a scowl pasted to his lips. Usually, a brooding Owen was a bad sign—and this probably was —but it beat the hell out of being questioned, or more like grilled, by his perceptive grandfather.

Finn gestured toward his brother. "The artist calls."

Owen strode onto the patio and balked at their grandfather. "That cigar's got to go, Gramps. I don't want that scent getting into the diploma paper orders."

Finn assessed their surroundings, calculating the distance and the amount of smoke it would take to taint a batch. "I think you're good, O. I wouldn't worry. Especially with the breeze."

"I can't take the chance of this paper smelling like a cigar bar," Owen shot back, his eyebrows shooting up to his hairline. "And you really think I'm good? Look around, Finnegan. Nearly every drying rack is filled. Do you know how many schools want their diplomas printed on Starrycard paper? Do you know how many colleges and universities are in Colorado?"

"There are approximately one hundred and five," Finn answered and bit back a grin.

Owen frowned. "Fine, yes. Do you know how many want Starrycard paper?"

"Roughly, two-thirds."

Owen ran his hands down his face and groaned. "Fuck my life, I forgot how good you were with numbers."

Of course, he knew the numbers. He and Owen were tapped to continue the family business. And he would be a part of it again, just not quite yet.

"How could you think I didn't know? I work here. I've been . . ." Finn fumed. He should have kept his mouth shut.

Owen sighed, a weary huff of a sound. "Yeah, I know, I know. Taking a break. Is the press calibrated? I can't have another delay."

"I checked each one. You're all set," Finn replied, glancing away from the man.

"*We're* all set. That's what you meant, right?" Owen countered.

Finn flinched. He was not winning Brother of the Year. "Yeah, that's what I meant."

Owen was barely thirteen months older than him. Goldie called them Irish twins. She was spot-on with the description. The Starrycard kids were close, but that didn't mean they didn't butt heads. They gave each other shit and could be downright pains in the asses, but that's what siblings did when they shared an unbreakable bond. But his connection with Owen went deeper—a connection they forged by sharing a bedroom until Owen left for college. Most people would say he and Owen were opposites or that he and Kieran were more alike, thanks to their analytical minds. But from the second they could talk, he and Owen could finish each other's sentences. They were different sides of the same coin, each passionate about the family business. Well, he'd been passionate until he started second-guessing his every decision.

"Nobody knows these machines like you, Finn. Nobody understands the process better. I could use you here a little more," Owen added.

Finn inhaled, and that damned rose scent was back, taunting his senses. He glanced away, breaking the connection with his brother. "I'm here today."

That was the best he could give the man.

"And I appreciate it, but we'll need to have a conversation if . . ."

Finn knew what the man couldn't bring himself to say.

If he didn't get his ass in gear and start acting like he worked there.

Rex ground out his cigar and joined his grandsons. "The artist needs the machinist. And the machinist needs the artist. Creativity and practicality. You two balance out this place. It's a new era for our family. Every Starrycard until your generation had one son. No daughters. No siblings. One son. One child, that's it. It's a miracle we made it this far. Now, I don't know what happened with your parents, but it's a gift to pass on our family's legacy to you kids and watch you work together."

"We're grateful, Gramps. We know what this company means to the town and to Colorado," Owen answered and held Finn's gaze.

Finn gave his brother the look for *I know damn well what you're insinuating. I get it. I just need some more time.*

His grandfather finished his last sip of whiskey and set the glass on a shelf next to a stack of feathery-edged paper. The old man stretched like a sly old cat, then rubbed his belly. "It feels like cherry turnover o'clock. I'm gonna head down to the restaurant and poke around the bakery case. You want to join me, Owen?"

Owen blew out a frustrated breath, resurrecting the stressed-out papermaker persona. "Gramps, this is crunch time. I can't do turnovers now."

A twitch of a grin curled his grandfather's lips. "There's always time for turnovers."

"Says the man who used to spend sixteen hours a day here," Owen tossed back.

"Yeah, and my wife used to come by and bring me turnovers. All the turnovers. You get my drift?" the man finished with a mischievous wink.

Finn and Owen groaned.

"Gramps, don't say another word! The last thing we want to

picture is you and Goldie doing whatever it was you were doing in the shop," Finn lamented while Owen playfully squeezed his eyes shut and pressed his hands to his ears.

Rex shook his head and clapped Finn on the shoulder, still rocking that ghost of a knowing grin. "It's good to see you here, young man. You've been missed."

The elder Starrycard strolled past the tour group and out the front as Kieran came in through the back with his eyes glued to his cell phone. The oldest Starrycard sibling looked up and met Finn's gaze before eyeing Owen.

"What's he doing here?" Kieran asked Owen, pocketing the device.

"Owen oversees creative. I'm in charge of operations and business expansion," Finn answered, surprised by the conviction in his voice.

"So, you're back?" Kieran asked, his features remaining unreadable.

That was his brother's superpower. His uncanny ability to remain muted and rock-solid. It's what made him an excellent city councilman. The man's sense of calm bordered on robotic, but it also allowed him to appear impartial. The town appreciated his steady hand. The fact that he was a lawyer like their mother added to his air of credibility. Finn studied his brother. Despite his stoic expression, a subtle unease crept over the man, and his usual composure wavered.

"Finn's here, Kier. We're taking it for what it is. What do you need? Wait, I know. Those folded cards, right?" Owen paused. "What do you do with them, man?"

A muscle ticked on Kieran's jaw. There it was—that flicker of unrest flashing in his brother's demeanor. The buttoned-up guy glanced at the creek. "Paper shit. What do you care?"

"Is it for city council business? I could have the town's logo embossed on them," Owen offered.

Another minute tic rippled Kieran's still-waters persona. "That's not necessary."

Finn studied the man. *What did he do with those cards?* It was a good question. "It just dawned on me how long you've been requesting this one special kind of paper for folded cards. It's been years. Christ, maybe a decade—long before you were elected to the council."

"Don't you have a roommate to pick up, Finnegan? A school-teacher, I believe?" Kieran posited with that same ghost of a sly grin his grandfather had sported.

And Eliza had gotten to Kier, too.

Kieran's phone buzzed. Thank the cell phone gods! He slipped it from his pocket, studied the screen, and sighed.

"What is it?" Owen asked.

"It's Christian."

"How's Major League Baseball's heartthrob power hitter?" Finn asked.

Kieran frowned. "It's his shoulder."

That was never good. Since joining the Rocky Mountain Rattlers, he'd become the team's home run leader. There was a hell of a lot riding on him to lead the team.

Finn frowned. "Is it acting up?"

"Yes."

"Is he going to rest it?" Owen pressed.

"Can he rest?" Finn mused. "The baseball season just got underway."

"Probably not. He doesn't want anyone in the Rattlers' management to know. I'll talk to him," Kieran added as his cell pinged again.

"Another text from Chris?" Owen asked, concern laced into the question.

"No. Town business. Developers are eyeing Starrycard Mountain. There's no way in hell I'll allow some money-grubbing corporate outfit to swoop in and ruin what we've got going here." He lifted his gaze from his cell. "Where are my cards?"

Owen surveyed the part of the shop where they placed the sheets to dry over long metal cylinders. "They're not quite ready.

Will you be at Starrycard Under the Stars tonight? I can bring them along."

Starrycard Under the Stars?

That was tonight.

With the arrival of Hailey, Finn had forgotten it was that time of year.

He'd loved these nights as a kid. And he'd especially adored the first Starrycard Under the Stars evening. William and Fiona had established the tradition starting on the third Friday in April in the early days of Starrycard Creek, when it was merely a rustic mountain town. Food, sweets, music, dancing at the pavilion beside the creek, and stars—and not only the stars in the sky. They were a paper town, and they had paper stars. His family provided their non-toxic, biodegradable paper for kids and adults to make simple five-pointed shapes and set them adrift in the creek. With about a half mile of the waters illuminated by twinkling lights, seeing a blanket of bobbing stars rushing through the creek marked the coming of enchanting summer evenings and sun-kissed days ahead.

Kieran growled at his cell. "No, I can't make it. I've got to deal with this council business."

Owen surveyed the buzzing shop. "I'll drop them by your place. It'll be late, though."

"That's fine," Kieran mumbled, his thoughts clearly elsewhere.

Owen rubbed his eyes. "Are you going tonight, Finn? The paper for the stars and wishing wall slips are ready. And someone needs to drop the summer banner choices off at the voting table."

Finn adjusted the tape measure on his tool belt. "I'm not sure—"

"Let me rephrase that," Owen said, weariness permeating his tone. "I'll be pulling an all-nighter. Can you please drop off the paper and banners at the pavilion?"

Finn had picked up two pounds of cherry licorice twists from the sweets shop. The plan—his plan—was to spend the weekend locked away on the mountain, naked and going at it like rabbits with his Sweet Miss Marmalade. But how the hell could he say no to Owen? The guy had been carrying the load for months.

"I can do it."

"Hey, guys," Kieran murmured with a smirk tugging at the corners of his mouth. He gestured toward their father, still leading the tour. "Prepare to cringe," the man added with a tinge of amusement.

The brothers shared a knowing look—a secret language known only to them, thanks to growing up a Starrycard.

And, oh boy, these boys knew what was coming.

CHAPTER
Eleven

FINN

NOSTALGIA WELLED in Finn's chest, an intoxicating mix of emotions reminding him how much he enjoyed being with his brothers.

They shared another round of knowing glances as their father waved the teens toward one of the humming conveyor belts, loaded with torn white strips.

The brothers watched the scene play out. A scene they'd witnessed countless times.

"Does anyone younger than fifty know what Dad's about to reference? Thanks to Mom and Dad's love of music from the nineties, we were subjected to it growing up. But these kids can't be more than fifteen or sixteen," Finn asked, keeping his voice low.

Owen crossed his arms. "We shall see."

"This," Hank Starrycard said proudly, "is one of our three conveyor belts. It brings the raw materials we use to make the pulp to the shredder—the first step in artisan papermaking."

The brothers looked at each other. And just like that, they were teenagers again, working in the shop, screwing around, and trying not to laugh when their father came to this part of the tour.

Hank turned off the machine, and the shredder halted its frenzied hacking rampage. Once the shredder had gone silent, their dad theatrically eyed the blades. "We follow MC Hammer's advice with this piece of equipment. Any guesses on what the lyrical legend says about the artisan papermaking process?"

And . . . crickets.

The kids stared at Hank like he was speaking another language.

"You can't touch this," Finn whispered as their father rattled off the same cringe-worthy joke he'd been using for as long as he could remember.

Kieran covered his mouth and turned away while Owen held a piece of Starrycard paper in front of his face to muffle his laughter.

"Finnegan," his father called in the same voice the man had used when they were kids, and he'd caught his boys involved in the shenanigans du jour.

"Yeah, Dad," he replied, doing his best not to break out into a giggle-fest. It was damned hard keeping a straight face with his brothers silently laughing like clowns in training.

"Would you mind giving our guests the Cliff's Notes version of how we make our handmade paper, son?"

"Who's Cliff Notes?" a kid in the back asked. "I thought William Starrycard was the papermaker who started Starrycard Paper?"

The question triggered another round of giggles between Kieran and Owen.

"*Break it down*, Finn," Owen rapped while Kieran turned the color of a ripe tomato.

Couple of jackasses!

But Finn had to pull himself together. He surveyed the teens and inhaled, smelling one botanical.

Cherries.

He lifted his chin, easing back into his leading role at the shop. "Let's forget Cliff and focus on the paper," he said, addressing the group, his body remembering, his mind unburdened. "Like my dad said at the beginning of the tour, we only use natural fibers.

This conveyor belt delivers material to the shredder." Finn touched the scraps. "Today, it's working on a batch of organic linen."

"From a local clothing manufacturer," his father added.

Finn nodded. "These materials could have ended up in a landfill. We repurpose them for paper. The remnants from the 'you can't touch this' shredder collect in a bin," he continued, picking up the old tub and showing the students the mound of tiny white fragments. "The next step," he said, falling into his old cadence, "is beating the rack."

"You hit it?" a skinny boy with glasses tossed out.

"Essentially, yes," Finn replied, not missing a beat. "This is the papermaking step where the remnants, the shredded organic linen in our case, are added to a large vat filled with Starrycard Creek water." He gestured for the students to follow toward a vat that was close to being done. "The blades in this Hollander beater break down the fibers and create pulp." He stuck his hand into the water and scooped out the wet, mushy substance. "Waterlogged gold," he said and sniffed it, reveling in the earthy scent. "This batch has been going for about eight hours. This is the stage when we can add botanicals, glitter, dye. You name it, we can put it in paper."

"What's going in this batch?" a kid near the back of the pack asked.

Finn met Owen's eye.

"You choose," Owen replied. "That's a bunch of broke for wishing wall paper."

"Broke?" a girl in the front repeated.

"Broke is what we call paper from previous batches," Finn explained. "It could be anything—the edges we cut off to make business cards, stationery, or diplomas. It's the unused parts that become useful again."

"So, it's not really broken. It's waiting to become what it's supposed to be?" the girl from the front continued.

Become what it's supposed to be.

"That's a good way of putting it," Finn answered. He'd heard the term used thousands of times but never thought of it like that. And he knew what botanical he'd be adding to the broke batch. He jogged to the wall of botanicals and scooped several cups of his new favorite scent into an old plastic pitcher. "Let's use dehydrated cherries minced into fine pieces." He added the botanicals to the vat and allowed the students to watch as the white pulp took on a pink hue, mirroring Hailey's cheeks when he made her blush.

An internal spark that had long been dormant reignited. He met Owen's gaze. "You want to be my vat man for this part of the tour?"

It was like his brother could sense the change, too.

The guy had a shit ton to do, but he nodded. "Why not? I am wearing this stylish waterproof apron," he joked as he picked up a large wooden frame fashioned with a screen. He dipped it into the pulpy mix.

Finn turned to the teens. "The process of removing the pulp in thin layers is like panning for gold. Watch as my brother dips the frame into the mix. He allows the pulp to settle, jiggling it to allow it to even out and fill the frame. Next, he'll lift the frame out of the water."

Owen did exactly that. He tilted the wooden rectangle from side to side and allowed the excess water to pool on the cement floor.

"It's messy," a tall brunette in the back remarked.

Messy.

Hailey had used the same word the night they met. The night he pitched the idea of a roommates with benefits situation as transactions. Nothing more, nothing less.

"Nothing more. Nothing less," he murmured.

"What was that?" a kid in the middle of the group called out.

Finn blinked, then scanned the group. All eyes were on him. "Creating something new can be messy but . . . beautiful," he replied, blissfully awash in the scent of cherries.

Owen cleared his throat.

"Sorry," Finn mumbled, getting his head in the game. "My vat man will remove the frame, called the deckle, and place the thin, rectangular pulp mold on a sheet of wet felt. He'll place another sheet of wet felt atop that," Finn continued as his brother carried out the age-old papermaking tasks. "The paper is ninety percent water. Once you've got a stack, it's time for the hydraulic press to remove much of the excess liquid."

Hank came to his side. "The ones we use here are fitted with a valve my son invented. A valve that can be highly calibrated to remove excess water without compromising the integrity of the paper fibers. It also reduced the drying time by thirty percent, which allows us to increase the amount of paper we produce," the man proudly interjected, blessedly without referencing nineties hip hop.

"Too much pressure and the paper will tear. Not enough, and it'll be too weak," Finn continued, speaking the same words he'd always used, but today, they sounded different, resonating in a way he'd never noticed. He stared at the vat, drinking in the pink hue, then checked the time.

3:19 p.m.

Shit! He had to get moving.

He caught his dad's eye and tapped his watch. "I've got to hand the tour back to my father. I have someone to be with . . . I mean somewhere to be."

His dad snapped his fingers. "Finn is leaving the old behind, new chapters to sow," the man continued in the most cringe-worthy, singsongy voice ever. Hank frowned and surveyed the group. "It's from 'Getting Jiggy Wit It.' Will Smith. Nobody knows this song? Ah, come on! It's a classic."

More crickets.

"Go, but don't forget the paper for tonight," Owen said, suppressing a grin.

"Get out while you can," Kieran added with a wink.

Finn grabbed the box marked Starrycard Creek Under the

Stars, then picked up one of the containers with slips for the wishing wall.

He jogged out the back and loaded the items into the bed of his truck. Moving like a man with naked plans that included cherry licorice, he hit the gas and drove the familiar route down Main Street, leaving the buildings behind and following the line of the creek past the pavilion. He was so damned close, and then a school bus moving at a glacial pace clogged the road.

He checked the time.

3:29 p.m.

Damn! He'd miss his favorite part of the day if they didn't get moving. He reached into the bag of licorice, pulled out a piece, and jammed it into his mouth. Minutes ticked away as he chomped like a stressed-out goat. After two painful blocks, the bus peeled away, turning onto the school's circle drive.

3:32 p.m.

His pulse kicked up.

He still had time!

He checked to make sure the route was clear when a pregnant woman pushing a stroller coasted to the edge of the sidewalk. He donned his best polite, go-ahead expression and waved for her to cross.

Come on, come on!

The second those stroller wheels hit the other side, he accelerated and zoomed around the corner, wheels squealing.

3:34 p.m.

He was a minute late.

He pulled into his usual spot, checked beneath the tree, and . .

.

No redhead.

No smile.

Instead, he saw gray-haired Mrs. Harris, who'd taught first grade at Starrycard Creek Elementary since the dawn of time. She stood with her students and Hailey's students beneath the great oak.

Where the hell was his Sweet Miss Marmalade?

He exited the truck, headed toward the dismissal location, and scanned the space like a soldier on a reconnaissance mission.

"Hey, Uncle Finn!" McKenzie broke free from the group of children gathered around the first-grade teacher and ran to him.

He ruffled her hair. "What are you doing out here? Don't you usually go to your mom's office after school?"

"Mommy's sick."

"So is Daddy, but at least I can still move," Jack said, sounding like death warmed over as he dragged his ass across the grassy space.

Finn reared back. "You look terrible, man."

"You should see your sister."

"Mommy's nose looks like she colored it with a bright red crayon. And she's moaning—and not the happy moaning she and Daddy make when they practice yoga at night. This moaning sounds like she's a ghost in a haunted house."

"Yoga, Jack? When have you and Eliza ever practiced—" Finn stopped himself, figuring out the code word. He pinched the bridge of his nose, but his friend looked too much like dog crap to give him shit. "I hope you and Liza feel better," he said, then eyed his niece. "Hey, Kenz, where's Miss Higgins?"

McKenzie's eyes went wide. "My class walked by Miss Higgins' classroom. The school secretary, Mrs. Larson, was whispering to her in the hallway, and then Miss Higgins turned this color," the girl continued and pointed to her stark-white knee sock. "Then she asked my teacher to take her students out for dismissal. Miss Higgins must be in big trouble. Mrs. Larson only whispers when something is really bad."

Finn ran his hand through his hair. "Oh, jeez, okay."

What the hell could have happened?

"Kenzie," a little boy with blond hair called, "see you at Starrycard Under the Stars."

"Okay, Cody!" she hollered back.

"Who's that dude?" Finn barked.

"Just Cody. He's my third-grade buddy."

Finn grumbled.

"Finn, she's six. He's eight," Jack supplied.

Finn eyed his best friend. "Eliza was six and you were eight once."

"Jesus, Finn," the man mumbled, then sneezed.

"I can't wait for Starrycard Under the Stars. You, me, and Mommy love those nights, huh, Daddy," McKenzie remarked.

Jack's already pitiful expression grew more pained. "Kenz, I don't think Mommy and I are up to taking you to Starrycard Under the Stars tonight."

McKenzie's shoulders slumped. "It's okay, Daddy. You and Mommy are super-yucky sick." The kid kicked a mound of dirt, then burst into an ear-to-ear grin. "But Uncle Finn isn't sick. He can take me. And after, I can spend the night at the cabin with Uncle Finn and Miss Higgins."

Oh, shit!

Finn plastered a nervous grin to his lips. "What, Kenz?" His cherry licorice sex-a-thon plans were disintegrating in front of his eyes.

Jack coughed, and it sounded like he had a chainsaw going off in his throat. "That would be a lifesaver, man. Liza and I could get some sleep without this little star waking us up at the crack of dawn."

"Please, Uncle Finn," Kenzie begged and batted her eyes.

Dammit! How could he say no to that face? And, of course, he wanted to give Jack and Liza a break.

He patted the girl's cheek. "All right, little star, I'll be by in a few hours. Right now, I need to go inside and see what's going on with Miss Higgins. I'm her . . ."

"Handyman!" the girl exclaimed. "Did you get her the rug? Remember when I saw you picking up that wood when Mommy had to take me to the dentist during lunch on Tuesday, and I told you to get Miss Higgins a floofy rug like you have?"

"Yes, I remember, and yes, I picked up a rug for her. I'm going to show it to her today."

"Because you drive her to school and pick her up every day?" McKenzie added.

"That's right."

"I bet it's fun to be in the car with Miss Higgins," the child mused. "Everybody at school thinks she's the nicest and the prettiest teacher. Do you wish she was yours, Uncle Finn?"

"What?" he stammered. "Mine?"

"Your teacher? Do you wish she could have been your teacher? You know if you could go back in time and be a kid again."

"If I went back in time, wouldn't Miss Higgins be a kid, too?"

McKenzie's brow furrowed like her brain was on the verge of overheating.

"I wish I could go back in time before your Mommy gave me this cold," Jack said, changing the subject from Hailey. "I owe you one, Finn. We'll have Kenz ready to go," his best friend rasped, looking like he needed a decade's worth of sleep. "Come on, little star. Let's get back to Mommy. She needs us."

Finn watched the pair head out. Longing, or perhaps jealousy, twinged in his chest. He ignored it. He didn't have time to bother with bullshit feelings. He zeroed in on the building and headed inside as a question formed.

Who was this unwelcome guest who'd wrecked his afternoon?

It couldn't be her ex, could it? He clenched his jaw. If it was, he'd make the jackass sorry he'd stepped foot in this town. He increased his pace, prepared to kick some ass. He shot past the office and raced down the hallway toward the primary-grade classrooms. He curled his hands into fists as he skidded to an abrupt stop outside her classroom. He parted his lips, prepared to call out to her, when a woman's terse and demanding voice shut him the hell up.

"Miss," the woman hissed, "as I said before, Golden Tech has invested resources into Starrycard Creek Elementary. It's an educational partnership. We provide the engineering enrichment curriculum and materials. You share it with your students and provide us with feedback. For the last three years, the second-grade teacher oversaw the program. We haven't heard a peep from your school in months. You're in danger of losing funding. I'm here as a courtesy since you haven't responded to our numerous emails. Are you following the lessons?"

The adrenaline coursing through his veins dissipated as his body relaxed. He recognized that exacting tone.

"No, I haven't taught any of these lessons," Hailey stammered.

"No?" the woman roared.

"Miss . . ." Hailey sputtered. "I—"

"It's Doctor Christine C. Schneider."

Finn grinned. He'd called her *miss* and had made the same mistake years ago.

"I apologize, Dr. Schneider," Hailey continued, "if you'd give me a moment to explain, I'm—"

"You are the second-grade teacher here at Starrycard Creek Elementary, correct?" Dr. Schneider snarled.

"I am, but—"

"Choose your next words carefully. I don't take kindly to excuses."

Finn chuckled. There was another familiar line. He stood in the doorway.

It was time to help out his Sweet Miss Marmalade.

He knocked on the classroom's doorframe and sauntered into the room.

Hailey locked onto his gaze. She was giving off serious S.O.S vibes.

He understood the sentiment.

He nodded to the woman, currently tearing his Sweet Miss Marmalade a new one, then tossed Hailey a playful wink. "Tread carefully, Miss Higgins," he said, suppressing a grin, "Dr. Christine C. Schneider's bite matches her bark."

CHAPTER
Twelve

HAILEY

HAILEY'S PULSE quickened as she stared—no, gawked—at her business card boyfriend. The pounding of her heart resonated in her chest, a telltale sign of the tornado of emotions swirling within her.

What was going on?

She had Finn, cool as a cucumber, winking at her while a terrifying senior citizen berated her.

In less than a week, another woman had crashed into her life, throwing a curveball her way. The positive? At least this gal wasn't waving around a positive pregnancy test.

The negative? This lady was upset and out for blood regarding some engineering enrichment program.

It didn't make any sense. Why had she incurred this strange woman's wrath? Eliza hadn't mentioned anything about an engineering curriculum.

But one fact was crystal clear. Finn was acquainted with this irate lady. A glimmer of hope flickered. Perhaps his connection to the stern senior citizen was a stroke of luck.

Nevertheless, this was not how she saw her Friday afternoon panning out.

Ten minutes before dismissal—before the classroom crasher barged in—she was as ready to start the weekend as her students.

And why was that?

She'd have two entire days with Finnegan Starrycard.

To everyone at the school, he was her roommate. Her handyman repairing her cabin. And her ride to and from school each day until her car was back up and running. If anyone inquired about the nature of their connection, she'd kept it light and hadn't made much of it. Eliza had done a little prodding, but she'd been able to deflect the woman's subtle questions that sounded innocuous enough but had a thread of innuendo woven into the words.

"How are things with Finn?"

It was an innocent question, but the mischief in Eliza's eyes gave away her intentions.

Fortunately, Hailey had the perfect answer.

She'd breezily report that the man was great. He was busy repairing the cabin, and she was equally busy pouring herself into her new job.

And pouring herself into Finn's T-shirt every night.

Not that it stayed on for very long.

The second she slipped it over her head, Finn would flip her around, fling the T-shirt onto the floor, and pin her against the wall with his hard body.

But she wasn't about to disclose that because that would be inappropriate, and her carnal activities with her handyman were simply transactions.

Still, her heart couldn't help but count down the minutes until his truck appeared. She was ready to don that shirt and get down and dirty with her scorching-hot handyman. She'd been keyed up since he'd dropped her off this morning. But it wasn't only her. Something was in the air today. The children were more wiggly than usual. Perhaps it was her energy rubbing off on them. It took everything she had not to explode from sweet anticipation.

Fifteen minutes before dismissal, while the kids were tidying their desks and packing their backpacks, she traced his route in her mind. She could see twists and turns coming down the mountain. She pictured his midnight blue truck cruising down Main Street. She knew he'd be parked in his usual spot. Her body ached for the moment when she'd emerge from the building. The weight of his gaze would sweep over her, igniting a deep yearning within, like a wildflower thirsting for the touch of the sun's vibrant rays. His focus never wavered from her. With each passing second, her breath would quicken as exhilaration bubbled up from within, flowing through her body like the rollicking Starrycard Creek, splashing and gurgling with vitality.

But that is *not* what happened this afternoon.

Minutes before the bell rang, the school secretary, Mrs. Larson, a petite elderly woman with silver ringlets dotting her brow, had hustled down to her classroom with an urgent message. The second-grade teacher had an appointment with the administrator from the Golden Tech STEM Sparks Enrichment Program.

Today.

After school.

Hailey's jaw had dropped.

This had been news to her. And with Eliza out sick, she couldn't get more information.

She'd barely had time to wave over the first-grade teacher and ask her to take her second graders out for dismissal before a towering woman with snowy-white hair fashioned into a tight French twist stormed into her classroom. Wearing large tortoiseshell glasses, a sleek navy blazer, and sporting a furrowed brow and a scowl that rivaled her growly handyman's expression, this smartly dressed senior citizen appeared ready to make heads roll. And the noggin on the chopping block appeared to belong to Hailey Higgins.

The question was, why did Finn look totally fine with the situation—giddy even? The classroom door was open. He had to have heard the woman's tirade. People in the next town probably heard the outburst.

It was time to connect the dots.

"You know Dr. Schneider—a woman who appears ready to claw my eyes out?" she stammered, holding the handyman's gaze. And, oops, she probably shouldn't have said that last part.

"Oh, yeah," he answered, beaming like he ate a bowl of rainbows for breakfast.

Who was this lady? A relative?

"Finnegan Starrycard," the woman cooed, her demeanor switching from a pissed-off barracuda to a doting grandmother.

"It appears you're still as feisty as ever, Professor Schneider. Retirement hasn't slowed you down," he replied and embraced the woman.

"I'm semi-retired. I still mentor graduate students and oversee the elementary enrichment outreach programs." Dr. Schneider's barracuda face returned. "And this school has been slacking off for months."

"I think I know the reason for that, Professor," Finn said gently. "Meet Hailey Higgins. The new second-grade teacher. Miss Higgins, this is Doctor Christine Schneider, the former dean of Golden Tech's School of Engineering and, once upon a time, my graduate advisor."

Hailey looked between the pair. Now the connection made sense.

"Your last name is Higgins?" the professor asked.

"Yes."

"Are you from around these parts?" She pressed. The woman appeared truly taken aback. Almost as if she'd seen a ghost.

How odd.

On the bright side, she wasn't yelling.

"No," Hailey answered, taking a moment to catch her breath. "I'm not from Starrycard Creek. I inherited my great-uncle's cabin and moved here last week because . . ."

How was she supposed to finish that statement?

Because she'd lost everything?

Because she'd chosen the wrong guy again?

Because she was clean out of options?

None of those would do.

"Because she's renovating it," Finn answered, filling in the blank.

The professor glanced out the window, then fiddled with her slim gold bracelet.

"Professor?" Finn asked gently.

"Sorry, I . . ." Dr. Schneider abandoned the jewelry. She reached into her bag, removed a sheet of paper, and cleared her throat. "Let's get down to business. Marcie Kimball is the second-grade teacher of record on the Golden Tech STEM Sparks application. She went through our training program, agreed to present the lessons to her class, and provide feedback. We haven't heard from her in months."

"Mrs. Kimball moved a few months ago and left her position," Hailey explained. "I was hired as a long-term substitute teacher to finish out the school year. This is my first week. Before that, the principal was covering this class."

"Eliza was teaching and running the school?" the professor asked, turning to Finn.

This woman appeared to know quite a bit about the Starrycards.

"Yes, and from what I can tell, it was a real mess. Following the engineering enrichment must have slipped her mind. She's out sick today. The intense workload caught up with her, and her body is paying the price," Finn added.

"I see," the woman replied and nodded. "When you next speak with her, please let her know I hope she's on the mend soon."

"I will," Finn answered.

Dr. Schneider observed Finn closely. "I understand why Miss Higgins is here. Not that I don't enjoy seeing you, Finn, but what are you doing here?"

Hailey froze.

Finn shifted his stance. "Miss Higgins is my neighbor. Her car is giving her some trouble. I offered to drive her down to town and bring her home. I'm also repairing the cottage. I'm living up at Starrycard Cabin. It's next door to Higgins Hideaway—her late great-uncle's cabin."

Dr. Schneider peered out the window. "Is she?" Her wistful expression gave way to a look of genuine concern. She zeroed in on Finn. "You're living in Starrycard Cabin on the mountain?"

The warmth rolling off Finn chilled. "Yes."

Her gaze lingered on him. "I heard about what happened with Susan. I'm so sorry, Finn. It must have—"

"I'm fine, Professor. Better than fine," Finn shot back.

Hailey studied her business card boyfriend. Who was this *Susan*? It had to be an ex.

"I'm glad to hear you're doing well," Dr. Schneider said, not missing a beat. "And it's fortunate you're here, Finnegan. I was going to give you a call. I could use your help."

"Name it," Finn replied, his icy demeanor thawing. "I owe you everything. You're the reason I hold a patent."

She waved him off. "You did the work. The valve design came from that magnificent brain of yours. In all my years, I've only known one other who could visualize a problem and execute a solution so masterfully. I simply made sure you lived up to your potential."

"Now that you've buttered me up," Finn said, his cheeks taking on a pink hue, "what can I do for you, Professor?"

"In a few weeks, we need engineering alums to come to the Golden Tech campus to judge the paper tower competition."

"What's that?" Hailey asked.

"It's a problem-solving competition for our seniors. Finn's team won back when he was a student, if I'm not mistaken."

Finn nodded and smiled, but the emotion didn't reach his eyes.

"The competition has been around since the nineteen forties," the woman continued. "Participants are given sheets of paper, kindly provided by the Starrycard Creek Paper Company, and a roll of tape. Judges award points based on the design and the amount of weight the structure can hold. It's a rite of passage for our engineering college students before graduation. Can I count you in, Finnegan?"

"Absolutely," the man replied.

Hailey's teacher-brain kicked in. "It sounds wonderful. I bet that idea could be modified for younger children."

"It is. It's part of the Golden Tech's STEM Sparks curriculum," Professor Schneider answered and pursed her lips.

Oh no! Was the lady about to go off again?

"You should come along when Finn joins us in Golden to judge the competition, Miss Higgins."

"Why? I can't be a judge," Hailey stammered. She was not expecting the woman to say that.

"We'll be running our elementary school STEM Sparks teacher training institute that weekend. A grant would pay for your lodging and materials. If your car is still out of commission, I'm sure Finn would be happy to bring you."

Hailey could feel Finn's eyes on her but concentrated on the professor. "That's a generous offer, but I'm not sure if I'll be teaching at Starrycard Creek Elementary next year."

The intensity of Finn's attention dialed up like a thermostat cranked to the highest heat level.

"You aren't going to live in the Higgins Hideaway Cabin?" the woman pressed.

"I'm not sure. I learned that Albert Higgins was my great-uncle less than a week ago. I'm at a bit of a crossroads in my life. I'm not quite sure where I'll end up."

It wasn't a lie.

Now, did she love it here in Starrycard Creek?

Yes, she was enchanted with the town and enamored with her students and the school's community. But how would she handle whatever this was with Finn? Would they go on *transacting* indefinitely? She'd been so sure she was done with love, done having her heart broken. And she was. She couldn't allow herself to become a doormat again. Yet, she couldn't deny that her steadfast resolve to shun the prospect of falling in love dwindled when Finn held her in his arms and called her his Sweet Miss Marmalade.

Stop! Do not give in to the sappiness. It never ends well. Love sucks, love sucks, love sucks.

"It doesn't matter where you teach, Miss Higgins," Dr. Schneider said with a flick of her wrist.

Hailey snapped back. This was not the time to imagine her extra-curricular activities with Finnegan Starrycard.

"If you don't stay in Starrycard Creek," she explained, "having this training and a connection to the university on your résumé will set you apart from other teacher candidates. It's a perk you can bring to any school. We have partner teachers across the country. And as I said, the program covers the cost of the training and provides meals and lodging during the long weekend. It's an opportunity I suggest you don't pass up."

The lady had a point.

Hailey mulled it over. She had to look out for herself, and increasing her STEM skills would serve her well as an educator.

"How far away is Golden from here?" she asked.

"Two hundred and twenty-two miles, to be exact," the woman answered.

222

The same number as Higgins Hideaway's address and the number of slips in the pickle jar.

It was as if her parents were nudging her to accept the offer.

Finn was still watching her. She tossed a glance his way but couldn't read him.

But this wasn't about him.

She held the professor's gaze. "I'd love to attend. I'm grateful for the opportunity. Thank you."

"I'm so pleased to hear it." The professor reached into her bag and produced a sheet of paper. "Here are the directions to sign up online." She checked her watch. "Oh, dear, I better head out. I'm on grandmother duty tonight back in Golden. I don't want to be late for that. See you soon, Miss Higgins," the woman said with a faraway lilt to her voice.

Hailey nodded, not sure what to make of it. It was probably nothing.

"I'll walk you to your car, Dr. Schneider," Finn said and followed the woman. He was halfway out the door when he stopped and looked over his shoulder. Heartbreaking pain flashed in his eyes. The man blinked, and it was gone, hidden behind his stoic mask. "I'll wait for you at my truck."

"The usual spot?" she asked.

"Uh-huh."

She surveyed the classroom. "I won't be long. I just have to pack up."

Finn watched her for a beat, like he wanted to say something. What was going on inside that man's head? She desperately wanted to ask about this Susan, but this wasn't the time.

Finn disappeared down the hallway. His voice mingled with Dr. Schneider's until only the hum of the fluorescent lights remained.

Hailey placed her planner, the sheet from Dr. Schneider, and the thick folder of items to be graded over the weekend into her tote. She turned off the lights and took a moment to drink in the darkened space. Every classroom she'd subbed in shared similarities. The little chairs. A space across one wall fixed with a dry-erase board or a chalkboard. The pleasing scent of construction paper and stubby crayons. Well-loved books with creased covers and dogeared pages.

If she did remain in Starrycard Creek, how would she make this room her own?

She'd add a cozy corner where children could sit in bean bags and escape into a story. Book baskets on the tables. Self-portraits done in watercolors lining the walls.

What would her life look like here?

She pictured sage-green eyes, hidden dimples, and a smile that took her breath away. Her lips tingled. She shook her head, dismissing the daydream. "He doesn't want me like that," she whispered.

"Everything all right, Miss Higgins?"

Hailey gasped and spun around.

The school secretary pressed her hand to her heart. "I didn't mean to scare you, dear. I see that woman has left."

Hailey gestured for Mrs. Larson to join her as she walked down the hall. "Yes," she said, closing the classroom door. "It was Dr. Schneider from Golden Tech. There was a bit of a misunderstanding, but it's resolved."

"Good to hear."

Hailey pointed toward the side door. "I better get going. My ride is here. Have a nice weekend."

"Will I see you at Starrycard Under the Stars, dear?" the woman asked.

With her hand on the doorknob, Hailey stilled. "I'm not sure what that is?"

"It's great fun. Tonight's the first one. Everyone gathers at the park near the amphitheater at sunset. It's a joyous celebration. You should go."

An air of disappointment settled upon her. "We'll see," she answered, mustering a grin. "I'm working on my cabin, so I'm not sure if I'll be able to make it." Her heart sank as she spoke the words. Finn hadn't mentioned anything about it. And why should he? It's not like he'd want to take her.

Nobody can know about us.

That's what he'd said, and she'd agreed.

Her phone pinged. She fished it from her bag and eyed the text from Nico.

Dinner tonight?

The man had messaged her every day this week, asking if she wanted to grab dinner. Each time, she'd gently turned him down. She sighed and dropped her cell into her bag. She'd text him back later.

Opening the door and exiting the building, she inhaled the fresh mountain air and spied Finn's truck. Like usual, he was in the driver's seat, but he wasn't looking out his window. His gaze was directed downward. What was he looking at? Her throat thickened with emotion, recalling how Grant had been glued to his phone while she walked down the aisle. She banished the thought. This was not her wedding day. And Finn Starrycard was most certainly not her fiancé.

"Bye, Miss Higgins," a little boy from her class called out of a passing car's window.

She waved as he went by, then looked up and found Finn watching her. For a fraction of a second, a charged expectancy pulsed between them like they were on the cusp of something that left her breathless.

And then it disappeared.

He broke their connection, hopped out of the truck, and slipped his wallet into his pocket. Going through the motions, he took her bag and helped her into the passenger seat.

He got in, fired up the engine, and shifted into drive. This is when he'd usually rest his hand on her knee and make slow circles with his thumb—and the reason she loved wearing dresses and skirts. The contact sent a delicious charge through her body she'd come to crave. But his hands remained at ten and two, gripping the wheel like he had a vendetta against it. They drove out of town, neither saying a word. The smoothly paved road turned to crunchy gravel as they wound their way up the mountain.

Minutes ticked by, and still, the man wouldn't even look at her. They turned onto Starryview Lane. His drive came into view, and she couldn't take the silence.

"This was not the start to the weekend I was expecting," she said with a nervous laugh, hating the shake in her voice.

Finn didn't reply. Instead, a muscle ticked on his jaw. He jerked the wheel to the right like he'd been possessed. The truck protested with an abrasive screech. Loose gravel scattered across the road as he slammed the vehicle into park.

She shrieked and braced herself.

Had he lost his mind? Was he trying to get them killed?

CHAPTER
Thirteen

HAILEY

HAILEY INHALED A SHARP BREATH, her heart pounding, adrenaline spiking. Before she could demand that Finn explain his reckless behavior, the man unbuckled his seat beat. He closed in on her. A predator swooping in on its prey. He cupped her face in his hands. His breaths came in ragged sips of air as if he depended on her very existence to breathe.

"Sweet Miss Marmalade," he whispered against her lips.

Despite wanting to throttle the guy for scaring her half to death, his words were like a salve to her battered heart. She studied him like a work of art. Beneath the shade of a towering evergreen, the sun-dappled light held his beautiful, pained face in a wash of flickering light and darkness.

She would have sworn she could hear his racing heart beating in sync with hers. Before she could utter a word, he kissed her with a hunger that brought tears to her eyes. The bittersweet intensity of his longing engulfed her. She returned his kisses, her lips tingling and her body on fire. Her hand rested on his leg as his hands tangled in her hair. Frenzied energy on the brink of igniting crackled in the snug space. Needing to know how badly he wanted her, she slid her hand up his thigh and then a bit further and found her thick, hard answer. She stroked him through his jeans, his cock straining against the denim.

"Hailey," he rasped, manhandling her name.

She clenched her core, her body wet and ready to welcome his hard length. He must have sensed the urgency coursing through her veins. In a trio of fluid movements, he pulled back, unbuckled her seat belt, and hoisted her onto his lap.

He couldn't wait, either.

She straddled him, pushing onto her knees as he undid his pants and shrugged them down enough to free his cock. He reached between her thighs, slipped his fingers inside her panties, and teased her entrance. She rolled her hips, riding his hand. Shamelessly giving in to her desire.

The corners of his lips curved upward as he slipped two fingers inside her. "This is for me. This is mine."

Heaven help her! This man's possessive, growly side had her writhing.

"It's yours," she breathed.

He pushed aside the slim strip of fabric between her legs, lined up his cock, then gripped her hips. His fingertips dug into her skin, claiming her, marking her. A zing of decadent pain laced with the sweet bite of pleasure surged through her as he pulled her in close, his cock filling her in one swift thrust. Her nipples tightened. Every muscle in her body tensed. Her body trembled, anticipating the pleasure to come.

"Look at me," he demanded, his voice laden with desire.

Her eyes locked onto his, drawn into the depths of the sage-green hues. They glinted with raw need.

He clenched his hands, forcing her to remain immobile like a pinned butterfly. "Tell me you want this."

What did that mean?

Was he talking about sex? Or could it be more?

"I want this," she whispered, unsure what she was agreeing to but powerless to deny him what he wanted.

He loosened his hold, and she released an audible breath. She had to move, had to lose herself in this man. She held on to his shoulders, giving herself the leverage to rise and fall. There was no ramping up. No foreplay. Working him hard and fast, she rode his cock in a crash of thrusts and groans. He slipped his hands from her hips to her ass and tightened his hold, lifting her and lowering her, urging her to dial up the pace, like if they made love forcefully enough, frantically enough, it would permit them to escape whatever they were running from.

What was *she* running from?

What was *he* running from?

Her thoughts dissolved into heated gasps as she swayed and lost herself in the rhythm of their bodies. He kissed her between breathy exhales. She could feel the pull of her release, like a roller coaster car edging closer to the top of the track.

Click, click, click.

With each rock of her hips and thrust of his cock, they inched forward until they teetered at the top. He squeezed her ass, his fingertips imprinting on her skin, as they hovered for a fraction of a second before momentum took over, and they rocketed toward carnal bliss.

"Yes, fuck, yes! Come for me, Hailey," he bit out, right there with her.

Caught up in the heady rush of release, she was free. Weightless, a buzzy euphoria propelled her through the imaginary track, ascending and descending, the wheels sparking and rattling. Her orgasm consumed her, driving her to buck harder and push every limit. He buried his head in the hollow of her neck, holding her in his muscled arms, pumping and thrusting as he spilled into her. She disappeared in the momentum, in the hum of their bodies. Breathless, she fell forward. He reached up and held her face in his hand, their breaths syncing and slowing as their eyes met.

He stroked her cheek. "I've got you."

"I know you do," she whispered, carelessly allowing herself to drift to that place where she yearned to be treasured, that space where she could pretend this was real.

"Marmalade?" he said with a sweet, sated bend to the word.

She kissed him and smiled against his lips. "Yes, business card boyfriend?"

"I want to show you something."

"You did show me something."

He chuckled. "It's hardwood."

"Yeah, I got that part."

"Not *that hard wood*, Sweet Miss *Sex-crazed* Marmalade."

She sighed, ecstatic to return to this lighter, looser place where it was just the two of them, limbs tangled and grinning at each other like blissful idiots.

"Sweet Miss *Sex-crazed* Marmalade? That's a mouthful," she teased.

He drank her in. "So is *business card boyfriend*, and you came up with that one."

"True," she conceded. She traced her fingers down his jawline, delighting in his scratchy scruff. "Wordy or not, I like the way it sounds," she answered, then chewed her lip as two thoughts—no, two worries—threatened to pop their post-sex banter-bubble.

He narrowed his gaze. "What is it, Marmalade? You're doing that lip thing."

She lifted herself off his lap and sat beside him, listening as he took care of his pants situation.

He stilled, and she could sense him watching her. "Hailey, tell me what you're thinking."

She smoothed her skirt, staring at the wrinkled fabric as a thread of jealousy wove around her heart. The first thought was about this Susan. She wanted to ask about her but wasn't about to go there. Still, she could tackle the other subject.

She toyed with the hem of her skirt, twisting the cotton around her index finger.

Finn rested his hand on hers. "Talk to me, Marmalade."

She concentrated on his beautiful face. "I could drive to Golden on my own—to the teacher training thing. And you don't have to fix my car. I can pay the mechanic in town to take care of it. When we were with Dr. Schneider, I got the feeling you . . ."

He laced his fingers with hers. "I'll get to your car. It just needs a new battery. But you're not driving up to Golden alone. We'll go together."

His reply set her body ablaze. Every nerve ending tingled with an intensity she couldn't ignore. She studied their hands, then met his eye. "We will?"

"Of course. It's no big deal, right? You'll do your thing, and I'll do mine," he answered, slipping his fingers from hers as he let go.

His words hit like a bucket of ice water to the face.

The hollowness in her chest eating away at her heart expanded. "Right, okay."

"Now, about the hardwood," he said, starting up the car, but he didn't turn down his drive. He'd cleared the driveway leading to Higgins Hideaway earlier in the week and took a right toward her cabin.

"We're going to my cabin?" she asked, ignoring the ache in her chest.

"There's a reason I asked you not to go into the cabin for the last three days."

"And that reason is *hard wood*."

"The hardest wood," he said in a dirty rumble.

"Keep talking like that, and I'll need you to pull over again," she replied. She couldn't let her love-sick side sabotage what she had with her handyman. She was creating new patterns and forging a new life outlook. She had to keep reminding herself to stick to the mantra.

Love sucks. Love sucks. Love sucks.

As much as she wanted, that sentiment didn't ring as true today as it had the day she was blindsided at the altar.

But it had to. There was no alternative.

He tossed her a wink. "Can you keep it in your skirt for five minutes, Marmalade?"

"I can try," she added, mustering a grin as he pulled up to her place. She surveyed the front yard. There was an actual path leading to the porch. "You cleared out a bunch of the brush."

"With it warming up, it's damned pleasant spending time outside. I've been bouncing between projects indoors and outdoors. It's going a lot quicker than I thought. The place has good bones."

She surveyed the little cabin. "My great-uncle built it, didn't he?"

"Yeah, and he was an engineer."

"How do you know that?"

"My grandpa mentioned it when I saw him at the shop before I picked you up," Finn added and exited the truck.

Hope sparked in her chest. He talked about her with his family. No, he didn't say that. He was probably updating them on his latest handyman project. She was his client. That was it.

He opened the door and helped her out.

"Did your grandfather know my great-uncle well?" she asked, swallowing her feelings and focusing on her relative.

Finn shrugged. "I don't think anyone knew Al Higgins that well. My grandad only knew a few things about him."

"Like what?"

"He might have gone to Golden Tech for college. He may have designed something that made him some money, but my grandpa thinks he might have given it away, then came to Starrycard Creek and built this cabin to live a solitary life."

They walked up the now sturdy porch steps, and Finn held open a new screen door that appeared to be firmly fixed in place and not a projectile hazard.

She tapped the door's shiny silver knob. "You fixed this, too. My, my, you've been busy."

He leaned in like he was going to kiss her, then stilled before his lips met hers. "I am a *very* handy man," he purred and pressed the key to her palm. "Open the door, Marmalade."

His gruff tone had her body purring for round two, but she mustered a little self-restraint. Whatever he wanted to show her, he was proud of it. She could feel the pride coming off him in waves. She could see the excitement of his accomplishment in his eyes, like when one of her students was sure they knew the correct answer to a question she'd posed.

She eyed the key, and a lightness took over. She couldn't help but recall how even her first impression of the bit of tarnished metal had lifted her spirits. The very weight of the solid object had comforted her. Inserting it into the lock, it turned smoothly, unlike the first time she'd done this.

She opened the door a few inches, listening for the telltale squeak as she slipped the bit of metal into her pocket. But the only sound was the breeze rustling through the aspens and evergreens.

She glanced at him.

Another wave of pride rolled off her handyman. "I got rid of the horror-movie-door soundtrack. Hope you don't mind."

"It'll keep me from jumping into your arms."

He frowned. "Add to handyman list," he murmured and pretended to write on his palm. "Make door squeak." He looked up from his fake pad of paper and flashed a boyish, panty-melter of a smile.

The butterflies in her belly flapped their wings. *Lord have mercy!* This must be the original expression that sparked the phrase weak in the knees. If it were possible for bones to spontaneously liquefy into a gooey mess due to the presence of an absolutely delectable man, she'd soon be one big lump of swoon.

"Go on, Marmalade. Your business card boyfriend has wanted to show you this all day."

She pushed up onto her tiptoes and kissed his cheek.

"What was that for? You haven't even seen it yet," he asked.

"Whatever it is, I know I won't be disappointed."

"How do you know?"

A spark danced through her body as she gazed into his sage-green eyes. "I feel it."

He watched her like he wasn't quite sure what to make of her.

That made two of them.

She eyed the door. Gently, she opened it, blinking a few times as her eyes adjusted to the light. She took a few steps inside, her flats tapping against the polished floor. And not any old water-damaged floor. She feasted her eyes on gleaming hardwoods. Skipping like a schoolgirl to the center of the empty space, she drank in the pockets of sunlight streaming through the windows. Like she didn't have a care in the world, she extended her arms, looked up at the beams in the ceiling, and twirled. She couldn't help herself. The floor demanded it. It was like walking on enchanted wooden planks, and each one held a different secret.

She finished her fourth or fifth rotation and screeched to a halt. "You put in this floor?"

He feigned surprise. "No, I just moved the junk to the shed, fixed the roof, and updated the plumbing. The raccoons must have done the floor."

"You know you did good," she countered, calling his bluff.

He attempted to school his features. "How do you know that?" he tossed back.

"I see it in your eyes. I see it in your smile, in the way you lift your chin. You take pride in what you do."

"You see all that?"

"I do. A teacher trait." She walked the perimeter of the living room and studied the hardwoods. A blend of chestnut, caramel, and amber hues intertwined with honey-gold planks to create a mismatched masterpiece. "This wood is unique. I've never seen anything like it."

Finn crossed his arms, still sporting a satisfied smirk, and leaned against the wall. "It's reclaimed wood. It comes from an old mining shack up near Starrycard Falls. Your uncle had several planks scattered around the property. That's what gave me the idea to use it. I'm familiar with sourcing recycled materials in the area through my work."

She cocked her head to the side. "As a handyman?"

"No, as the head of operations and expansion at my family's company."

In their time together, he'd never mentioned his official role in the family business. It sounded quite comprehensive. She wanted to press him for more details, but sensing his unease, she simply nodded.

"Hold on," he said, brightening, then entered the bedroom.

She craned her neck, watching him disappear. "What are you doing back there?"

"Close your eyes."

"Why?" she called.

"Just close them, Marmalade. I have a surprise."

"Fine," she answered sharply, but on the inside, butterflies were having another flap-fest in her belly.

The clap of Finn's footsteps followed seconds after she'd closed her eyes. She concentrated on the sound as he whipped past her, then stopped somewhere in the middle of the room. There was a heavy shake—a blanket, perhaps—then silence.

"Now you can look," he called.

She opened her eyes and giggled as she peered at the white, floofy sheepskin rug gracing her gorgeous new floor.

"Now we each have a sex rug," he said and sauntered toward her, his green eyes darkening as he drank her in.

Her body ignited beneath his gaze. "It appears we do."

Carnal mischief glinted in his eyes before he did an emotional one-eighty and frowned. But this was not his growly handyman frown. No, this sulking was for show. Hamming it up, he deepened his scowl and scratched his chin. "Actually, no, this sheepskin rug is brand-spanking new. I must apologize. You don't officially have a floofy sex rug, Sweet Miss Marmalade."

"I don't? Oh no!" she replied coyly, understanding exactly where he was going with this.

He moved toward her like a moth drawn to a flame as she took a few steps back. Her heels brushed against the bottom of the bookshelf.

He held on to the side of the shelf with one hand and tilted her chin up, forcing her to meet his eyes. His breath was warm against her lips. "You don't officially have a floofy sex rug . . . yet."

Yep, that's what she'd hoped he'd say.

He leaned in a fraction closer, his lips a whisper away when—

"Shit!" he exclaimed, jumping back.

A craggy creak accompanied his outburst.

"Was that the cabin? Is the roof about to cave in?" she stammered, raising her arms to the duck-and-cover position.

But Finn didn't look like a man concerned with being crushed by thick wooden beams. Quite the opposite, in fact. He peered past her shoulder where he'd gripped the bookcase. The panic on his face gave way to an appraising nod. "I'll be damned. But I'm not surprised."

"What is it?" she eked out with her hands clasped above her head, not ready to forgo head protection.

He pointed to the top of the bookcase.

Cautiously, she lowered her arms and went to Finn's side. She assessed the hulking wood structure. The crown molding was no longer attached to the top. It had popped open.

She cocked her head to the side. "Is it broken?"

"I don't think so. There must be a hidden hinge in the back we can't see. I must have triggered it to open when I pulled on the piece of trim."

"Why would tugging on a piece of decorative trim pop the top?"

He reached up and slipped his hand inside. "Well, look at that."

She pushed onto her tiptoes but couldn't see a thing. "What is it?"

Wonder overtook his features. "It's a secret compartment. And there's something in there." Finn removed a compact, battered metal toolbox, a bit slimmer than a shoe box, from the stealthy storage space.

She stared at the little dents in the metal. "What do you think is in there?"

"There's only one way to find out," he replied and handed it to her.

She shook it like a kid trying to decipher the contents of a wrapped present. "It's not that heavy, and there doesn't seem to be tools inside. But it's definitely full of something." She looked around the snug space. The place was empty. Finn had moved the furniture and knickknacks to a shed behind the cabin. She eyed the rug, then sat on the soft surface. Placing the box in front of her on the white faux fur, she rested her hands in her lap.

Finn followed and sat across from her. "Don't you want to open it?"

She focused on the tarnished latch with rusted screws holding it in place. "Do you think my great-uncle would want me to see what's in here? Is this for me?"

"You're his only living descendent. If not you, then who else?" Finn asked, watching her closely.

The man had a point.

She lifted the clasp, unlocking a new-found connection to her family. Carefully, she opened the toolbox and inhaled the soothing scent of old paper and photographs. She lifted a black-and-white photo of a young man with his arm around a young woman. They were outdoors. A large letter G was emblazoned on the side of the mountain face behind them. She turned over the photo and read the writing on the back.

Golden Tech, 1963

Al and Cookie

"This must be my great-uncle," she said, handing the photo to Finn.

"And that's Golden Tech, for sure." He pointed to the enormous letter. That's the G on Mount Evermore in Golden. It's been there since the school opened. I'd know it anywhere."

"It looks like he did attend your college." Hailey studied the man in the photo. "He looks a little like my dad. They share the same cut of their jawline." She slid her gaze to the young woman with light hair that brushed past her shoulders. "My uncle never married, did he?"

"I don't think so."

"Hello, Cookie, who were you to my great-uncle?" she asked, eyeing the beaming girl in a miniskirt and boots with bracelets lining her wrists.

Finn handed her back the photo and dipped his hand into the toolbox. "Look at this. It's from nineteen sixty-five," he said, removing a sheet of paper.

"US Patent Office," she read from the top of the certificate with a gold seal affixed to the side.

Finn scanned the text. "Your great-uncle must have been a metallurgical and materials engineer."

"A what?" she asked. "I've never even heard of that."

"You might not have heard of it, but I guarantee you've seen the results of it. It's a field of engineering that focuses on using different materials to construct objects, like buildings or bridges." He skimmed the page. "This patent is for a material used to reinforce beams and columns. This must be how he made his fortune. Even though my degree is in mechanical engineering, I'm familiar with this process, thanks to Dr. Schneider's class."

Hailey peered inside the toolbox. She removed two bundles of letters, each an inch or so high, tightly bound with twine. The top envelope on the first bundle had one word written across the center.

Cookie.

"There's that name again," she said, showing Finn.

She turned over the second bundle and gasped at the return address. "These are from my dad."

"Hailey, is this you?" He plucked a few photos from the bottom of the toolbox and examined them. She could only see the back, but from that vantage point, she could tell they weren't aged like the photo of her great-uncle and Cookie. Finn turned the photo so she could see it.

She pressed her hand to her heart. "That's me in grade school. Probably first or second grade."

His expression softened. "And are these your parents?" he asked gently, passing her the second picture.

It was a shot from her high school graduation. She stood between her mother and father, smiling an easy smile, not knowing she'd soon lose them. "I graduated from the school my parents taught at. They were so excited I wanted to follow in their footsteps and study education." Emotion welled in her chest. "This is one of the last photos taken of the three of us."

"I think this letter went with it. It wasn't in an envelope," Finn said and handed it to her.

> Dear Uncle Albert,
>
> I enjoy getting your packages with the beautiful handmade paper. I wish you'd pen a note with the gift. I'd love to know how you're doing. Perhaps we could visit Colorado before Hailey starts college in the fall. She wants to be a teacher. She has such a gentle, loving heart. We're so proud of the young woman she's becoming.
>
> Your nephew,
> David

She stared at her father's handwriting. "I didn't know my dad corresponded with my great-uncle."

Finn touched the corner of the paper. "It doesn't sound like your great-uncle wrote back. He just sent the Starrycard paper."

She untied the twine and fanned through the letters from her father. The postmarks were in chronological order. She slipped the folded paper from the first letter her father had sent to his uncle.

"My dad was still in high school when he got his first Starrycard paper package."

Dear Uncle Albert,

The paper you sent is like nothing I've ever seen. Your note said to write meaningful words on it. I have the perfect use for it. It's for a girl. But she's not just any girl. Even though we just met, I know I'm going to marry her.

Your nephew,
David

"The pickle jar notes. I didn't know that my great-uncle was the inspiration behind them," she said and brushed a tear from her cheek.

"Are you all right, Marmalade?" Finn asked and rested his hand on her knee.

"I don't know." She focused on the letters and photos scattered on the white rug. "I thought of something."

He stroked his thumb across her knee in a slow, comforting motion. "Let's hear it."

"My great-uncle died two years ago, right?"

"Two years and give or take a couple of months."

"Do you know what happened?"

Finn nodded. "He had a heart attack in his sleep."

"Who found him?" she pressed gently, peering at the black-and-white photo of the young smiling Al and Cookie.

"The mailman. His box was full. After a couple of days of knocking and getting nothing, he tried the door. It was unlocked, and the guy found your great-uncle in his bed, unresponsive."

She brushed another tear from her cheek. The man was utterly alone in his last moments.

"Hailey, what is it?" Finn pressed.

"I thought I'd been alone these past six years—not having any family. But I did have family. I had a great-uncle. I would have liked to have known him. Maybe that would have made these last years . . ."

What was she trying to say?

Maybe they could have helped each other. Maybe her last six years wouldn't have been so lonely. Perhaps if she hadn't been isolated like a boat adrift in the big, wide ocean, she wouldn't have tried to fill the hole in her heart with uncaring jerks who'd only added to the void in her chest.

Without a word, Finn removed a letter from the stack. He slipped a folded page from the envelope. "It appears he knew about you," he said and handed her a birth announcement with her name printed on the card and a snapshot of an infant wrapped in a pink blanket clipped to the back of it.

Finn went through the stack of envelopes. "I know Starrycard paper. These envelopes are quite worn. They've been handled repeatedly. I think your great-uncle spent a lot of time with them. Maybe in his own way, he did care about you."

"Why do you think he never responded to my dad's letters? Why do you think he shut himself off from the world?" she asked, trying to make sense of the man's choices.

Finn concentrated on the stack of paper. A muscle twitched as he clenched his jaw. "I don't know. Stuff happens, and people can get lost and lose their way. You can get caught up in just trying to make it through the day."

Is that what happened to Finn? And was some woman out there named Susan to blame?

"What are the other letters? The ones marked with Cookie," he asked, clearing his throat.

She untied the twine, picked up the envelope on top, and peered inside the envelope. "There's a slip of paper inside. It looks like Starrycard paper." She removed it carefully. "Critical component, number one." She read, then met Finn's gaze. "Those are odd words."

"Critical component is an engineering term. If a critical component fails, the whole system is compromised. Critical components require special attention to keep the system working."

She nodded and reread the message. "Critical component, number one. You smiled against my lips when I kissed you." She opened the second envelope. "Critical component, number two. You were the only one who could make me laugh." She stared at the letters, written in sharp, bold strokes. "I think he wrote these notes to her but never sent them." Needing to test her theory, she plucked an envelope from the bottom and removed the piece of paper. The handwriting was similar to the first note but shakier, like time had eroded the precise engineer's pen strokes.

Finn leaned in. "What does it say?"

"It doesn't say critical component. But there's a date." She showed him the slip.

"That had to be a few days before your great-uncle died."

She peered at the last message the man wrote. "Remember the gift I gave you? I was worried you wouldn't like it. The tears in your eyes told me you loved it. Did you keep it? Do you wear it and think of me? I should have shouted my love for you from the rooftop. I should have tended to it diligently. It's my greatest regret." Hailey tucked the note into the envelope. "I wonder why they didn't end up together?"

"I don't know," Finn answered, pain laced through the words, like the longing in that last note struck a chord deep in his soul. He cupped her face in his hand and stroked her cheek.

"Do you think Cookie ever learned that Albert still loved her? What happened to her?" she whispered.

In the cozy cabin, she lost herself in Finn's eyes as the world faded away until footsteps snapped her back to reality.

"And I have wondered what happened to you, Hailey Higgins," came a man's voice with a rolling Italian accent.

"Nico!" she shrieked and pulled away from Finn. She blinked. The short-shorts-wearing man was the last person she'd expected to see standing in the doorway. Nervous energy took over. She hastily collected the mementos, letters, and photos from the rug and returned them to the box. She rose to her feet. "What are you doing here?"

The man greeted her with a wide grin. "I decided to surprise you, *bella*. You promised you'd allow me to show you the town and take you to dinner. You always seem to be working. But you can't be working tonight. It's Friday, and it's the first Starrycard Under the Stars. I'm here to whisk you away and introduce you to my canoe."

She felt the waves of irritation rolling off Finn as he rose to his feet and loomed a half-step behind her.

"Your . . . what?" She zeroed in on her business card boyfriend. Stone-faced, the man reverted to grump mode.

"My canoes and kayaks in the boathouse near the water," Nico explained. "What did you think I was referring to?"

God help her.

"So, what is this about whisking me away?" she asked, changing the subject from anything shaped like a canoe.

"I thought we could take a walk along the creek. The light catches the water beautifully this time of day." The man directed his liveliness toward Finn. "Finn would know that better than me. Have you taken Hailey on a walk along the creek?"

"No," the man mumbled.

"Then it would be my pleasure," Nico exclaimed, oblivious to Finn's icy reception. "And we can have dinner together at the park." The man looked from her to Finn. "Unless you two have plans."

"We don't have plans," Finn reported robotically. "I'm helping my family with something. I'm busy."

It took everything Hailey had not to let her jaw hit the floor. That was news to her. All he'd been talking about that week was having her to himself for two whole days. And holy moly, what an about-face! An hour ago, they'd made love. Minutes ago, he'd tenderly wiped tears from her cheek. And they were talking—really talking. But that man was gone. She needed to accept that there were two versions of Finnegan Starrycard. When they were alone, he was affectionate and attentive. When anyone was around, he was an aloof grump. Which was the real Finn? Her head and her heart were at odds on that one. And then a word materialized in her mind.

Transaction.

What they shared was nothing but a transaction to him—an opportunity to play the part of a doting business card boyfriend when they were alone. She recalled what he'd said when he'd slipped his hand inside her panties.

This is for me. This is mine.

She'd forgotten the caveat.

She was his, but only when it was just the two of them.

He wasn't her boyfriend. She was a hidden indulgence. She was his little secret—like she'd been to Grant. There was a difference, though. She'd agreed to their roommates with benefits situation, but she'd be lying if she said she didn't want more. She'd claimed that love sucked—that she was done with it. Still, her heart longed for something deeper. Falling asleep in Finn's arms and waking to his kisses had clouded her mind. She'd let herself believe Finn's feelings about her had evolved and grown into something more.

She was wrong.

At least she'd caught herself before she let him know she was on the cusp of falling in love with him.

She forced a smile as the void in her chest expanded. "It appears I'm free for dinner."

"Hailey Higgins, you're mine tonight." Nico studied the cabin's interior. "The place is looking good. And I can help you with it, too."

"She's already got a handyman," Finn answered, maintaining his frigid edge.

"I leave that work to you, Finn. Everyone in town sings your praises. I don't think there's a shop or a building you haven't fixed. And you were so kind when you replaced the broken window on the boathouse. You're truly a gifted craftsman," Nico gushed. "What I am offering is something else. I recently obtained my real estate license. If you're considering selling, I'm your man, *bella*. Now, shall we?" he said and gestured out the door.

She looked between the men. "You want to leave now?"

"Why not?" Nico tossed back, enthusiasm bubbling off him like he was the human equivalent of fizzy champagne. "Let's seize this beautiful day."

She looked at Finn, but he wouldn't meet her eye. "What about Sweetie and Whiskers? We should check on them."

"Who?" Nico asked.

"Our kittens," she supplied and instantly understood her error.

"They're not our kittens," Finn bit out, finally acknowledging her. "We're fostering them. I can feed them and lock up your cabin. You can go. We're done here, right?"

She stared into his eyes. The warmth had drained, leaving a sheen of cold detachment that mirrored his hardened exterior. And that's when it hit, like a wrecking ball to the gut. There would never be a place for her in his heart, and there was only one way to answer his question.

She reached into her pocket. "Yes," she replied, willing her voice to remain even as she pressed the key to his palm, "we're done."

CHAPTER

Fourteen

FINN

FINN TUGGED at his sports coat's lapel, fussing with the fit of the charcoal gray garment. "What's Hailey doing now, Kenz? But don't stare. Act naturally."

McKenzie fluffed her puffy, Pepto-pink dress. "Miss Higgins laughed again, Uncle Finn. Just like she did five seconds ago when you asked." The child huffed and squirmed on the bench. "Can I play on the playground and make paper stars with my friends? I want to show everybody how fancy I look in my dress. We're fancy-pants people tonight, Uncle Finn."

He peered at the shiny black loafers McKenzie had insisted he wear to celebrate the first Starrycard Under the Stars event. "Not yet, kid."

"Then can I have more cherry licorice?"

Crunch!

Finn eyed his niece. "You're eating a pickle. You want to eat pickles with cherry licorice?"

"Yeah," she lobbed back, addressing him like he was the dumbest dude on the planet, which he might actually be after his jerk-tastic handyman-special performance a few hours ago. Kenzie presented her palm, knowing she held all the cards.

He pulled a twist from the bag on the bench and handed it

over. "I don't get eating pickles and licorice together. Seems like a gross combo."

"You said I could eat whatever I wanted, and Mrs. Brimble from the sandwich shop has the best pickles in all of Starrycard Creek. She has a whole table full of them for Starrycard Under the Stars, and she wanted me to thank you for fixing the sliding door on her display case. She says it's not leaking cold air anymore. Then I told her in my sweetest voice, 'Mrs. Brimble, you make the best pickles.' And then she said I could take a jar and share them with you. Want a pickle?" The kid held out the glass jar.

His heart jumped into his throat. All he could think of was Hailey and her pickle jar and how he was a colossal idiot.

We're done here, right?

Sparked by the gnawing voice in his head and the unrelenting vice clamped around his heart, he'd spoken those damned, cruel words. Sure, he could feign ignorance and say he was talking about their time viewing the new floor, but that's not how it had gone down or how she'd interpreted his douchebag behavior.

Despite sharing a tender moment with her—a moment when he wanted to hold her in his arms and assure her she wasn't alone in this world—he'd been powerless to respond differently. The pain he'd wrapped himself in like a thorny blanket had intensified the second Nico showed up.

It wasn't even like Nico was a bad person. The tiny man shorts were a little weird, but the dude was a good guy. He volunteered in the community and had beefed up the water sports program, bringing more revenue to the town. But the second Mr. Short-Shorts showed interest in Hailey, he'd become Finnegan the Terrible—a man prepared to thwart humiliation at any cost. Every insecurity he'd harbored over the last year had amplified. It was as if his heart hardened with each prick of anxiety and every slash of self-doubt.

He was a goddamned mess.

He could still see the searing disappointment in Hailey's eyes and the heartbreaking confusion etched on her face. But that wasn't what had sent an icy tremor through his body. It was the finality in her tone when she answered him.

Yes, we're done.

And she had every right to be angry and hurt.

He wasn't a total idiot. He saw the way she looked at him through her lashes, those amber eyes welling with hope and whispers of love.

But what was he supposed to tell her?

The truth?

Hell no!

He couldn't tell her that from the second he'd laid eyes on her, he'd been a goner. He couldn't say that her sweet smile, cherry scent, and those freckles dusting her cheeks took his breath away.

He couldn't let her in—not all the way.

He couldn't let her see who he truly was.

Or maybe he could?

Maybe she was his way out of this shitshow he'd been living.

Dammit! He was all over the place.

He messed with the sleeves of his tailored jacket.

Did he have a plan to apologize?

No.

All he could do was watch her from afar and stew in a sea of conflicting emotions that threatened to shred what little control he had left. And by control, he meant no fucking control. The proof? He'd roped his niece into helping him spy on her.

"Uncle Finn?" McKenzie said, shaking the pickle jar in front of his face. "Want the big one?"

He waved her off. "No, Kenz, I'm good sticking with licorice," he answered, plucking another twist from the bag and shoving it into his mouth. He glanced at the candy. While Kenz had eaten her fair share, he'd started his sugar binge seconds after Hailey left with Nico. And he hadn't let up.

Crunch!

He checked on his niece. Double-fisting a pickle and a licorice twist, McKenzie wiggled on the bench, tapping at the tiny sequins sewn into her dress's frilly fabric with the candy rope. He should have said no to her fancy dress-up requirement. But it wasn't the kid-sized gown that was the problem. The child was getting more restless by the second, but he couldn't let her hit the playground yet.

"Let's get back to our *game*, Kenz. Can you see Hailey and Nico? Are they still eating dinner?" he asked, eyes on the creek as McKenzie peered in the other direction, lifting a tree limb to get a better look.

He'd purposefully picked this bench for their surveillance location. A cluster of rocks and feathery aspens created a curtain, allowing them to remain hidden but still giving them a decent view of the picnic tables where residents were enjoying dinner not far from the band and makeshift dance floor.

"Okay, when Hailey laughed, did she lean in toward Nico?" he pressed.

"Huh?" *Crunch!*

"Did Hailey move closer to Nico?"

McKenzie switched to licorice. "No."

Good, good, good!

His skyrocketing anxiety dialed back a few notches.

"What's happening now? Are they still eating?" he asked as the band concluded a lively melody and transitioned into a slow, jazzy tune.

"No, they're done eating. They're standing up, and Nico's pointing to the dance floor."

Shit!

"What's Hailey doing? Does she look like she wants to dance?"

"She's shaking her head like she's saying no, and . . ." His niece paused. "Uncle Finn?"

"Yeah?"

"Are you sure Miss Higgins and Nico know we're playing super spies?"

"Yeah, they know," he lied.

Crunch! "I don't think they know."

"They know. Focus. What's happening now, Kenz?"

"Der manding old mans."

He stared at the girl. She'd wrapped the licorice around the pickle and was going at it. "Kenzie, don't talk with food in your mouth," he chided.

"You sound like Mommy," the kid grumped. "And for your information, Miss Higgins and Nico are standing, and he's holding her hand."

Dammit to hell!

"He's holding her hand?" Finn shot to his feet and hid behind the rocks, trying to see for himself, but a family stood in his line of sight, blocking the view.

"Yeah, Nico is holding her hand and walking with her to the dance floor." *Crunch!* "Uncle Finn, my belly feels weird."

"Go easy on the licorice and pickles." He craned his neck but couldn't see past the people. "Kenz?"

A guttural groan escaped the kid's mouth. "My burp stinks, Uncle Finn. Want to smell it?"

"No, Kenz, are Miss Higgins and Nico dancing?"

"Uh-huh."

Shit! Dancing meant touching, lots of touching.

"Where are Nico's hands?" he asked, doing his best to keep his tone even as every cell in his body freaked out.

The kid frowned. "His hands?"

"Yeah," he replied, irritation flooding his system at the thought of anyone but him dancing with Hailey.

"They're attached to his arms. See, Uncle Finn," she said, extending her pink-puffy-sleeved arm. "Here's my arm, and here's my hand, stuck on the end of it."

He mustered a grin for his niece. *Christ, what the hell was he doing?* He should abandon this cockeyed plan, put himself on a licorice detox, take McKenzie to the park, and let her play with her friends. He should be a doting and responsible uncle.

Emphasis on the *should be* part.

He smashed another cherry twist into his mouth. "Where are Nico's hands touching Hailey's body?" he demanded, going all-in on the total-fucking-lunacy option.

"One hand is holding her hand."

"Okay, and the other?"

"Kind of on her back and kind of above her butt."

Every muscle in his body tensed. "Above her butt or touching her butt?"

"I don't think it's very nice for me to be staring at Miss Higgins' butt—or anybody's butt."

Holy hell! His sister wouldn't be pleased with this stunt. But he was a desperate man.

"You're not looking at her butt. You're looking at Nico's hand. Concentrate, Kenz."

"Maybe his pinky finger is close to her butt."

That was enough for him.

"Oh no!" he cried, feigning concern as he pointed toward the darkened, gurgling waters of Starrycard Creek.

McKenzie spun around. "What is it, Uncle Finn?"

"Some of Nico's kayaks must have gotten loose. I think I saw a few headed down the creek."

The child gasped. "That's terrible! Nico loves his kayaks. He told us all about them at the water safety class at my school."

Finn maintained what he hoped was a look of deep distress and not the expression of a man capable of diabolical deception. "You better get Nico and let him know. He'd be so sad if they were gone forever."

Eliza was going to kill him. At least she was still under the weather. That gave him a few days before his sister was healthy enough to tear him a new one. And there was a chance he could load McKenzie up on so much candy, pickles, and ice cream her kid-brain might block out this bullshit quasi-creepy game of snooping on Hailey and Nico.

"Nico, there's a kayak emergency!" McKenzie exclaimed as she blasted from beneath the aspen curtain.

Finn ducked behind the rocks to watch the scene play out.

Waving her arms in a tumble of pink, McKenzie darted past dancing couples, then pointed to the creek. An alarmed Nico reared back. He pressed his hand to his heart and appeared to thank McKenzie. The man spoke to Hailey. She nodded, then pointed to the creek. *Shit!* Was she offering to help find the not-missing kayaks? Finn breathed a sigh of relief as Nico waved her off, then sprinted down the path.

Finn couldn't suppress a grin. He was a goddamned genius.

"Hey, Uncle Finn, I did what you asked me to do," McKenzie bellowed, waving him over as she stood beside a stern-faced Hailey Higgins.

Perhaps he'd been hasty in claiming the brainiac title.

Feeling his cheeks heat, he rose from behind the rocks like some kind of formalwear-clad pervert who hides out in bushes to spy on people, which was precisely what he'd been doing. With trepidation building in his chest, he left his secret spot and weaved through the tables. He stuffed his hands into his slack's pockets. "Hey, what a coincidence seeing you here," he said, going for casual. He met her fiery gaze. "You look nice."

"I'm wearing the same clothes you saw me in earlier."

He shifted his stance. "Yeah, but they also look great under the hanging lights."

Jesus, he sounded like a moron.

"Do you like my dress, Miss Higgins?" McKenzie chimed.

"It's beautiful," she answered, gifting the kid with a warm grin.

"Uncle Finn and I are fancy-pants people, like he used to be. See his shiny shoes."

"You both look very nice," Hailey replied, focusing on his niece.

It didn't matter if he wore eight-hundred-dollar shoes, a jacket tailor-made in London, or a Superman cape that gave him the power to fly. He was in the doghouse. Big time.

McKenzie scanned the dance floor. "Since Nico is gone, you should dance with my uncle Finn, Miss Higgins. He likes you."

Hailey raised an eyebrow. "Does he?"

"Yeah, you're the one who helped him find his real smile."

Where the hell was this coming from?

"Kenz—" he stammered, but the kid was on a roll.

"You didn't smile a real smile for a long, long time," his niece continued, "and then I saw you sitting at the table at Goldie's with Mom and Grandma the day Daddy brought the kitties to the table, and anytime Hailey looked away from you, you stared at her and smiled like you were looking at a big tub of cherry chocolate chip ice cream."

"You can go play now, Kenz," he said.

"I can?"

"Yeah."

"Where's my pickle jar?"

"Pickle jar?" Hailey repeated.

"We got pickles because I used good manners, and Uncle Finn fixes everybody's broken stuff in town. He might seem growly, but he's a good helper, Miss Higgins."

Great! Now it looked like he'd coached his niece to brag about him.

"Your jar is on the bench, Kenz."

"I want to bring it back to the cabin. We're having a sleepover. I'll let you have the last pickle, Miss Higgins," McKenzie gushed.

Hailey caught his eye. "You're watching McKenzie tonight?"

"Yeah, Jack and Eliza are under the weather."

"You're watching me, too, Miss Higgins, because you and Uncle Finn live together in the same cabin," McKenzie clarified. "We're gonna have so much fun!"

Hailey smiled at the girl, but it wasn't her easy grin. This smile didn't reach her eyes.

"Go play, Kenz," he said, patting her on the back. "Show your friends your fancy pink dress."

His niece narrowed her gaze. "Are you going to ask Miss Higgins to dance?"

He might as well do it. McKenzie was not one to let up.

He turned to Hailey. "Would you like to dance with me, Miss Higgins?"

Hailey glanced at McKenzie. "One dance can't hurt." Her voice sounded sweet as pie, but something lemon-suckingly sour glinted in her eyes. She took his hand. "This will give me some time to chat with your uncle. I have a feeling he's been keeping you busy. I noticed you in your pretty dress. You were by the creek—at that bench next to the rocks and trees."

Finn cringed. All he could do was brace for impact.

McKenzie nodded enthusiastically. "Yeah, I was playing our game."

"And what game is that?" Hailey pressed, back to sounding deceptively sweet as pie.

"The spy game."

"The spy game," the woman echoed.

"Yep, the one we were all playing—you, me, Uncle Finn, and Nico."

"I think I see your buddy—that Cody kid," he said. He wasn't really lying. There were a ton of children swarming the play equipment. Cody could have been one of them. "Go show him your dress. I bet he'll like it."

"He'll love it!" she exclaimed. She turned on her heel and sprinted toward the kids. "Cody, look at me," the girl exclaimed.

"Stay on the playground," he called after her.

"And don't wander off," Hailey added.

Damn, they weren't half-bad at taking care of—

"The spy game?" Hailey pressed, cutting off another premature celebration of his adulting skills. "You tricked your niece to help you spy on Nico and me?"

He gathered her into his arms, but he didn't hold her close. A ruler—and then some—could fit in the space between them. "I can explain—"

"Finnegan Starrycard," came a man's voice, blessedly buying him some time to devise a non-psychotic explanation.

Finn turned toward the sound. "Hello, Mr. Perry."

"I wanted to thank you for fixing the railing on my bookshop," the older gentleman said, swaying to the beat a few feet away with his wife in his arms.

"It was no trouble, sir."

"And you must be Miss Higgins," the man continued. "The new second-grade teacher."

"Yes, I am."

"Our granddaughter, Brinlee, is one of your students. She can't stop going on about you."

Hailey beamed at the couple. "Brinlee is a delight to have in class."

"Finnegan, dear," Mrs. Brimble, the Starrycard Creek Pickle Queen, called as she danced over with her husband. "I hope your niece conveyed my appreciation."

"She did, ma'am. I'm glad the display case is working properly."

"My darling boy, and hello, Hailey," his mother called as his father twirled her like this was Dancing with the Starrycards.

Jesus Christ, this dance floor was busier than Free Cherry Turnover Day at Goldie's restaurant.

"Don't you look dapper," his mother cooed, giving him a once-over. "How's babysitting McKenzie going?"

"Good, I mean, great. McKenzie's on the playground in one of her dress-up ballgowns." He cleared his throat. "And we're definitely not engaging in quasi-illegal or morally questionable activities," he blathered like an idiot.

His parents studied him like they were assessing if a screw had come loose on their third-born son.

"Have you voted for the Starrycard Creek Sunshine Jubilee street banner?" his mother asked, thankfully not dwelling on his word salad of an answer.

"Not yet, Mom."

"What's that?" Hailey asked.

"Each year, the town votes on the image for the banners along

Main Street for the Starrycard Creek Sunshine Jubilee. It's a celebration of the end of the school year and the sunny days ahead. The town narrows it to two designs. The local business owners pick the final one. It's great fun. They're printed on Starrycard paper. We place them into slim plastic cases to protect them from the elements and attach them to the lamp posts." His mother pursed her lips. "That reminds me. Finnegan?"

"Yeah, Mom?" He knew what was coming.

She eyed his jacket. "We'll need someone to hang them for us. Are you still the local handyman?"

The woman was fishing for information. And he couldn't help her. He honestly didn't know what he was. But handyman or not, he could do the job.

"I can hang the banners."

"You'll get to see them before most of the town, Hailey," his father added, giving his mother another twirl.

"And why is that?" she asked, the tension draining from her body.

"The teachers lead the children into town just after the banners go up," his dad replied, reeling his mom back in.

"Like a parade?" Hailey asked, perking up and relaxing into his arms, which had to be a good sign. Not making a big deal of it, he drew her in closer.

"Exactly! There's food and games. The children play in the creek and enjoy the sunshine—just like when Fiona Donnelly-Starrycard opened the town's first school."

"It sounds lovely. And the more I learn about Fiona, the more it sounds like she was a force of nature," Hailey replied.

"A demure force," his mother slipped in. "It's said that she was a quiet woman—an artist. But she knew what she wanted for herself and this town." His mom peered across the crowd. "I remembered something. Official mayoral business. You'll have to excuse us. Hank, dance us over to the Brimbles. I hear she has a new batch of pickles, and we're not missing out. She sold out completely last week."

"That's mayoral business?" Finn asked, eyeing the woman.

"My business is mayoral business." His mother tossed him a cheeky wink as she faded into the crowd with his dad.

He couldn't worry about his family or what plan his mother was cooking up. With Hailey in his arms, he relaxed. But when he met her fiery gaze, it was clear he wasn't out of the woods yet.

She scowled. "Did you set that up?"

"Set what up?"

"Everyone singing your praises. Your parents sharing the town's charming history."

"No," he shot back, "I didn't set that up. I don't think there's one small business or local government building in this town that I haven't patched up. And history is just history."

"So, the only thing you were up to tonight was dressing up like a businessman and spying on me?" she asked, using her I-know-that's-not-the-whole-story teacher voice—a voice he'd heard her employ a few times at dismissal.

"Yes, ma'am. I mean . . ." *Damn!* How could he lie when she looked at him like if he said the wrong thing, he'd land his ass in detention? "You're right about the spying. I recruited McKenzie to help me keep tabs on you and Nico," he conceded.

"What about the kayaks?" she pressed.

He stared at the water. "There aren't any kayaks floating down the creek."

Her jaw dropped. "You asked a six-year-old to lie?"

Christ on a bike, the more it sank in, the worse his little stunt sounded.

He grimaced. "I told her I saw the kayaks floating down the creek and asked her to tell Nico. She didn't know she was lying. She believed me."

"That doesn't make it okay, Finn. You took advantage of her trust."

"It was a shitty thing to do. I won't do that to her again. I wasn't thinking."

Hailey didn't look convinced. "And what about Nico? How far does the creek go?"

Finn shrugged, playing like he didn't know. But he knew. Of course, he knew. The creek originated at Starrycard Falls in the mountains, wound its way into the valley and through the town, then continued. It went for hundreds of miles before it merged with the Arkansas River—which went even farther. Nico could be running along the creek bank for hours or days.

Shit!

He had to figure out a way to lighten the situation. Nico was a grown man. The guy wouldn't run himself into the ground.

Think, man!

He cleared his throat and glanced at the playground. A few kids racing back and forth on the playground caught his eye and gave him an idea.

"Nico loves to exercise," he began cautiously. "I see him jogging all the time. He'll be getting in many more steps to make his quads even *quadier* in his tiny man shorts."

A twitch of a grin graced Hailey's lips. The barely-there movement sent his pulse racing. He had to take advantage of this crack in her icy demeanor.

"I'll text him and let him know I made a mistake," he offered.

"Thank you."

"But in twenty minutes. Let's let him get in a partial workout."

That ghost of a grin returned. "Finnegan Starrycard," she chided, and Christ, he loved hearing her say his name, even if she was still half pissed off at him.

"Come on, Marmalade. Think of Nico's quads."

She shook her head, but the smile remained.

"Listen," he said softly, bringing her in another inch closer. "I'm sorry for spying on you. I was a little out of my mind."

She watched him like a hawk. "Why were you out of your mind?"

His heart knew the reason, yet he couldn't get his damned brain to allow his mouth to deliver it. He opened and closed his pie hole—or, in his case, his cherry-licorice-twist hole—a couple of times like a beached sugar-obsessed flounder.

It was a terrible move.

Her hint of a smile disappeared. Pain shined in her eyes. She stepped back, breaking their connection. Her bottom lip trembled as she left his side and wove her way to the edge of the dance floor.

Dammit!

He followed her, wanting to punch himself in his flounder mouth.

What was wrong with him? Or perhaps the real question was what *wasn't* wrong with him.

"Hailey, wait . . . give me a second to explain."

She stopped at the wishing wall, not far from the playground, and rested her hand on the rocky surface. He stood beside her, trying to find the right words to explain what was going through his head, when McKenzie spied them from atop the play structure. She had a licorice twist hanging from her mouth and the pickle jar tucked under her arm as she waved from her spot. How much could one six-year-old eat? When it came to junk food, his niece could put away as much as a competitive eater. He waved back, and Hailey did the same. He glanced at the enticing woman. She'd put on a smile for the child, but the second his niece disappeared down a tunnel slide, her expression darkened.

She turned toward him and rubbed her eyes. "I can't do this, Finn."

The vice on his heart tightened.

"Do what?" he asked, knowing damned well what she meant.

"I can't *transact* with you. I thought I could handle whatever this is we're doing and keep it casual. But when I'm with you . . ." She stared at the creek. "My heart isn't built for *transactions*. It longs for the real thing. I don't know why I attract men who are embarrassed to be with me, who want to use me, who only want me on their terms."

A knot twisted in his belly.

Was that him?

Dammit, it was.

"I know I agreed to this," she continued. "I thought I could give up on love. I wanted to. But I can't. I can't let this be all there is for me. I have to believe there's someone out there meant for me."

"Like the opposite of what the wallpaper said?" he offered.

"You remember me telling you that on the night we met?"

He remembered everything.

"Yes."

Curiosity glinted in her eyes.

He flicked his gaze to the creek. "Do you think Nico's meant for you?"

"No, he's sweet, but no." She huffed a sad little laugh. "You see, I'm sort of cursed."

He studied her and observed the gentle upward curve of her lips as the lights lining the creek held her in a shimmery glow. "How are you cursed?"

"I know what real love looks like. I know how beautiful it can be. My parents were a shining example." She raised her gaze to the sky. "My mom and dad met on an evening like this in high school at an outdoor astronomy talk. It was held up on some hill and a decent hike to get there. After it finished and everyone returned to the parking lot to have snacks and drinks, my mom stayed to take in the view. My dad was there with a few friends, but he told them to go ahead. Even though he didn't know my mom, he didn't want to leave her. She was new to the school. She'd just moved to town to live with her grandmother. He'd noticed her in the halls. And it was a good thing he'd stayed. When my mom decided to head back to her car, she lost her footing and tripped."

"Was she okay?" he asked gently.

"Yeah, my dad swooped in and caught her before she could fall. He insisted on carrying her all the way down. There'd been food and drinks that the astronomy club had brought for the event, but it took my parents so long to get down the only thing left to eat was a jar of—"

"Pickles," he supplied.

Hailey sighed as a wistful grin bloomed. "From that moment, they were inseparable. Love at first sight." Her expression dimmed. "I may never find that type of love, but I can't keep allowing men to treat me like I'm barely a blip on their radar—like some booty-call side-chick."

Her words hit like arrows piercing his heart.

"You think that's all you are to me?"

Her eyes shined as she drank him in. "You're the one who said nobody could know about us."

The screws on the vice crushing his heart turned, clamping down harder. Pain radiated through his chest. "I didn't say that because of anything you did or who you are."

She shook her head. "What else could it be? I don't understand you, Finn. You make me feel like I'm the center of your universe when it's the two of us. But you turn into this grumpy, sullen, sulking man the minute we're not alone, and you treat me like I mean nothing to you—like you'd treat a random stranger on the street with more kindness."

How could he make her understand without speaking the words he couldn't even say to himself?

A muscle twitched in his jaw as an emotional powder keg threatened to explode within him. He schooled his features and pegged her with his gaze. "It's because I don't want to be nice to you."

"What?" she breathed, incredulity coating the word as the pound of footsteps drew closer.

"I want to be everything to you," he bit out, his words gruff, ragged, and the absolute truth.

He pictured himself on bended knee, slipping a ring onto her finger. The sun in her auburn hair. Her amber eyes welling with tears of joy. And that smile that owned him stretched across her beautiful face.

He had to touch her—had to make her see that while he was a gruff, sullen, sulking jerk, he was her gruff, sullen, sulking business card boyfriend. He moved to touch her cheek and cup her beautiful face in his hand. He wanted, no, needed to kiss her. He had to show her what his words couldn't convey.

"Uncle Finn! Miss Higgins!" McKenzie called, barreling toward them.

He startled and pulled back, abandoning his plan to kiss her as a frilly tornado with pigtails and a pickle jar skidded to a stop before them.

McKenzie set down the container and held out her closed fist. "Look what I got when I voted for the version of the banner I liked the best." She opened her hand, revealing slips of Starrycard paper. "We get to make our first wish tonight." She gave them each a strip of paper, then went to town using a crayon to write on her slip. "*Stegosaurus. S-T-E-G-O . . .*" she murmured as she wrote. The child finished and handed Hailey the crayon. "Go ahead, Miss Higgins. Write your wish. I wrote the same wish I always do. Goldie says that you only get what's meant for you, but I think if you wish real, real hard and keep on believing, that has to help."

Hailey shot a look his way, then concentrated on the fragment of paper in her hand. Gently, she rested the slip on her palm and turned away from him as she followed Kenzie's lead. The woman finished writing and folded her strip in half. "What do we do now?"

"Keep folding until it's super-duper tiny," the child instructed, demonstrating with her slip.

Hailey mimicked the movement. "How's this?" she asked, holding out the tiny square.

"That's perfect. You're a good wish folder. Do you want me to stuff it in the wall for you? I know the luckiest spot. My great-grandpa Rex showed me."

"That would be very kind of you, McKenzie. Thank you."

The little girl took Hailey's tiny square and the crayon, then ran down to a spot about twenty feet away. She crouched, jammed the folded papers into crevices, then bolted back all grins. "Did it. Now Uncle Finn has to do his, and then we can make paper stars to float on the . . ." McKenzie stilled and pressed her hands to her belly.

"Are you all right, honey?" Hailey asked.

He slipped the piece of paper into his jacket's pocket as his niece took a few steps toward him. She looked up, eyes bulging. "Uncle Finn," she eked out, then puffed up her cheeks.

He knew what was coming.

And it wouldn't be pretty.

Before he could move a muscle, McKenzie pitched forward.

"Look out below," she croaked as an explosion of putrid cherry-pickle vomit spewed past her lips and splattered all over his shiny shoes.

CHAPTER
Fifteen
FINN

FINN STOOD on the back porch of Starrycard Cabin and hosed off his shoes, fighting the urge to gag at the scent of the cherry-pickle-stomach-acid combo permeating the expensive footwear. For the millionth time, he couldn't help thinking this was not what he expected to happen that evening.

Then again, he should know better than anyone how quickly life can throw a curveball.

He held out the shoes, allowing the water and the remaining contents of his niece's belly to pool on the ground beside the deck. He leaned against the sturdy cedar railing. He'd built this outdoor area with seating and a fire pit. It had been the first project he'd completed after he'd hit rock bottom. And like his weekend plans, he hadn't expected it to be used for vomit decontamination, but nevertheless, it worked. He released the trigger on the spray nozzle and cut the water. He examined the dripping loafers. Once polished and refined, they now looked like they'd returned home from one hell of a bender. He sighed. There was no saving these shoes. Shaking off the excess moisture, he dropped the nozzle and walked over to the bear-proof garbage bins on the side of the cabin. He unlatched the lid and flipped it open, but paused before dropping the ruined items inside. An unwelcome memory returned. He pictured the fancy shoebox and the extravagant bag they'd been placed inside. As if he'd slipped through a ripple in time, he could hear the roar of traffic, the honking cabbies, and the wailing sirens—New York City pulsing around him as he sat in an expensive leather chair in the high-end men's shoe store. His stomach did a flip-flop, but not because of the smelly loafers in his hand. Suddenly, the pungent floral scent of roses assaulted his nostrils, and all he could hear was the voice he'd worked so damned hard to forget.

You should buy the loafers, Finn. They suit you.

The muscles at the base of his neck tightened. He scrutinized the sad shoes and shook his head. Without another look, he dropped them inside the bin and slammed it shut, cursing that damned voice and those fucking aggravating memories.

He ran his hands through his dark hair and stared up at the sky—at the same sparkling points of light that had enticed William Starrycard to stop in this part of the country. The stars that led him to Fiona.

"What am I doing? How do I move forward?" he whispered into the wind, his question hovering in the night air.

The stars didn't answer, but something rustled in the darkened woods. It was probably a fox or a rabbit.

He sighed and strode across the deck when the sound of someone opening his bedroom window stopped him.

"Anytime I had a sour belly, my mom and dad would open my window to let in a little bit of fresh air," Hailey said softly, her words carrying on the breeze as she spoke to his niece.

The tension drained from his body. Her warm and tender voice called to him—a melodic life preserver plucking him from the tumultuous sea of memories that threatened to drag him into the depths of his tortured mind. He stepped closer to the window and caught a glimpse of her through the curtains. She'd twisted her hair into a messy bun. Tendrils kissed her cheeks. He took another half-step closer and drank her in. She was a beacon, radiating love and compassion. He couldn't look away.

"Let's get you tucked in, little one," she continued.

"My mommy and daddy call me little star, and my grandma Maeve and Goldie call everybody with Starrycard in their name little star, too."

"Would you like me to call you that?" Hailey asked, fluffing the pillow.

"Yeah, I would."

"All right, *little star*, you are squeaky clean and ready for bed. Cuddle in. Your pillow is fluffy and soft and ready to give you sweet dreams," Hailey replied in her honey and molasses tone.

"What do you think my mommy and daddy are doing?" Kenz asked with a melancholy note weaved into the question.

"I bet they're sleeping. That's the best thing to do when you're sick."

"My mommy and daddy feel super sick. But they'll want to see me in the morning. What if I sleep too long in Uncle Finn's bed? They'll be missing me a lot. They might get worried."

Hailey brushed a damp lock of hair from McKenzie's cheek. "Are you missing them a lot, little star?"

"Uh-huh," the kid croaked.

Finn's heart sank. He was worried she might get homesick.

Hailey leaned forward and waved in his niece. "Can I tell you a special secret about moms and dads?"

"Okay," Kenz whispered back.

"They're always right here," Hailey replied and patted her chest above her heart.

McKenzie copied the movement. "In your heart?"

"That's right. My dad used to say that's where the love lives."

"Why doesn't he say it anymore?"

"Because he and my mom are up in heaven, but they're always in my heart."

Finn swallowed past the lump in his throat as he drank in this quiet powerhouse of a woman. It was easy to see her kindness. It rolled off her in cherry-chocolate waves. Her strength was subtle, but Jesus, this woman was strong. She'd endured a hell of a lot more than he had, and look at her. Her goodness and beauty still shined through.

"I have lots of love in my heart," McKenzie said, lifting her little chin.

"I bet you do, and I have an idea," Hailey replied and picked up her cell from the bedside table.

"How about we set the alarm on my phone so you don't sleep too long." She concentrated on the screen. "Let me just close out of my email."

McKenzie sat up and stared at the device. "*You have un-sub-scribed from Shoot-ing Stars Love Stories,*" she said, sounding out the words on the screen. She looked up at Hailey. "What's that?"

It sounded oddly familiar. He squinted but couldn't see anything from his vantage point.

"That's some great reading, McKenzie. They're stories with happily ever afters."

"Like my mom and dad," the kid remarked, perking up. "My daddy loves my mommy super-duper lots. And he's loved her with his whole heart for his whole life. I hear him tell her that when they think I'm asleep. Are the stories like that?"

A wistful grin graced Hailey's face. "Yes, very much like that."

McKenzie pursed her lips. "But you unsubscribed."

"I did. I needed a little break from them."

McKenzie rocked from side to side. "Did you like the stories?"

"Quite a bit."

"Has anybody ever written a story like that about you?" McKenzie continued.

"No," Hailey answered, trying to mask the sadness encapsulating the syllable, but he detected it.

Could he give her what she deserved?

"Now, enough about emails. Let's set the alarm," Hailey said, smiling at McKenzie, but it didn't hold her signature warmth. She tapped the screen, then set the phone on the side table. "All ready to go. How's your belly feeling, little star?" she asked and patted the pillow, signaling for his niece to get under the covers.

"The crackers feel good in my tummy. My throat doesn't burn, and I don't feel like puking on Uncle Finn's shoes. But maybe I should puke on his work boots."

"Why do you say that?" Hailey asked with a thread of amusement as the warmth returned to her expression.

"I bet when he takes them off, they're super stinky because he wears them so much."

Finn suppressed a chuckle. He looked from the window to the back door. He should go inside and help Hailey with his niece. Jesus, she'd already done so much.

Hailey had sprung into action after McKenzie finished tossing her pickle-licorice cookies. She'd scooped the child away from the putrid splatter and into her arms. Before he could blink, she'd commandeered a napkin, a glass of water, and a paper bag from one of the picnic tables, then directed him to get the truck and meet her and Kenzie on the corner. Minutes later, he'd pulled up to find Hailey still holding the girl and patting her back. She'd hummed and rocked the whimpering child in her arms for the entire drive up the mountain. Her quiet steadiness had kept what could have been a traumatic night for the kid low-key—peaceful even.

That was Hailey's magic. She made everything better. He'd known this from the second the woman stepped into his truck's headlights. Simply holding her in his arms could silence the noise in his head.

A prickle spider-crawled down his spine. He needed to remind himself that he was on the verge of losing her.

Or maybe not.

I don't want to be nice to you. I want to be everything to you.

The words had tumbled past his lips—his heart overriding his head.

Again, the question taunted him. Was he capable of giving her everything?

Did he have anything left to give, and would she even allow him to try?

He stared at the door, but his legs were rooted in place, drawn by the allure of her presence, the melody of her voice, and the sweet gift of existing in this perfect slice of time, giving him a chance to catch his breath and observe her.

Meow.

"Can one of the kitties sleep with me?" McKenzie asked, her tone growing groggy.

"It's both of them or neither of them, little star. They don't like to be separated."

"Can both of them sleep in bed with me? Sometimes, at home, all my animals sleep in my bed, and there's barely any room for my legs. But I'm real good at staying super still so nobody gets knocked onto the floor."

"Let's ask the kitties," Hailey said and lifted the balls of fuzzy fur onto the bed. "Would you like to sleep with McKenzie tonight?" Hailey held the girl cat up to her ear and pretended to listen. "She says yes." She held up the boy kitten to her ear. "He also says yes."

McKenzie pushed onto her elbows and stroked the boy cat's head. He snarled but allowed her to continue. "The cats are like you and Uncle Finn. My uncle used to be super grouchy like when Mr. Whiskerfrown can't find Sweet Miss Marmalade. And you're nice and pretty and kind of orange like Sweet Miss Marmalade. I know I came up with their names, but those are a lot of letters for cat names. Like McKenzie Fiona Starrycard-Dunleavy."

"Your uncle and I shortened their names and call them Sweetie and Whiskers."

McKenzie yawned. "Sweetie and Whiskers. I like those names." She sighed and sank into the pillow. "Will you sing to me? My mommy sings 'Twinkle, Twinkle, Little Star' to me before I fall asleep."

"I know that one. It's one of my favorites," Hailey replied, resting the kittens next to McKenzie. She hummed the tune in that soothing honey-molasses tone, then sang the words. Cast in a golden glow of the lamp on the bedside table, she was like something out of a dream—something his heart had ached for this last year.

A home.

Of course, Starrycard Creek was his physical home. But he'd been adrift, mindlessly seeking things to fix, items to mend, unsure of how to undo what had been done to him. Uncertain of where he'd gone wrong. He closed his eyes. Her voice washed over him like a spell, setting him free.

A question rose to his consciousness. A question that had lived in his heart since the moment he pressed his lips to hers.

Could her love fix someone as messed up as him?

Just as the notion materialized, he felt her. He opened his eyes as Hailey looked up. She peered through the fluttering space between the curtains, and their eyes met. It was as if she could see into his soul. He'd known her less than a week but couldn't imagine his life without her.

She broke their connection and rose from the edge of the bed. He listened to her footsteps. The doorknob turned, and there she was. She exited the cabin and joined him on the deck.

Crossing her arms, she rubbed her hands against her sheer sleeves. "McKenzie's asleep," she reported, peering into the woods, and not meeting his eye.

He took a step toward her. "Are you cold?"

"A little." She glanced over her shoulder into the cabin. "I can get my jacket."

"No, take mine." He unzipped his worn Golden Tech gray hoodie and draped it over her shoulders. "And there's a fire pit, too. We can warm up there," he added awkwardly, sounding like a fire pit salesman as he flipped the switch. A blue flame trailed along a line of coals. "See, it's real fire."

Holy hell, where was a roll of duct tape when a man needed it?

"It's cozy." She sat on the log bench across from the flames and scanned the deck. "I haven't been out here yet."

"We've been too busy *getting busy* inside," he replied, inwardly cringing as he sat beside her.

What was wrong with him? Barely an hour ago, she'd told him she believed all she was to him was a booty call, and idiotic utterances like *we've been too busy getting busy* didn't help him change her interpretation of their situation.

He leaned forward. "I heard you singing to Kenz."

She nodded, still not meeting his gaze.

And he was still on her shit list.

He rubbed his hands on his sweatpants. "Thanks for taking care of her so I could clean up."

Hailey stared at the flames. "Would you mind if I borrowed a blanket and a pillow?"

Why would she ask that?

He tried to get a read on her. The flickering flames created dancing shadows, masking her expression. "We have pillows and blankets in our bedroom—in the bedroom," he stammered. "With Kenz here, I figured I'd take the couch, and you could stay in the guest room."

"I'm sleeping at my place tonight," she answered, eyes locked on the fire pit.

"At Higgins Hideaway?" he shot back. "I had to get rid of most of the furniture. Everything that's left is in the shed. Where will you sleep?"

"I'll be fine on the floor." She turned to him. Her bottom lip trembled for a fraction of a second before she regained control. "I don't think McKenzie will get sick in the night. She ate some crackers and drank half a cup of peppermint tea. It seems to have settled her stomach. But if she needs anything, you can call me. I'll hurry over."

"Are you serious?" A knot in his stomach twisted, the physical manifestation of the pain ripping through his chest.

"I am," she said and rose to her feet.

He stood and clasped her hand in his. "Don't go. Marmalade, please don't leave me."

She offered him the saddest smile he'd ever seen. "I don't have a reason to stay."

Fucking hell! This was all his fault.

She started to pull away, but he wouldn't let her go.

"McKenzie was right about my smile. Remember, she mentioned it when we were on the dance floor," he began. "She was right about how you're the reason it's back."

Hailey stilled, allowing her slender hand to remain in his grasp. "What made you lose it?"

"Are you sure you want to know?"

"I want to know everything, Finn. I want to understand. You're a puzzle to me, and I've only got a handful of pieces."

"If I tell you the whole story, will you stay with me?" Christ, he sounded desperate—but he was. He was stuck between losing her and regurgitating a truth he'd barely acknowledged over the last year.

The firelight caressed her features, amplifying the intensity of her gaze. "I'm here now, Finn. That's the best I can give you."

He'd take it. He couldn't let her leave. If these precious days with her had taught him anything, it was that he needed this woman.

He stroked his thumb across her knuckles. "I was engaged to a woman named Susan Randall. The night I met you on the road—when I thought you were a deranged bride and you thought I was an axe murderer—was a year to the day since . . ." He recalled standing in the hallway as the door to his fiancée's hotel room swung open, and his life crumbled around him.

"Start from the beginning," Hailey suggested gently.

She was his lifeline—a lifeline giving him one final chance.

He tightened his grip on her hand. "I met Susan in college. Met is probably the wrong word. Everyone knew who Susan was. There's a building on campus named after her family. They own a publishing and media conglomerate. When I was a senior, Susan and I were on the same team that won the paper tower competition."

"The one Dr. Schneider spoke about today?"

"Yes," he answered, slipping back in time. "Everyone liked Susan. She was funny and attractive. I was a kid from a little mountain town. Coming from New York City, she was like a celebrity—this worldly, wealthy heiress. But she wasn't a snob. I appreciated that she wanted to understand her family's business and learn how the machines in her family's publishing company worked."

Hailey nodded, listening intently. "You two were college sweethearts?"

"No, she had a boyfriend. He was going to school in New York. Susan and I were friends. It wasn't until about three or four years after I graduated with my master's degree that we connected again. I was living with my brother Owen here in Starrycard Creek. We're the ones who stepped up and said we wanted to take over Starrycard Paper. He'd run the artistic side. I took on business development and operations. I worked twenty-four seven, attending events and looking for new avenues for expansion. Thanks to my patent design bringing in some cash, we had some money to play with. But it wasn't enough to propel an entire company to the next level. The thing about Starrycard paper is it can't be mass-produced. To maintain the quality, I needed to find a niche market that would value the time, care, and craftsmanship that goes into our paper. It would have to be a market catering to events with great sentimental meaning. I researched the wedding industry and decided to put my energy there and focus on wedding invitations."

Hailey listened closely. "That makes sense."

"I was at a trade show—a luxury wedding expo in LA—and I looked across the room and saw Susan. She was heading up business development for her family's business. They'd recently acquired three of the largest wedding websites and corresponding printed publications. I asked her to dinner to talk business and learned that she was still living in New York, but she and her boyfriend had just broken up, and he'd moved to Georgia for work. That weekend with Susan was a whirlwind. We were insep-arable. I had some cash now. I wasn't a penniless student anymore. I was able to take her out and we started dating." He paused, preparing himself.

"Go on," she encouraged.

He peered at the fire. "We started meeting at different trade shows. I was making good connections with top wedding plan-ners. I was working my ass off, but I was also growing enamored with Susan and with this flashy life of luxury hotel suites and gourmet meals. We decided to date exclusively. After about six months, we were invited to an alumni dinner event at Golden Tech. It was a big deal for high-dollar donors. I'd donated so I could be there with Susan. That's where I proposed with a dozen roses in one hand and a ring in the other. Looking back, I should have known better. Panic had flashed in her eyes when I opened the ring box. I chalked it up to shock. But she said yes." A brittle little smile curved his lips. "I thought I was on top of the world. We were still doing the long-distance thing, but I figured that had to change. For someone who methodically plans every step, I'd tossed that thinking out the window. I was caught up in growing the business and being engaged to this woman who was so out of my league." He stared up at the sky. "Owen warned me that I wasn't acting like myself. That the expensive suits and thousand-dollar shoes weren't me, wasn't Starrycard Paper. I didn't listen. I thought he was being short-sighted and accused him of not seeing the opportunities I was bringing in. I said I had to look and dress the part. He said the product should speak for itself."

"Did you get any deals?" Hailey asked.

A coppery taste invaded his mouth. "No."

"What about your ex-fiancée's connections—the websites and magazines?"

"There were talks, but they ended one night in Atlanta."

Hailey cocked her head to the side. "Atlanta, Georgia?"

He tightened his grip on her hand. "Susan had a meeting there."

"I don't understand. Did she decide to partner with another paper company?"

A lump formed in his throat. "She decided to choose a different partner."

"A different partner?" Hailey repeated, then rested her hand on his knee. "Wait. The ex-boyfriend was in Georgia. Oh, Finn."

"My family doesn't know what I'm about to tell you. All they know is that Susan and I broke up and called off the engagement after I went to see her in Atlanta."

"What happened?"

"I'd gone to surprise her and show her the wedding invitations I'd made on Starrycard paper and embossed myself. I had it in my head that this was it. This was how the world would be introduced to my family's company. It was late when I got to her hotel. My flight had been delayed. I figured it didn't matter. She didn't know I was coming. So, I'm holding the invitation in my hand like I'm transporting a vital organ. I knocked, and to be funny, I said, 'Room Service,' then slipped the card under the door. But Susan wasn't the one who got it."

"The ex," Hailey said, reading between the lines.

"The door opened and there was this guy in a towel, hair still wet from the shower, holding the invitation. I looked past him, thinking I had the wrong room, but then I saw Susan in a robe. Wet hair. Disheveled bed sheets. A vase of roses on the end table. I stood there like a fool. She said that they reconnected a few weeks after we got engaged. They ran into each other in New York, and she realized he was her soulmate. She kept telling me she never meant to hurt me, that she cared for me, but she loved someone else. Then she handed back the invitation. That was the last time I had any contact with her. She left messages and emailed a few times, but I never read or listened to them. Just delete, delete, delete." His shoulders slumped. The crushing weight of his humiliation settled upon him. All he had to do was look in his wallet. The constant reminder was always with him.

"I'm so sorry, Finn," Hailey said tenderly.

He sighed. "Leaving the hotel, I swore to myself I was done with weddings and invitations and lofty business development ideas. Done with love. Done with everything that reminded me of what a chump I'd become. I came home, moved up here, and started fixing whatever didn't work. It was all I could do. Fix, mend, repair, replace. It didn't matter what it was. I could fix it. What I couldn't fix was my shit judgment. My shame. And then, on the one-year anniversary of the breakup, you show up in the middle of my street. I'd been numb for so long, then for the first time in ages, I felt a spark, a flicker of desire. It was this over-whelming need to keep you close to me, to help you, to care for you. I . . ." He swallowed the word.

"What is it, Finn?"

"I'm *falling* for you," he said, amending what his heart wanted him to say.

"You are?"

"You're what's holding me together. I need you. I need what we have. You and your big heart and the brush of your lips against mine are bringing me back, fixing me, bit by bit. I'm sorry for how I acted and what I said. I know it was cruel. I don't want whatever this is—what we have—to be over. I get hung up on my insecurities when people are around. I can't stop remembering what it felt like to have Susan tell me she didn't want me while her boyfriend stood there, staring at me. That's why I lose my shit when we're around people. Why I act like—"

"A grumpy, sullen, sulking business card boyfriend?" Hailey supplied, but there was nothing but kindness in her voice.

He released a nervous chuckle. "Yeah, a grumpy, sullen, sulking business card boyfriend." He angled his body toward her and took her hands in his. "You have to know what you mean to me, Marmalade. You have to feel it." He stared into her eyes, trying to see if she understood. He watched her. Anguish marred her features—the result of the push and pull of her emotions battling in her head.

"Finn, I don't know what to say."

He cupped her face in his hand. "What do you feel when you're with me?"

Tears glistened in her eyes as that sweet slide of a smile bloomed on her lips.

Joy rippled through his chest. He knew that smile. It was the same expression she gave him every day when he picked her up from school. She still cared for him. She couldn't hide it.

He tipped her chin, prepared to kiss her full lips, when Hailey winced.

"Ow! That was painful," she yelped and pulled away.

"Being with me is painful?" he asked, utterly confused, then mirrored her behavior as a sharp object collided with the top of his head. "Ow! What was that?" he exclaimed and rubbed the tender spot.

Hailey pointed at the roof. "It's them."

He followed her line of sight. Four pairs of raccoon eyes glared at them. The light from the fire pit distorted their little bodies. He peered at the pair of prickly pinecones at his feet. "Are they really dropping stuff on us? Ow!" he cried again as the colossal jerk raccoons answered his question with another pinecone to the noggin.

"I think they're mad because we evicted them from my cabin."

"They're raccoons," he exclaimed. "They don't get to live in a cabin." He zeroed in on the mischief makers. "Your home is in the forest. You're wild animals. And if I'm being honest, you're a bunch of asshole wild animals."

"Finn?" Hailey uttered under her breath.

"Yeah?"

"We need to get inside."

An onslaught of pinecones rained onto his deck. *Was this normal raccoon behavior?* He wasn't about to wait around and find out. Muscle memory kicked in. He whisked Hailey into his arms and sprinted toward the cabin. Adrenaline coursed through his veins as he balanced her on one arm, threw open the door, then slammed it shut behind them.

Breathing hard, they stared out the window as the masked bandits scurried onto the porch and took off into the woods.

"At least it was only pinecones and not raccoon poop," Hailey offered, back to gazing at him like he was her entire world.

For what had to be the millionth time in six days, he found himself lost in the depths of her amber eyes. "I've been projectile puked-on tonight. What's a little scat?"

Hailey's laughter sparkled like stars, illuminating the darkness in his heart. She wrapped her arms around his shoulders, then kicked her feet. "I always seem to end up here."

"Which is exactly where I want you."

She observed him as if trying to decipher the unspoken feelings etched on his face. "Do you mean, where my *business card boyfriend* wants me or something else?"

"We know what we mean to each other," he replied, dodging her question.

He knew what she was asking. Was he her boyfriend—without conditions? The vice on his heart tightened, holding him back from putting a label on their relationship. It damn near killed him. He wanted to say more—wanted to pour his heart out to her. But he'd done that before and gotten burned. Would his words be enough? Could she see that he was trying? A thread of fear wove itself around his heart. She deserved more—and in time, he could be that man, couldn't he?

What if this went to hell like it did with Susan? What if Hailey saw how broken and pathetic he truly was?

He swallowed past the lump in his throat and ignored the voice in his head and the sickening twist in his belly.

She touched his cheek, and like magic, her caress banished the clawing voices in his head. "I know what you are to me, Finnegan Starrycard, local handyman," she said softly, her caramel gaze conveying the depth of her feelings. "I'm in—"

"What are you guys doing out here?" McKenzie chirped.

He spun around and nearly dropped Hailey on her ass.

McKenzie stood in the middle of the kitchen with a kitten tucked under each arm and a crease to her brow.

The child cocked her head to the side. "Why are you holding Miss Higgins like a baby?"

Think, think, think!

"We were outside on the deck, and this is how I sometimes help Miss Higgins come inside."

Jesus, that was bad. But would the kid buy it?

"Thank you for your assistance," Hailey added, grinning like a spokesmodel for being ushered over a threshold. "We're safely inside. You can set me down."

"Right, yeah," he stammered and returned her to the ground.

"McKenzie," Hailey said, dropping to a knee to be at eye level with the child. "How are you feeling? Do you feel like you're going to get sick?"

"No, I feel okay, but . . ." the child looked from Sweetie to Whiskers. "The kitties and I want to make a smooshy sandwich."

Hailey glanced up at him, looking for a translation. He shrugged. Smooshy sandwich? He didn't know what the kid was talking about.

"Are you hungry, Kenz? Do you want a regular sandwich? Like a PB and J?"

"No, a smooshy sandwich isn't food. It's when I climb into Mommy and Daddy's bed and wiggle in between them, and we smoosh together."

"I see," he replied. The homesickness was kicking in. He kneeled, then took her little hand in his. "Kenz, your mom and dad aren't feeling well. We get to have you here with us tonight for a sleepover so they can rest."

"I know, Uncle Finn. The kitties and I don't want to make a smooshy sandwich with them. We want to make a smooshy sandwich with you and Miss Higgins in your big bed."

"Oh," he answered. He turned to Hailey. "What do you think?"

"I think it's a terrific idea."

McKenzie beamed. "You do?"

"Sure," Hailey replied and guided the girl toward the bedroom. "You're in charge, little star. Tell us where we're supposed to go to make this smooshy sandwich."

McKenzie surveyed the bed. "Uncle Finn can be on the left side, and Miss Higgins, you can go on the right side."

Hailey smoothed the kid's bedhead. "How about you call me Hailey when we're at the cabin."

The wattage on McKenzie's grin cranked up a few more notches. "Okay, *Hailey*, you're on the right side. And you guys can hold the kitties. Uncle Finn, take Sweetie, and Hailey can hold Whiskers."

He caught Hailey's eye as they took their usual spots in bed. "I bet you didn't think you'd be making smooshy sandwiches in bed with me tonight."

She pressed her lips together, holding back laughter, and flashed him a look—one of her teacher looks—that said, zip it, mister.

Now, he was on the cusp of a giggle-fest.

"Are you guys ready for the best night of your life?" McKenzie asked, standing at the foot of the bed as she lifted the bottom of the comforter.

It took everything he had not to burst into laughter. He wasn't alone. He caught Hailey biting her lip, working damned hard to hold it together.

He regained control, schooled his features, and eyed his niece. "Bring it on, Kenz. It's Smoosh City time at the Starrycard Cabin."

With a triumphant clap, the child wiggled under the covers, moving toward them like a determined inchworm set on smooshy sandwich world domination.

He watched the tiny lump move closer to the pillows and turned to his bedmate. "Ready for the best night of your life, Marmalade?" he teased.

She cracked, her cheeks growing rosy as a tumble of laughter escaped past her lips. "Is that what you're promising?"

What was he promising?

There it was, that prickle determined to ruin his happiness.

He disregarded it. "Something like that."

McKenzie's head popped out from beneath the blanket. "Here I am. Let's get smooshy."

"How does getting smooshy work?" he asked.

"I lie like this in the middle," the girl said, flat as a board on her back. "You and Miss—I mean, Hailey—lie on your side and look at each other."

They adjusted the kittens and snuggled in, gazing at each other over the top of McKenzie's head.

"And you hold hands on my belly," the girl added.

With her auburn waves framing her face, Hailey Higgins was so damned beautiful. He drank her in and offered his hand. She peered at it for a beat, then rested her left hand on his palm. He focused on her ring finger—on that thin strip of lighter skin he'd homed in on that first night. It seemed to have disappeared, like each day in Starrycard Creek had helped erase the damage that asshole Grant had done to her.

"Just like that," his niece said, resting her little hands on theirs. She yawned and relaxed between them. "This is a smooshy sandwich," she continued, losing her second wind as her words slurred together like a sleepy stream.

He lifted his head to check on his niece. Her chest rose and fell as she drifted off peacefully.

"Miss Smooshy Sandwich is out for the count," he whispered, then met Hailey's eye. "This wasn't what I had planned for tonight, but my niece is right about one thing."

Hailey yawned, her eyes growing heavy. "And what's that, handyman?"

"This might be the best night of my life," he confessed.

She smiled that smile that was just for him, then closed her eyes and hummed a sweet, sleepy sound. "I was about to say the same thing."

He watched her succumb to slumber. He'd done this every

night she'd been with him, but tonight was different. If McKenzie hadn't interrupted them, he knew Hailey would have told him she loved him.

Did he deserve her affection?

He swallowed hard and concentrated on her like if he looked away, she might disappear, and life would revert to that dim, dark place he'd existed this past year.

"Marmalade?" he said softly.

Nothing. She'd joined his niece in the land of sweet dreams.

He stroked his thumb across her knuckles. "This is the best day of my life because even though I've only known you for six days, I'm so in love with you, Hailey Higgins. I can barely breathe without you."

There. He'd said it. Now, he had to find the courage to speak those words when she was awake.

Meow.

He peered down at Mr. Whiskerfrown. The kitten had poked up his head and glowered at him like the tiny beast could read his mind. The cat appeared ready to claw his eyes like he was warning him not to hurt the sweet Miss Higgins.

Did the cat know something he didn't?

An unsettling question crept into his mind. Did he have the capacity to give his heart to Hailey fully and without reservation? That's what she'd want—and deserve. It's why she read those love stories. It was why she kept her parents' pickle jar with her.

He tightened his grip on her hand and drank in her whisper of freckles and those auburn lashes against her porcelain skin.

Don't fuck this up.

He'd get there. He'd figure it out. He'd tell her how he felt. He would. What he couldn't do was allow the raw, bitter part of him, the brokenhearted sap, fearful of looking like a fool, to lead him astray. He closed his eyes, heavy with exhaustion, and recalled the first time he kissed her. The warmth. The safety. The desire.

The love.

Jesus, that cherry-chocolate moment had turned his life upside down and cracked open his fortress of a heart.

She was never a transaction.

She was a goddamned treasure.

That was it. Focus on Hailey. It was the only way. He swallowed past a lump in his throat, concentrating on the angel of a woman. "Sweet Miss Marmalade, you're the only one who can save me," he whispered like a prayer.

CHAPTER
Sixteen

HAILEY

"TO all the educators in the room, I'd like to congratulate you on officially completing the Golden Tech STEM Sparks Elementary Enrichment Training. You've been exposed to a plethora of new information these past few days. It's normal to feel overwhelmed and excited simultaneously," Dr. Schneider said from the podium in the cavernous lecture hall. "Take a look at the final page in your training binder," she continued. "We've listed every participant's name, school, and location. I encourage you to connect with the educators in your area. We strongly support collaboration. And remember, my team and I are an email or call away. We're grateful to have you onboard. That'll do it for the training portion. I look forward to seeing everyone later today for the farewell reception."

Hailey clapped for the woman along with the other teachers. Dr. Schneider was correct. Taking in the new information was like drinking from a fire hose. Nevertheless, she couldn't wait to put what she'd learned into practice in the classroom. Two jam-packed days of hands-on training from eight in the morning until eight at night and a half-day session today had her brain buzzing with ideas and possibilities. She shifted in her seat and inhaled a sharp breath. It wasn't just her brain that was on overload. Thanks to sharing a hotel room with her business card boyfriend, her body buzzed, deliciously aching due to nights spent in orgasmic bliss.

That wasn't quite right.

Finnegan Starrycard had rocked her world in the early morning hours as well. Her pulse kicked up as her body yearned for his touch. This morning, she'd mounted him like she'd majored in naughty rodeo arts. With her hands pressed to his bare, muscled chest, she'd ridden his magnificent cock, taking all of him, reveling in his heated breaths and gruff moans. She could still feel his rough hands on her ass, her breasts, her hips, her face. He'd gazed up at her, eyes glittering with carnal lust. He'd whispered sweet nothings and filthy-dirty nothings in her ear. But he hadn't uttered the four-letter word he'd whispered when he thought she was asleep a little more than two weeks ago.

Yes, she'd heard him profess his love.

Should she have pretended to be asleep?

It wasn't an easy question to answer.

When he'd called her Marmalade, she'd heard the conviction in his tone, the clawing need in his voice to confess what was going on inside his head—and possibly his heart.

I'm so in love with you, Hailey Higgins. I can barely breathe without you.

She'd waited so long to hear those words, but what he'd said next sent a shiver down her spine. He'd said she was the one who could save him.

Could she do that?

He'd been hurt and thrown for a loop when it came to love. He'd retreated from his life and questioned his every choice.

Would he question how she felt about him, too?

She could only hope he'd trust her.

She'd wanted to tell him she'd fallen in love with him at least a million times over the last sixteen days.

But she hadn't.

That would change today.

As they showered together this morning, a soaped-up Finn

had mentioned he was working on a surprise for her. He'd tried to school his features, but she'd seen the excitement glinting in his eyes.

Would he proclaim his love here, at his beloved college?

Or perhaps she should make the first move and tell him she'd fallen in love with him. Sharing her feelings first might give him the strength to do the same. But he loved her. He'd spoken the words.

If she was right about her feeling, this trip could be the turning point. They could return to Starrycard Creek as a committed couple. It could be the beginning of her happily ever after—her Shooting-Stars-worthy love story. She could build a life with Finn in Starrycard Creek and gain a family. She adored Eliza. Goldie and Maeve were lovely, and she'd met Owen, Kieran, and Rex when they'd dropped by the school to watch McKenzie's first-grade music recital.

Could she see herself as a Starrycard?

Could the quaint mountain town become her home?

Finn had to want that, too, right?

A tiny seed of unease festered in her heart at the thought of their current situation.

Nobody knew they were anything more than roommates.

They'd remained hidden away on the mountain. Besides running into town to grab groceries, she and Finn hadn't been out and about together. But it wasn't entirely his fault. She'd been swamped with work. The end of the school year was always chaotic, but it was especially busy for a substitute teacher. She had to familiarize herself with the school's testing protocols, and each child had to be assessed in reading, writing, and mathematics. And she still had to plan engaging lessons for each subject. One teacher did the job of three people this time of the year. And she wasn't the only one with a lot on her plate. Finn had been equally busy, dividing his time between renovating her cabin and putting in hours at the paper company. When they were together, they spent the bulk of their time wrapped up in each other. She wasn't complaining, but something inside her knew their situation was on the brink of change. She could feel it in her bones.

She thought of her parents' pickle jar and all those words of love her father had penned to her mother. And then there were the romantic, heartbreaking notes her great-uncle had written and never sent to his Cookie.

I should have shouted my love for you from the rooftop.

That twist of unease returned when someone tapped her shoulder.

"Why are you listed like this, Hailey?"

Hailey met the gaze of Jana Diaz, a lovely teacher from Denver, Colorado, whom she'd gotten to know over the last couple of days. The two were close in age and had been assigned as partners in one of the STEM workshops and ended up striking up a fast friendship.

Jana tapped a page in her binder. Hailey peered at the piece of paper and spied her name.

Hailey Higgins
School: To be determined
Location: To be determined

Jana tucked a lock of dark hair behind her ear. "I thought you said you were from a little mountain town a few hours south of Golden. Starry, something."

"Starrycard Creek. That's where I'm teaching now. But it's a substitute teaching position. When Dr. Schneider invited me to the training, she understood I might not continue there," Hailey answered as that seed of unease in her chest grew. Her phone pinged an incoming text—a welcome distraction. She pushed past the pickle jar—yes, she brought it with her—and fished her cell from her tote. What she saw distracted her from her worries.

"Is it important?" Jana asked.

"It is. It's my best friend. She works for a conservation organization. She's been in the field for weeks. I haven't heard from her in a while. I should reply. Her internet connection is often pretty spotty."

Jana closed the binder. "I understand."

"Jana and Hailey," a woman called from the aisle. She gestured to a few other teachers attending the training sessions. "We decided to take a walk around campus before the farewell reception. Do you want to join us?"

"I'm in," Jana chimed.

Hailey glanced around the near-empty lecture hall. "I'll have to pass. I should hang back and message my friend. But you guys have fun."

Jana slipped her binder into her bag and stood. "So, you're not sure where you'll be teaching next year?"

Hailey plastered a smile on her lips. "No, nothing's been decided."

That wasn't exactly the whole truth.

Hailey assessed her oversized canvas tote and zeroed in on an envelope slipped inside her planner. It wasn't just any old envelope. It contained a Starrycard Creek Elementary teaching contract. The school secretary had given it to her the day before she and Finn left for Golden. All she had to do was sign it, and the job was hers. But she hadn't. And she hadn't mentioned it to Finn either. Trepidation wove itself in with the seed of unease. She ignored the foreboding feelings. After whatever special surprise he had planned for her, she'd tell him about the job offer.

"Let's talk later, Hailey. I'd love for you to meet my mom," Jana said.

Hailey cocked her head to the side and eyed the woman. "Your mom is coming to the campus?"

"She lives in Denver, and the city is only about twenty minutes from here. She's in education, too. She's a principal at a school not far from mine."

"Sure," Hailey said warmly. "My parents were teachers. It's always great to meet families who dedicate themselves to education. I'd love to meet your mom."

"Good! We'll catch up later," Jana replied, then joined the masses exiting the lecture hall.

Hailey tapped her screen and scanned the message.

> Isabelle: OMG! I'm sorry it's taken forever for me to get back to you. We had to spend a couple of extra weeks in the field. I'm just seeing your bonkers text. That was not the message I expected to get from you, Hails.

Hailey read the last text she'd sent her best friend.

> Hailey: Grant and I broke up at the altar. He knocked-up his side chick and married her instead of me. I know that sounds insane, but I'm okay. I'm living in a cabin with a handyman in Starrycard Creek, Colorado, and teaching at the local elementary school. Text back when you can.

She'd sent the message to her friend on her first day at Starrycard Creek Elementary during her lunch break.

Dots appeared on the screen as Izzy wrote another message.

> Isabelle: Starrycard Creek, Colorado? I know of that place. There are a few endangered species in the area. But forget about that. Why are you there?

Because the universe has one bizarro sense of humor. Hailey chuckled, then knocked out a reply.

> Hailey: I had a long-lost great-uncle pass away, and I inherited his mountain cabin in Starrycard Creek.

> Isabelle: WOW! I was not expecting that either. Are you living in this cabin with the handyman? What's going on there?

Here's where it got a little thorny.

Hailey chewed her lip.

> Hailey: No, I'm living in the handyman's cabin next door. My cabin needs some work before I can move in. The handyman is helping me with that.

> Isabelle: Did you know him before you got there?

Hailey exhaled a slow breath. Izzy wouldn't like this answer, but she had to stick with the truth.

> Hailey: No, not exactly.

> Isabelle: Hails! Details NOW! I'm at a tiny airfield with a dirt runway in one of the most remote locations on the planet. I've only got a few minutes with WiFi before we fly out.

"Buckle up, Isabelle," Hailey whispered to the cell as her thumbs moved at light speed.

> Hailey: His name is Finnegan. I thought he was an axe murderer, but he's a handyman and helps run his family's artisan papermaking company. I've been living with him while he fixes my cabin. We're fostering a pair of kittens.

She hit send, then cringed. *Heaven help her!* Her message sounded insane.

> Isabelle: Did you hit your head, girl? You thought he was an axe murderer but agreed to live with him?

Hailey: He's not an axe murderer. It was a mix-up on my part. It was dark, raining, and my car broke down. When I met Finn, he was holding an axe and standing on the side of the road.

Isabelle: That sounds exactly like where an axe murderer would be. Woman's car breaking down in the middle of nowhere encountering a man wielding an axe sounds like a horror movie plot.

Hailey chuckled and typed out a reply.

Hailey: I promise you. He's not an axe murderer. He's wonderful. He's my business card boyfriend.

Isabelle: Wonderful? Your business card boyfriend? Hails, I ask again, are you sure you're okay?

Hailey: Yes, I know it sounds nuts, but I like him, Mel. His family makes the paper my dad used to write the pickle jar notes.

Isabelle: Seriously!?!?! What are the chances? That's a crazy coincidence.

It was pretty amazing.

Hailey sighed as an invisible cocoon of warmth and joy wrapped around her. She knew what she needed to tell her best friend and typed the message.

I've fallen in love with Finn and the town. I'm happy here. So happy.

She reread her message, but before she could hit send, dots appeared, and another text from Izzy populated.

> Isabelle: My time is up, Hails. We have to take off before the weather rolls in. I'll call or text when I can. Don't get axe murdered. Still, I'd rather you shack up with a serial killer over the nimrod Rimnod. Love you! Signing off for now.

Hailey reread the unsent text. Should she send it so Izzy could read it the next time she had WiFi?

"Miss, cell phone use is prohibited in the lecture hall. And you might want to look up from your phone. I believe your class ended."

Hailey gasped and dropped her cell. It clattered on the table desk that ran the length of each row, then fell into her tote. She looked up to find her handyman.

"You scared me." She pressed her hand to her chest, her heart beating a mile a minute.

"You were smiling at the screen."

"I was texting with Izzy."

"Your environmentalist friend out in the field?"

"Yeah, she had WiFi for a few minutes. We got to message each other."

Finn sank into the seat next to her, rested his elbows on the writing ledge, and dished out a cocky grin. "Did you mention me?"

It took everything she had to maintain a neutral expression. "Maybe," she purred.

"Maybe?" he echoed, raising an eyebrow.

"I told her I met an axe murderer."

He chuckled. "I'm sure that sparked quite a conversation. I wondered what happened to you, Marmalade."

She loved the thought of him camped out in front of the lecture hall.

"Were you waiting for me, handyman?"

He set his satchel on the chair to his right. "I was, and I learned something new about you."

She held his gaze. "And what's that?"

He drank her in, those sage-green eyes twinkling with mischief. "I've always pegged you as a good girl. I didn't take you for one to text during class. Very bold—especially when Schneider's at the podium. I would never have dared set my cell on the table in her class. You're a naughty schoolteacher, Miss Marmalade."

Oh no! She was not *naughty* when it came to her profession.

"Finn," she whisper-shouted and scanned the room. A few stragglers, several rows ahead of her, were left. They remained in the hall, staring at their phones as she'd been doing. But she sure didn't want any of her colleagues thinking she was a naughty-girl schoolteacher. "I wasn't texting during class. I'd never do that. And I am not a," she glanced around to confirm no one was close enough to hear her, "naughty schoolteacher," she mouthed.

"You're not?" he asked with a crafty twist to his lips and rested his hand on her knee.

Her core clenched at his touch. Her skin tingled as he stroked his thumb across her bare skin. The weather had been gorgeous, and she'd chosen to wear a red dress that brought out the highlights in her auburn hair. It hit slightly above her knee, and Finn was taking advantage of her choice.

He slid his hand up her thigh a few inches, edging up the scarlet fabric.

She inhaled a shaky breath. "What are you doing? We're in a lecture hall."

"I know where we are, Marmalade. I sat in this very seat many, many times when I was a student."

"Did you engage in this type of hands-on behavior back in college?" she asked, her breathing growing shallow as he slid his rough hand farther up her thigh.

"Hell no. I was too much of a nerd back then. But I fantasized about doing this to a sexy redhead. I guess that makes you my ultimate fantasy girl. Now, I need you to do something for me."

"What's that?" she asked, eyeing the two participants several rows in front of them, focused on their phones. They didn't seem to notice the hanky-panky—thank goodness.

"Open your legs, Sweet Miss Marmalade," he whispered against the shell of her ear.

The breath caught in her throat. "But we're not alone."

Finn glanced at the stragglers. "That's what's going to make this so hot. Nobody will know what we're doing. I'm just some guy conversing with a beautiful woman. Come on, Marmalade. You want to come as badly as I want to make you come. Show me your naughty side, Hailey Higgins."

That voice manhandling her name would be her undoing.

And her business card boyfriend wasn't wrong. She ached for his touch. Unable to resist, she parted her thighs, giving him complete access to her most sensitive place.

"What will we talk about?" she rasped.

Lust gleamed in his eyes as he pushed aside her panties and teased her entrance, warm and so wet thanks to his touch. He worked her sensitive bud in maddeningly slow circles, winding her up like a horny Jack-in-the-box.

"You're going to tell me every nerdy engineering word you remember from your training."

Okay, she could manage that. Her brain hadn't completely turned to orgasm-obsessed mush yet.

"Thermoelectricity," she breathed, staring into his eyes.

"That's a good one. Keep going," he purred, dialing up his pace.

The door slammed, and she checked the room. They were the last two in the hall.

"Eyes on me, Marmalade," Finn demanded, which amped up her arousal.

She rocked against his hand. "Photo-elasticity," she got out between heated breaths.

"Altering visual properties when a material is exposed to a load. One of my favorites," he added, working her like the attentive machinist he was.

She gripped the edge of her seat. His low, gruff voice had her teetering on the edge.

"One more, Marmalade. Then I'll make you come so hard you'll wish you could halt and catch fire." He leaned in. "That's a term for when a machine malfunctions to the point where it becomes so potentially destructive, and the only option is to—"

"Let it burn," she answered, recalling the term. Not to mention, she was on the verge of combusting.

"Look at you," Finn said and slipped a finger inside her as he continued his relentless assault between her thighs. "Give me one more."

She bit her lip, on the brink of losing control. "Last term," she said in a wisp of an exhale. "Electromechanical resonance."

The deliciously devilish smirk stretched across his lips, signaling she'd chosen a good one.

She tightened her grip on the side of the chair. She couldn't hold back much longer.

"Electricity and vibration. Nice touch, Marmalade. See you on the other side."

This man.

She could hear the note of arrogance in his tone—so sure he could get her off on command. It would have been infuriating if it weren't one hundred percent true. He increased his pace and pressure, and she couldn't hold back. Unbridled, a jolt of titillating electricity and a heady vibration tore through her core. Swells of heat and ripples of pleasure washed over her, reaching every cell in her body. She held Finn's gaze, marveling at the man, who looked downright spellbound.

Pure wonder graced his face. "Christ, you're beautiful," he murmured, watching her like he could never get enough.

His eyes widened, mouth slightly agape, as she wound down from her release. "I live to make your body ache for my touch," he rasped in a gravelly, sensual, manhandling tone.

What does a gal say to that?

Nothing.

She blinked, bleary-eyed, unable to put a sentence together as she mooned over her ecstasy exporter.

Ecstasy exporter?

She chuckled.

He stroked her cheek. "What's so funny?"

She sighed. "My addled brain called you my ecstasy exporter."

"Your addled brain is damned right. I should put that on a business card."

She sighed again, drinking in the man. *And Lord have mercy!* He cleaned up well. Dressed in a crisp white button-up with the sleeves rolled up, exposing his muscled forearms and dark gray slacks, he was business card boyfriend sex-on-a-stick.

A door slammed, and the clap of footsteps echoed through the room.

Oh no!

They weren't alone.

CHAPTER
Seventeen

HAILEY

HAILEY GASPED as Dr. Schneider strolled toward the podium.

"Finn, I need your hands where I can see them. Now," she whispered-shouted, her gaze ping-ponging between her ecstasy exporter and the professor.

He teased her sensitive bundle of nerves with the pad of his thumb. "Are you sure? Schneider may want to watch."

Wide-eyed, she couldn't believe the man. "Finn," she mouthed.

"Finnegan? Is that you up there with Miss Higgins?" the professor called.

"Yes, it's me," he answered. Casually, like he didn't have a care in the world, he removed his fingers from her vagina. *And yowza!* Thank the stars for gigantic lecture halls with ample table desks to obscure any beneath-the-belt antics.

"Could you come down? I was hoping to speak to you." Christine Schneider raised her hand to block the lights illuminating the podium and stared straight at them. "Miss Higgins, you look like you've been put through the wringer."

Hailey froze, lips opening and closing like a mortified goldfish.

"Your training has wiped her out, Dr. Schneider. I don't know what else could have left her looking so spent," Finn replied with a devious smirk as he stood and looped his satchel over his shoulder.

Hailey tossed the man a look that said, Stop it, you super-freak and possible axe murderer!

It only enhanced the mischief glinting in his sage-green eyes.

Doing her best to exit the row like the sweet schoolteacher she usually was—and not someone who just experienced carnal bliss in a classroom—she smoothed her skirt, gathered her materials, and met Finn in the aisle.

"After you," he said, gesturing with the hand he'd used to export her earth-shattering orgasm.

"You're asking for trouble, handyman," she said under her breath as she passed him.

What did the cheeky man do? He tossed her a wink.

But she could not worry about Finn. She had to act like a professional.

Dr. Schneider picked up a few pieces of paper she must have left on the podium and joined them near the exit. "I hope you've both enjoyed your time here."

"I certainly have," Hailey replied. "I've learned so much these last few days."

"She has," Finn added. "I was testing Miss Higgins' knowledge of engineering terms. She was able to hold up under pressure."

This man deserved to be throttled. Still, that didn't stop the butterflies working overtime in her belly.

"That's wonderful to hear. It's helpful to get that type of feedback. I've also been given feedback from the students about you, Finnegan," the professor remarked.

"Really?" he replied, losing his devious edge.

"Turns out, you're their favorite judge. They appreciated your guidance."

"Guidance?" Hailey repeated, studying the man.

Finn shrugged. "It was nothing."

"Finn's being modest. He worked with the teams before the official judging began to help them understand the strengths and weaknesses of their design. The students knew who he was, thanks to the Starrycard valve. Now, they know how dedicated he is to helping others."

"Look at you," Hailey said, borrowing Finn's words.

The sweetest blush colored his tanned cheeks. "The students are terrific. I've thoroughly enjoyed my time with them."

"I'm glad to hear it. And that brings me to why I needed to chat with you, Finnegan. I'd love for you to return to campus and speak at the mechanical engineering dinner the night before graduation."

A grin stretched across the man's face. "I'd be honored."

"I'll have my assistant send you the details. And Miss Higgins?"

"Yes?"

"We'll be emailing you a survey to rate the quality of the training and update your employment information."

"I'll keep an eye out for it."

Christine Schneider checked her watch. "I need to get going. I'm meeting with a few alums in town for a board meeting, but we'll talk soon."

They said their goodbyes, and the professor headed out.

"Employment information?" Finn asked, opening the door for her.

"Just something for teachers to help us collaborate."

He nodded with a slight furrow to his brow.

She'd talk to him about her employment status later. After they shared their feelings, she would bust out the contract and sign it with him.

"Is it surprise time?" she asked, changing the subject.

The man's expression brightened. "It is absolutely surprise time. I had a little extra time today to do a bit of research. There are two surprises," he explained as they left the building and strolled across the quad, lined with sleepy oak trees. Students milled about the open space, and the mountain campus vibe seemed to put Finn at ease. "Follow me," he said, veering off the main walkway and onto a gravel path. He pulled out a hand-drawn map and then glanced around.

She peered at the rudimentary drawing. "Did you make that?"

"No, the woman at the alumni office did. It's directions to surprise number one. She said this spot wasn't easy to find since they'd made some landscaping changes about twenty years ago."

Hailey flicked her gaze from the slip of paper and eyed the man. "Why were you at the alumni office?"

"Part of the surprise. I went looking for information about your great-uncle since we know he went here. In a stroke of luck, I happened to know the woman working in the office. I went to school with her grandson. I asked her to search for your great-uncle's name. She wasn't supposed to, but she made an exception because Albert was deceased, and I told her I was asking on behalf of his great-niece. She came up with two donations. He'd gifted a hefty sum to Golden Tech back in the sixties and bought an on-campus donor gift more recently."

"How recent?"

"About five years before he passed away."

"What did he buy?" she pressed.

"That's what we're about to see, Marmalade."

"You don't know what it is?"

"I only know where it is. Are you up for a little adventure with your business card boyfriend?" he asked, taking her hand as they disappeared into a secluded, twisting and turning sea of green.

She glanced up to get her bearing and spied the mountains. They had to be on the periphery of the campus.

She watched her step as the greenery thickened. "This isn't a trick, is it? You don't have an axe in that satchel of yours, do you?"

"Do you feel like I'm leading you to your demise?" he teased.

She ducked beneath a rogue limb. "A little."

"Rest assured, I did not pack my axe," he said, pocketing the map as they entered a small clearing. "And here it is. Welcome to surprise number one."

Finn stepped aside, and Hailey took in a wooden bench among a burst of spring greens and towering trees.

"This is what my great-uncle donated to the school?"

"It is according to the alumni records."

She studied the object. "It's a beautiful bench, but I wonder why he chose to put it here. Who would know about this place?" she mused, wiping loose twigs and dead leaves from the seat. She was about to sit when a lone ray of sunlight cut through the foliage. It glinted off something attached to the back. She brushed off a smattering of dirt and uncovered a clue. "There's a little plaque with an engraved message."

"Does it say his name?" Finn asked.

Hailey chipped away at a dried coating of mud. "It says For Cookie, always my critical component." She turned to Finn. "It has to be my great-uncle's Cookie."

"It must be." Finn stood there and grinned like someone told him he'd won the lottery.

"Everything okay?" she asked.

"More than okay. I'm really happy to be here with you, Hailey."

"Me too."

Alone in this wooded refuge, he tipped up her chin and pressed a whisper-soft kiss to her lips.

"My Sweet Miss Marmalade," he purred.

He wrapped his arm around her shoulders and examined the gift. "There's something familiar about this bench. I can't place it, though."

She leaned into him. "I wonder if Cookie knows about it."

"I don't know, Marmalade. Cookie might not even be alive."

He was right.

"Always my critical component," she repeated, reading the words aloud. "He loved her for his entire life. And there's a chance she never knew."

"That's no way to live," Finn said softly.

Her heart hammered as heady anticipation set in.

Was this the moment he'd proclaim his feelings?

He kissed the top of her head. "Ready for surprise number two?"

"Sure," she replied, hating that she had to force a smile. Perhaps the next location was where he wanted to proclaim his undying love.

They left the quiet sanctuary and returned to the quad.

She tried to read him. "Do you need a map?"

"No, I know where to go."

They passed a few buildings before she figured out their destination. She peered at the giant *G* on the side of the mountain.

"Stop right there," Finn said, holding her shoulders and positioning her like a mannequin.

Hailey complied as the people around them stopped and snapped pictures in front of the campus landmark.

"Why am I standing in this exact spot?" she asked, eyeing the activity.

Finn opened his satchel and removed her great-uncle's metal toolbox.

She'd had no idea he'd packed it. "You brought that with you?"

"You travel with a pickle jar, Marmalade," he countered.

He wasn't wrong.

She peered into her giant tote. "It's for sentimental reasons."

"So is this." He opened the lid and handed her a photo. "You're standing where Cookie stood. Your great-uncle would have been to your left."

She examined the pavement as a strange other-worldly sensation overtook her, like she'd tapped into the energy of the moment Al and Cookie had shared. It was as if their love and excitement transferred to her. She concentrated on the picture of the smiling couple. A mix of competing emotions washed over her. She could feel their hopes, dreams, and their profound loss—a love story that never fully bloomed. It echoed in her chest, in the empty space around her heart. The wave of emotion overtook her, and she wiped a tear from her cheek.

"I was ready for that, too," Finn said softly.

She watched the man open the flap on his bag. "Ready for what?"

"You, getting all sappy and tender-hearted." Again, he reached into his satchel. This time, he produced a packet of cherry licorice twists. "These always make you happy, and a little candy can turn your day around. Isn't that something someone you loved very much used to say?" he said, borrowing her mother's words.

This perceptive man.

She laughed and shook her head, unsure her heart could take much more sweetness. "Do you have cherry chocolate chip ice cream in your bag, handyman? That would be quite a feat."

"Sorry, Marmalade, just licorice."

She held his gaze. "I'll take just licorice. I love just licorice."

Did he understand what she was trying to tell him?

He stepped into the place where her uncle had stood. "Is that right?"

"It is," she answered, lost in this man as time stood still.

He swallowed hard. She watched his throat constrict like his body was doing everything it could to hold him back.

"Hailey?" he said, his voice barely a whisper.

"Yes?" She could barely breathe. This was it. This was the moment.

"I—"

"Hey, Mr. Starrycard!"

Finn stepped back, leaving Albert's spot and breaking their connection.

"I wanted to thank you. My group appreciated your help," a young man with a backpack slung over his shoulder called as he jogged up to them.

Finn shook the guy's hand. "You guys were already ninety-nine percent of the way there. All you needed were a few tweaks."

Finn turned to her. "This is Shawn. He and his group took second place in the contest. Shawn, this is Hailey Higgins."

Just Hailey Higgins? Not Hailey Higgins, the woman I love, or Hailey Higgins, my girlfriend? Okay, that would have been weird. She couldn't fault him for that.

She mustered a grin. "Hi, Shawn. Congratulations."

"Thanks. It's nice to meet you, Hailey." The student gestured toward the mountainside. "Would you guys like me to take a picture of you with the *G*?"

"That would be great," Finn replied and handed the young man his phone.

Finn rested his hand on the small of her back as the student took their picture.

"Does that work?" Shawn asked, returning the phone to Finn.

"It's perfect. Thanks, man."

"Anytime," Shawn said and headed out, blending into the crowd.

Hailey held the black-and-white picture next to the screen. "This is exactly where Al and Cookie stood."

"It is. You wouldn't believe the math I had to do to be one hundred percent positive this was the precise location. But you're worth a little math, Marmalade."

She handed him the photo. "Is that so?"

This was it.

"Hailey!" a woman called.

Come on, universe! She'd been waiting years to have a man speak those three little words to her.

She looked over her shoulder as Jana approached with an older woman by her side.

"Hi, Jana! And you must be Jana's mother. I'm Hailey—"

"Higgins. Yes, I'm Maria Diaz. Jana's told me about you, Miss Higgins."

"What have you said to your mom about me?" Hailey asked as an icy prickle danced down her spine.

"You might be the answer to my prayers since you're not staying on at your current teaching assignment," Maria answered.

Hailey could feel Finn's eyes boring into her. "I'm not following," she said, praying this wasn't what she thought it was.

"Remember, I told you that my mom is a principal at a school near where I'm teaching," Jana explained.

Hailey plastered on a nervous grin. This was what she feared. "Yes, you mentioned that."

"Our second-grade teacher gave notice that she won't be returning, and Jana tells me you'd be a perfect fit for the job," Maria Diaz finished. "I'd love to talk more with you."

"Oh . . . wow! That's kind of you to consider me," Hailey stammered.

Maria turned to Finn. "I'm sorry. Where are my manners? I'm Maria, and this is my daughter Jana. We're educators from Denver. Are you with Hailey?"

A muscle ticked on Finn's jaw. "No, it appears that *I am not* with Hailey."

No, no, no!

Hailey's mouth went dry. It was as if she'd entered a nightmare—a nightmare where her world crumbled around her. But she was awake. This was her real-life hopes and dreams shattering in front of her. The crush of fear and disillusionment settled in her chest, rendering her immobile and ill-equipped to reply.

"If you'll excuse me," Finn said, his voice eerily steady, "I see some people I know and should say hello." Without another word, he set off down the sidewalk and melted into the crowd.

"Should we find a bench and have a chat?" Maria asked. "Jana tells me your parents were also teachers."

"My parents . . ." Hailey tried to take a breath, finding it hard to breathe. She stared into the crowd. Finn was nowhere in sight. "My parents were high school teachers. They taught at my . . . my . . . my high school." She peered into her tote and zeroed in on the top of the pickle jar.

"Do you need to sit, Hailey? You look as if you've seen a ghost," Maria remarked, concern in her tone.

Hailey could feel the blood whooshing in her ears. She hadn't seen a ghost. What she'd witnessed was more frightening than that. She'd just observed the man she loved sever his connection with her.

"I don't need to sit down, but unfortunately, I'm not able to chat," she got out.

"Take my card," Maria said, handing over the item. "Give me a call, and we can talk more about my elementary school in Denver."

Hailey nodded. "Thank you, and again I apologize," she stammered as she dropped the card into her bag and started down the sidewalk.

Her thoughts whipped through her mind. Had she ruined everything? She had to fix this. She could fix this.

Weaving through the crowd, it was as if her body was on autopilot, desperate to find Finn and explain that what he'd seen and heard was a misunderstanding. Her throat thickened with emotion. The void in her heart grew and grew. With each step, the emptiness that had gripped her since she lost her parents expanded like a black hole, sucking the light from her life.

Do not fall apart.

A sign pointed toward the Randall Engineering building. *Could he have gone that way?* She took a gamble, veered off the main walkway, and headed down the less populated route. And it paid off. She spied Finn and Dr. Schneider. They were with a few other people. Two men and a woman—a stylish blonde in linen pants and a smart navy-blue sweater. Hailey focused on Finn, observing his tight posture and crossed arms.

She walked up to the group. That telltale muscle in his jaw twitched, but he didn't look her way.

Another man joined the group and greeted Dr. Schneider.

"Craig," the professor said, embracing the new arrival. "We're bursting with alumni, thanks to the board convening this same weekend as the paper tower competition."

Hailey scanned the group. Most of them were wearing name tags. Joe Tollens, Reed Lake, Craig Allen, and the blonde was . . . Susan Randall.

Oh, no!

Hailey's heart sank. She glanced at Finn, but the man had donned an iron mask.

"Are you a student?" Susan asked, directing her blue-eyed attention her way.

Hailey held the woman's gaze, hardly able to believe she was face-to-face with the woman who'd wrecked Finn's world. While she was coiffed and put together, she didn't give off an air of heartlessness.

"Hailey is one of our elementary teachers taking the STEM training," Dr. Schneider answered.

"It's a wonderful program. The board is delighted to fund it," Susan offered warmly.

"I'm excited to implement the curriculum in the classroom," Hailey replied, grateful she could form words.

She shot another glance Finn's way. He appeared collected, but the twitch on his jaw told her he was spiraling, shattering into a million tiny pieces beneath the surface. She had to get him alone. She couldn't let him shut her out.

"Somebody misses their mom," a man with a fussy baby in his arms said as he came to Susan's side.

Holy moly!

That had to be the ex from Atlanta. Hailey did a quick check of their left hands. Both wore wedding rings.

"Is this little Everett?" Dr. Schneider asked.

"It is, and it's well past nap time," Susan replied, taking the baby from her husband. Once the child settled, a sheepish grin bloomed on the woman's lips. "Where do you teach, Hailey?"

Hailey braced herself. There was no worse question Finn's ex could have asked her at this very moment.

"Starrycard Creek Elementary," she answered, grateful she could get the words out without passing out.

Susan offered Finn a ghost of a grin. "Are you two here together?" There wasn't any malice or ill-intent in her tone. Her wistful expression gave the impression she wanted Finn to have found someone.

"We—" Hailey began.

"No, we're not," he said, cutting her off. "Hailey was having car issues. I offered her a ride here since we were both expected at Golden Tech. But Hailey's got another way home. Excuse me, I misspoke. She's got another way to get back to her *temporary* home. She's only a substitute teacher at Starrycard Creek Elementary."

Temporary home. Only a substitute teacher.

The breath caught in Hailey's throat, rendering her mute.

"I see," Susan replied with what sounded like a touch of sadness. The baby fussed, and she shifted the bundle in her arms. "We should be going. It was good to see you all," she said to the group of alums and Dr. Schneider, then turned to Finn. "Take care. I wish you the best."

The man nodded but didn't show an ounce of emotion. "Yeah, you, too."

Susan and her family left the group as Dr. Schneider and the men's conversation shifted to recent updates to the engineering labs.

Hailey touched Finn's arm. "Can we talk?"

His phone chimed. "Yes, we need to talk."

She exhaled a relieved breath. "Good, I'm glad you agree. And are you okay after seeing Susan? That couldn't have been easy," she added, lowering her voice.

He focused on his cell. "I've got the information for your ride back to Starrycard Creek."

What was he talking about? What information?

Worry creased Dr. Schneider's brow as she glanced away from her companions and eyed Finn.

"Let's find a quiet spot to discuss the changes to your travel arrangements," he said in an I-don't-give-a-fuck-about-anything tone.

She walked beside him. It was like accompanying a block of ice.

"Finn," she said softly.

His phone pinged again, and he stepped onto a grassy spot off the walkway and stared at the screen. "Kieran's in Denver, dealing with some regulation bullshit. I sent him your cell number. He can bring you back to Starrycard Creek later today. Perhaps he could take a detour and drive you around Denver so you can see if you'd like to move here."

She tried to look him in the eyes, but he wouldn't look away from his phone. "What you heard about Denver Schools was a misunderstanding. I want to be with you." She looked around as families and students strolled through the picturesque campus. This wasn't how she pictured doing what she was about to do, but she had no choice. "I love you, Finn. I've got the contract to teach at Starrycard Creek Elementary right here. I wanted to sign it with you." She slipped it from the confines of her planner and held it out.

He crossed his arms. "Don't stay in Starrycard Creek for me."

The sulking, sullen version of the man reared its ugly head. His words stung like a thousand hornets descending on her heart.

"How can you say that? How can you say that after what I told you?" she asked, hating the shake in her voice.

He finally met her gaze, but his eyes were void of emotion. "Because love sucks, Hailey. Love rips you apart and lets you down."

She had to call him out. It wasn't like her—but she had to speak, like a dormant part of her had awoken. "Love doesn't have to suck, and I know you love me, Finn. I heard you say it. You thought I was asleep, but I wasn't. I heard every word."

Pain flashed in his eyes. "I was wrong. I shouldn't have said that."

A cruel statement like that would have wrecked her a little over a month ago. But she didn't crumble. She held her ground.

Finn was in pain. He'd just encountered his ex-fiancée, her husband, and child. She wanted to extend grace to him. She yearned to wrap her arms around him and tell him he didn't have to punish himself. He didn't have to punish her for loving him. But she didn't speak those words. Instead, she peered at the pickle jar in her tote. She touched the lid and took comfort in the cool metal.

"I was wrong, too," she said, her voice barely a whisper.

"At least we're in agreement," Finn grumped, slipping farther into his sullen handyman act.

"No, we're not in agreement about everything," she countered.

Once upon a time, another version of herself would have begged Finn to reconsider, pleaded with him to maintain their hidden-away, nobody-can-know-about-us relationship. But she wasn't that woman anymore.

"I was wrong about love. Love doesn't suck. Love is a risk. It's a journey of vulnerability and growth. Even if I crash and burn a thousand times when it comes to love, I'll know I've embraced hope and courage and goodness. And that takes strength." She thought of the notes her uncle had written to Cookie—all the dreams and touching observations that had gone untold, unspoken, hidden away in a locked chamber inside a recluse's heart. It broke her heart. But that was on her great-uncle Albert. He'd had a choice. He could have fought for love.

He didn't.

Finn appeared to be on the same lonely, bitter path.

She studied her business card boyfriend's hardened expression and recalled what she'd written on a scrap of Starrycard paper. "Love was my wish for you, Finn. I wrote it on the slip of paper McKenzie gave me at Starrycard Under the Stars. I wished you could comprehend the massive amount of love that surrounds you—from your family, from the town, and from me."

Finn's mask slipped, and for the space of a breath, pain flickered beneath his eyes, veiled but unmistakable.

"I know you have the capacity to love," she continued. "I've felt it. I've witnessed it. But you can't see it. You think cutting yourself off from love is the answer. But what has that gotten you?"

He didn't reply.

And that was okay. She didn't need to rely on him.

"I'll tell you, Finnegan Starrycard, local handyman. You've got bitterness and fear. So much fear. I was ready to shout my love for you from the rooftop. Ready to let the world know my heart was yours. I wanted to help you. I wanted to be your safe place. But that's not what I'm *meant* to do."

The word triggered a memory of a flapping strip of dingy wallpaper. *He's not meant for you.*

Unyielding, she held Finn's gaze. "My happily ever after might not look like the Shooting Stars Love Stories I read online. But I understand the risk I've got to take for love."

She studied the man. It was as if she were seeing him with new eyes. No, that wasn't quite right. It wasn't her perception of Finn that had changed. What had been altered was her view of herself. Her job wasn't to turn frogs into princes and hope they would love her. Her path to happiness had nothing to do with them.

"What do you have to do for love?" he asked, his voice cracking.

But she didn't crack. Her breath steadied, syncing with a newfound calm. "I have to love myself enough to walk away from you. And that, Finnegan Starrycard, is what you can print on my business card."

CHAPTER
Eighteen
FINN

"FOR THE LOVE OF CHRIST, what's the problem? What am I doing wrong?" Finn growled through gritted teeth, crouched a few inches from the ground as he glared at Eliza's minivan's spare tire and zeroed in on the rogue lug nut. "What the hell is wrong with you?" he asked the piece of uncooperative metal—or perhaps the question was directed at himself.

It wasn't like it was the first time he'd asked himself that over the last twelve days. The question had played on repeat in his head since Hailey had walked away from him, leaving him with nothing but his demons and doubts.

His analytical mind tried to make sense of it.

Was she right?

Had he allowed bitterness and fear to cloud his judgment?

Of course, she was right.

At the mention of a teaching job in Denver, that switch in his head had flipped, thrusting him into survival mode. His walls went up, and his capacity to behave like a decent human being plummeted.

And again, he'd become the worst version of himself—the version that was supposed to shield him from the excruciating ache tied to matters of the heart.

But sweet Jesus, between learning Hailey might leave Starrycard Creek, and then seeing Susan, her husband, and child, the collision of those events had left him reeling and had sent the message loud and clear. His judgment was fucked. Maybe Hailey could believe in love, but he had to shut it out. It only messed with his head. He couldn't live like this. He had to double down on cutting himself off.

That meant putting Hailey out of his mind.

And how was he doing on that front?

He was fucking failing.

Hailey Higgins was everywhere.

It didn't matter that by the time he'd returned to Starrycard Creek, she'd moved out of his cabin and into hers. It didn't matter that the only time he saw her was when he drove past the school and caught a glimpse of her through her classroom window. When he slept, she visited him in his dreams. When he was awake, she starred in his fantasies. Even though she hadn't left a trace, every corner of his cabin held a memory of her.

Christ, he missed her!

He missed the little sighs she made each morning when he kissed her. He longed to see her seated at the kitchen table, licorice in one hand as she graded papers with the other. He missed her freckles. He missed the sweet twist of her lips when she caught him watching her. He yearned to bask in the heady lightness she cast everywhere she went like a walking and talking ray of auburn sunshine.

He had to stop thinking like a man who was hopelessly in . . .

Don't even entertain thoughts of that word.

He eyed the recalcitrant lug nut. "What the hell is wrong with us? What are we doing wrong?" he whispered, wishing the tarnished lump of metal could tell him how to move forward.

"Do you need to use all the lug nuts?" Liza asked.

"Yes, the last thing you want is to lose a tire. It's a critical component of driving," he shot back.

Critical component.

He'd thought that was what Hailey had become to him. The piece that allowed him to function, to love again.

He was wrong.

What drove him to near madness was that he couldn't decipher what exactly was life's critical component.

"Let Kieran help, Finn," Eliza said as she paced back and forth on the sidewalk. "You'll get grease and tire juice on your nice sports coat. I love that charcoal gray one on you. You can't address the engineering students looking like a smudged-up handyman."

"Tire juice isn't a real thing, and I can screw in a lug nut. Anyone could do it. I'll fix it myself," he grumped, unable to figure out where he'd gone wrong. But he couldn't think straight. His goddamned mind was flooded with questions about Hailey Higgins.

Where was she right now?

Was she preparing to sell her cabin?

Was there any reason she'd stay?

Was she thinking of him?

Did she miss him the way he missed her?

Fuck!

"I'm right here, Finn," Kieran said, leaning against a light post. "Say the word, and I'll finish up."

Ping!

"Caroline's texting me," Eliza relayed. "I let her know about the tire situation."

Ping!

"Caroline wants to know if you need her help?"

Finn glared at the lug nut. "Caroline doesn't know how to change a tire. Every time she got a flat, she called me."

Ping!

"Caroline, again?" Finn asked.

"Yes," Eliza replied. "She says that if you forgot how to do it, she can send you a link to an empowering video."

"Are you kidding me? An empowering video?" he grumbled.

Ping!

The sound came from the cell in his pocket.

"That's the link," Eliza reported.

Finn rested his head against the side of his sister's minivan. "I'm a mechanical engineer. I can change a freaking flat tire. Hell, I could take the car apart and put the whole damned thing back together if I had to."

"You're certainly taking as long as someone putting together an entire minivan," Kieran mused, injecting his dry sense of humor.

Ping!

"Caroline says she texted Christian and told him about the flat," Eliza continued, giving the play-by-play of the Starrycard siblings text-a-palooza.

Ping!

"Chris says he can drive up and help. The Rattlers aren't playing tonight, but he's ninety minutes away."

Finn cursed under his breath. "I don't need any help. But a little peace and quiet would be nice."

They were five miles from Golden Tech when the front passenger-side tire blew out on a quiet residential street. And while he wasn't running late, this wasn't the day to be stuck on the side of the road battling a stubborn lug nut with his siblings in tow. He was scheduled to speak to the engineering students—to motivate and inspire them in their endeavors, which was pretty rich coming from a man who spent his days actively seeking out objects in need of repair, then passing out in front of the TV after ingesting an insane amount of ice cream. But he'd told Dr. Schneider he'd do it. He, however, wasn't planning on caravanning with his siblings. When Eliza showed up at his cabin with Kieran—an hour before he had to leave and announced that his ride had arrived—he'd told them to buzz off. But the pair wouldn't take no for an answer.

Bloop! Bloop!

He glared at the lug nut. "Is that your phone again, Liza?"

"Yeah."

"What's going on?"

"We're trying to help, Finn," came Caroline's fluttery voice.

He looked over his shoulder at Eliza. "You've got Caroline on a video call?"

"Yes," Eliza balked, "she's worried about you."

"Jesus, next you'll say Christian is worried, too," Finn grumped.

"He is. I've got Chris on video," Kieran announced.

Finn pinched the bridge of his nose. "Where's Owen? It's not a Starrycard roadside shindig without him."

"I'm right here, bro. I'm on Eliza's phone with Caroline," Owen answered.

"I added him to the group video call," Eliza explained, holding out her cell.

"Of-fucking-course you did," Finn grumbled.

"We couldn't leave Owen out," Eliza shot back.

Finn shook his head. "How many Starrycards does it take to change a tire?"

"One, if you'd stop brutalizing that lug nut and allow me to finish," Kier answered.

"That's actually a hella deep question, Finn. You might want to meditate on that," Caroline suggested.

Meditation. That had to be Care's purpose du jour.

Finn stared at the tire. Screw meditating. Maybe he could bang his head on it a few times. Perhaps that would keep the last lug nut in place.

"I'm in Bali," the youngest Starrycard continued, "and I think I've finally found my meaning, and that's thanks to deep meditation and contemplation. I can't recommend it enough. I might go into yoga or become a guru or something."

Great! Now, he was getting advice from his lovable, yet extremely flighty, baby sister. This had to be the definition of hitting rock bottom.

"Finn, did you hear me? Liza, can he hear me?" Caroline asked.

"Oh, he can hear you, honey. Perhaps he's meditating," Eliza replied, biting back a grin.

Finn exhaled an exaggerated breath. "I hear you, Care. You want me to contemplate a tire."

"I think she wants you to contemplate what it's like to be a flat tire," Christian added.

"I wasn't, Chris. But I agree," Caroline gushed. "Finn, picture yourself as a flat tire. What would you do to get *un-flat*, or would it be blown up? No, don't get blown up."

"Inflated?" Eliza offered.

The sibling shindig had evolved into an all-out bullshit word salad spectacular.

Owen groaned. "I've got too much to do to contemplate the inner workings of an *un-flat* tire. I need to prep the paper for the jubilee banners for Main Street, but I'm thinking of you, Finn. Good luck tonight."

"Thanks, O," Finn answered and breathed a sigh of relief. One onscreen Starrycard down, two to go.

"One more thing, Finn," Owen called.

"Yeah?"

"Don't fuck up your speech, man. You are representing the family and the business. Just saying."

Finn rubbed the knots at the base of his neck. "Got it. Don't fuck up. Avoid crushing embarrassment."

"I second that advice. Don't fuck up," Christian said. "And I've got to go, too. My shoulder is screaming to be iced."

"I still think you should meditate," Caroline added, "but I need to go so I can call Dad and see if he'll give me a teeny, tiny loan. I'm so close to figuring out my grand purpose. One quick jaunt to Italy or maybe South Africa, and then I'll know exactly what I'm supposed to do with my life. Love you, little stars! Oh, and Finn?"

"Yes, Care?" He knew what was coming.

"Don't fuck up. Get un-flat. And . . ."

"Yeah, Care?"

"We want you to be happy, Finn, and sometimes, happiness wears a borrowed red fleece coat in my size."

A muscle ticked on Finn's jaw.

Confirmed.

His siblings had been talking about him. But he should have known they would.

"I love you, little star. You always figure out how to solve the puzzle. Except this time, you're the puzzle," she added and blew him a kiss.

And shit, for being flighty as hell, Caroline could always drill down to the heart of the matter.

"Love you, too, little star," he replied, his chest muscles tightening.

He'd grown up hearing that term of endearment more times than he could count, but family memories didn't come to his mind when Care said it. He heard Hailey's voice as she spoke quietly, then sang to his niece.

Bloop, bloop, bloop.

"Are they gone?" he asked, his gaze growing glassy as he concentrated on the lug nut.

"Yes, it's the three of us," Eliza replied. "But don't you feel better?"

He swallowed past the emotion in his throat. "I had three people tell me not to fuck up."

"And aren't you the better for it," Eliza added. She was trying to keep it light, but he could hear the note of concern in her voice.

He hadn't talked to anyone about what had happened with Hailey. Had Hailey said something to Eliza? The pair had grown close and worked in the same building.

But he wasn't about to ask.

Focus on the tire.

He had to concentrate on what he could fix.

That's what he should do. Instead, he stood. "We wouldn't be in this predicament if I could have taken my truck and headed to Golden alone. But no, you insisted on making this a sibling road trip."

"You need us, Finn. Your *handymaning* is out of control," Eliza tossed back.

"*Handymaning*? That's not a real word. And I'm not out of control."

She lifted her chin defiantly. "I'm an educator. If I say it's a word, it's a word. And yes, you are out of control!"

"I'm not!"

"You are!"

"I'm not!"

"You are!"

"Take a breath," Kieran murmured, raising his hands like a boxing referee. "You two have to stop. As the oldest, I'm the tie breaker, and it goes to Liza."

Finn stared at his brother. "I'm not out of control, Kier. I've been quite productive since . . ."

Since he fucked up the one thing that made him feel like a person again and allowed the worst part of him to ruin everything.

Maybe he did Hailey a favor. She deserved to be put on a pedestal, to be loved and cherished.

Jesus, he couldn't say any of that. But he sure as hell could think it—and feel it. His chest ached as the vice tightened around his heart.

"You say productive," his brother mused in his lawyer voice. "Keen observers might label it as manic."

"Manic?" he shot back.

"It's why Owen didn't come with us," Eliza continued. "He needed some time at the shop without you. It's crunch time, and he's behind on the banners. He could barely do anything with you tweaking every valve and taking apart the vats."

"It's called necessary maintenance," he countered. It was a

bullshit answer, but he couldn't let his siblings think they knew what was going on inside his head.

"At the city council meeting yesterday, Mrs. Brimble said you tightened every screw in her refrigerated display last week," Kier stated, his tone deceptively even.

Finn eyed the elder Starrycard. "Yeah? So?"

"She said you went back the next day and tightened them again, like you couldn't stop moving. She also told us that you bought every jar of pickles in the place."

Shit! There was a decent chance he had gone in two times. He'd been on one hell of a handyman bender—and pickle-eating bender to boot.

He shifted his weight. "Again, I was being thorough, and I was low on pickles."

That was a lie. In the last week, he'd purchased enough pickles to live off them for the next twenty years. Pickle jars lined every flat surface in the cabin. Hell, he had so many he'd left a jar outside for the asshole raccoons.

"And were you low on cherry licorice?" Kieran continued.

Finn crossed his arms and glanced away. "Maybe."

"The candy shop said you bought them out," he stated in his lawyer voice—not judgmental but irritatingly all-knowing. "Goldie mentioned you stopped by the restaurant to check the plumbing and left with a hell of a lot of her orange marmalade."

Marmalade.

It took everything Finn had to keep his features neutral. "It's delicious on turnovers."

"And don't forget the ice cream," Eliza chimed. "Someone whose name rhymes with 'begin-again barley-yard' bought out the cherry chocolate chip."

Finn fumed. "Is everyone in town keeping tabs on me?"

"Honestly, you might get voted man of the year by the Starrycard Small Business Guild for all the work you've done for the merchants and the small fortune you've spent on junk food. Mr. Perry suggested we print your face on the jubilee banners. I cautioned that image may frighten the schoolchildren when they parade down Main Street," Kier added with the ghost of a grin.

Finn cocked his head to the side. "Ha-ha, quite a joke."

"No, I'm serious. The motion was raised," his brother replied evenly.

Finn studied his perma-stoic brother. Was Kier telling the truth? Hell, if he knew. Before he could ask, Eliza jumped in.

"Let's get back to our beloved brother's handyman hysterics. Kier, did I tell you how much time Finn spent fixing the completely fine flagpole at the elementary school?"

"Is this in addition to replacing the window trim?" Kieran asked, like the pair had practiced this shtick.

"Yup, Kier, it is," Eliza replied with a touch too much gusto.

Finn watched a motorcycle zoom by, wishing he could commandeer it and head off into the sunset. Alas, the speedy bike disappeared down the street. He sighed heavily for what had to be the hundredth time. "I noticed that the pulley mechanism was squeaking when the kids raised the flag each morning back when I was . . ."

"Taking Hailey to work," Eliza supplied.

He glanced away. "It needed a little lubrication."

"You were there for three hours," Eliza countered.

"Again, I'm thorough," he answered, losing steam.

Thoroughly fucked, he needed to get this lug nut to cooperate so they could get to this event and he could get a break from his brother and sister.

Eliza raised an eyebrow. "The second-grade classroom looks out onto the flagpole."

Finn stared intently at a dandelion growing from a crack in the sidewalk. "Does it?"

His sister came to his side. "Finn, we know you miss Hailey."

"What do you know about me and Hailey?"

Kieran stepped forward. "I helped her move her things into Higgins Hideaway when we got back to Starrycard Creek. And I connected her with the guys at the auto shop who replaced the battery in her car. Liza works in the same building with her. We know what's going on."

"Kenzie watched your kittens while you were in Golden," Eliza added, worry etched on her face. "Hailey texted and asked me to return them to her place. We know she hasn't been staying with you. We know you're hurting. If you would just talk to her, I bet she'd—"

"I'm fine," he blurted. "Hailey was just somebody I helped out. A deranged bride whose car broke down and needed a place to stay."

More damned lies.

Eliza raised an eyebrow. "Are you sure that's all she is to you?"

"Liza," he said in an exasperated breath.

"Finn, you asked me to drive her back to Starrycard Creek," Kieran continued as the sibling verbal beat-down continued. "You sent me a text that said Hailey requires transportation from Golden Tech to Starrycard Creek as soon as possible. The last two lines spoke volumes," his brother continued, eyeing his phone. "You wrote, I need you to do this for me and not ask why. I'm hanging by a thread."

Finn bit the inside of his cheek—needing to feel pain that didn't radiate from his heart. "How was she during the drive? You never said anything."

Kieran held his gaze. "Did you want me to report back to you on her wellbeing?"

Finn kicked a rock on the ground. "No, but I wouldn't stop you if you had something to say."

Lies, lies, lies! He'd been dying to know if she was okay. He'd only gotten glimpses of her since he'd returned.

It was pure torture.

"Hailey is a lovely person, Finn," Kieran said, his annoyingly neutral tone warming. "My job is to remain impartial and act in the best interest of our town. By nature, I keep my distance from people. It allows me to do what I have to do without emotion swaying my perception."

"Yeah, you might want to work on defrosting the iceman act occasionally, Kier," Eliza murmured.

"But this allows me to read people," Kieran said, plowing ahead and ignoring Liza's comment. "I can see bullshitters coming from a mile away. I can tell you Miss Higgins is a genuinely gentle and unwaveringly kind person. Now, there was something of interest about her I noticed."

"Was she sad or distressed?" Finn rasped, his voice a husk of a sound.

"Before I drove her home, I'd only met her briefly at the elementary school before Kenzie's first-grade performance, but she was different on the drive back to Starrycard Creek."

"Super calm, right?" Eliza tossed out.

Kier nodded. "Yes, I'd use the word *serene*."

Finn raked his hands through his hair. He'd seen what Kier and Eliza had described moments before she'd walked away from him. He couldn't have missed it. The conviction in her voice. The hope shining in her eyes. Christ, he'd wanted to run after her. But his feet became cement blocks. Stuck. Fucking stuck. He'd ended up at that hidden away bench—the Higgins bench. He'd sat there for hours. His mind—a mind that understood the inner workings of any machine—couldn't chart a path forward. He couldn't figure out how to get over himself and be the man Hailey deserved. What was the critical component? He thought it was her. But he'd blown up that theory.

He turned to his sister. "Has Hailey signed the contract? Did she take the second-grade position?" he asked, hating the pathetic lilt to his voice.

Liza crossed her arms. "I can't disclose that, Finn. Hailey's my friend, but I'm her boss when it comes to school matters."

"You can ask if the position is still open," Kier suggested in lawyer mode.

Finn took a step toward his sister. "Is it?"

She crossed her arms. "It is."

"She doesn't want it?" he asked, the words hitting like a sledgehammer to his heart.

Eliza looked at Kieran. "Can I say what I want to say? The thing I told you about?"

Finn took a step back. "You've talked to Kier about Hailey?"

"He's on the school board."

"All we can say is that the top candidate for the second-grade position is weighing another job proposal. She has until noon on the last day of school to declare her intentions," Kier replied.

Finn's pulse kicked up. "That's eight days from now."

Kieran nodded.

"Denver wants her, right?" Finn tossed out, eyeing his sister.

"My guess is any school she'd apply to would want her. I called and checked with the principals at all the schools she'd subbed at. They all sang her praises and wanted to keep her on," Eliza said gently. She touched his arm. "You know you can talk to us. It's okay to share how you feel about her." She offered him a sad smile. "Come on, Finn. You made a smooshy sandwich with her."

Kieran's maddeningly neutral demeanor cracked. "What the hell is a smooshy sandwich?"

"Simmer down, Kier. It's something Jack and I do," Eliza explained, waving off their brother.

However, Eliza's assurance didn't alter the eldest Starrycard's gobsmacked expression. In fact, Kier's reaction was the opposite of simmering down. "Jesus, Eliza, I don't want to hear about my little sister like that, or about Finn smooshing one of the nicest people on the planet."

Finn eyed Eliza. "See, I'm not the only one who doesn't want to hear about you and Jack, but take a breath, Kier, it's not a sex thing. It's . . ."

It was the night every piece of his life fell into place—where he felt whole and home and loved. It was the night he couldn't hold back. The night he'd spoken the words he'd promised himself he'd never say again. A knot twisted in his belly. For all the warm fuzzy moments that evening included, look where it had gotten him. Love did suck—maybe Hailey still held out hope, but how could he?

"What happened when you and Hailey were in Golden?" Eliza asked.

He studied his sister. "She hasn't said anything to you?"

"She's not like that, Finn. When I asked about her plans for the future, she said she had some personal and professional matters to consider and that she believed she'd end up where she was meant to be."

"Meant to be," he echoed. "Like a wish written on Starrycard paper." ·

"It can only be yours if it's meant for you," Eliza replied, reciting the old prophecy.

He stood there, as useless as the uncooperative lug nut.

"You care about Hailey. We all saw how you looked at her that morning at Goldie's, and you'd just met her the night before. And don't think I don't know about your night enlisting my daughter's help to spy on her and Nico."

Finn cringed. "Yeah . . . sorry about that."

"What happened, Finn?" Eliza pressed. "You're crazy about her, and anyone can see she feels the same way about you. Watching you drop her off at school was like something out of a Hallmark movie. You guys were enamored with each other. What changed?"

He sighed. Every damned thing.

He ran his hands down the scruff on his cheeks. "I screwed up. A teacher from Denver wanted to hook Hailey up with a job. I heard the entire conversation. I lost my shit, and then I ran into Susan."

"Susan?" Kieran and Eliza repeated, pure disbelief coating the word.

Kieran was the first to recover. "What was she doing at Golden Tech?"

"An alumni board thing. But she wasn't alone."

"Who was she with?" Liza asked.

"Her ex. The ex that she left me for," he confessed.

He might as well put all the cards on the table.

Kieran raised an eyebrow. "We thought you guys just broke up."

"I didn't tell you everything. The night we broke up, I went to her hotel room. She was there with her ex." Finn stared at the lug nut. "The ex who is now her husband. When I ran into them at Golden Tech, they were there with their baby."

"Oh, Finn," Liza said softly.

He looked up as dusky wisps of purple and midnight blue stretched across the sky. "It was like everything was closing in on me—all my faults and fears," he continued, using Hailey's words. "I became the worst version of myself. Petty. Thin-skinned. A snarling wounded animal. That's when I texted you, Kier. I couldn't be around Hailey. I had to be alone."

"What else? I get the feeling there was more to the story," Kieran replied, knowing him well.

Finn's battered heart ached as he swallowed past the emotion. "Before she walked away from me, she told me she loved me."

Eliza gasped. "What did you say to her, Finn?"

Bitter regret left a salty, acrid taste in his mouth. "Not what I should have said."

Eliza rubbed his back. "You must know that every relationship isn't like what happened between you and Susan. And when you were with her, you weren't . . ."

"What?" he pressed.

"You weren't yourself when you were with Susan," Kieran supplied. "You never even brought her home. You didn't let us know you were going to propose to her. You made the wedding invitations when nobody was at the shop."

"It was like you wanted to hide your true self from her," Eliza added.

Finn pinched the bridge of his nose. He was not up for a road-side psychoanalysis session.

"It doesn't matter. Whoever the hell I was, Susan didn't want it," Finn grumbled, feeling the folded square in his wallet like a hot coal burning into his soul.

His shit judgment had gotten him here.

He was floundering, bitter, and fearful of love.

His once Sweet Miss Marmalade had called him out correctly.

His cell pinged. He sighed, grateful for the distraction.

"Could it be Hailey?" Eliza asked, perking up.

As much as he wanted to see Hailey's name and picture pop up on the screen, he knew she wouldn't text him. She'd made herself clear. She was walking away from him—walking away from a man who sucked at love.

He pulled his cell from his pocket. "It's Dr. Schneider. She wants to chat with me at her office before the event." He returned his cell to his pocket and scrutinized the lug nut. "But before we can go anywhere, I've got to figure out what the hell is wrong with this damned thing."

"If one way doesn't work, try another," Kieran suggested, that hint of a grin cracking his stoic demeanor.

For Christ's sake!

Finn stared at the lug nut in the waning light and cursed under his breath as he rotated the bolt clockwise. "I was turning the damn thing the wrong way. What a rookie mistake," he mumbled as the once uncooperative piece of metal fit into place. He returned the wrench to the back of the minivan and smoothed his sports coat. "Why didn't you say something if you knew I was doing it wrong, Kier?"

"You've always had to figure it out yourself, Finn. It's your curse and your blessing," Kieran replied.

"Come on, little stars," Eliza called, jumping into the driver's seat and assuming the role of minivan mom. "We can't be late."

The trio loaded up. Kier and Eliza took the front, and Finn

hopped in the back. Doors slammed shut, and they headed down the tree-lined street toward Golden Tech.

"Do you know what you're going to say to the students?" Eliza asked and hit the gas.

Jesus, the speech!

"I wrote down a few notes when I had a second, here and there." He picked up his satchel and unbuckled the flap to retrieve his better-than-nothing notes when a clank from inside his bag cut through the stagnate minivan air.

Kier looked over his shoulder. "What do you have in there?"

Finn stared at the battered metal toolbox. He'd hoped Hailey would have reached out to ask him to return it. She hadn't, and while he longed to see her and hear her voice, holding on to her great-uncle's keepsakes and letters had provided him some comfort—and a connection to her.

"Finn, what are you carrying around?" Kieran pressed.

"Is it for your speech?" Liza asked.

His siblings had entered the micro-management phase of the road trip intervention.

"Just stuff," he mumbled, cramming the cards into the pocket of his charcoal blazer. "Don't worry about the speech. Something will come to me. I'll figure it out. You're the one who said that's how my mind works, Kier," he replied as the engineering building came into view. "Let me out here, Liza, so I can meet up with Dr. Schneider. The event is outdoors on the side of campus closest to the *G* on the mountain. Do you know where to go?"

"Yes, we'll park and see you in a bit," she replied. "And Finn?"

He exited the vehicle and peered in through the open window at his sister. "Yeah."

Eliza held up her phone and snapped a pic.

"What was that for?"

"I'm texting Jack for McKenzie. I almost forgot. She wanted a picture of you."

Ping!

Eliza grinned at the screen. "McKenzie says you're wearing

her favorite jacket. The same one you wore on your super spies sleepover night."

He nodded, unable to escape the memory of that night.

"You'll figure out what to do. I know you will. And . . . don't fuck up," Eliza added, tossing him a wink before shifting into drive.

He wasn't sure if she meant the speech or his life. It didn't matter. As much as he appreciated her kind words, he'd fucked up almost everything.

He watched the minivan disappear around the corner, then headed toward the building. His shoes clapped against the sidewalk as the toolbox tapped against a few pens at the bottom of his bag.

This side of the campus was quiet, and the rattle inside his satchel soothed his addled mind until he spied the spot when he'd last spoken with Hailey. At first glance, there was nothing remarkable about a patch of grass off the walkway—no sign that it was the location of his searing heartbreak. He trained his gaze on the engineering building and took the familiar route to Dr. Schneider's office.

"Just get through the speech," he muttered, entering the small sitting area.

Barely a second passed before the door to her private office swung open. "That might be easier said than done, Finnegan. We've got a problem," Dr. Schneider said with a frown.

He'd just walked in. How could he have fucked up already?

"What's the problem?"

She eyed him warily. "You."

"Me? Why am I the problem?" he exclaimed.

She waved for him to join her inside her private space. "You were supposed to send in a headshot for the event program—a program we're giving to everyone in attendance."

"I did that." He had. The email had come in after he'd checked the pipes at Goldie's restaurant and before he'd hit the elementary school to address the flagpole issue.

"This is what you sent, and it's printed on two hundred sheets of paper. We just received them," Dr. Schneider said, holding up a page. "I believe that's Miss Higgins holding what looks to be a very grumpy cat where your headshot should be."

"She's holding Mr. Whiskerfrown."

"Who?"

"The cat," Finn stammered. "His name is . . . never mind. I'm sorry. I must have selected the wrong image on my phone."

He might have been—okay, he absolutely had been—perusing Hailey pics on his phone when the email request had come in.

"You have pictures of Miss Higgins holding kittens on your phone?" the professor asked, raising an eyebrow.

Knock, knock!

Dr. Schneider flicked her gaze from him and waved in the man in the doorway. "Shawn, tell me you have good news."

"We think we can get new programs printed quickly. Hey, Mr. Starrycard," the kid said.

Finn recognized him from the tower competition. "Hey, Sh—"

"Say cheese!" the kid called, holding up his phone.

Finn stared at the device like he'd never encountered a cell phone. "Huh?"

"Got it," Shawn said and turned to go.

"Wait . . . I didn't smile."

"You look . . ." The guy stared at his phone and cringed. "Pretty decent."

"Pretty decent?" Finn echoed.

"It's gonna take a bit to get these printed and folded." Shawn checked his phone and turned to the professor. "We've got about half an hour until everyone arrives. The volunteers and I will make it work, but I better go."

"I'll walk you out, Shawn. Finn," Dr. Schneider said, eyeing him like one would stare down a flighty teenager. "Stay here."

"Yeah, no problem." He could use a moment. The last twenty minutes had put him through the wringer. He set his satchel on a chair and walked up to the professor's bookshelf. Framed shots of her grandkids and older photographs of her with her children and husband lined the shelves, mixed in with engineering textbooks and an array of plaques and awards. He was no stranger to her office. Thanks to her being his thesis advisor, his ass was probably indented into one of the conference table chairs. But tonight, a photo he'd glazed over every time before stuck out.

A framed black-and-white picture of a young woman in a miniskirt standing with three other men. Summer Research Program 1963 was printed on a metal tab affixed to the frame.

He studied the people in the photo, and his heart leaped into his throat.

One of the men in the picture was Albert Higgins. He'd recognized the man because he'd seen the picture of Al and . . .

He lifted the frame from its spot on the shelf and zeroed in on the young woman in a miniskirt. Bracelets stacked on her right arm. Holy shit, he recognized her, too.

"Finn, I was hoping we could chat about your speech. I was thinking . . ." The woman froze, her gaze trained on the picture frame in his hand.

He looked between his mentor and the photo as the pieces came together. "Dr. Schneider, I know who you are."

CHAPTER
Nineteen

TIME SLOWED, stretching every second, as Finn processed the information that could not be denied. He held his mentor's gaze. "Dr. Schneider, you're Cookie."

The professor's lips quivered, curving gently upward with a hint of sorrow in her eyes as if hearing him call her Cookie had unlocked memories that had been tucked away for a very long time. "Only one person ever called me by that name."

"And that one person was Albert Higgins," Finn answered.

A puzzled crease formed between her eyebrows. "How did you figure that out? Nobody knew that—not even my late husband."

He returned the framed photograph to the shelf and went to his satchel. "The cabin near mine—Higgins Hideaway. I've been working on it for Hailey. We found a secret compartment in a bookshelf Albert must have made when he built the place." He removed the slim metal box from his satchel. "This toolbox was what he had stored inside. It contained some personal items. We found it by chance."

The woman pressed her hand to her chest. "I never expected to see that again. And it's not a toolbox. It was Al's field kit. It contained the implements we used to take rock and soil samples. He was a—"

"A metallurgical and materials engineer," Finn supplied and removed the patent from the box. "This is how I figured that part out."

"And he was a mechanical engineer," Dr. Schneider added.

"He had two engineering degrees?" Finn asked.

"The man was brilliant," she replied, a thread of regret woven into her words.

He handed her the photo of the pair posed in front of the G. "This is how I figured out you were Cookie. Albert didn't have any tools in the kit. Only mementos and letters. This picture was one of the items. Were you two together?"

She concentrated on the image. "That would depend on how you define *together*. Are two people together if nobody can know about them?"

Finn stood there, unable to answer, taken aback at her reply.

"We had a summer," she said softly. "But whatever we had, it didn't last or end well."

Should he mention the letters? Would it help or hurt her to know Albert cared for her until the very end of his life? Before he could utter a word, the professor spoke.

"It wasn't easy being a woman working toward an engineering degree in the early sixties," she began, gaze still trained on the photo. "There were only four women in my class. Two of them weren't serious about their studies. They were sent to college to find husbands. I couldn't fault them. It was how it was back then. My parents wanted the same for me. I had a boyfriend back in Wyoming. They wanted me to marry him."

"That's where you're from, right?" he replied, seeing a whole new side of the professor. No longer the no-nonsense academic, but the young woman, pining for a different trajectory.

"And that's where my parents wanted me to stay. They wanted me to marry Carl, my boyfriend from down the block, have kids, and become a housewife. But it wasn't what I wanted. Luckily, my grand-mother, Granny Cook, was ahead of her time. She liked to tinker in the garage and let me tag along. When I was eight, she taught me how to rebuild a carburetor. She'd fix the old Buick and let my grandfather take the credit. When I told her I wanted to study engineering, she helped me apply to Golden Tech and even sold a few pieces of jewelry to pay my tuition. My parents tried to object, but Granny was pushy, slightly grating, and quite headstrong. I'm told I take after her."

"That explains a lot," Finn said with a low chuckle, then paused. "Did you meet Albert Higgins here, in Golden?"

That smile tinged with regret graced her lips. "I met Albert when I was a freshman, and he was working on his doctorate. He was looking for research assistants for the summer. He was one of the few who'd considered allowing a woman to join his team. I needed something to keep me out of Wyoming. I didn't want to go home. I didn't want to see Carl. He'd written to me about the two of us getting married. I couldn't let my mind go there. I didn't write back."

"You didn't care for Carl?"

"He wasn't a bad person, by any means, but I wanted this," she replied and gestured to her office. "The picture on my shelf was the team Albert assembled. Al was brilliant and a bit quirky. He liked nicknames." She tapped the photo above one of the men. He called Dan Jones, Jonsey. Bill Mack was Mackey. My maiden name is Cook."

"You were Cookie," Finn supplied.

"For one summer. Yes. We traveled to every corner of Colorado, taking samples. Albert and I grew close. We all did, but Albert and I had that instant chemistry. It's hard to explain."

Finn pictured a woman soaked to the bone wearing a torn wedding dress. "You don't have to explain. I know what that's like."

Dr. Schneider nodded. "Albert treated me like an equal. He listened when I spoke. I'd never had that before from a man. After the first month, Al wanted more mineral samples, so we decided to break into teams of two. Jonsey and Mackey went west, and Albert and I found ourselves in the southeast, near a town called Starrycard Creek. Al had heard the story about the waters teeming with minerals. He was intrigued. He wanted to check it out and take samples. We drove down and rented a secluded cabin on the side of a mountain called Starrycard Cabin."

The air in the office crackled with a strange energy, causing the hairs on his arms to stand on end, a testament to the uncanny coincidence. "I'd forgotten that my great-grandparents used to rent it out," he replied, thrown by the woman's admission.

"We stayed for over a month, using it as a home base. Starrycard Creek was where Albert began brainstorming the building material formula that would become quite lucrative for him. We also fell in love there."

"I understand if you don't want to disclose what I'm about to ask you, but what happened? I know how the story ends. Albert became known as Old Man Higgins to everyone in Starrycard Creek. A recluse. An eccentric hermit. A man completely alone," Finn said, ice prickling in his veins like he was describing his foreshadowed fate.

Dr. Schneider toyed with her bracelets, then released a low, pained sigh. "It doesn't have a happy ending, but of course, you know that."

He kept his mouth shut, giving her space to gather her thoughts.

"Everything fell apart on our way back to Golden at the end of the summer," she began. "I'd wanted to talk about our future. But Albert was quiet, contemplative. He'd told me he loved me when we were at the cabin. I, perhaps foolishly, thought that spark of new love would sustain us." She peered out the window. "When we pulled up to the engineering building, Carl was there with a bouquet of roses. My parents must have told him I was on my way back. The second I stepped out of Al's car, he dropped to his knee and proposed."

"What did Albert do?"

Dr. Schneider met his gaze. "Nothing."

"Nothing?" Finn echoed, disbelief infused into his reply.

"I hadn't told Albert about Carl. When I finally got Al to talk to me, he was livid. He said I'd lied to him. How could I love him if I had Carl waiting in the wings? It was an ugly fight. Albert said he didn't love me. He'd made a mistake. His judgment had been flawed. The last thing he said to me was that I wasn't a *critical component* in his life."

Critical component.

"That had to have hurt," Finn said, pulse racing as his mind connected the similarities between himself and the bitter old recluse.

"It did," she replied, sadness welling in her eyes. "Albert moved out of state a few days later to continue developing his formula. Carl returned to Wyoming without a fiancée, and I stayed in Golden to continue my studies. I wrote to Albert. I never heard anything from him. My letters came back unopened, return-to-sender. I'd read about his success and the patent. He couldn't hide that from me. I knew he'd made quite a bit of money. I was happy for him, but he made it clear how he felt about me. Six years after that summer, I met Doug Schneider."

"Your late husband. The physics teacher. I had him. He was . . ."

"Less demanding than me?" she challenged, her veil of sadness lifting.

"I don't know about less demanding. But he was less terrifying, for sure," he added, grateful to lighten the mood, if only for a moment.

The professor chuckled and gestured to a picture of a young woman in a white pantsuit standing beside a man in a tuxedo. "Doug supported my desire to remain in academia. Not long after we married, I learned Albert had donated a substantial sum to the school and disappeared from the engineering world. He didn't publish any research or write articles. For a very long time, I didn't know where he'd gone, until many years later, a Finnegan

Starrycard landed in my class. Your last name got me thinking of my time in Starrycard Creek. A quick internet search revealed an A. Higgins on 222 Starryview Lane."

His heart broke for his mentor. "That had to have hit like a punch to the gut. Did my presence bring you pain?"

She grazed her fingers over the delicate bracelet adorning her wrist as if she were lost in a memory. "Yes and no. Getting to know you and then guiding your research was like having a little piece of Al near me again."

"Was that a gift from Albert?" he asked, recalling what the man had written on his last note to Cookie as he eyed the slim line of gold.

Remember the gift I gave you? I was worried you wouldn't like it. The tears in your eyes told me you loved it. Did you keep it? Do you wear it and think of me? I should have shouted my love for you from the rooftop. It's my greatest regret.

"I kept it to remember the man he once was." She paused, studied the bit of gold, then met his gaze. "You ask if your presence was a painful reminder. I need to amend my answer. I wouldn't describe it as painful. When I met you, yes, it brought up memories. My heart broke for Albert, but not like when I was younger. I mourned the loss of a great inventor. I mourned what he could have contributed to the field, the minds he could have inspired. But I'd be lying if I said that was all. A part of me always wondered what drove him to a life of solitude. Was it regret? Was it madness? Was it love? Did he ever truly love me? I'll never know."

Finn glanced at the metal kit. "Would you like another piece of him—a piece that comes with closure?"

She narrowed her gaze. "What do you mean?"

"I can answer your question, but there's something you need to see. Somewhere we need to go."

She checked the clock on the wall. "We don't have time to go anywhere. You're due to give the opening remarks in twenty minutes."

"What you need to see is on the way to the event," he replied, returning the kit to his bag. He went to the door and held it open while she slipped her purse strap over her shoulder.

They walked in silence as they left the building. The night air greeted them with a light breeze. Not needing a map this time, he led her off the main path and onto the narrow gravel trail that snaked into the foliage. He couldn't help but think of Hailey. But he didn't feel the gnawing emptiness that plagued him these past days. Oddly, he felt her light, her warmth, her genuine excitement. She'd want Dr. Schneider to see the bench and learn the truth.

He pushed a branch out of the way and allowed the professor to go ahead of him. It was dark, but the lighting for the outdoor event on the other side of the secret enclave cast a golden glow into the small clearing.

Finn focused on the bench. It sat quietly, like a keeper of secrets. "Albert bequeathed two gifts to Golden Tech. You knew about the first gift—the large endowment. This is the second gift. He donated this bench about five or so years before he passed away."

Dr. Schneider ran her hand along the curved wood and glanced around, surveying the area. "My goodness," she said softly. "This is a different bench, but I believe this is where Al brought me when he interviewed me for the research position. This part of the campus used to be wide open—an extension of the walkway. Over the years, the landscape has changed. I didn't even know this was still here."

"There's more," Finn said, removing his cell from his pocket. He turned on the light and illuminated the small plaque. "It says for Cookie, always my—"

"Critical component," she finished, her gaze trained on the starry sky. "That's what Al called me. He'd say Cookie, you're my critical component. He never figured it out. That thinking is what must have led to his demise."

What did that mean?

The professor sat and patted the spot next to her. "Join me, Finn."

He sank onto the bench, feeling an odd kinship with the wood, and now he understood why. He'd pulled planks of it out of Al's cabin. "I didn't recognize this when I was here before, but this isn't any bench. I believe Al made it with the same materials he'd incorporated into his cabin."

"That doesn't surprise me. Albert couldn't sit still. He was always moving, tinkering, building. His mind required it."

"I can relate," Finn murmured.

She nodded and ran her hand down the armrest. "Oh, the twists and turns of life. When you get to my age, you see things differently. You get a better view of the whole picture. I married a wonderful man who I loved ardently," she began, her words floating in the cool air like the petals of a heartfelt confession. "He gave me over fifty wonderful years of marriage. I have beautiful children and grandchildren, but a part of me always wondered what my life would have been like if Albert had figured out what the true critical component was. If he'd fought for me, fought for our love instead of letting his pride and ego stand in the way."

"Maybe he'd been hurt before," Finn offered, hating the shake to his voice.

"Like you'd been hurt?" the woman tossed back.

Of course, she knew about Susan and had connected the dots. She'd been at the dinner where he'd proposed. He shifted his weight and rested his elbows on his knees. "What's the critical component Albert got wrong?"

"That's not something I can answer. It can't be told or explained like an equation or a lesson in a textbook. It's got to be realized and acted upon."

Well, shit. That didn't help.

"I can tell you this, Finn. No matter what thorn pricked Albert's heart, it wasn't fair to make me pay the price for loving him."

Finn flinched. Hailey could say the same thing about him. But he couldn't allow that truth to cloud his mind. He was here for Dr. Schneider—for her closure.

"Albert Higgins did love you," he said, reaching into his satchel. "I have written proof that reveals his greatest regret was losing you," Finn said, feeling the weight of Albert's pain as he handed her the slim stack of envelopes and then turned on his phone's flashlight. "You'll want to open the last one addressed to Cookie. We think it was written a couple of days or weeks before he died."

He positioned the light from his cell so she could read the shaky scribbles of an old man.

She removed the slip of paper and peered at the message. *"Remember the gift I gave you?"* she read. *"I was worried you wouldn't like it. The tears in your eyes told me you loved it. Did you keep it? Do you wear it and think of me? I should have shouted my love for you from the rooftop. I should have tended to it diligently. It's my greatest regret.* Oh, Albert, you finally understood," she whispered, her voice laced with the melancholy wisps of what could have been. She touched the paper reverently. "For a scientific man, he adored the legend of Starrycard Creek paper. He liked thinking that the minerals in the water could make dreams come true." A lone tear trailed down her cheek. She brushed it away and glanced at the stack.

Finn pocketed his phone. "Losing you was his greatest regret."

Dr. Schneider turned to him, and the dim camera light caught her solemn expression. "And it appears you're on the brink of making the same mistake as Albert."

"What are you talking about?" he stammered. "There's nothing that can be done with Susan. She's married and has a child."

"I'm not talking about Susan. I'm talking about Hailey Higgins."

"Why would you say that?" he rasped, but he couldn't hide the emotion in his voice.

"I saw how you looked at her that day I visited Starrycard

Creek Elementary. I saw it again when you were here less than two weeks ago. It was the same way Albert Higgins used to look at me. You love that woman. I also watched her walk away from you. I saw your face, Finn. It was the same expression Albert had after he told me he never loved me."

Finn swallowed past the lump in his throat. "And what face was that?"

"The face of a liar. The face of a man who couldn't determine the critical component until it was too late. The face of a man who, decades later, finally realized what he should have done."

"Maybe he wasn't built for love. Maybe I'm the same way," Finn replied, unable to rein in the razor-sharp edge in his voice. "Look what happened with Susan. You were there when we got engaged. And now she's married to another man and has a baby."

Dr. Schneider hardened her features, going into professor mode. "You're going to let one negative test result derail your entire project?"

Finn shook his head. "This isn't a thesis meeting."

"No, it's more important. This is your life, Finn. And you're smart enough to evaluate the data. You must see the parallels between yourself and Albert Higgins as clearly as I do. You have a chance to change—but that change must come from within." She held up an envelope with Cookie scribbled on the front. "What would you write on a slip of Starrycard Creek paper right now?"

He waved her off. "It's a moot point. I don't have any Starrycard paper. It would have to appear out of thin air. And a wish can only come true if it's meant for you. What if Hailey isn't meant for me?"

"You'll never know unless you risk your heart, figure out what matters, and fight for her."

He exhaled a frustrated breath. "What does that mean, professor? I'm an engineer. I need to understand the pieces I'm working with to get it right."

"Let me ask you this. What does Hailey want? What gift could only the man who truly knows and loves her give her?"

He hung his head. Grief set in as a whirling state of confusion took over. "I don't know."

"Don't they say love is always in the cards in Starrycard Creek?" she continued.

He peered at the picture in her hand. "It wasn't in the cards for you and Al."

"It's not too late for you and Hailey. You can solve this, Finn."

"What if I can't?" Frustration and an ache of longing strained his voice as he grappled with the puzzle of how to win back the heart of the woman who meant the world to him.

Ping.

Dr. Schneider pulled her phone from her purse. "We'll have to table this discussion, Finn. Shawn texted. Your opening remarks start in five minutes. We need to go. May I keep these?" she asked and rested her hand on the photo and the letters.

He ignored the clawing irritation of being unable to solve the professor's critical component riddle. "I know Hailey would be thrilled to know these items made their way to the real Cookie. She was quite touched when we discovered them. I'm sure she'd want you to keep them. I think she'd like to talk with you. She expressed a desire to learn more about her great-uncle."

Dr. Schneider stood. "Thank you, Finn. And I'm sorry you're hurting. I can feel your frustration. But I know how your mind works. I remember when you made the final calibration on your valve. When it clicked, you were positively euphoric, grinning ear to ear. You were unstoppable. You can have that again. The only person who has the power to take away the ability to experience love and joy is you."

He nodded to appease her, but he couldn't see a way back to that person.

They followed the path out of the clearing, joined the main walkway, and headed toward the hum of voices and clinking glasses. The outdoor area twinkled beneath a cascade of lights. Round tables with ivory tablecloths dotted the open-air space. Waiters crisscrossed the area, handing out drinks and an array of appetizers. He scanned the crowd and found his brother and sister standing in the back, near the catering tent. He nodded to them, then followed Dr. Schneider onto a stage. Several faculty members sat at a rectangular table on the prominent spot. A podium equipped with a microphone completed the space.

"That's your seat, Finn," Dr. Schneider whispered, pointing to the chair beside the podium. "I'm on the other side."

The emotional weight of what he'd endured hit. His hands trembled. His mind spun, unable to let go of his inability to figure out the secret to love. He set his bag on the chair and concentrated on a glass of water at his place setting. A little drink, and then he'd muddle through his speech. He lifted the glass to his lips and gulped down the liquid like a dehydrated Labrador.

What the hell was wrong with him?

Plenty, actually.

Water trickled from his stubbled chin, marking his charcoal gray sports coat with a smattering of dark spots. He rubbed his wrist across his mouth, mopping up the excess, and gazed into the crowd. Students weren't the only ones in attendance. Several cameramen were sprinkled around with their cameras pointed his way.

"What's that about?" he asked, meeting Dr. Schneider's gaze, then gesturing to the closest cameraman.

"The school started filming these a few years ago. I'm told the students and families enjoy watching them. They're also used in promotional materials. That's not a problem, is it?"

"No," he stammered.

Shit! He needed to get himself together. But all he could think about was not knowing what the hell to say to the students and not having a clue about how to win back Hailey. Not to mention— if he didn't figure it out, he was on track to become a crazy recluse riddled with regret.

Just get through the speech.

Notes. He had notes. He took another drippy, Labrador-esque sip of water and dragged his fist across his lips like a Neanderthal.

He focused on Eliza and Kieran. The pair gave off strong what-the-hell-is-wrong-with-you vibes. But he couldn't worry about his siblings. Dr. Schneider was at the mic. It was go-time.

"Welcome, Golden Tech seniors," she said as the hum of conversation died down. "To start things off, we've got your favorite judge from the paper tower competition and successful inventor of the Starrycard valve, Finnegan Starrycard, here with us tonight. Finn's going to share some words of wisdom."

The students clapped with a few whoops thrown in.

Okay, that was a good sign. Or the college students were already hammered, which was a possibility. Still, he'd take it as a win.

"Finn," she said and gestured to the podium.

Get your head in the game, man.

"Hello, good evening," he stammered, adjusting the microphone.

He should have kept his hands to himself.

A jarring band of feedback pierced the air. The audience cringed and covered their ears.

"Are you okay?" Kieran mouthed.

It was a good question.

Finn answered his brother with the universal fuck-if-I-know shrug and took another sip of water. At least it remained in his mouth.

He reached into the pocket of his sports coat and removed a few note cards. "It's an honor to speak to you on this special occasion." He glanced at his first card. "This is an exciting time in your life, but it's also a time to make measured decisions. Life doesn't always meet your expectations. Be prepared to live with a degree of disappointment."

Holy mother of God! This is what he'd written?

He should have googled motivational quotes and recited them like an automated message.

He rearranged the cards, praying he scribbled something that didn't evoke doom and gloom, when a slip of paper fell from between his horrendous talking points. "Excuse me, I dropped something." He bent down and spied a slip of Starrycard paper.

Where the hell did that come from?

Picking it up, he brushed his thumb across the familiar texture and placed it immediately. It was the piece McKenzie had given him before she puked on his shoes. He'd tucked it into his pocket. He'd never made his wish. Was the universe telling him to make that wish now? Could he dare hope that Hailey was meant for him? That she was the answer to his happiness? No, that wasn't it. It wasn't about him. What was the gift she truly wanted?

Think, think, think!

A charged jolt of aggravation tore through him. He shot up and banged his head into the corner of the podium. "Motherfucker!" he exclaimed. But he couldn't focus on the pain. He grabbed the teetering podium from plummeting onto the ground, then noticed something shooting through the air. He blinked. Damn, it was the microphone. It careened into the audience and crash-landed in a pitcher of water on a nearby table.

"Shit," he mumbled, scrambling off stage after it. He reached into the water and pulled the mic from the icy liquid. "Hello? Hello?" he said into the soaked stick. And nothing. Double shit! He broke the damned thing. He spun around to ask Dr. Schneider if there was a backup mic and slammed into the side of a waitress.

Ooph!

Cocktail shrimp flew into the air like confetti. One smacked him in the face while a few lodged themselves in his hair and beneath his collar.

Clang! The shrimp platter hit the concrete like a renegade gong.

"Your shoes!" the waitress exclaimed.

Finn pulled a chilled crustacean from behind his ear and examined his feet. Tomato-red cocktail sauce doused his last pair of fancy shoes. "That's all right. This happens to me quite a bit. And it's not puke. Then again, the night my niece puked on my eight-hundred-dollar loafers was the best night of my life."

"Okay," the woman replied, eyeing him like he should be restrained in a straitjacket. She picked up the platter and the empty cocktail sauce bowl, then looked him up and down and cringed before scuttling toward the catering tent.

At least she wasn't hurt.

He stared at the doused mic, then scanned the table with the half-filled water pitcher. "Do you mind if I leave this here?" he asked the unfortunate inhabitants sitting front row of the Finn Starrycard shitshow.

No one said a word.

That was as close to receiving permission as he would get. Gently, he rested the microphone on the table. He exhaled an audible breath and caught a glimpse of Eliza and Kieran. The pair looked on wide-eyed and slack-jawed.

So much for not fucking up.

He took a few steps, sloshing in the chilled shrimp dip. "That was unexpected, but if we don't have another mic," he said and glanced at the faculty table, whose expressions mirrored Liza and Kier's dumbfounded countenance, "I'll speak up. Can everyone hear me?"

"You'll have to speak loudly," Dr. Schneider said, still wide-eyed but able to form a sentence. She pointed toward the top of the engineering building. "They're filming this from a few different vantage points."

Shit! He'd forgotten about the cameras.

Finn shielded his eyes, looking above the Golden Tech banners hanging from the lamp posts, and zeroed in on a man on the roof of a two-story building with a camera on his shoulder.

"Shout so we can hear you on the rooftop, dude," the camera guy called, waving his free hand.

Rooftop.

"Shout it from the rooftop," Finn whispered like it was the equivalent of "open sesame" because, for his brain, it was.

Albert had wished he'd shouted his love from the rooftop.

Hailey had spoken those very words. She was prepared to shout her love from the rooftop.

That was it. He'd deciphered love's critical component. His lug-nut-brain haze lifted—or perhaps this was the effect of being concussed. Whatever the trigger, the mechanics of love came together in his mind in a symphony of moving parts. No person could be another's critical component. That's not how the machinery of love worked.

Love was action.

Motion.

Maintenance.

Love keenly acknowledged the little things, the looks, the sounds, the scents.

Love noticed. Love learned.

The critical component of love was action, and the action he needed to take was to become the man who was worthy of Hailey Higgins.

Adrenaline zinged through his body, a euphoric rush that had him grinning like a kid on Christmas morning. He waved to the guy on the roof. "I'm the one who should be shouting from the rooftop," he shouted from the ground to the guy on the rooftop, then scanned the crowd. "Forget everything I just said to you about life."

"Louder, dude," the rooftop guy called.

Louder was right. He had a message for these students. A message they needed to hear as badly as he needed to deliver it. He focused on the table with the dead mic. This table would be his platform—quite literally. He stepped onto an empty chair, then hoisted himself onto the table, his shoes marking the pristine surface with cocktail-sauce footprints.

"This guy might be nuts," a young man at the unfortunate table said to the woman beside him.

"I'll message campus security," the young woman replied.

"You're right," he said, pointing to the pair. "I'm nuts. Lug-nuts nuts. Everything makes sense." He raised his arms. "Students, you're embarking on a new chapter. Don't let fear hold you back," he called as the guy on the roof waved and gave him a thumbs-up. "You've got one life to live," Finn continued. "Live deeply. Follow your dreams. Dream big. Dream wild. And this is the most important part. Let your actions define you. By doing this, you'll probably fail spectacularly. That's good. That's how you'll grow and learn. Take it from me, it won't be easy. But when you figure out what matters. When the critical component in your life is revealed," he added, peering over his shoulder at Dr. Schneider, "you will never look back with regret."

"I regret sitting at this table," a young woman murmured.

But Finn couldn't worry about her. He was on a roll. "Let the people you care about know how you feel. My brother and sister are here with me tonight. They came with me because they were worried about me."

"I'm worried about you, man," a guy at the table murmured.

"I love you guys," Finn called. Jesus, this was freeing.

"We love you, too, buddy," Liza replied and looked over her shoulder. "You might want to wrap it up. Campus security appears to be headed this way."

"Finn," Kieran called with a note of urgency. "Seriously, we should get going."

Finn gazed at the slip in his hand. "I'm almost done." He held up the paper. "This is Starrycard paper from my hometown of Starrycard Creek, Colorado. We believe that this paper is capable of extraordinary feats." He smiled. This paper and his business card had led Hailey to him. "People write their dreams and desires on this paper, hoping their wish will come true. I didn't know what to write on this paper. But I do now. I need a pen," he said, scanning the tables. "Who has a pen?"

Eliza darted in from the side.

When had she gotten so close to him?

"The minivan will be ready to go in thirty seconds," she whispered.

"Do you have a pen? I have to do this, Liza. It's for Hailey."

"What the hell happened to you? Besides the probable head trauma?"

"I love Hailey, and I know what she deserves."

Eliza exhaled an exasperated breath. "Here." She reached into her purse and handed him a pen. "Write fast. If we get arrested, I'm telling Mom and Dad it's your fault," she grumbled, but her ghost of a grin revealed her true feelings.

He scribbled out his dream, his wish, his promise to himself and to Hailey.

Finn looked out at the students. "I'll bring my opening remarks to a close with this. Nothing matters without love. Love isn't stagnant. Love requires maintenance and attention. Nurture your love of your profession. Nurture the love in your lives." He pointed to the guy on the rooftop. "You get all that?"

"Yeah, dude. We got it. And you really might want to run."

Three officers rushed past the catering tent.

"Finn, we've got to go," Eliza growled and slapped her hand on the table.

"I just need my bag." He hopped off the table, cocktail sauce flicking from his feet, and headed toward the stage.

Dr. Schneider handed him his satchel. "That's certainly one way to deliver opening remarks."

"Thank you. Thank you for helping me understand," he said, so damned grateful to know this remarkable woman.

"And thank you." She patted his cheek. "I know this look, Finnegan Starrycard. You've put the pieces together. I had a feeling you would. Good luck."

"I'm gonna need it," he replied, glancing over his shoulder as security rushed toward him.

Beep, beep!

"That's Kieran in the minivan," Eliza called.

Finn peered down the walkway and spotted the vehicle. Its sliding side door was open, and Kieran sat in the driver's seat.

"Kier drove onto the quad? That's not allowed."

"And I'm willing to bet neither is launching college property into a pitcher of water, assaulting a waitress, then tap dancing on a table covered in shrimp cocktail sauce while showcasing a nervous breakdown. That's why we have to go, genius," Eliza shot back and grabbed him by the arm.

They hoofed it down the walkway, which was no small feat when running while marinating in shrimp dip. But he didn't give a damn about his feet. He was still flying high. "I wasn't having a nervous breakdown. I had a breakthrough. I have a plan to win Hailey back," he bit out, sprinting alongside his frighteningly fast sister.

"Does it include shrimp cocktail?" she asked between breaths.

"No."

"Thank God, now get in," she ordered, diving into the kid-mobile.

Finn was right behind her.

"Hit the gas," Eliza called, slamming the sliding door like they'd just robbed a bank.

Eliza looked out the back. "I don't see any flashing lights."

Finn hoisted himself into one of the bucket seats and caught his breath. "What a night."

"Yeah, on a scale of one to what-the-actual-fuck, I'd say you broke the scale with that performance," Kieran said, taking a sharp right, then a fast left, tires squealing as they headed toward the interstate.

"I get it now, guys. I hit my head, then there was shrimp, and my shoes are fucking ruined, but when the guy on the roof said *rooftop*, it came together. Everything clicked. I know what the critical component is."

Kieran glanced over his shoulder at Eliza. "Do we need to take him to a hospital?"

"No," Finn exclaimed, laughing, light as a feather. "Don't you get it? I love Hailey. I love her and I've got a plan to win her heart —a complex sequence of events to prove to her I won't let her down again."

"Even if he is rocking a concussion, I haven't seen him this happy in ages," Eliza said, plucking a shrimp from beneath his collar and popping it into her mouth. "What's your plan?"

"A multi-prong approach culminating on the last day of school."

"Go on," Kier replied, catching his gaze in the rearview mirror.

"I know I've been playing the I-alone-can-fix-it card, but I can't be that guy anymore. I'll need help. A lot of help. We'll need to get Owen on the phone. I have a print request that can't wait." He turned to his sister. "You'll need to call Jack. I'll need him onboard. And Kieran?"

"Yeah?"

"I need to speak with the Starrycard Creek small business owners."

"All of them?"

"Uh-huh. And we'll need to loop Mom in, too. And Nico. Remind me to apologize to him. I was a giant asshat. And I should do something nice for him." He sat back and sighed, a steely resolve surging through him. "I won't end up a crazy recluse."

"You might not end up a recluse, but I'm not so sure about the crazy part," Kieran answered, but there was nothing but warmth in his usually tepid tone. "Wow, look!" he exclaimed, pointing out the window.

"A shooting star. Isn't that something," Eliza commented.

"Shooting star," Finn echoed, catching the tail end of the faint line of magical light as another piece to winning Hailey back clicked into the love machinery cranking away in his head. He pulled his cell from his pocket. "There's a call I need to make. I should have made it a long time ago." Finn removed the folded square from his wallet. "Do you have a trash bag in here, Liza?"

"It's a minivan. Of course, I do. It's in the pocket in front of you."

He dropped the square into the bag, like a drowning man, releasing an iron chain from around his neck and rising to the surface.

"Finn, seriously, are you okay?" Eliza asked, concern coating the question.

He inhaled a sweet breath. "I've never been better." He looked between his siblings. "What do you say? Are you guys in? Are you willing to help Finnegan Starrycard, local handyman, get the girl?"

Eliza and Kieran shared a knowing look.

"Little star," Eliza replied and squeezed his hand, "we're Team Love-Is-Always-In-The-Cards. So yes, big brother, we're in. We're always in."

CHAPTER
Twenty
HAILEY

"I KNOW YOU'RE SCARED. I know you're not sure where you'll end up, but I believe you'll be fine. No, better than fine," Hailey said, swallowing past the emotion in her throat as she peered at the kittens. Whiskers and Sweetie looked up at her from their spot in the milk crate on the front seat of her sedan, listening like furry little students. "The rescue organization matched you with your forever home. Our time together was always going to end. But our happy times will always live in our hearts. That's something my dad would say." She glanced at her tote. The mid-morning light poured in through the car window and glinted off the top of the pickle jar. She unscrewed the lid, closed her eyes, dipped her hand into the papery sea, and selected a random fragment.

Julianne, the first time I kissed you, I knew my purpose in this world was to spend my life loving you.

She exhaled slowly, dropped the slip into the jar, then returned her attention to the kittens. "You'll be loved, so loved, in your new home. This is a happy day. A momentous day. A day of new beginnings."

Sure, she was giving this pep talk to the kittens, but the message also echoed in her heart.

It was the last day of school. The day of the Starrycard Creek Sunshine Jubilee. Her class had been busy making sunshine signs out of paper plates and popsicle sticks and practicing their parading skills on the playground. Eliza had texted her last night, letting her know the school would be on a delayed schedule today —a late start—due to an emergency construction project on Main Street, which turned out to be helpful. Seconds after the text came in, a woman named Annie had called from the animal rescue organization on the outskirts of Starrycard Creek. An application had been approved for Whiskers and Sweetie. Annie had suggested they meet in the school's parking lot to do the handoff.

And that's where Hailey and the kitties were, sitting in her sedan, inhabiting this limbo, unsure what the following days and even hours would bring. The situation was similar to her life after she'd been blindsided at the altar.

Could she trust that a handyman's business card and some handmade paper would show her the way again?

It didn't seem likely.

She scratched beneath Mr. Whiskerfrown's chin. He was living up to his name this morning. His kitty perma-scowl deepened like the cat knew she was sugarcoating the situation. "I know," she confessed. "You're calling me out. Moment of truth," she continued, looking between the pair. "I'm nervous, too. How about this? It's safe to say we're in the same boat when it comes to not knowing what the future holds. But we're hopeful, and we're different now from where we started, up on the side of that mountain road, soaked to the bone. We're different because of the time we've spent together. You guys are healthy, and I . . ." She reached into her tote and removed a card from the side pocket. She couldn't bring herself to part with it. The card had comforted her when her life in Kansas had gone sideways. She smiled at the kittens and began again. "You're bigger and stronger, and I know my worth and understand the kind of love and life I want." She brushed her thumb across the bumps of the embossed letters on the business card and inhaled the hint of fresh-cut wood. "Oh, Finn," she said, each syllable carrying an undertone of longing.

Of course, she missed him. But she'd changed. Standing on that patch of grass at Golden Tech, she'd tapped into a strength, a sureness about herself. A steady stillness she hadn't experienced since before her parents had passed. It was as if a veil had been lifted, and as much as her heart yearned to be with her business card boyfriend, to gaze into his sage-green eyes and lose herself in his kisses, she understood she couldn't compete with the sullen and bitter version of himself—not if she wanted to love and honor herself in the way her parents would want. She wouldn't allow herself to become a man's secret girlfriend again.

Goodbye, Doormat City!

The man meant for her would shout his devotion from the rooftop. That's what she'd wanted to do for Finn, and she'd meant it. A life partner would want the same.

It didn't mean the pieces of her life had come together and revealed a precise roadmap to her happily ever after. Still, from the moment she walked away from her handyman, she'd known she'd made the right choice.

From there, life had moved quickly.

She hadn't been sure what the drive back to Starrycard Creek with Kieran would be like.

It had turned out to be exactly what she needed.

The reserved man seemed to have had quite a bit on his mind. They'd made small talk, and he'd asked about her family and where she grew up. She'd told him about what it was like having teachers for parents and how she'd had the same best friend for most of her life. He was a good listener, and talking about her parents solidified her resolve. About an hour into the drive, the conversation ebbed. They'd existed in an easy silence, which had turned out to be the perfect precursor to what happened after he'd gotten her back to Starrycard Creek.

Kieran had checked her car and insisted on calling the local mechanic to come to the cabin and switch out the old battery. After that, and again without mentioning Finn, he'd helped her move her things from Starrycard Cabin and into her place.

Alone in the snug space—her cozy cabin—with the scent of the new hardwood floors permeating the air, she'd thanked Kieran and bid goodbye to the man. She'd listened to the rumble of his SUV as it crunched along the gravel, then faded into stillness when he hit the main road and headed back to town. In that silent slip of time, she'd invited the quiet into her heart and explored. She'd taken her time investigating the space.

Before that day, Finn had been with her every time she'd visited the cabin. On her own, she connected to the man who'd built this cabin and promised herself she wouldn't allow her heart to harden. Still, she couldn't help but think of Finn. He'd meticulously brought the cabin back to life. His fingerprints marked every surface, every pipe, every hinge, every outlet. His intensity lingered in the air. Feeling him around her, she could only hope he would find a way to let go of the pain that held him back from being the man she knew he could be.

Her Starrycard paper wish.

And then, in line with turning over a new leaf, that meant working on her happiness, she focused on the cabin. Aside from the faux sheepskin rug, the place was a blank slate. She'd considered removing the floor covering, but she didn't. She'd stroked the silky surface and smiled. It was no wonder McKenzie liked it. It was girly, comfy, and just plain fun. She wanted to add to that vibe and make this place a home. As if the universe wanted to tell her she was on the right track, when she'd gone to check the mail, she'd found a letter from the Bank of Colorado with a hefty check enclosed. Her great-uncle had nearly eleven thousand dollars in savings when he'd passed. That money had become hers.

Hello, retail therapy.

The next day, she'd headed to downtown Starrycard Creek. And she kept going into town, exploring the quaint community, ducking into shops, and learning how to enjoy her own company with the delicate babbling and splash of the creek soothing her senses as she strolled down the streets.

That didn't mean she was over Finn. She loved him. She did. She couldn't turn off her heart as if it were a switch. And she missed him. But it wasn't her job to fix him. Still, it didn't mean she had to ignore him. He'd cleared much of the overgrown brush between their properties. Taking advantage of the view, she'd allow herself one thirty-second indulgence every evening. She'd gaze out the window toward his cabin and take in the pulses of light from his television. When the thirty seconds were up, she'd concentrate on her cabin.

Over the last three weeks, she'd spent a good portion of her new windfall purchasing items to decorate and furnish the space. She'd learned that while Starrycard Creek had a reputation for producing high-quality handmade paper, the town was also home to many talented artisans and merchants. She'd gotten to know the shop owners. She'd seen her students out with their families. The children made her feel like an instant celebrity when they'd spot her on the street. She'd even enjoyed dinner alone, eating at Goldie's restaurant. Still, she wasn't sure where she was meant to be in this world. She'd invited Nico to the cabin for his realtor advice. He'd assessed the property and advised that she could sell the cabin and walk away with a sizable chunk of change. He'd mentioned developers were itching to pick up mountainside properties in this rustic and untouched part of Colorado.

She couldn't discount this information. Selling was a possibility. Starrycard Creek Elementary wasn't the only school that had offered her a teaching contract. There was a chance she'd need to start looking for a home in another city.

She removed two envelopes from her tote. Each contained a teaching contract. One from Starrycard Creek Elementary and one from Denver. Neither signed.

And the question she'd been ignoring the last few weeks swirled in her mind.

Should she stay in Starrycard Creek, or should she go?

She removed the contracts from their corresponding envelopes. While they were for two different schools, each had the same verbiage and directions written below the contract's language. She looked between them and studied the last few lines above where she was supposed to sign.

Check the statement that applies.
__ I accept the position.
__ I decline the position.

She folded the contracts and returned them to the envelopes when her phone pinged. Emotion welled in her chest. "That could be Annie from the rescue," she said to Whiskers and Sweetie. She checked the screen. Nope, it wasn't Annie. An alert for a new love story on the I Said Yes Shooting Stars blog had posted. She'd resubscribed to the emails the night she'd returned from Golden. But she didn't click the link. Unable to stop herself, she raised her gaze from her phone and surveyed where Finn used to park his truck when he'd picked her up from school.

"What is that?" she whispered as the breath caught in her throat. She blinked as if she were trying to reset reality. "No! It can't be."

But there was no denying it. A red Porsche 911 with a distinct dent on the driver's side door—the same red Porsche she and Grant were supposed to purchase after they'd become man and wife—was parked in Finn's spot. From her vantage point, she couldn't see if anyone was in the car. Her heart hammered in her chest as actual hammering—well, knocking, to be exact—pulled her attention from the dented car. Hailey gasped and whipped her head toward the banging on the passenger side window, again, barely able to believe what was right in front of her.

A wisp of a woman with an unlit cigarette hanging from her

hot pink lips peered through the half-open window and winked. "Hello, sugar tits. We meet again."

"Flo . . ." Hailey stammered, still not sure if this was happening. "Flo from Stu's Weddings and Funerals 4 Less?"

"The one and only!" The woman removed the cigarette from between her lips and slipped it behind her ear. "I saw you admiring my new car. A Porsche 911 from nineteen ninety-seven. A real classic. She's a beauty, isn't she?"

Hailey opened her car door and walked to the passenger side, moving cautiously like she'd entered the twilight zone. Slack-jawed, her gaze bounced between the tiny woman she never expected to see again and the old sports car she also never expected to see again. "I know that car."

"I thought you might," the woman answered, her painted pink lips twisting into a sly smirk. "You see, someone else wanted to buy it. I've had my eye on it but didn't have the cash to snap it up. The car lot guy said he'd hold it for me unless another buyer came forward. To my dismay, one did. But when this potential buyer came in with his new pregnant wife to do the paperwork, it turned out they both had terrible credit. The rates for a loan on a sports car were sky high, let alone the cost of insurance. The buyer was forced to walk away. The dealer called me after they left. I'd been saving up for it, and the timing was perfect. I had just made the last twenty bucks to buy that beauty."

"Twenty dollars?" Hailey repeated.

"The cash you left in the bride's room to cover the cost of your girls popping out at the altar. Yep, sugar tits, your sugar tits got me over the finish line. I'm in charge of enforcing the nudity clause, and Stu lets me keep the cash."

Hailey glanced down at her sage-green A-line dress with a demur neckline. She'd seen it in a shop window on Main Street last week and purchased it. Thankfully, there was no chance of a boobalicious reveal in this number.

"That's fascinating," she replied, blown away, gobsmacked that her R-rated altar disaster had played a part in the Porsche.

But what was Flo doing here?

"How did you end up—"

"And there's more," Flo interrupted, her eyes twinkling with mischief.

"More?" Hailey blathered, still thrown for a loop.

Flo pulled the cigarette from behind her ear and used it to wave in Hailey. "There's gossip going around town about the newlyweds."

"What are people saying?" Hailey asked, riveted. Might as well go with it. If she'd been rendered insane and was currently hallucinating, at least this was one heck of a delusion.

"Stu's cousin maintains security surveillance videos for some local businesses back in Kansas."

"Okay," Hailey replied, enthralled.

"He said that this newly married couple worked for the same company, and Stu's cousin monitored this company's security feed. The newly married couple's boss asked Stu's cousin to check the building surveillance videos and found footage of the couple engaging in explicit behaviors that are frowned upon in the workplace. Namely, on their boss's desk and desk chair."

"Wow," Hailey breathed.

"They were fired. And there's no baby."

Hailey took a step back. "What?"

"More juicy stuff on video. Stu's cousin said he heard the newlyweds talking on the surveillance video. Apparently, the bride went to her sister's house to use one of her pregnancy tests. This sister had been trying to get pregnant for years. The bride took a test with her sister, then picked up the wrong one. A knocked-up switcheroo."

"That's . . . wow," Hailey replied, relying on *wow* quite a bit—because, *wow,* Flo was serving up one heck of a story.

"Last I heard, they're both unemployed and living in the bride's mother's basement. Lucky thing you didn't end up with that nimrod. *I guess he's not meant for you,*" the woman added and winked.

He's not meant for you.

Hailey gasped. How many more jaw-dropping nuggets would Flo drop?

She studied the woman, and like when she'd first laid eyes on Flo, she made note of her pale blue eyes. "That's what was written on a strip of wallpaper in the bride's room. Did you write it?"

Flo tapped the tip of her cigarette to her chin as the whisper of a grin graced her pink lips. "Did I tell you I have a granddaughter, Miss Higgins?"

Hailey cocked her head to the side. Where was Flo going with that question? "Yes, I believe you did," she answered, wracking her brain. "You said you couldn't run behind schedule because you were taking her to the park with your sister."

"My granddaughter drew this." Flo pulled a folded square of paper from her pocket. "Take a look," she said, handing it over.

Hailey brushed her thumb across the fibrous surface and placed the paper immediately. "This is Starrycard paper."

"It is. My sister sends it to my granddaughter. She likes the texture for drawing."

Hailey unfolded the page and peered at a child's drawing of two people. It featured a tall stick figure with red hair, brown eyes, and a green dress. This stick lady was placing a bandage on a smaller stick figure's leg. This child-sized stick person had long hair, light blue eyes, and shed dark blue tears. A thick red line was drawn on her hand.

"That's you and Misty, my granddaughter, with the fish-sized tears falling off her face," Flo explained and chuckled, but her expression grew serious. "Misty talked about you for a week. She called you the nice substitute teacher, Miss Higgins, who gave her a piece of licorice and put a Band-Aid on her boo-boo when she fell on the playground."

"I remember Misty," Hailey said, recalling the blue-eyed girl. She met Flo's gaze. Flo and Misty's eyes were the same color. "I thought there was something familiar about you when you came into the bride's room. You knew who I was. You knew I'd been a substitute teacher in your granddaughter's class. Did you write that message on the wallpaper to warn me about Grant? How would you know to do that? We'd never met."

"Let's just say I might be a crusty old broad, but anyone who's good to my Misty is aces in my book. And . . ." the woman continued, her smirk reappearing, "when you and Mr. Rimnod came in to book Stu's place, your nimrod went outside to take a phone call. I was on a smoke break and overheard him talking about the Porsche 911—the one I'd wanted to buy. He was telling whoever was on the line that he'd figured out a way to get it. Then he said they needed to fix the office chair they'd broken doing-the-dirty on it the night before so their boss wouldn't think they were up to any hanky-panky."

Hailey blinked back tears. She'd thought she'd been alone that day. She'd been unaware that anyone was looking out for her. "Thank you," she whispered and hugged the tiny woman.

"None of this touchy-feely stuff. I see enough of that garbage at work. I'm no do-gooding angel. I had a feeling your credit wasn't in the toilet like your nimrod's. If you'd married him, I wouldn't have my dream car. I'd say it worked out for the good gals in the end, right, sugar tits?" Flo tossed back, harnessing her no-nonsense persona, but she brushed her fingertips across her cheek when she turned away.

"Is that why you're here?" Hailey asked softly. "Did you track me down to let me know what happened? But how would you even know where I went?"

Beep, beep!

Flo gestured to the street toward a van with *Rescue Pet Alliance* written on the side. It pulled onto the side of the road and parked in front of the Porsche. "That's how I knew. Well, how I guessed you were here."

A woman got out of the driver's seat and waved. "Is that Misty's Miss Higgins, Flo?"

"It's her, Annie."

"Annie?" Hailey echoed, staring at another familiar face from her botched wedding day.

"This is my sister," Flo explained, gesturing to Annie as the woman crossed the street and joined them. "I believe you met her shortly after you snuck out the window at Stu's."

Hailey looked between the women, then focused on Annie. "You're the Rescue Pet Alliance lady."

"And you're the crying bride from the side of the road," Annie lobbed back.

"What are you doing here?" Hailey asked.

"Rescue Pet Alliance is a national volunteer program. I help with animal transportation. I volunteer to pick up animals at overcrowded shelters and drive them to rescue centers in different states. We often make trips to the rescue shelter outside Starrycard Creek. I'm retired, and doing this allows me to see other parts of the country. I try to raise a little money for them in each town I stop in. Sometimes, my sister comes along. Except this time, she drove behind my van in a flashy red sports car. How'd you end up here, Miss Higgins?"

"Right after we spoke, I opened a letter and learned I'd inherited my great-uncle's cabin in Starrycard Creek. I drove straight here."

"Albert Higgins?" Annie asked.

Hailey's eyes widened. "Yes."

"I believe he donated quite a bit of money to the local animal rescue. It takes a kind soul to do that—like you," Annie added.

"Me? I only gave you ten dollars."

"Don't think I didn't notice that you gave me the last bill in your wallet. You Higgins folk are good people. Good hearts." Annie peered into the sedan. "Now, I believe those orange beauties are the precious cargo I'm here to transport."

This was it. Time to say goodbye. A wave of sorrow washed over her as her gaze lingered on the sweet balls of fluff.

"Do they have names, honey?" Annie pressed.

Hailey brushed a tear from her cheek. She opened the

passenger side door and picked up the crate. "Sweetie is the girl, and Whiskers is the boy."

Flo frowned. "That boy looks ornery."

"He's like that when he's scared or unsure. He's a fuzzy lump of love beneath that scowl."

Like a handyman she knew. But she left out that part.

"It's too bad it didn't work out with you keeping the kittens. I got a real cat vibe from you, Miss Higgins. You even look alike," Annie remarked, taking in the redheaded trio.

Hailey scratched beneath Whiskers' chin. "Now isn't the best time for me to adopt a pet. I'm not sure where I'll be in the next few months. I might leave Starrycard Creek," she answered as a rush of conflicting emotions washed over her.

"Well, don't you worry about these cuties. I'm told they're going to a good home. A newly engaged couple—very much in love. Time to go. Say goodbye to nice Miss Higgins," Annie crooned, speaking to the animals.

Hailey nodded, a lump forming in her throat. "We had quite an adventure, didn't we, little stars?"

"Little stars?" Annie repeated.

Hailey cocked her head to the side. "What?"

Annie smiled. "You called the kittens little stars."

She hadn't realized she'd used the term of endearment. "It's something I heard from a student at the elementary school."

"Well, good luck to you, Miss Higgins," Annie said and headed toward the van. "Are you coming, Flo? We're on a tight schedule."

"Just saying my goodbyes," Flo answered, then set her pale blue gaze on Hailey. "Let's keep in touch. Take my card." She reached into her cleavage and removed the paper rectangle.

Hailey studied the item. "This is Starrycard Creek paper."

"My sister had them made for me. She says there's something special about the paper, special about this town and the creek that runs through it."

"She's right. This is a special place." Hailey turned the card over. "Florence LaMont, independent bridal consultant," she said, reading the embossed words. She eyed the woman. "Independent bridal consultant? Are you leaving Stu's Weddings and Funerals 4 Less?"

"I'm broadening my horizon, and I like it here. I bet my expertise would be helpful in a little place like this. I'm pretty good with brides, don't you think?"

Hailey blinked, again on the verge of tears. "You were good to me."

Flo slipped the cigarette between her lips and frowned. "I feel like you're about to get mushy again." She stepped back and gave Hailey the once-over. "That dress looks more like you. That shade of green suits you."

Hailey smoothed the fabric. "What do you mean, it looks more like me?"

"In the bride's room, you told me your wedding dress wasn't really you. I said, 'Who are you?' You didn't have an answer then, but I'd reckon you have an answer now."

"What makes you say that?" Hailey asked, not sure of anything.

Flo pointed to the picture. "You look more like Misty's drawing."

Hailey studied the crayon strokes. "How do I look in the drawing?"

"Happy, like you might have figured out who you are and what's meant for you. Am I right, sugar tits?"

Hailey exhaled a slow, steady breath, feeling the void in her heart mend as she embraced the woman her parents would want her to be. A woman who understood her purpose. A woman who knew her value.

She returned the drawing to Flo, then glanced at the envelopes in her tote. "Will you be going past the post office on your way out of town?"

"I'm sure we'll pass by one."

"Would you pop a letter in the mail for me?" She grabbed her tote from her car and removed the envelopes and a pen. Using the hood of her sedan as a table, she signed each contract and checked the correct corresponding box. An electric thrill coursed through her veins. Her body tingled, moving as if guided by an invisible, other-worldly force. She sealed both envelopes, fished a stamp from her wallet, and affixed it to the one going to Denver. She held out the Denver-bound envelope. "I know what's meant for me."

Flo plucked the letter from her grip. "Good for you, sugar tits," she said with an appraising nod before heading toward the Porsche.

Hailey watched the cars disappear down the street. "Last day," she said, gazing at the envelope containing the Starrycard Creek teaching contract. She picked up her tote and headed toward the building. The second she opened the door, something felt off. She took a few more steps, then stopped dead in her tracks. It was quiet, too quiet. According to Eliza's email, the children weren't due at school for another hour, but the teachers and staff should be here. Their cars were in the parking lot. She walked down the empty hall, her flats the only sound echoing through the corridor. She peered into every room. Empty. Empty. Empty. Was there a faculty meeting scheduled? She kicked up her pace, her heart racing. Rounding the corner, she entered the office and skidded to a halt. Her jaw dropped when she locked eyes with the room's lone inhabitant.

What was he doing here?

CHAPTER

Twenty~One

HAILEY

"KIERAN?" Hailey exclaimed, trying to clear the fog of utter confusion clouding her brain.

Finn's brother sat in the school secretary's chair, his hands folded on the desk. "Hello, Miss Higgins."

She scanned the space. "Where is everyone?"

"Not here," he replied.

No kidding!

Still dazed, she held up the envelope. "I need to give this to Eliza. It's due today."

"Is that the Starrycard Creek teaching contract?" he asked, his face not giving anything away.

"It is."

"Hold on to it. You can deliver it to Eliza. She's downtown," he said with a twitch of a grin.

What was going on here?

"Downtown? She's there now? I thought there was a delayed start. Where are the other teachers?"

"With the students downtown," he replied in a maddeningly mild tone.

These unreadable Starrycard men would be the death of her.

A prick of anxiety emanated through her chest. "They've already left? The parade started? What about my students?"

"They're with Eliza, down—"

"Yes, downtown," she finished, hating to cut the guy off, but she needed more information. "What happened? Why did they leave before I arrived?"

"A last-minute scheduling change."

An unsettling unease took hold. "Nobody mentioned that to me."

"It must have been an oversight. Perhaps the email notification went out to permanent staff and not to you because you're listed as a substitute teacher with our school."

All the Starrycard siblings shared the same sage-green eyes, and as much as the oldest Starrycard was trying to hide it with his placid demeanor, excitement glinted in his gaze.

She watched him closely. "Perhaps," she answered. Something was up. But she wasn't getting any answers here. "I should get downtown to be with my class. It is the last day."

"It is, indeed. Let me walk with you. You can't drive. Main Street is only open to foot traffic today on account of the jubilee."

"Okay," she replied warily, still trying to figure out what Kieran had up his sleeve and why the entire school would leave without her on purpose.

He came to her side, and the pair exited the building. They strolled down the sidewalk. Golden sunlight bathed the Colorado landscape, casting dappled shadows as the mountain breeze rustled through aspen leaves along the creek's edge.

She and Kieran walked without speaking for the first few minutes, the splash and gurgle of the creek filling the space until she couldn't take it.

She held up the envelope with the contract. "Do you want me to tell you what I decided?"

"No," he replied, looking ahead and not missing a beat.

"No?" she exclaimed.

"It's prudent to ensure a comprehensive review of potential

additional information that may impact your decision before turning over a legally binding contract."

She studied the man. "Huh?"

"We want to show you something before you turn in your contract," Kieran said, thankfully dropping the lawyer-speak.

"We?" she replied, reduced to one-word utterances.

His cell phone chimed before she could form a question with more than one syllable.

He held it so she could view the image. "This is for you."

"Me?" *Ugh!* She had to stop communicating like a befuddled cavewoman. But she couldn't help it. When she looked at the screen, she couldn't believe her eyes. She peered at two familiar smiling faces, a man and a woman she'd seen but never met.

"Hi, Hailey," the smiling brunette crooned, "I'm Caroline Starrycard. I heard you've been wearing my clothes."

What a way to meet Finn's little sister.

Hailey blinked, praying her mind and mouth would cooperate. "Yeah, yes, I did wear some of your clothes. They're great—comfy, super-comfy. I hope you don't mind," she blathered, but that word salad was better than nothing.

"I don't mind at all. You probably wonder why my brother and I are calling you," she continued.

"Yes, I am."

Caroline's bright expression grew serious. "We're calling to tell you that Finn is not a flat tire."

Hailey glanced up at Kieran. The man appeared to suppress a grin.

She returned her attention to the cell phone. "I'm not sure what that means."

"Let me help," Christian Starrycard said. "Finn is a fully functioning tire—a tire with purpose. And don't mind the cameras today. They can be jarring at first, but just ignore them."

"Cameras?" Hailey eked out, returning to one-word utterances.

Christian offered up a sparkling grin. "I know a lot about them. You might recognize me. I'm—"

"You're Christian Starrycard. I know who you are," Hailey said, finishing his sentence.

His million-dollar smile widened. "You're a baseball fan?"

She shook her head. "No. I don't know anything about baseball. Finn showed me a picture of his brothers and sisters. I recognized you from it."

The wattage on Christian's grin dialed down a few notches. "You know me from a family photo?"

"Chris, let it go," Kieran said, still seeming to work overtime to bite back a grin.

"Our brother is a good guy," Caroline explained. "He cares about you. We thought you should know that."

What had Finn done over these last few weeks? What had he said to his family? What happened to keeping their *transactions* on the down low? She mustered a grin, needing to play this close to the vest. "He's lucky to have siblings who care about him as much as I can tell you all do."

Kieran scanned the street. "All right, time's up, gang," he said to his siblings, sounding very much like the oldest. "The rest is up to Finn."

"Bye, Hailey," Caroline chimed.

Christian's brows drew together. "If you were interested in learning about major league baseball, I could—"

"Not today, Chris," Kieran quipped and ended the video call.

Hailey tried to read Kieran, but the man's expression remained neutral. "Can anyone ever tell what you're thinking? Family, friends, girlfriends?" she asked.

A muscle ticked on his jaw. It must be a Starrycard trait. "I don't date. I'm too busy working to keep developers from trying to turn this town into a gaudy tourist attraction."

"Can you at least tell me what that call with your brother and sister was about?" she asked, changing gears as they neared the park and outdoor amphitheater. A few more minutes, and they'd pass by the first row of shops on Main Street.

He glanced at her. "Just a typical Starrycard shitshow." His words flowed in a monotone stream, again lacking any hint of emotional inflection, but he couldn't hide the love shining in his eyes. He cleared his throat. "I'd like to share something with you about Finn."

"All right."

"From a young age," he continued, his voice softening, a warmth overriding his tone's usual neutrality, "Finn loved puzzles. He adored taking things apart and putting them back together. He loved machines—the sounds, the smells, the textures. He'd work for hours to figure out how parts came apart and went together. It wasn't always easy for him. He'd make mistakes, and often, the assembly became ten times harder than it had to be. But once he saw the whole picture, once he understood the mistakes he'd made and could see the path forward, there was no stopping him."

Her heart couldn't take much more. She loved Finnegan Starrycard, but he'd made himself clear the last time they spoke.

Don't stay in Starrycard Creek for me.

His words had cut to the bone. He'd embraced his sullen, sulking side. He'd chosen to harden his heart.

Perhaps something had changed.

"Why are you telling me this, Kieran? Why is it so important for you and your siblings to tell me about Finn?"

"Because as much as we love our brother, we're also looking out for you. We know he hurt you. You didn't deserve that."

She trembled as emotion welled in her chest. Aside from calls and video chats with Izzy, she'd been so very alone in this world these last few years. She glanced into her canvas tote at the top of her pickle jar, then focused on the envelope in her hand. She met Kieran's gaze and nodded, worried her words would unleash a torrent of tears if she spoke.

"And I'm here to prepare you," the man added with a slightly ominous edge to the warning.

"To prepare me for what?" she asked, coming to a halt.

Kieran stopped beside her. "That additional information I mentioned earlier. You'll have to—" His phone pinged. He slipped it from his pocket and glared at the screen. "I'm sorry. I need to take this. It's a pressing matter for the town." He held the cell to his ear. "Yes. What do you mean it's a requirement of the land trust? Hold on," he murmured, then pointed down the street. "Keep walking. The banners will explain what's coming."

"The Sunshine Jubilee banners?" she asked.

He nodded, then turned and resumed his call.

She stared down the road. There wasn't much else to do other than keep going.

What had Finn orchestrated for her? The scope seemed to be widening by the second.

She continued down the sidewalk. She'd expected to see someone—anyone—but the place was a ghost town. Where was everyone? She concentrated on her breath, her steady footsteps, and the soothing sound of the creek. Just when she was about to turn back and demand Kieran tell her exactly what was going on, a pair of light brown pigtails peeked out from inside the Brimble's Deli.

"Hey, Miss Higgins," McKenzie called, leaping onto the sidewalk.

Hailey gasped. "Hello! You startled me. What are you doing here by yourself?"

"Giving you this," the child replied and handed her a large empty wicker basket that could easily hold a few pieces of firewood.

"What's it for?"

"I told you. It's for you. It's part of the plan," the child chirped, then skipped down the street. "Keep walking, Miss Higgins, and don't forget to read the banners," she called over her shoulder.

"Finnegan Starrycard, what have you done?" Hailey whispered, then spied the first paper banner hanging from the light post. Her brows knit together. Her class had seen the approved design—a lovely sun dotted with stars over a mountain with a creek running through the center. But that wasn't what was embossed on this giant sheet of handmade paper set in a protective clear sleeve. The banner in front of her had only words— words meant for her.

To: Hailey Higgins
From: her business card boyfriend.

Her pulse kicked up as she approached the next banner.

I'm sorry.

The next.

I love you, Hailey Higgins.

"Oh, Finn," she breathed, her heart ready to leap into her throat. She could hear murmurs and footsteps woven in with the rush of the creek, but she couldn't take her eyes off the banners.

She continued down the street and read the next message.

I figured out life's critical component.

Had he? Her heart wanted it to be true.

She peered ahead. Main Street ended at the Starrycard Creek Paper Company, where the valley met the mountain. The final banner hung on the lamppost across from the two-story blond brick building.

I should have done what I'm about to do sooner.

Her already elevated pulse jumped. What was he about to do?

The thought barely registered when the thunderous beat of footsteps drowned out the rush of the creek. She turned and watched wide-eyed as her second graders sprinted toward her with their paper plate sun signs in one hand and something red in another.

"We've got presents for you. We brought you some of your favorite things, Miss Higgins," a little boy called.

Hailey knelt so the crush of children could easily slip their treats and paper treasures into the basket.

"I made you a paper star. Lots of us did."

"I've got a little jar of pickles for you, Miss Higgins."

"I've got cherry licorice. I took a bite, but the rest is for you."

Grinning from ear to ear, she glanced around as children from other grades, teachers, and many of the shopkeepers she'd come to know over the last few weeks added treats and folded paper designs to the basket.

Finn's parents, Eliza, and his brother, Owen, joined the mix.

"You *can* touch this," Finn's father, Hank, said, beaming as he added a cherry licorice twist to the basket.

"Dad, you gotta stop with the nineties music references. It's getting creepy," Owen murmured, shaking his head as he added a little jar of pickles to her basket.

"Yes, excuse my husband," Maeve offered, placing a licorice twist into the basket. "It's not time for hammers, honey," she said and kissed Hank's cheek.

"Ignore them," Eliza mouthed.

Hailey couldn't wipe the smile off her face as the Starrycards mixed into the mass of people who seemed to be in on whatever Finn had planned. She thanked everyone, her heart nearly bursting with gratitude. As the voices died down, she searched the sea of faces, expecting to see her handyman, but he wasn't with the group.

"I've got another licorice twist for you, Miss Higgins," McKenzie said, setting the candy in the basket.

The crowd went silent like McKenzie's words were code for something.

Hailey observed as everyone's gaze shifted to the paper company.

"And I've got the marmalade," a man called.

Finn.

She turned toward the Starrycard Paper building and spied the man standing on the roof of the two-story structure. With a jar of orange marmalade in his hand and an axe in the other, he rocked work boots, a denim shirt, and a tool belt like the handyman gods had anointed him their chosen one. It was the same outfit he'd had on the night they met.

Invisible strings pulled tight within her chest as her heart raced. "What are you doing up there?"

He smiled, and the action lit up his face. The man's exuberance rivaled the brightest star. "I love you, Hailey Higgins. I'm shouting it from the rooftop."

Hailey shielded her eyes. "Who's up there with you?"

"My grandparents."

"Hello, dear," Goldie called, rising from a folding chair. "Rex and I haven't been up here in ages."

"Quite a view," Rex said, cigar in hand as he waved.

"Hailey Higgins," Finn continued, "I'm proclaiming my undying adoration for you in front of my family and before the town I love. You were right about everything."

"As an attorney and a woman, I'd advise you to get that in writing," Maeve remarked, eliciting a few whoops and claps from the crowd.

Hailey nodded to the mayor, then peered up at her handyman. "You're shouting from a rooftop." It's what she'd wanted, metaphorically, but it was literally happening right before her eyes. And it was like something out of a dream.

Eliza came to her side. "How are you doing?"

Hailey swallowed hard as two men with cameras swooped in and aimed them straight at her. That must have been what Christian had warned her about. "I'm not used to being the center of attention. Is Finn okay? Did he hit his head?"

"Oh, he hit his head," Eliza replied with a wry twist to her lips, "but he's never been better."

"I'm coming down," Finn called.

Hailey gasped. "He's not going to jump, is he?"

"No, he's taking the stairs," a woman answered.

Hailey turned to find Dr. Schneider and a slew of young men and women in Golden Tech T-shirts. The crowd parted, and a group pushed a rolling flatbed with a giant paper staircase extending at least thirty feet into the air toward the building.

"What a surprise to see you, Professor. And what is that?" Hailey asked, eyeing the paper monstrosity.

"It's an engineering project," Dr. Schneider explained, pride written all over her face. "Finn worked with a group of students to construct a staircase using paper and duct tape as a sort of community service project for . . ."

"For causing mayhem and property damage to the Golden Tech campus," Eliza supplied.

"Mayhem?" Hailey asked, again reduced to one-word utterances.

Eliza cringed. "It's a long story—for another time."

"We can add it to the list of surprises," Hailey murmured, finding her voice.

"It appears you're on the receiving end of quite a few revelations today," Dr. Schneider remarked. The professor's gaze flashed with a wistful gleam as if she were momentarily lost in a memory.

Hailey nodded. "It does appear that way, Doc—"

"Why don't you call me Cookie," Dr. Schneider said and touched the thin gold bracelet on her wrist.

What?

Everything went topsy-turvy. Hailey was lucky she was still standing. "Cookie? You're Cookie. My great-uncle's Cookie?"

"I am. We'll talk later, dear. In the meantime, there's a shabbily-dressed handyman who's desperately in love with you headed your way."

Hailey blinked, but the scene remained the same. She watched as Finn descended from the rooftop. The sunshine held him in a near-blinding glow as the mountain air ushered in a woodsy scent —the scent of his business card.

She pinched her arm. This was really happening.

She'd always been the girlfriend in the shadows.

The afterthought.

Not anymore. Finn was making sure of it.

He stood before her, donning his tool belt. He held a jar of orange marmalade in one hand and the axe in the other. "Hi, Marmalade," he said, and God help her, she loved that nickname.

"Hi, handyman." She looked over her shoulder at the pair of cameramen. "So much for keeping us hidden. Who are those guys?"

"One is from Golden Tech. He's doing a before and after video."

She cocked her head to the side. "Before and after? Before what?"

"I had a sort of public epiphany. I'll explain later. And the other cameraman is from the I Said Yes website."

How many shocks to the system could one woman endure? It appeared she was about to find out.

"The website that hosts the Shooting Stars Love Stories?"

"Yes."

She peered at the cameraman wearing a shirt with I Said Yes printed on the pocket. She'd missed it before. "How did you get them here?"

"The family of someone I know owns several wedding websites. This is one of them. I called in a favor and made peace with someone that wasn't meant for me."

Susan.

"Finn," she said softly, staring into his sage-green eyes.

He shifted his stance. "And I should apologize for the pickles and licorice shortage. I wasn't sure if you'd tried to buy any over the last couple of weeks."

"I did. They were sold out."

"That's my fault. I bought all the orange marmalade and cherry chocolate chip ice cream, too. I've been eating a pint for breakfast each day like a drunk toddler."

She laughed. He was laying it on the line. "It's okay." She glanced at the basket. "I've got plenty of snacks now."

"There's more," he continued and grimaced. "I want to tell you everything."

"Okay."

"I've been feeding the raccoons and built them a house. We're kind of bros now." He gestured to the roof of the paper company, where four raccoons sat munching on pickles not far from Goldie and Rex.

"Are your grandparents safe?"

"Oh yeah, as long as the pickles don't run out."

She stared wide-eyed at the furry quartet, her expression a mix of disbelief and amusement. "Raccoons like pickles?"

"They also ate a pair of my shoes doused in shrimp cocktail sauce."

What in the world had happened to this man?

"It's better than having them pelting us with pinecones," she said through a chuckle.

"I apologized to Nico for lying and making him run seventeen miles, and I got him a gift."

"A subscription to Thigh Trekker," Nico announced, stepping forward.

Hailey took in the beefy man, who was hard to miss in his unique outfit. "What is Thigh Trekker?"

"Every month, they send me a new pair of shorts. I'm wearing this month's pair," the man answered, rocking neon orange short-shorts.

Finn bit back a grin. "The man can wear a pair of shorts."

"He certainly can," she answered, working overtime to keep a straight face. She eyed her handyman. "You've been busy."

He set the jar of marmalade into the basket, then took the weighty item from her. He handed it and the axe to Owen. "I had a lot to do. A lot to make up for and a lot to learn." He took her hands into his. "I've missed you so much."

Emotion built in her chest as her bottom lip trembled. "I've missed you, too."

"I meant it when I said you were right about everything. I was scared and bitter. I didn't appreciate the love and support that's always been with me. I thought you could fix me. I thought your kindness and your goodness would wipe out my pain. But that's not your job. That's my job. Love isn't a series of empty transactions. It isn't expecting another to take away the pain. It's selfish to behave like that, and it's not love's critical component."

"What is love's critical component?" she asked, breathless.

He tightened his hold on her hands. "To be the man you deserve and spend every day on this planet proving that you're meant for me. The critical component is the doing—the loving, the listening, the supporting. It's believing in us. It's the beat of my heart moving with one purpose, and that purpose is to love you like I know your parents would want you to be loved."

Tears filled her eyes as the world dissolved, leaving only her and Finn and the connection that had sparked between them the second their eyes met that rainy night.

He released her hands and pulled a slip of paper from his pocket. "This is my Starrycard wishing wall wish. My wish is that you'll allow me to be the man who's meant for you. Say you'll be mine. Give me another chance. Tell me you want me to be more than your business card boyfriend."

"And what would that be?"

"Kenz?" he said with a sly grin like he'd anticipated she'd ask the question.

McKenzie zigzagged through the crowd with an empty glass jar in her hands. She passed it to her uncle. Hailey stared at the container. A container nearly identical to the one in her tote, except this glass jar held one slip of paper. Finn unscrewed the lid. He removed the fragment and pressed it into her hand.

The breath caught in her throat as she brushed her thumb across the fibrous snippet with pink and purple flecks. "I know that paper," she said, a tear trailing down her cheek as she pictured her parents.

"I borrowed a sheet from your uncle. I hope you don't mind. Open it, Marmalade."

Speechless, she peered at the paper.

Hailey Higgins, my Sweet Miss Marmalade, will you marry me?

"We don't have to stay in Starrycard Creek," he said. "I'll follow you wherever you want to go. I've already talked with my family. I can work remotely and travel back to Starrycard Creek. I know you've been offered a position to teach in Denver."

She nodded. "That's right."

"Of course, they did. You're amazing. I don't care where we go. You're my home, Hailey Higgins. You're my forever," he continued.

She drank in this beautiful man as a slight shimmery sound whispered in the wind.

A wish can only come true if it's meant for you.

She exhaled a slow breath, feeling the magic of this mountain town all around her. "Do you remember the first time you kissed me?"

Warmth cascaded across his face as if he slipped back to the moment their lips first met. "The first time I kissed you," he began with a swoon-worthy, boyish grin, "was when I learned forever tasted like cherry chocolate bliss and spring rain. The first time I kissed you, I knew my purpose in this world was to spend my life loving you."

A hushed "*wow*" escaped her lips. She stepped back. "The first time you kissed me, you knew your purpose in this world was to spend your life loving me?"

"Yes, it took me a while to understand the rush of emotions. My heart always knew we were meant for each other. My head took a little longer to catch up."

She unscrewed the lid on her parents' pickle jar and plucked a specific slip from the top. It was easy to find. She'd read it in her car with the kittens less than an hour ago. She handed it to Finn. "You spoke the exact words my father wrote to my mother."

Finn examined the snippet as a tear trailed down his cheek. "I promise to love and protect your daughter," he whispered to the paper. "Where she goes, I'll go." He held the slip to his ear, then pursed his lips.

That started sweet and got weird fast. Was he communicating with the paper?

She frowned. "What are you doing, Finn?"

"Listening. Your parents are saying that I sound like a real keeper."

Okay, he was conversing with the note, but he wasn't wrong. Her parents would have loved him.

She laughed through her tears. "Here's another piece of paper you should see," she said and handed him the envelope containing the Starrycard Creek teacher's contract.

He ripped open the top and unfolded the sheet.

"I already decided to stay," she said, watching a grin stretch across his face. "Looks like I'm getting more than a job and a business card boyfriend out of this town."

"So, your answer is yes, you'll marry me?"

Her gaze swept over the buildings and the mountainous landscape. The soft melody of the creek mingled with the murmurs of the kind townspeople who'd welcomed her with open arms. She could feel her parents smiling down on her, their love infused in the sunshine. This is the kind of love they'd want for her.

"Yes, I'll marry you."

A twitch of a grin revealing his dimples brightened his expression. "Then it's a good thing I brought my axe."

"Your axe?" she replied, not expecting that response.

As if on cue, he reached out and opened his hand. Owen swooped in and placed the axe's handle on Finn's palm.

She shook her head. Mischief and excitement and everything else that made her love this handyman glinted in his eyes.

"Don't move, Marmalade," he said and strolled to the paper staircase. He nodded to the students gathered around Dr. Schneider. "Are we good to go?"

"We're good to go," a young woman called.

He raised the axe, swung it like a seasoned lumberjack, and sliced through a rope she hadn't noticed anchored to the flatbed. Before she could take another breath, the top of the staircase burst open. Pink rectangles exploded into the air, filling the sky like confetti with a delicate cherry scent. They rained down like papery snowflakes. The children hooted and hollered, chasing the cards as they carried on the breeze toward the creek. Finn came to her side as she plucked a rectangle from the air. But these weren't just slips of Starrycard paper. They were business cards—cherry-scented business cards.

And not just any cherry-scented business cards. They were her business cards.

Hailey Higgins-Starrycard
Second Grade Teacher
Starrycard Creek Elementary School
Cat Mom

She eyed Finn. "Cat mom?"
Meow!

McKenzie walked toward them with Whiskers and Sweetie in her arms. "A lady with bright pink lips from the animal rescue said the cats were for you and Uncle Finn."

Hailey checked the crowd and found Flo and Annie. She

waved to the women, then pegged Finn with her gaze. "You're the one who adopted the kittens?"

He shrugged, playing it off like he hadn't just done the sweetest thing. "We both know I have a thing for redheads, Marmalade."

This man!

"Can I take Sweetie and Whiskers to play in the creek?" McKenzie asked.

"We'll keep an eye on them," Jack said, coming toward them with Eliza by his side. "Good job, man," he continued and clapped Finn on the shoulder. "And Miss Higgins," Jack continued, "we're glad you're staying in Starrycard Creek."

"So glad," Eliza gushed. "And now you'll be part of the Starrycard family craziness forever."

"You should have run while you had the chance. Once these folks have got you, there's no escape," Jack teased as Eliza swatted his arm.

"Come on, Mom and Dad, let's show Whiskers and Sweetie around their forever home," McKenzie called.

Hailey drank in the sea of pink covering the ground as Finn wrapped his arms around her. She melted into his strong embrace. Enveloped in a cocoon of love, she basked in the glow of being cherished and adored. Grateful for a quiet moment, she rested her head against his chest. They watched the schoolchildren climb on the rocks, play in the water, and collect her business cards. The townspeople clustered in groups, laughing and chatting as musicians set up under a tent, and Goldie and Rex had left their spot on the roof. The pair set out plates of turnovers and jars of marmalade alongside trays with sandwiches and bowls of pasta salad.

Finn held her business card in his hand. "I took a leap of faith when I made these. I hoped you'd be okay with what I had embossed on them."

"Of course, I'm okay with them, Finn. They're perfect."

He looked her over and frowned. "You're missing something."

"What could I possibly be missing? You enlisted the help of the entire town to propose to me. You got up on the roof and proclaimed your love. You helped university students build a staircase volcano that spews business cards with my name on them. You made sure Sweetie and Whiskers were ours." She glanced over her shoulder and chuckled. "You even have cameramen documenting the whole thing."

"But what's a proposal," he said, taking a knee, "without one of these?" He opened a flap on his tool belt and removed a ring.

Hailey gasped. It was like nothing she'd ever seen.

He slipped it onto her ring finger. "It's a pink diamond to match your business cards. It's also the color of your cheeks when I make you blush, and it matches the pink flecks in—"

"In the paper my great-uncle would send to my dad," she finished, admiring the gem. It sparkled with a soft, ethereal radiance like it was meant just for her. "Finn, it's beautiful and enormous."

He stood and took her hand with a possessive glint in his eyes. "I want everyone who sees you to know that you're taken and that you're my Sweet Miss Marmalade."

She wrapped her arms around his neck and sighed. "It's hard to believe we're here because of a business card."

He pursed his lips. "I might need a new one."

"And what would it say?"

"Finnegan Starrycard," he purred, his warm breath sending a delicious tingle down her spine, "local handyman, not an axe murderer, and the papermaker who can't wait to make Hailey Higgins his wife." He gathered her into his arms and smiled that dazzling smile that melted her heart. "It looks like love was in the cards for us. And our love story is sure to be one for Starrycard history books," he added, then brushed his lips across hers, celebrating their engagement with a cherry chocolate kiss.

Epilogue

FINN

FINN RAN his hands down his fiancée's torso, gripped her hips, and kissed her neck. "How am I supposed to pack for our trip and get a few things done around the house when you're prancing around in my Starrycard Creek Paper Company T-shirt?"

He had to stop working on the kitchen cabinets when he'd caught a glimpse of her. The possessive, caveman side of him had taken over. Not to mention, she happened to be standing on his favorite white floofy rug. But this wasn't just any white floofy rug. This was the *new* floofy faux sheepskin rug in their *new* home.

That's right. New home.

It was safe to say they'd been busy these last two weeks since he'd put a ring on it.

After the town kindly allowed him to hijack the Starrycard Creek Summer Jubilee and turn it into a business-card-laden wedding proposal extravaganza, he and Hailey had gone all-in, charting a course for their life as a couple in Starrycard Creek.

Their first move was an actual move.

With him returning to work at the shop and her accepting the teaching position at Starrycard Creek Elementary, they wanted a place in town. Thanks to Nico, the best short-shorts realtor in all of the West, the pair purchased a three-bedroom blond-brick bungalow down the street from Jack and Eliza. Equidistant from the school and the shop, they'd each have a short walk to their place of employment. And speaking of real estate, Hailey decided not to sell Higgins Hideaway. It was her connection to her great-uncle Albert—the man who'd changed the trajectory of her life. Along with Starrycard Cabin, they offered the cozy cottages to their friends and family whenever they required a mountain escape. Dr. Schneider and her daughter were scheduled to arrive in a few days.

But they weren't about to jump right back into work. Hailey had the summer off, and he wanted to spend part of that time learning more about her roots. She'd already gotten the whole Starrycard initiation. His family adored her, and due to the extensive sharing of Starrycard history and folklore by his parents and grandparents, the woman had essentially acquired a PhD in all matters related to Starrycard Creek.

Now, it was his turn.

He wanted to see where she'd grown up in Arizona, visit the school where her parents taught, and pay his respects to the people who raised the woman who helped him become the man he was meant to be.

And that's where the packing came in.

They were leaving for Arizona today. But far be it for his family to allow the newly engaged couple to slink out of town without a proper Starrycard sendoff. On the cusp of summer, his mother had suggested brunch at Goldie's. And this gathering was slated to start in less than an hour.

Had he expected his blood supply to head south before a family get-together? No. Wait, strike that! He lived with a redheaded goddess. It was a fucking miracle he was able to leave the house without a stiffy. What he hadn't expected was to find his fiancée with her hair in a ponytail and rocking his Starrycard Creek Paper Company T-shirt in the middle of the living room. With the addition of the pink diamond ring glinting on her finger, that combo had him raring to go.

"What's going on with the wardrobe, Marmalade?" he asked, expecting she'd be dressed. He kissed her neck as he tightened his grip on her hips. "Not that I'm complaining, but why are you still wearing my favorite shirt? Are you trying to see how many orgasms I can give you in twenty-four hours?"

It was a legitimate question. They'd greeted the day, knocking out two in a sweaty tangle of limbs.

"Am I provoking you?" she asked, a teasing edge to her voice.

"Yes, but for the record, you could provoke me in a potato sack."

She reached up and threaded her fingers into the hair at the nape of his neck. "A potato sack, huh?"

"Any type of sack. You know what you do to me. And you must know you're also standing on my favorite rug."

Yep, he had to buy another for their new home.

The little minx rubbed her ass against him. "Am I?" she replied, feigning mock surprise.

What did she have up her sleeve?

She turned to face him and flashed a doe-eyed expression. "You'll have to excuse my behavior. You see, I'd just taken a shower and finished blow-drying my hair. I had every intention of getting dressed. But then I heard a commotion and threw on the first thing I could find. When I peeked out to see what was going on, I noticed a handyman in my kitchen."

"A handyman, huh?" he replied, pretty sure he knew where his naughty schoolteacher was going with this sultry performance.

She nodded. "He was fixing a squeaky hinge on one of the cabinets."

"A squeaky hinge will stop any do-it-yourself enthusiast clean in their tracks. Tell me about the handyman in your kitchen," he coaxed, more than happy to play along.

"He was tall, dark, and ruggedly handsome. And he was wearing a tool belt. I've got a thing for men in tool belts who are good with their hands. I must admit, watching him got me a little hot and wet."

He drank her in, falling deeper under her spell as he inhaled her cherry scent. "Mind if I assess your situation, ma'am? You see, I'm a handyman, too. I might be able to help you with your heat and moisture issues."

She gazed at him through her lashes. "How fortunate. Go ahead."

He came up behind her, assuming his original position. Getting harder by the second, he skimmed his handy hand down her stomach and slipped it inside her panties. He inhaled a tight breath, lust coursing through his body. "You're not a little wet. You're soaked," he rasped, working her tight bundle of nerves in lazy, taunting circles.

She hummed her pleasure. "Then it's a good thing you came along."

"Your situation is quite dire. I better get to work," he said against the shell of her ear.

She rocked her hips. "Would you happen to have a business card? I need to make sure you're the real deal."

He spied her canvas bag hanging from a hook near the front door. Pausing his handyman foreplay, he turned her around in his arms. Face-to-face, he guided her toward the entrance to the bungalow. It only took a few steps before he had her back against the front door. Not missing a beat, he reached into her tote's side pocket and produced the same business card she'd had tucked in her cleavage the night they met. And Christ, he loved that she kept the card with her everywhere she went.

He held the slim rectangle in front of her. "My card. I'm Finnegan Starrycard. Local handyman and . . ." He paused and bit back a grin. "An accomplished ecstasy exporter."

"I don't see *ecstasy exporter* on your card, Mr. Handyman," she said and wrapped her arms around his neck.

"It's a new title I was given not long ago. One of my *clients* coined the phrase. She gives me rave reviews. Unfortunately, I haven't had a chance to update my cards."

Mischief glinted in her eyes. "Did I ever tell you that I licked that card?"

He raised an eyebrow. "You didn't mention that to me. But I'd love to know more," he replied as they abandoned their steamy role-play.

"I opened the letter with the information about Higgins Hideaway, saw the card, and sniffed it. Then I licked it." A wicked grin spread across her lips. "Want a demonstration?"

His cock twitched as a fresh surge of lust hit his system. "We get into a lot of trouble when you demonstrate things. So, yes—absolutely—demonstrate away," he replied, holding the card a whisper away from her lips.

Slowly, she drew the tip of her tongue across the back of the paper.

He drank her in. "I've been around paper my entire life, and I will never look at it the same way again. God help me, I love your mouth, those full lips, and that tongue."

A blush graced her cheeks. "It wasn't exactly that sexy when I did it in my car. But I did taste it. I guess that makes me a paper super-freak."

This woman. This beautiful, vulnerable, hilarious, sexy, and tender-hearted woman. Her cherry-sweetness was infused in every part of her. Her adorable reaction to her paper-licking confession had him beaming.

He slipped the card back into her bag and pinned her against the door with his body. "It's a good thing I'm a handyman who's also part owner of a paper company. We can indulge your every paper-licking desire."

She gifted him with the grin that was only for him.

He kissed the corner of her mouth. "Every time I think it would be impossible to want you more, you prove me wrong. Do you know how much I love you, my Sweet Miss Marmalade?" He pulled back and held her gaze, enamored with the woman who was going to be his wife, his partner, his everything.

"Why don't you show me with this," she answered, cupping his cock through his khakis.

Oh, hell yes!

He'd turned her into a sweet little sex monster, and he wasn't about to deny her. He dropped to his knees, removed her panties, and tossed them over his shoulder. He rose, caging her in and capturing her mouth. The world dissolved into a symphony of sensations. The softness of her breath and the hint of cherry licorice on her tongue stoked his desire with every brush of their lips. Electricity coursed through him. Revitalizing him. Fueling his need to consume her.

"Finn, I want you inside me . . . now," she demanded.

See, a real sex monster.

He undid his pants and freed his cock. Lifting her into his arms, he pressed her back against the door and thrust his hips, filling her in one fluid motion. She moaned, greedily welcoming his hard length. But he needed a second. He stilled, basking in the fiery rush that ignited like a flame the second their bodies became one.

He stared into her eyes. "I love you."

Affection swirled in the depths of her gaze. He could see their future—a future ripe with shared dreams. But now was not the time to wax poetic about the depth of his feelings. He squeezed her ass. "You'll want to hold on for this. It's going to be a rough ride."

Desire shined in her eyes as she arched her back, her full breasts straining against the faded cotton.

"Let's see what you've got, handyman," she challenged.

And game on!

He pumped his hips, giving it to her hard and fast. Their heated breaths and wanton moans joined the soft thud of her body bumping against the door. Like an attentive machinist, he focused on his fiancée, adjusting his pace to the furious rhythm that had her digging her nails into his back. The sweet bite of pain fueled his desire. He fine-tuned each kiss, each thrust, each slap of skin meeting skin. And Christ, she felt like heaven. His muscles flexed as he delivered a hot, titillating, down-and-dirty slice of before-brunch quickie sex. And there was no doubt he'd live up to the ecstasy exporter title.

He drilled into her, rubbing against her sweet spot as friction built between them. He knew her body. He understood her tells. She tightened her core, her lithe frame going rigid as she teetered on the precipice of release.

A jolt of carnal delight tore through him. She was close—so close.

He dialed up his pace, changing the angle. And fuck, he was right there, hovering inches from ecstasy. His world centered on one thing. Hailey Higgins. She was everywhere. She was everything. He tightened his grip on her ass and breathed her in, dissolving into her sexy sighs.

Harder. Faster.

Thud-thud-thud.

The relentless sound reverberated through the air, each impact echoing with urgency and desperation.

"Finn," she whimpered against his lips, flying over the edge to meet sweet oblivion.

Her seductive rasp of a voice was his undoing. He couldn't hold back. Claiming her mouth, he joined her, plunging into a sea of rippling waves. Roiling and writhing, pleasure washed over him. Pulsing, it cocooned them in a blanket of heat, light, and love —a connection so profound it brought tears to his eyes.

Exquisitely spent, she collapsed, sighing as she allowed him to hold her close and support her body. She chuckled against his neck, a feathery sated sound. "Don't drop me."

He shifted her weight, supporting her with one arm and cupping her face in his hand. "Oh, Marmalade, I've got you. I will always have you."

It was the truth—in every facet and season of their lives, he'd be there to love and support her.

She leaned back and studied his face.

"What are you thinking?" he asked and stroked her cheek with the pad of his thumb.

She gifted him with a sultry smirk. "That I'm really glad you're not an axe murderer."

He shook his head, zeroed in on her full lips, and prepared to kiss that expression off her pretty little face when a sharp *pop* cut through the sex haze.

They stilled.

Knock, knock, knock!

There it was again. It was the door.

"It's me, McKenzie. We're here to walk down to the shop with you."

What? That was news to him.

"We're walking down to Goldie's with Kenz, Liza, and Jack?" he whispered, wide-eyed.

Hailey chewed her lip. "Oops, yes, Eliza texted. I was on my way to tell you when I found you doing your handyman thing in the kitchen. And then I got . . . derailed."

"Are you saying that my sexy handyman prowess scrambled your brain?" he asked, feeling pretty damned good about himself.

A naughty twist of a grin curled the corners of her lips. "Yes, but now you need to answer the door and buy me a minute to get dressed. Your niece is only inches away from us."

He stared at the door. Oh shit! At least it wasn't a glass door.

Bang, bang, bang!

"Uncle Finn?" the little girl called, knocking away like the Big Bad Wolf coming for the Three Little Pigs.

"We should probably do something about this," she said, glancing down at the spot where his cock was still inserted inside her. "You should put me down."

He blinked. "Yeah, good thinking." It wasn't his fault he was a little slow on the uptake. Blood had only recently returned to his brain.

He pulled out, then carefully lowered Hailey to the ground. She hightailed it to the bedroom as he fastened his pants and prayed Kenzie hadn't heard anything through the door.

He did a quick check of his wardrobe.

His shirt was slightly wrinkled. Pants, too. But no visible genitals meant he was good to go.

No visible genitals? Now, there's something he hadn't expected he'd be on the lookout for today.

Meow!

He glanced down as Sweetie and Whiskers emerged from the bedroom.

"I look presentable, right, guys? Nothing hanging out that's not supposed to be hanging out?"

Whiskers eyed him warily.

Jesus! He was talking to the cats about his junk. He needed to get it together. He had to get moving. The longer he waited, the more shit he'd get from Jack and Eliza.

He opened the door. "Hey, Kenz," he said. Blessedly, Eliza and Jack were on the sidewalk a good twenty feet from the covered front porch.

McKenzie looked him up and down. "It sure sounds like you were getting some, Uncle Finn."

Oh fuck! Fuckity, fuck, fuck, fuck!

He cleared his throat and double-checked his fly. It was zipped. He shifted his stance. "What are you talking about, Kenz?"

"All that pounding on the door. Uncle Finn is sure getting some, right, Daddy? Right, Mommy?" the kid called, looking over her shoulder.

Could six-year-olds see through solid wood?

Finn felt his cheeks heat. Eliza pressed her hand to her mouth, and Jack crossed his arms and glanced away, the pair working overtime not to bust out laughing.

Finn mustered his last ounce of dignity and zeroed in on McKenzie. "I'll probably regret asking this, but what do you think I'm getting?"

"You're getting some handyman work done on your new house. You like to fix things. I heard you. You were fixing the door. That's what that pounding was."

Oh, for the love of Christ!

The kid peered inside. "Does Whiskers have underwear in his mouth?"

That was it. Jack and Eliza lost it and broke out into laughter.

Dammit, Whiskers!

"What's funny about underwear?" the little girl called to her parents. "Remember when I found Mommy's underwear hanging from the chandelier in the dining room?"

Boom!

Finn pointed to Eliza and Jack, who'd stopped laughing.

That serves them right!

He eyed the pair. "I don't want to hear a word from you two."

Eliza mimicked zipping up her lips.

"These are mine," Hailey said, swooping in and swiping the undergarments from the cat. "I must have dropped them when I was packing my suitcase. So much packing going on here. Only packing. No funny business. Thanks for helping out, Whiskers," she finished and tossed the panties onto the couch out of McKenzie's line of vision.

"You guys are packing and pounding, huh? Both those words start with *P* and end with *I-N-G*," McKenzie chimed.

Could this get any more embarrassing?

"Those are some super-smart word skills, McKenzie," Hailey remarked, using her magical teacher powers to steer the conversation to a less X-rated topic. She grabbed her tote. "How about we head out, and you can tell me some other words you know that end in *I-N-G*."

"We better hurry. We don't want Uncle Owen and Uncle Kieran to eat all the turnovers, do we, Kenzie?" Eliza called.

"Come on, Almost-Aunt Hailey," McKenzie exclaimed, taking his fiancée's hand and guiding her down the porch steps to the sidewalk.

Eliza, Hailey, and McKenzie headed down the street as he hung back and walked beside Jack.

"How are you doing, man? It's been such a whirlwind since I proposed to Hailey, but we'll settle into a routine when we get back and have you guys over to the new house," Finn said, taking in the warmth of the morning sun on his cheeks.

Jack tossed him a cheeky grin. "Are you kidding? I'm married to the best Starrycard of the bunch. Of course, I'm doing well."

Finn clapped his friend on his shoulder. "I'm glad."

"Are you finally okay with me marrying your sister?" Jack asked, skepticism coating the question.

"Hell no. But I'm *less bad* with it," Finn teased, knowing damned well Jack Dunleavy was the best man for Eliza. Still, he had to give the guy a little shit now and then.

The men settled into a leisurely pace as Hailey, Eliza, and McKenzie's voices drifted in the gentle breeze.

"We're damned lucky," Finn said, catching Hailey's eye as she glanced back at him.

"We are indeed, my friend," Jack agreed.

And damn, life was good.

It didn't take long before they turned onto the street that led to Goldie's, and McKenzie took off like a shot.

"Uncle Owen! Uncle Kieran!" the kid exclaimed, "save a turnover for me!"

"Duty calls," Jack said with a wide grin before jogging to catch up with Eliza and his daughter.

The trio disappeared around the corner, and Hailey came to his side. He took her hand in his as they walked the familiar route. He soaked in the moment. It was as if he were seeing his hometown with new eyes. He listened to the creek. Its gentle babbling stirred memories of his childhood. That familiar gurgle of water winding through the valley was a window to his past.

Starrycard Creek would always be where he was from. His last name connected him to the land and the family business, but having Hailey by his side was what would make this place his forever home.

"Are you ready for a Starrycard family get-together?" he asked.

"It should be interesting. Eliza says your mom and grandmother are wagering on which Starrycard sibling will find love next."

"They never quit. Lucky for me, I don't have to worry about that anymore," he replied and kissed the crown of her head.

They turned the corner, and Goldie's was hopping. He spied his family. The group sat at a long rectangular table with a billowy white tablecloth. Trays of pastries, jars of marmalade, bowls of fruit, and an assortment of savory breakfast staples dotted the pristine surface as the hum of his family chatting and laughing mingled with the rush of the creek.

A humbling sense of awe overtook him as he surveyed the scene. "Thank you, Hailey."

"For what?"

Warmth spread through his chest. "For helping me see how fortunate I am to be a part of this family and this place."

He took in his parents. His gaze drifted to Eliza, Jack, and McKenzie before landing on Owen and Kieran. He thought back to the photo of his siblings he'd shown Hailey when he had to prove he wasn't an axe murderer who kept his victims' clothing as souvenirs. He was a Starrycard—one of six. He and his brothers and sisters had the opportunity to strengthen the town, the business, and their reputation. And he would get to be a part of securing their legacy with the love of his life by his side.

He returned his attention to his fiancée. Peering into the depths of her amber eyes, he found a lifetime of love reflected back at him. "I wouldn't be here, feeling on top of the world, if it wasn't for you, Marmalade." Lost in the moment, he leaned in to kiss her when his mother's voice rang out.

"There's the newly engaged couple," she announced and waved them over.

"To be continued," he whispered against Hailey's lips.

"Absolutely," she said with the hint of a mischievous grin.

"Did you see this?" his mom asked, holding out her phone.

"Love, Stars, and Pickle Jars," Hailey read, eyeing the screen as they settled into their seats.

"It's the feature love story on the I Said Yes website," his father gushed.

"And check out what's right below it," Owen added.

His mother scrolled down and gasped. "A picture of a Starrycard wedding invitation."

"Finn, what a triumph!" his father exclaimed.

Hailey touched his arm. "Did you know this was coming out today?"

He shook his head. "I didn't know the exact date. Susan mentioned it would probably be posted a couple of weeks after the proposal. It's at the discretion of the website's editors."

Yes, he'd reached out to his ex.

When he'd called Susan to ask about having the Shooting Stars Love Stories cover his proposal to Hailey, she'd mentioned wanting to partner with the Starrycard Creek Paper Company. And there was more. He and Susan had talked—a real heart-to-heart. He'd wished her well, and she'd expressed the same sentiment. It was the closure they needed.

He rested his hand on Hailey's knee and admired the image on the screen. The old version of himself wouldn't have been able to stomach seeing anything connected to his ex-fiancée. But he wasn't that angry, grudge-holding man anymore.

"I'm so proud of you," Hailey said, her signature tenderness woven into her words as she pressed a kiss to his cheek.

"Good job, bro," Owen added. "This is huge for the company."

"A toast," his mother announced as Grandpa Rex and Goldie emerged from the restaurant.

His grandparents handed out mimosas to the adults and a champagne flute filled with orange juice for Miss McKenzie.

"To the newly engaged couple, congratulations. Hailey, we're so pleased you'll be a part of our family. The adage is true," Maeve continued. "Love is always in the cards in Starrycard Creek."

"That's because, here in our beautiful mountain hideaway, you'll always find what's meant for you," Goldie added, standing beside his mother.

Maeve met Goldie's eye. "Two Starrycards down. Three bachelors and one bachelorette to go," she said with a cheeky grin as the women clinked glasses.

"Really, Mom? That's how you're ending the toast?" Kieran deadpanned as his cell phone pinged. He concentrated on the screen. A muscle ticked on his jaw. "Excuse me. I need to take this," he grumbled, abandoning his mimosa, and headed toward the creek.

"And speaking of love," Maeve continued, not letting up on the subject. "I'll open it to the group. Who do you think will be the next little star to follow in William Starrycard's footsteps and find their true love?"

All eyes fell on Owen.

The man glanced down the path that ran along the creek toward the Starrycard Creek library, then raised his hands defensively. "No way. That old saying won't work for me. I'm married to a vat of pulp."

"It's me," Kieran roared, not missing a beat. The man stood near the wishing wall with his cell pressed to his ear and pinched the bridge of his nose.

What?

Finn, along with everyone else at the table, eyed the oldest Starrycard sibling. The guy kept his personal life private—super private. He had a good idea Kier hooked up with women when he traveled for work, but he'd never mentioned a girlfriend or even that he was dating or interested in someone.

"I'm going to go out on a limb and say that Kieran didn't hear you and isn't vying to be the next Starrycard Creek Bachelor to fall," Eliza offered.

"And his birthday is coming up. I doubt his birthday wish is to fall in love," Owen added.

"I disagree, little stars," Goldie replied, sharing a look with Maeve. "If anyone needs to be rocked off his axis, it's our Kieran." His grandmother pulled a pen and a slip of Starrycard paper from her apron. She jotted a note, folded the fragment into a little square, and handed it to McKenzie. "Will you find a good spot for this on the wishing wall, dear? Kieran has a birthday coming up, and I have a feeling, this year, he'll find out what's meant for him."

Read the Bonus Scene

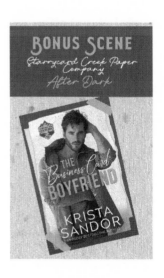

When Finn and Hailey sneak into
The Starrycard Creek Paper
Company for a little after-hours
hanky-panky, they're interrupted
by another couple looking to score.
Download at https://dl.bookfun
nel.com/g0t90n5cly

Books by Krista Sandor

The Starrycard Creek Bachelors Series

A small town rom-com series set in the mountains

Book One: The Business Card Boyfriend

Book Two: The Birthday Card Boyfriend

Book Three: The Baseball Card Boyfriend

Book Four: The Christmas Card Boyfriend

The Nanny Love Match Series

A nanny/boss romantic comedy series

Book One: The Nanny and the Nerd

Book Two: The Nanny and the Hothead

Book Three: The Nanny and the Beefcake

Book Four: The Nanny and the Heartthrob

Love Match Legacy Books

Nanny Love Match Series Spin-off Books

Mistletoe Love Match

The Sebastian Guarantee

The Oscar Escape

The Bergen Brothers Series

A steamy billionaire brothers romantic comedy series

Book One: Man Fast

Book Two: Man Feast

Book Three: Man Find

Bergen Brothers: The Complete Series+Bonus Short Story

The Farm to Mabel Duet

A brother's best friend romance set in a small-town

Book One: Farm to Mabel

Book Two: Horn of Plenty

Farm to Mabel: The Complete Duet

The Langley Park Series

A suspenseful, sexy second-chance at love series

Book One: The Road Home

Book Two: The Sound of Home

Book Three: The Beginning of Home

Book Four: The Measure of Home

Book Five: The Story of Home

Box Set (Books 1-5 + Bonus Scene)

Own the Eights Series

A delightfully sexy enemies-to-lovers series

Book One: Own the Eights

Book Two: Own the Eights Gets Married

Book Three: Own the Eights Maybe Baby

Box Set (Books 1-3)

STANDALONES

The Kiss Keeper

A toe-curlingly hot opposites attract romance

Not Your Average Vixen

An enemies-to-lovers super-steamy holiday romance

Get the Newsletter

DON'T MISS THE NEXT BOOK RELEASE

Sign up for Krista's newsletter to get all the up-to-date Krista Sandor romance news. Learn more at www.KristaSandor.com.

Acknowledgments

PEOPLE KRISTA HOLDS CLOSE TO HER HEART

To:

Becky, Leah, Carrie, Tera, Marla, Wander &
Andrey, Najla, Dani, and David

With love and deep gratitude,
Krista

After I finished writing the Nanny Love Match Series and the Love Match Legacy spinoff books, I wasn't sure what was next for me. I had an idea and a title, but not much more than that.

That's where Becky comes in. Becky is a romance Jack-of-all-trades. It would take another ten thousand words if I wrote everything she does for the romance community and romance readers. She's knowledgeable, kind, and always there to lend a hand and share her opinion.

Taking this little nugget of an idea, we brainstormed a concept. This concept grew and grew. And boom, thanks to the word *card* being in the title of that flicker-of-an-idea book, a fictional family running a papermaking business in a small town in Colorado emerged.

Now, did I know a damn thing about artisanal handmade papermaking when I started planning this series?

Oh, hell no!

Thank goodness for the internet.

I dove into the research. Papermaking is truly an art form and a labor of love. And while I was reading up on techniques and watching videos, I remembered something that happened when I was teaching second grade.

A parent came to class to share papermaking with the children. She had old beat-up blenders that worked the pulp we made from tap water and paper scraps. As soon as this memory hit, I recalled the earthy scent and the cool grittiness of the pulp. But it was my class's reaction that resonated the most. The children were enamored with the process. Even my most rambunctious and wiggly students were gentle and patient as they carefully transferred their water-laden sheet from the deckle to the felt.

Holding on to that precious memory and weaving in what I'd learned watching videos and reading articles, I created an origin story for the town, and William Starrycard and the legend of Starrycard Creek paper was born.

Now, I don't do this alone.

It takes quite a bit of work to get this story into your hot, little hands.

The women who help me whip my work-in-progress into shape go well beyond editing. They help me work through rough spots and keep me consistent. Carrie always gets the manuscript first. I depend on her guidance, and I am *always* in awe of her ability to keep every element of the story in her head. As a writer, if I decide to change something—while I'm dropping the kids at school or running an errand—it doesn't always get changed in the book. Carrie keeps me in line!

Marla and Tera work their magic, combing through the manuscript. And let me tell you. I'm the queen of missed words. I could read a sentence fifty times and think it was perfect. Nope, I forgot a word or switched tenses. I'm grateful for the time and precision they put into their work.

I must also thank Leah. She and Becky are partners in romance crime and collaborate on many projects. We've got a chat where I ask them questions, show them covers and swag designs, and basically drive them crazy with my insanity. I'm so fortunate to call these women my friends.

Let's talk about this gorgeous cover. Wander and Andrey's photographs are simply breathtaking (Wander Aguiar Photography).

Is it difficult sifting through page after page of handsome male models?

That would be a no.

What's hard is choosing from their buffet of beautiful men.

Once we've found the right model, Najla Qamber (Qamber Designs) takes over the cover design. I adore the concept she created for this series.

When it comes to PR and marketing, I know I'm in good hands with my publicist, Dani (Wildfire Marketing Solutions). She always has a plan, and I'm grateful for her guidance.

And I must thank my husband, David. He's always there, cheering me on and running out to buy me Diet Coke and espresso when I'm cranking to finish a book.

About Krista Sandor

If there's one thing Krista Sandor knows for sure, it's that romance saved her. After she was diagnosed with Multiple Sclerosis in 2015, her world turned upside down. During those difficult first days, her dear friend sent her a romance novel. That kind gesture provided the escape she needed and ignited her love of the genre. Inspired by strong heroines and happily ever afters, Krista decided to write her own romance series. Today, she's living life to the fullest. When she's not writing, you can find her running 5Ks with her husband or chasing after their growing boys in Denver, Colorado.

Never miss a release, contest, or author event! Visit www.KristaSandor.com to sign up for her romance newsletter.